PALE MOON

RED MOON SERIES, BOOK FIVE

ELIZABETH KELLY

EK PUBLISHING INC.

PALE MOON

(Book Five, Red Moon Series)

A dangerous power. An undeniable love.

Unlike his siblings, Nicholas Williams has no desire to find a mate. But when a group of strange Lycans and a human woman named Max arrive at his home, Nicky is undeniably attracted to her.

On a dangerous quest to the outskirts to save his birth father's life, Nicholas is drawn to Max in a way he does not understand. His urge to protect her and claim her as his own grows stronger with each passing day. But when Max reveals her strange powers – powers that can harm the people she cares about most – he must find a way to convince her to trust him.

CHAPTER 1

Nicky held out his hand and watched as the snowflakes landed on his open palm. They melted quickly, and he stared at the cloudy sky before dropping his gaze to the ground before him. The ground was stained with his father's blood, and he closed his eyes and took a deep breath before reaching for the shovel he had brought out from the barn.

He thrust the shovel into the hard ground, dug up a chunk of the blood-stained grass, and transferred it to the wheelbarrow. As he dug grimly, his thoughts returned to the silver haired Lycan's visit earlier in the day.

NICHOLAS STARED IN SURPRISE AT THE LYCAN STANDING before him.

"My birth father," he repeated.

"Aye. He needs your help," Meridan said.

Avery moved to Nicky's side and took his hand. "How do you know his father?"

1

"We work for him." Meridan indicated the two women standing next to him.

"Why did he not come himself?" Nicky asked.

"Your father has been taken by the leeches deep into the outskirts. We need your help in getting him back."

"Why would I help a man who abandoned me as a child?"

"He only learned of your existence three moons ago. Your mother's cousin, Saredina, fell ill. Before she died, she sought out your father and told him about you. She told him that a Lycan named Tristan Williams had taken you and your sister away from the city. Your father was preparing to come here when he was taken by the leeches.

"If he was taken by the leeches to the outskirts then he is already dead," Nicholas said.

Meridan shook his head. "No. The leeches have not killed him. I can assure you of that. They are holding him prisoner."

"You're wrong. The leeches do not take prisoners," Nicky replied.

The female Lycan frowned at Meridan. "How can they not know? Do they not care what happens to their own kind?"

"Quiet, Pavina. You forget that news does not travel as quickly in the country as it does in the city," Meridan replied.

"What are you talking about?" James led Bree toward Kaden and Sophia, standing her close to her brother and giving Kaden a brief look. Kaden put his arm around his sister, holding her protectively against him.

James stood next to Nicholas and Avery and gave Meridan a hard stare. "Tell us what you mean before I lose my patience."

"In the last year or so, there has been a surge in the number of humans the leeches have taken. They've been turning the humans in an attempt to increase their own kind. Four moons ago, it became clear why they were so desperate to increase their numbers. They needed larger numbers to take the Lycans. They've been abducting our kind and taking them to the outskirts."

"Why would they do that?" Avery asked.

"They are experimenting on them."

"What do you mean?" Nicholas frowned.

"They are attempting to make a hybrid of our kinds. Leech and Lycan mixed together. They believe they can use the Lycans to create a new race of vampires. They seek many of the Lycan's unique abilities, but what they desire most is the Lycan's ability to walk in the sun.

"The gods be damned," Avery breathed.

"Indeed," Meridan said. "If the leeches are successful in their quest, if they create a new hybrid of leech and Lycan, then we are all in grave danger."

"How do you know they have not already succeeded?" James asked.

Meridan shrugged. "We do not know for sure that they have not, but the rumour is that they are running into…issues."

Pavina snorted. "The leeches are ridiculous for believing they can create a hybrid. The Lycan gene is too powerful to be diluted by the leech's filth."

"What are the issues?" Nicky asked.

"Lycans who have been infected by the leeches die with a moon or two of being bitten. Their healing powers go into overdrive trying to destroy the leech infection within their bodies. The constant attempt to heal takes an enormous toll on the Lycan. It saps their energy and strength and eventually kills them."

There was a horrified silence in the room and Meridan sighed. "Despite their failure, the leeches do not seem to be giving up. More and more Lycans are being taken."

"Including my birth father," Nicky said.

"Aye. He was taken from the city nearly a moon ago. We are traveling to the outskirts to rescue him. Before he was kidnapped, your father confided in me about you and I made the decision to find you."

When Nicholas didn't reply, Meridan smiled briefly. "We have gathered many of your father's friends and employees to help us, but we could always use more Lycans. It will only become more dangerous the closer we get to the outskirts."

Nicky ran his hand restlessly through his hair. "You want me to help a man I've never met?"

"He is your father!" Pavina said. "What kind of Lycan leaves his own blood to die?"

"Hush, Pavina," Meridan said. "Nicholas, we believe there is a good chance that your father is still alive and has not been bitten yet. Your father is a good man, and there are many who are willing to risk their lives to save him. He is anxious to meet you."

Meridan paused. "If he has been bitten, then at least give him the chance to meet his son before he dies."

Nicky turned to his mother and her face paled at the look on his face. She cupped his face. "Nicky, you do not know that they speak the truth."

"We're not lying!" Pavina growled deep in her throat and her eyes turned a dark yellow. She took a step toward Avery and glared ominously at her. "You would be wise to hold your tongue, human. Not all Lycans are so complacent toward humans."

Pavina shrank back against Meridan, her eyes widening with fear, when a chorus of low growls answered her. Every Lycan in the room began to shift, their eyes glowing fiercely, as they stalked towards the three strangers. James and Nicky stood in front of Avery and used their large bodies to block

4

her completely from the gaze of Meridan and the two women.

"Threaten our mother again and you will die in this room." James voice was thick with rage. His beard was heavy on his face and his upper body had swelled to nearly twice its size. His shirt ripped across his shoulders with a low, purring sound as Meridan put up his hands in a calming gesture.

"Please, she meant no offense. Pavina speaks without thinking."

Nicky approached the female Lycan until he was standing only inches from her. He sniffed at her hair and then snarled under his breath. He bared his teeth at her, and a small whimper escaped her throat at the sight of his sharp fangs. She lowered her gaze to the floor.

"Keep your eyes on the floor. If you even look at my mother, I will pluck your eyes from your head and give them to her as a gift," Nicholas growled.

Pavina whined in submission as Nicholas continued to stare at her.

"Puppy!"

Nicholas turned. The human female was standing frozen with fear, but the small child strapped to her back was giving him a look of pure delight.

"Puppy!" she said again and before her mother could stop her, reached out and stroked the hair on Nicky's cheek with her small hand.

"Violet, no!" the woman gasped.

She pulled the child's hand away and took a step back. "I'm sorry."

Nicky cocked his head and stared into the woman's oddly coloured eyes. He waited for her to drop her gaze like Pavina and when she didn't, he leaned in and inhaled deeply. She smelled delicious, he thought hazily. Underneath the smell of her fear, there was an exotic blend of vanilla and jasmine and the good clean scent of her child.

"Hi, puppy," the little girl said, and her mother made a quiet moan of dismay.

Nicky, his body shrinking and the hair on his cheeks fading away, suddenly grinned at the toddler. "Hi, baby."

He gently pinched the girl's chubby cheek before stepping away. Sophia, Vivian, and Evan had joined James and were standing in a tight cluster around Avery. They stepped back as Nicky stood next to his mother. He put his arm around her and stared at Meridan.

"We speak the truth, Nicholas. I swear it," the silver haired Lycan said.

He didn't reply and Avery squeezed his waist. "Nicky, we must speak to your father first. He is still in the barn with Leta."

"Aye, I know," he replied.

Avery turned to Evan. "Evan, go the barn and get your father. Go quickly."

"Aye, mama." Evan started for the door of the common room.

He paused, his eyes widening, when the faint sound of Leta screaming could be heard.

"Leta?" Avery whispered. She stood frozen for a moment and then bolted from the room.

CHAPTER 2

"Papa!" Leta shrieked at the top of her lungs. "Papa, wake up!!"

She shook her father and, sobbing loudly, rested her small hands on the wound on his chest.

"Please, Papa," she whispered and closed her eyes.

There was nothing and then Tristan's entire body shuddered under her hands. He took a deep, gasping breath and his eyes fluttered open. They stared hazily at his youngest child.

"Leta?" he whispered weakly.

"Hi, Papa," Leta sobbed.

He groaned before his eyes rolled up in his head and he slumped against the hard ground. Leta cried out in dismay and then Avery, screaming Tristan's name, was dropping to her knees beside him. She was followed closely by Nicky and James, and Nicky snatched Leta away as James knelt next to his father.

Avery was already touching him, her hands pulling at his blood-soaked shirt and with a soft growl, James knocked her hands away and ripped open Tristan's shirt. Avery, crying and shaking, wiped at the blood, smearing it into her hands and Tristan's skin as she searched for his wound.

His chest was normal and the skin smooth and unbroken. Avery pressed her fingers against Tristan's throat as James stared at her in surprise.

"Mama?"

"He's alive," she whispered. "I can feel his pulse."

"Thank the gods," James said. He stared at the large amount of blood smeared into Tristan's chest and soaking into the ground beneath him. "Where is his wound?"

Avery stared at Leta in Nicky's arms. The young girl's hands were covered in her father's blood, and her tanned face was pale as she stared at Tristan's face.

"Mama? Is Papa all right?" she whispered.

Avery nodded slowly. "Aye, my love. He's all right."

The others were crowding around him and Sophia gave a soft cry and knelt at her father's head as Evan leaned over Avery's shoulder. Sophia stroked Tristan's long hair back from his face. "Mama, what happened?"

"Your father will be fine," Avery said. Still staring at Leta, she reached out and gripped James' shoulder. "James, carry your father to our bedroom, please."

"Aye, Mama."

"Sophia, take Leta and get her cleaned up. Kaden, can you help James?"

Kaden nodded and he and James lifted Tristan carefully. Evan supported his head and the three of them carried Tristan into the house as Avery followed. The rest of the family rushed into the house after them, leaving Nicky alone with the three strangers.

Nicky bent and picked up the discarded arrow, studying it carefully, as Meridan touched his shoulder. "Nicholas. I am sorry about your -"

He hesitated and Nicky, his eyes glowing with a mad light, glared at him. "My father. He is my father."

Meridan took a step back. "I do not mean to be disrespectful, but we need to finish our discussion. It is imperative that we move quickly if we are to save your father and I -"

"Meridan!" The human woman said sharply. Meridan glanced back at her and she shook her head. "Not now."

Meridan stared impatiently at her. "We must -"

"No. We can return tomorrow," the woman said.

The door opened and Maya stepped into the yard. She held her hand out to Nicky. "Nicholas, come inside please."

He nodded and, without looking at the strangers, disappeared into the house.

"My lady," Meridan said.

Maya shook her head. "No, leave now."

"Please tell Nicholas that we will return tomorrow," Meridan said.

Maya nodded as Meridan and Pavina turned towards the carriage. The human woman paused when her little girl said, "Potty, mama?"

The woman glanced at Maya. "I'm sorry. Do you have a bathroom we could use? It is easier for her if she has an actual toilet to sit on."

Maya hesitated, staring at Meridan and Pavina, before nodding. "Of course. Come with me."

The woman smiled gratefully and twisted around to glance at Meridan. "Five minutes, Meridan."

"Aye," he said and climbed into the carriage.

Maya led the woman into the house. Most of the family was in the common room and the woman glanced in briefly before following Maya down the hallway to the kitchen. Marian was standing at the sink, wringing her hands nervously. Maya pointed to another doorway at the other end of the kitchen. "There is a bathroom down that hall. Second door on the left."

"Thank you," the woman said. She walked down the hallway and disappeared into the bathroom as Marian approached Maya and took her hands.

"Maya, is the Lord Tristan…" Tears slid down her plump cheeks.

Maya squeezed her hands reassuringly. "He is alive, Marian. Avery and James are with him now."

"Thank the gods," Marian whispered.

Maya smiled at her. "I'm going to join the others in the common room. Show the human to the door when she's done, all right?" Marian nodded and Maya hugged her before leaving the kitchen.

———

LETA STARED GRAVELY AT THE PEOPLE GATHERED AROUND her. She was sitting on the couch and she bit her bottom lip nervously when Sophia and Nicky sat on opposite sides of her.

"Am I in trouble, Sophia?" Leta asked.

"No, my love. You are not in trouble," Sophia said.

"Then why is everyone staring at me?" Leta gave the group of Lycans and humans an uneasy look.

"We want you to tell us what happened, Leta." Sophia smoothed the young girl's hair back.

"Tell us everything." Nicky took her hand and rubbed it between his. "Start from the beginning."

Leta nodded. "I saw the carriage in the yard and Papa said we should find out who was here. We were walking toward the house and I was holding his hand. We were talking about when it would snow. I want it to snow so you can build me a snow slide again. Remember, Nicky?"

"Aye, I remember," Nicky said.

"Papa stopped and there was a weird noise and then, Papa, he… he…"

The little girl was beginning to tremble and Sophia put her arm around her, pressing Leta's head against her breast and kissing her forehead. "It's all right, my love."

Leta took a deep breath. "Then Papa gasped and there was an arrow sticking out of his chest." She started to cry, and Sophia made another soft, soothing noise.

"Papa pulled the arrow out and then he fell on the ground. I screamed and begged him to wake up but there was so much blood, Nicky."

The little girl stared up at Nicky's pale face. "I knew he was dying, and I was so scared. But then I remembered that I'm a healer like Mama, so I put my hands on his chest and I thought really hard about healing Papa."

She suddenly smiled through her tears. "Then I healed him."

"Leta, honey, you are too young to be a healer," Sophia said.

Leta frowned. "I am not. I healed Papa."

Sophia stared helplessly at Kaden. He shrugged and glanced at Maya.

"Maya, is it possible that Avery gained her healing powers before she was a teenager?"

Maya shook her head. "No. She did not gain her powers until after she started her monthlies. I am sure of it."

"James didn't get his healing powers until he was in his teens," Evan said. "Mama said so."

"I healed Papa!" Leta said stubbornly. "I saved Papa's

life. Why don't you believe me?" She crossed her arms with frustration and glared at the group.

"Perhaps the adrenaline and the fear jumpstarted her ability to heal," Marshall said.

"Is that possible?" Bree said.

"There's only one way to find out." Kaden held out his hand. "Evan, give me your knife."

Evan pulled the knife from the sheath around his belt and handed it to Kaden. As everyone watched, Kaden pressed the tip of the knife to his forearm and made a short but deep cut. He hissed with pain and Sophia frowned as blood immediately flowed from the cut.

Kaden crouched in front of Leta and held his arm out. "Heal me, Leta."

MAX SMILED AT HER DAUGHTER AND KISSED HER SOFT CHEEK. "Is that better, Violet?"

The little girl nodded, and Max lifted her into her arms before carrying her from the bathroom. She entered the kitchen and the plump woman stared nervously at her. "I'll show you out."

"That's fine. I know the way." She gave the plump woman a friendly smile and walked out of the kitchen before she could argue. As she approached the common room, she could hear voices and she paused and peeked inside, holding Violet firmly against her.

A large, dark-haired man was crouching in front of the young girl who was sitting on the couch. As she watched, he held out his arm and she could see the blood flowing from a wound on his arm.

"Heal me, Leta," he said.

LETA STARED APPREHENSIVELY AT KADEN'S ARM AND THEN shrugged. "Okay."

She pressed both of her hands on the cut and closed her eyes, and Kaden grunted under his breath. After only a few seconds, Leta pulled her hands back. She grinned happily at Kaden.

"See, I told you so."

"The gods be damned," Sophia said faintly as she stared at Kaden's arm. The wound was gone with only the blood dripping down his arm to remind them it'd been there.

There was a sharp gasp from the doorway. Nicky jumped to his feet and stalked across the room. He pulled the human woman into the room and pushed her back against the wall. Her hip bumped a small stand next to her and a yellow vase teetered on the edge. Without releasing the woman, Nicky reached out and caught it as it fell. He set it on the stand before cupping the back of the human's neck firmly. The little girl in her arms stared wide-eyed at him as he lowered his head until his face was only inches from her mother's.

"How long have you been standing there?"

"Only a few moments," she whispered.

"What did you see?"

"I – nothing." She swallowed.

"Do not lie to me, human," Nicky said. "What did you see?"

"I saw the little girl heal his arm."

Nicky's hand tightened on the back of her neck and she stared wide-eyed at him as she held her daughter closer.

"What's your name?" Nicky demanded.

"Max." She was squeezing her daughter so tightly the

toddler made a soft cry of discomfort. She loosened her grip as Nicky stepped closer.

"You saw nothing. Do you hear me, Max?" he said in a low voice. He stared into her eyes, at the odd combination of brown and blue, and growled softly. "Do I have to tell you what I will do to you if you speak a word of what you saw here today?"

Max stiffened and an odd sensation flowed through Nicky's hand and up his arm. The hair on the back of his neck stood up and his grip loosened. He flexed his arm as the vase on the stand beside the woman fell to the ground with a loud crash. It shattered into pieces and the baby twitched in her mother's arms before peering at the broken vase.

"Do I?" Nicky asked.

She shook her head as Nicky searched her face. Satisfied with what he saw, he released her and stepped back. Max backed towards the doorway as the baby smiled cheerily at Nicky.

"Bye, puppy," she chirped.

"Bye, baby," Nicky replied as Max nearly ran down the hallway.

CHAPTER 3

"Brother, are you all right?"

Nicky twitched, drawn out of his memory by James' voice. "Aye, I'm fine."

James watched as Nicky heaved another shovelful of dirt into the wheelbarrow.

"How's Dad?" Nicky said.

"Good. He hasn't woken yet, but his pulse is steady and he's breathing fine. Mama is about to clean the blood off of him."

James hesitated. "Mama believes Leta healed him."

"She did," Nicky replied.

"Nicky, Leta is too young. It isn't -"

"She did, baby brother. While you were with Dad, we questioned her about what happened. Kaden cut his arm with Evan's dagger and told Leta to heal him. She did. It took only a few seconds for her to heal him."

James grunted with surprise. "If that's the case, then she's more powerful than me."

Nick nodded. "Aye, she is."

TRISTAN OPENED HIS EYES. AVERY WAS BENT OVER HIM, wiping his upper body dry with a soft towel, and he stared silently at her for a moment. He took a deep breath and reached up to touch her hair, a little dismayed at how weak he was. At the touch of his hand, she jerked and stared up at him.

"Hello, girl," he rasped.

She began to cry. "Hello, my lord."

"Don't cry, my love."

She cried harder and he watched with bewilderment as she tossed the towel to the floor and pressed her head against his chest. He stroked her hair, threading the long red strands through his fingers as she sobbed brokenly.

"Don't cry," he repeated. "I'm fine. You saved me."

She sat up and wiped the tears from her face. "I did not, Tristan."

"What do you mean?"

"I did not save you. Leta did," she whispered.

"That's not possible."

She laughed jaggedly. "You're sitting here, are you not? You're breathing, talking – that is because of Leta."

"She's a healer," he said with soft wonderment.

"Aye," she said. "Sophia just left. She said that Kaden cut himself with a knife and asked Leta to heal him. She healed him in only a second or two. They believe that her fear and adrenaline brought out her healing ability."

"The gods be damned," he said.

Avery slipped off the bed and poured a glass of water from the ceramic jug by the bed. She handed it to him, and he sipped at it before resting back against the pillows.

"How do you feel?" she asked as she climbed up beside him.

"Tired and weak," he admitted.

She curled her body against his, stroking his chest as warmth tingled through him. He sighed contently and kissed the top of her head.

"You almost died, Tristan," she whispered.

"I believe I did die," he admitted.

She sat up and stared wide-eyed at him. "What do you mean?"

"The arrow was meant for my heart and it did not miss its mark," he said. "I could hear my heart beating in my ears and then it just…stopped. I don't remember anything after that."

She shook her head. Her face was completely devoid of colour and it made her red hair even brighter against her skin. "No, that is impossible. We – we cannot bring back the dead, only heal the living."

She was trembling violently, and he stared at her in alarm before tugging on her arm. "Lie against me, girl."

She did as he asked, and he rubbed her back as she wrapped her arms around his waist. They laid in comfortable silence for awhile. Avery's gift was doing its work, already he felt stronger and more alert, and he squeezed her hip.

"How do you feel, Avery?"

"Fine. Leta did all the hard work, remember?" There was an edge of hysteria to her voice and Tristan frowned before tilting her head up so he could look at her face.

"Avery, are you all right?"

"Aye. Why would I not be? My husband died and my child brought him back to life. Just another normal day, is it not?"

"I could be mistaken. Perhaps I was only close to dying."

"Perhaps. Or perhaps Leta is more powerful than we could ever have imagined."

He could hear the panic in her voice, and he cupped her face and kissed her firmly on the mouth. She kissed him hard in return, her tongue snaking into his mouth to rub against his as she ran her fingers through the hair on his chest. Despite his worry for her, his body responded to her touch. He groaned and gathered her closer, one hand reaching down to cup her breast through her shirt.

She pulled back and stared at him with regret. "I'm sorry, my lord. I should not have done that. You need rest."

He rubbed his thumb along her lower lip, and she moaned a little. "Please, my lord. This is not a good idea."

"Say my name," he murmured as he cupped the back of her neck and pulled her towards him.

"Tristan," she whispered.

His gaze dropped to her mouth and he smiled when her lips parted. "You know what I need most, girl. Give it to me."

"Aye, Tristan," she said.

She slid off the bed and he watched as she pulled off her clothes. When she was naked, she moved back toward the bed and he shook his head.

"No, let me look at you for a moment."

He stared at her, his eyes lingering first on her hardened nipples and then the red curls between her legs. When he lifted his gaze to her face, her cheeks were flushed, and he was secretly delighted that he could still make her blush.

"You're so beautiful, Avery."

She smiled. "Thank you, my love."

She pulled back the covers and stared admiringly at his hard cock before she straddled him. He moaned when her core brushed against his erection and she smiled again.

She bent her head and licked his throat before trailing wet

kisses down to his chest. She sucked on one flat nipple, making him groan, before he cupped her breasts. He rubbed his thumbs over her nipples and then pulled lightly on them.

She gasped and arched her back, her hands tightening on his shoulders, as she rubbed herself against him.

"Avery, please," he said hoarsely.

She smiled at him and grasped his cock. She stroked it firmly until his hips were rising helplessly and then rose up on her knees and guided him to her warmth. She rubbed the head of his cock against her clit and they both moaned.

"Does it feel good, girl?"

"So good," she moaned again.

He put his hands on her hips and pulled her forward until he was at her entrance. He pushed and slipped into her. Her pussy gripped him firmly and he groaned as he sheathed himself entirely inside of her.

"Tristan," she moaned when he didn't move.

"Aye, my love?"

She didn't reply. Instead, she braced her hands on her shoulders and rode him slowly. She rotated her hips, her pussy tightening around him, and he made another loud groan.

"Gods, girl," he muttered.

She grinned and moved faster, squeezing and releasing him with rhythmic movements as she moved up and down. He grasped her hips and helped her to move, pumping his hips against hers as she reached down and caressed her clit with the tips of her fingers.

She was panting now, her face flushed and her eyes closed with pleasure. He pulled her closer so that he could take one hard nipple into his mouth. At the feel of his warm tongue and lips, she shuddered and arched her back. She climaxed around him and he shouted with pleasure, his pelvis rising up as warmth surged through him and he joined her in climaxing.

He collapsed against the bed, panting harshly. She smiled down at him. "Do you feel better, my lord?"

"Aye, much better." He winked at her and she laughed before sliding off of him and pulling the sheet and quilt around them both.

"I love you, Tristan," she murmured as she wrapped her warm body around his.

"I love you too, girl."

———

MERIDAN WAS ON RYKER THE MOMENT THE CARRIAGE returned to their campsite. Max flinched and held Violet a little closer when Meridan nearly leaped from the carriage. His eyes glowing and hair sprouting on his face and hands, he grabbed Ryker by his shirt and shook him roughly.

"You fool! What in the gods name were you thinking?"

The man gave him a look of contempt. "You would be wise to release me, Meridan. Unless you want an arrow in your chest as well?"

"You're a fool, Ryker!" Meridan shouted. "You know we need Nicholas."

Ryker drove his hand into the bridge of Meridan's nose. It broke with a sickening crack and Meridan howled with pain as blood gushed down his face.

Ryker stepped back, straightening his shirt and dusting off his pants as Pavina crouched beside Meridan and patted his back helplessly before staring with fear and loathing at Ryker.

"The Lycan's adopted father would have convinced him not to go. You know that, Meridan. I believe the Lycan will be more inclined to help us find his birth father now that his adopted one is dead."

"Bullshit," Max said. Ryker turned his gaze to her, his eyes darkening with anger and something else she refused to identify.

"You shot that arrow at him because you were angry that Meridan would not allow you to come with us."

Ryker stalked past the moaning Meridan and stood in front of Max. He reached out and stroked her short hair gently before smiling at Violet. The toddler shrunk back, hiding her face in her mother's throat as Ryker leaned closer.

"Clever girl," he whispered as his thumb lightly stroked her temple.

He straightened and looked at the carriage. "Where is the Lycan? Did he need time to bury the man he believed to be his father?"

"He's not dead," Pavina said. "You missed."

Ryker blinked in surprise. "I never miss. My arrow found its mark."

Max smiled coldly. "Not this time, Ryker."

"That's impossible." Ryker stared at her in disbelief. He glanced at Meridan and Pavina before looking around the campsite. He eyed the large pack of Lycans, some in human form and some in wolf form, staring back at him before snorting angrily and storming to his tent. He disappeared inside of it and Max released her breath in a quiet rush.

Violet stared at her for a moment before whispering, "Bad man, Mama."

"Shh, Violet. It's okay." Max kissed Violet's soft cheek as a teenage girl, her long blonde hair braided and her pale skin flushed with the cold, approached them. She pulled Violet from the carrier on her mother's back and hugged the toddler.

"I'll take Violet to my tent and give her something to eat," the young girl said as Violet threw her arms around her neck.

"Thank you, Nina." Max smiled gratefully at her. "I'll join you in a moment."

As Nina disappeared into the tent with Violet, Max knelt next to Meridan. "Sit up, Meridan."

Pavina helped him sit up and Max wiped the blood from his face with the edge of her shirt. "How does it feel?"

Meridan turned his head and spit blood on to the ground. "How do you think it feels? It hurts."

"Will it heal on its own?"

He shrugged. "I don't know. I'm an old Lycan. My healing powers are not what they used to be."

He touched his nose gingerly. It was canted to the left and Max examined it carefully before giving him a sympathetic look. "This is going to hurt as well. Hold still."

He nodded and Pavina took his hand and held it as Max reached out and gripped his nose with her fingers.

"On the count of three," she said.

He nodded.

"One -"

She twisted her fingers sharply to the right and Meridan made a short howl of pain as his nose straightened.

"Gods be damned, Max!" He snarled at her as he cupped his aching nose.

"Sorry, my friend." She squeezed his shoulder before standing and walking to Nina's tent.

"HELLO, NICKY."

Nicholas looked up as Tristan sat down next to him. He

stared at the frozen lake in front of them as Nicky stared worriedly at him. "You should be resting, Dad."

Tristan shook his head. "I'm good. In fact, thanks to Leta and your mother, I feel about ten years younger." He stretched and the bones in his back cracked as he smiled at Nicky. "How are you feeling?"

Nicky shrugged. "Fine. Did Mama tell you who they were?"

"Aye, she did."

Nicky stared moodily at the lake for a few minutes. "You are my father. Nothing they said today will ever change that."

Tristan placed his hand on the back of Nicky's neck and squeezed. "Aye, and you are my son. I love you, Nicky, as does your mama."

"I know. I love you too." Nicky ran his hand through his short blonde hair.

"Will you go with them?"

"No. I have no wish to meet the man who abandoned me as a pup."

"Your mama said that he did not know about you until three moons ago," Tristan pointed out.

Nicholas stared at him. "Do you want me to go? Is that what you're saying?"

Tristan shook his head. "You are an adult, Nicky. It is not up to me to tell you what you should do." He hesitated and then squeezed Nicky's neck again. "But I believe there has always been a part of you that wondered about your real father."

Nicholas stared angrily at him. "I have been perfectly happy with you and Mama. You are my family, and I am grateful for everything you have done for me. I know that you did not have to take me as a baby, and if you think that I don't thank the gods every day that you -"

"Stop, Nicky," Tristan said.

Breathing hard, Nicky stared at the lake again as his father spoke. "I do not mean to say that you are unhappy with us. I know you are not. But it is not a betrayal to us to be curious about your birth father. It is natural and to be expected."

"I can't go," Nicky said. "You were attacked in our home. I need to stay and protect you, protect our family."

"What do you think the odds are that the arrow came from the people who are working for your father?" Tristan said.

"High." Nicky picked up a rock and threw it. It bounced across the frozen lake and he turned to Tristan, his eyes glowing with a fierce yellow light. "I will kill the man who tried to take you from us."

When Tristan didn't reply, the light faded from Nicky's eyes and he stared at the ground. "Sorry, Dad."

"Nicky -"

"It is another reason I should not go with them. If my birth father's men would try and kill you, the man who raised me when he did not have to, they cannot be trusted."

"We do not know for sure it was them," Tristan said. "You're right not to trust them though. You will have to be careful and keep your guard up always."

Nicky frowned at him. "You act as though I will go with them. I already told you I would not."

Tristan sighed. "Will you take my advice, Nicky? I realize you are no longer a child, but I would give you counsel if you will take it."

"Of course."

"If what these Lycans are saying is true, if the leeches have bitten your father with the purpose of creating a hybrid, then he will most likely die as the other Lycans before him have. If you do not go, if you do not try and meet him before he dies, I believe you'll regret it. My father has been dead many years but not a day goes by that I do not miss him. I was close to my father, as close as you and I are, and I thank the gods that I had as many years with him that I did."

He squeezed Nicky's neck until the Lycan turned toward him. "You are my son and I am your father. Nothing will change that – not even meeting your birth father. But I believe it would serve you well to meet the Lycan who gave you life."

He took a deep breath and smiled at his son. "Maya says they are returning tomorrow. It does not give you much time to make your decision but know that whatever you decide, I will stand behind you. All right?"

"Aye," Nicky said.

Tristan stood. "Come, it will be dark soon and you have been out here long enough. Your mama is worried about you. Come back with me and ease her worry."

He held out his hand and Nicholas took it, allowing Tristan to haul him to his feet. He hesitated and then embraced Tristan. Tristan returned his embrace and kissed him roughly on the forehead.

"I love you, Dad."

"I love you too, Nicky."

CHAPTER 4

They returned the following afternoon. Nicky, his arms folded across his chest and his eyes narrowed, watched as they stepped out of the carriage. The silver haired Lycan and the Lycan with the light brown skin had returned, as had the short-haired woman. The toddler was once again strapped to her back and she smiled gleefully when she saw him.

"Hi, puppy!" she called loudly, and her mother hurriedly hushed her.

A thin and frail-looking blonde girl stepped out of the carriage. Her skin was pale, and she couldn't have been more than fourteen. She looked nervous and she stumbled a bit as she stepped down from the carriage.

The short-haired woman caught her by the arm and gave her an encouraging smile. The girl nodded and took a deep breath before staring at Nicky. He returned her look without smiling, and after a moment she dropped her eyes to the ground before her.

Tristan stepped forward and held out his hand. "My name is Tristan Williams."

"Hello, lord Williams." Meridan shook his hand. "I am

Meridan and this is Pavina, Max, and Nina. The small one strapped to her mother's back is Violet." He swept his hand toward the women.

"Come inside, it is freezing out." Tristan studied Nina's pale face and Violet's chubby, rosy cheeks. "We would like it if you stayed for dinner this evening."

Meridan blinked in surprise. "That – that is very kind of you, lord Williams. Thank you." With a quick look at Pavina, he and the others followed Tristan and Nicky into the house.

———

MAX COULD FEEL NINA TREMBLING BEHIND HER AS THEY followed the lord Williams into the house. She took the young girl's hand and squeezed it. There were not as many people in the room as there were yesterday. The giant red Lycan was there, a tiny blonde woman standing by his side, as well as the pretty dark-haired Lycan. She gave them a cool look as the large man standing next to her took her hand before placing a gentle kiss on the top of her head. The redheaded woman from yesterday stood next to Tristan.

"This is my wife, Avery. These are my children and their mates. This is James," the red Lycan gave a brief nod, "and Bree. This is my daughter Sophia and Kaden."

"It's nice to meet you," Meridan said. There was an awkward silence and then Avery smiled at them.

"Can we take your coats? We were just about to have some tea. We would like it if you joined us."

Meridan hesitated. He obviously was surprised by their hospitality, and Max stepped forward and smiled at the Red.

"Aye, that is very kind of you. We would love some tea." She held her hand out to Avery. "I'm Max."

"It's nice to meet you, Max. And who is this?" Avery

stroked Violet's cheek. The toddler was staring at Avery's hair and before Max could stop her, she had stretched her chubby arm out and tangled her hand in Avery's hair.

"Pretty," she giggled.

"Violet, no!" Max gave Avery an apologetic look. "I'm so sorry."

Avery laughed before untangling Violet's hand from her hair. She gently kissed the baby's palm. "It is fine. It's a far nicer reaction than my hair normally gets."

An older woman stepped into the room. "Avery? The tea is ready. Shall I bring it in?"

Avery nodded. "Yes please, Marian. Do you need my help?"

Marian shook her head. "No. Renee and Laura will help me."

MAX TOOK ANOTHER SIP OF HER TEA AND TRIED TO KEEP THE squirming Violet on her lap. Avery had given the toddler her own cup of tea, sweetened with honey, and a warm biscuit slathered in butter. The little girl had eaten the biscuit eagerly and drank the sweet tea, but she had quickly grown tired of sitting on her mother's lap.

As she squirmed again, Avery smiled at Max. "Why don't you let her down to explore. It has been a few years since we had a small child in the house, but I remember their energy."

"Thank you." Max kissed Violet's head and released her from her lap. The child immediately slid to the ground and carefully toddled around the room.

"How old is she?" Sophia asked as Violet cautiously approached her.

"Nearly three."

"Hello, little one." Sophia smiled at the little girl and reached out to tickle her belly. Violet giggled and pushed at her hand before walking past her to the redheaded Lycan and his mate. She stopped a few feet away and stared up at him. Although she wasn't normally shy, she kept a healthy distance from him. Max didn't blame her. The Lycan was one of the biggest she'd ever seen and as she eyed the tiny blonde woman sitting next to him, she wondered idly how it worked between them in bed. The Lycan looked as though he could crush her easily, but it was obvious that she had no fear of him.

The blonde woman, Max thought her name was Bree, held out her arms. "Hi, Violet. Will you come and see me?"

Violet took a few steps forward, stared at the Red, and reconsidered. She backed away as Bree glanced up at him. "She seems to be frightened of you, James."

James smiled at her. "Aye, the small ones often are."

Violet continued to back up. She glanced briefly at Tristan and Avery before her gaze fell on Nicky. He was leaning against the wall, his arms still folded against his chest. He'd refused tea and food and had not spoken a word since they arrived.

Max took another sip of her tea and stared discreetly at him. He looked very similar to his father but, despite that, she found him handsome. His hair was short and, as she studied him, he raked his hand through it making it stand nearly on end. He had light blue eyes and although not as big as James, he was broad shouldered and muscular.

Violet, her face breaking out in a grin, toddled toward him. "Puppy!"

She stood in front of him and lifted her arms up. After a moment's hesitation, Nicky bent and scooped her up. He settled her in the crook of his arm, and she patted his smooth cheek happily.

"Hi, puppy."

"Hello, baby."

"Violet, his name is Nicholas," Max said.

Violet frowned at her mother. "Puppy?"

"No, honey. Nicholas," she said his name slowly and clearly and Violet returned her gaze to Nicholas."

"Nico-as?" she said hesitantly.

A small smile crossed his face as Avery laughed. "I believe Nicky would be easier for her to say."

Nicholas smiled at Violet. "Nicky. Can you say Nicky?"

"Nicky." Violet parroted obediently.

"That's right, baby." Nicholas kissed her soft cheek and Violet grinned happily at him.

She squirmed in his arms and he set her down. She smiled up at him. "Bye, puppy."

Avery and Bree laughed as Max sighed. "Oh, Violet."

Meridan cleared his throat. "You seem to be doing well after what happened yesterday, lord Williams."

"Aye," Tristan said evenly. "My Lycan healing powers served me well."

"Indeed. Do you know why you were attacked or who attacked you?" Meridan asked.

"We have our suspicions," Nicky said. He stared at Meridan.

"Well, I hope you find the culprit," Meridan said.

"I'm sure we will," Nicholas said.

Meridan cleared his throat again. "I realize this has been a bit unexpected, but have you had time to think on what we have asked of you?"

Before Nicholas could reply, a sharp barking was heard in

31

the hallway. A small dog, its tail wagging furiously, darted into the room and a young girl came barreling in after it.

"Tia, come back! Bad dog!"

The girl was the one who healed the dark-haired man named Kaden, and Max glanced at Nicholas. He was giving her a hard look and she looked away, her heart thumping.

The dog made a beeline for Violet who was standing in front of the fireplace. She jumped on the toddler and although the dog was small, the little girl staggered on her feet and fell backward. Her head hit the hearth with a loud thud. Max jumped to her feet and hurried forward as Violet's face screwed up and she wailed loudly.

The girl gently pushed the dog away before she bent and picked up Violet. "There, there, little baby. Did you bump your head?" She placed her hand on the back of Violet's head and kissed the wailing toddler's face. "You're okay, baby bird. Don't cry."

Max watched in amazement as Violet immediately stopped crying. She stared with wide eyes at the girl holding her and paid no attention when Max crouched beside her and examined the back of her head. From the force of her fall, she should have had a bump on her head, but Max could feel nothing under the baby's soft hair. Violet didn't wince or cry out when Max pressed gently on her skull, and the girl holding Violet smiled at her.

"She's all right."

"Aye," Max said.

"Leta?" Avery said gently. "We asked you to stay in your room, remember?"

"Aye, Mama. I'm sorry." Leta was still holding Violet and she jiggled the little girl in her arms. "Tia escaped and I was chasing her."

She put Violet down and the baby made a soft whine of disappointment and grabbed onto Leta's leg. "Up!"

Leta picked Violet up again, grunting softly with the effort, and smiled at Max. "She likes me."

"Aye, she does," Max replied.

"Do you like me, little baby bird?" Leta cooed. "Are you the sweetest baby ever?"

Violet giggled and placed a sloppy kiss on Leta's mouth. Max blinked in surprise. Violet wasn't shy but it wasn't like her to take so quickly to a stranger.

Leta carried Violet to a chair in the corner of the room, Tia trailing after them, and placed the girl in it before she picked out a picture book from the shelf on the wall. She climbed in next to Violet and heaved the little girl onto her lap. "Here, baby bird. I'll read you a story."

Violet leaned contently against Leta and stared at the book as Leta opened it and read quietly to her. Frowning a little, Max returned to the couch where Nina was sitting. She sat next to the Nina and took her hand as Tristan turned his gaze to Meridan.

"You say that Nicky's father was taken by the leeches nearly a moon ago?"

"Aye, give or take a few days," Meridan replied.

"It was take you at least half a moon to get to the outskirts. If they have bitten him, do you believe he will still be alive?"

"I do. Nicky's father is strong and healthy. And there is the chance they have not bitten him yet."

"Doubtful," Pavina sighed. "They like the strong ones, you know that. The leeches believe they have a better chance of turning them."

Nina made a small sound of dismay and Max frowned at Pavina. "Hold your tongue, Pavina."

Pavina shrugged. "I am only being truthful. Nina is not a child. We should not have to coddle her." She stared at Nicky. "Have you made your decision, Lycan? Will you go with us to rescue your father?"

"You ask me to risk my life for a Lycan I do not know? One who, despite your assurances, is most likely dead already. And if he is not, he will be shortly," Nicholas said.

Nina, her body trembling wildly and tears beginning to slide down her cheeks, jumped to her feet. "How can you be so cruel? He is our father! You do not know how -"

Nicky strode across the room and grabbed the girl by her arms. He shook her roughly as Max jumped to her feet.

"Our father?" He stared at the girl and shook her again. "What do you mean, our father?"

Nina gave him a frightened look as Max put her hand on Nicky's arm and pulled. He glared at her, growling under his breath, and she scowled at him.

"Let her go. You're frightening her."

"Be quiet, human."

"Make me," Max said sharply.

Nicky growled again and Tristan stood up. "Nicholas, enough."

He dropped Nina's arms but continued to stand in front of her. She stared up at him, her entire body trembling wildly as Max put an arm around her shoulders.

"She is your half-sister," Max said.

Nicky inhaled deeply as he stared at Nina. "You are human."

Nina swallowed. "Aye. My – my mother was human."

"You did not receive any of the Lycan genes?" Nicky said.

"No."

"How old are you?" Nicholas asked.

"Fourteen."

"Do we have any other siblings?"

"No," Nina said.

"Is your mother here? Has she come to rescue her mate as well?"

Nina bit at her bottom lip. "My mother and father were not married. She died two years ago."

Nicholas looked her up and down before stepping back. He gave Meridan a hard glare. "Why would you bring a child on a mission such as this? Are you that foolish?"

"I am not a child!" Nina said. "I have every right to go with them to rescue my father."

Nicky rolled his eyes. "The outskirts are no place for a young girl."

He looked to Meridan and pointed at Max. "You would be wise to force her to stay with this one and her baby while you go on your ridiculous rescue mission."

Nina glared at him. "Max is going as well, and I will not be left behind like some invalid. I will go and rescue our father with or without your help!"

Nicholas ignored her as he stared first at Meridan and then Max. "You're going to rescue my father?"

"Aye, I am," Max said defiantly.

Nicky snorted with disgust. "Then convince this one to stay with your child. She will need a nanny."

"Violet stays with me," Max said.

"What?" Nicky stared incredulously at her as the others glanced at each other in surprise.

Avery stood and approached them. "Max, surely you realize that the outskirts are no place for a child."

Max flushed a little. "Aye, my lady. I know."

"Yet you would still take her there?" Nicky said. "Knowing the danger? It is not safe for her." He glanced at

35

his mother who nodded. "Leave her here. My mother will take good care of her and keep her safe."

"Violet is safest with me," Max said.

Nicky snorted again. "You're a fool. You and your daughter will die in the outskirts." He stepped closer and closed one firm hand around her upper arm. "How do you think it will feel to watch your baby be fed on by leeches, or her essence sucked away by the faeries? Is that what you want for her?"

Max wrenched her arm free and glared furiously at him. "I told you I would keep her safe."

Nicholas looked her up and down. "How? Do you have some skill with the sword? You're fairly thick through the middle so I can't imagine you are planning on running."

"Nicholas!" Avery said sharply as Max raised her hand to slap him in the face.

He caught her wrist before she could slap him and, his eyes glowing, stared down at her. "You should not -"

Max tried to control it, tried not to let it overwhelm her, but like always when she was afraid, her power refused to be stopped. She could feel the air changing between her and Nicholas, and a weird look crossed his face as he stared at his hand around her wrist. Nina cried out with fear when the teapot, sitting on a cart next to them, suddenly exploded. Max and Nina were splattered with hot liquid, and Max winced when shards of ceramic embedded themselves in her arm and hand.

Violet made a loud cry and wiggled down from the chair she was sitting in with Leta. She stumbled across the room and latched onto her mother's leg. "Mama?"

"I'm okay, Violet." Max smiled shakily at her as Nicky dropped his grip on her arm and stood back.

Avery went to take Max's arm and Nicholas caught her

arm. He shook his head lightly at her and she frowned at him. "Nicky -"

Tristan pulled Avery back gently as Bree stood in front of Max. "You've been cut." She took Max's hand and examined the small cuts in her flesh before smiling at her.

"Nothing too serious but we should wash it and pull out the bits of ceramic. Here, come with me to the kitchen."

Max glanced down at Violet who was still clinging to her leg. The little girl was staring with fright at the trickles of blood on her mother's forearm and Max smiled reassuringly at her. "Mama's fine, Violet. I just need to wash my arm."

"Up, Mama." Violet held her arms up and gave her a pleading look.

"I need to wash my arm first, honey."

Violet's lip pouted out, and Max made a soft soothing sound. "Go to Meridan, honey. You can sit with him."

Violet turned to Nicholas and held her arms up to him. "Up, puppy."

He picked her up and she snuggled into him, resting her head on his shoulder and slinging her chubby arms around his neck. He rubbed her back a bit awkwardly as Bree turned to Nina.

"Nina, have you been cut?"

The young girl shook her head and Bree glanced at Sophia. "She has tea all over her. Will you take her to my room and give her one of my shirts? It should fit her."

"Aye." Sophia held her hand out to the young human. "Come with me, Nina."

Nina hesitated and glanced at Max. She nodded. "It's all right, Nina. They won't hurt you."

CHAPTER 5

"There, that's better." Bree had pulled all of the small shards of ceramic out of Max's arm and washed it carefully. She blotted it dry and placed a small bandage on the largest of the cuts. "It should not take long to heal."

"Thank you," Max replied.

"You're welcome." Bree smiled at her in a friendly manner before beginning to clean up.

Max glanced at the ring on Bree's finger. "How long have you and your husband been married?"

Bree grinned a little. "Almost three days."

"You are newlyweds."

"Aye."

"Are you a Lycan?" she asked.

Bree shook her head. "No. I am human."

"Your husband is one of the biggest Lycans I've ever seen. Do you – are you not worried he will hurt you accidentally?"

Bree hesitated and Max gave her an apologetic smile. "I'm sorry. I'm being nosy."

"It's fine," Bree replied. "James is big and looks rather

fierce, I know, but he would never hurt me. He is sweet and very gentle."

After witnessing the way the Red had threatened to kill Pavina yesterday for insulting his mother, Max wasn't so sure about that but she kept her thoughts to herself and smiled hesitantly at Bree. "I have never met a particularly sweet or gentle Lycan."

Bree laughed. "Aye, until I met James and his family, I hadn't either."

"How did you meet them?"

"James saved my life," Bree said. She stared at Max's tea-stained shirt. "You need a new shirt as well. Come with me. Sophia should have an extra shirt for you."

Bree led her out of the kitchen and down a long hallway and grinned when Nina and Sophia, carrying a shirt in one hand, stepped out of a room.

"I was just coming to find you, Sophia."

"Aye. I thought she would need a shirt as well. Mine should fit her well enough."

Sophia handed the shirt to Max and Bree opened the door they were standing in front of. "You can change in here. We will take Nina back to the common room. Can you find your way back?"

"Aye, thank you," Max replied. She closed the door behind her and stared curiously around the room. It was a good size with a fireplace on the far wall and a large walnut-coloured bureau on the opposite wall. A bed, covered in a blue and grey quilt, was pushed under the window. She walked toward it and laid the shirt on the bed before staring out the window. It was a nice view, she could see glimpses of the ice-covered lake through the trees, and she decided it would be an absolutely gorgeous view during the warmer months.

Sighing, she stripped off her shirt and reached for the one on the bed. She hesitated and stared down at her half-naked body. The Lycan had called her thick and she supposed it was a bit true. She wandered to the mirror that was on the wall and stared at herself. Her stomach was flat enough, but she had wide hips and since giving birth to Violet, her breasts were bigger and heavier than she cared for.

She turned sideways and stood on her tiptoes, examining her ass in the mirror. Her pants were too big, and she pulled them tightly across her body. Compared to Pavina, she did have a large ass. Although, she thought irritably, every woman compared to Pavina was thick looking. The Lycan was drop dead gorgeous, and Max couldn't ignore the niggle of jealousy that went through her.

She hasn't had a child, remember? Would you honestly give up Violet in order to have perky breasts and a small ass to impress a bad-tempered Lycan you just met? Gods, girl. You're being a fool.

She rolled her eyes at herself. She was being a fool. She had no –

The door to the room opened and Nicky, holding a sleeping Violet against his shoulder, walked in. The two of them froze and Max felt a hot blush rising in her cheeks when Nicky's gaze dropped to her naked breasts.

She stood frozen for a moment longer until the screaming in her head could no longer be ignored.

You're half-naked! Cover yourself, you fool!

She whipped around until her back was to him and covered her breasts with her hands for good measure.

"Turn around!" she snapped at Nicholas over her shoulder.

He turned obediently and stared at the wall as she hurried

over to the bed and snatched up the shirt. She pulled it over her head and glared at his back.

"Do you always walk in on half-naked women?"

"It's my bedroom," he replied. "Your child fell asleep and I thought she would be more comfortable napping in a bed."

He took a cautious look over his shoulder and Max crossed her arms over her chest when he glanced at her shirt-covered breasts. "You could have knocked."

"I didn't know you were in here," he said. "I thought you were in the kitchen with Bree."

She didn't reply and he carried Violet to the bed. He pulled back the quilt and sheet and placed the sleeping child gently on the bed. Max, her cheeks still burning, covered up Violet and brushed a gentle hand across her forehead. The little girl sighed and blinked sleepily before sitting straight up in the bed.

"Mama?" she whimpered.

"Hush, Violet. You're okay."

The little girl held her arms out and without looking at Nicky, Max lay down on the bed beside her and cuddled the little girl. Violet's thumb inched towards her mouth and Max pulled it gently away. "No thumb sucking, Violet. You're a big girl now."

Violet pouted up at her and then yawned widely. "Sleepy, Mama."

"I know, honey. Close your eyes."

"Sing, Mama?" Violet said hopefully.

Max, acutely aware of Nicky still standing next to the bed, began to sing Violet's favourite lullaby. The little girl buried her face in Max's neck and slung her chubby arm across her chest. Without speaking, Nicky turned and left the room, closing the door quietly behind him.

Max rested her head against Violet's soft hair and inhaled

deeply before closing her eyes. She had lost control earlier, for the second time in as many days, and she had just flashed her boobs at the Lycan. Could the day get any worse?

"Excuse me?"

Nicholas looked behind him. After leaving Max and Violet in his bedroom, he had grabbed his jacket and escaped to the back yard. He needed some time alone and he frowned irritably at the blonde girl standing behind him.

The girl, his half-sister he reminded himself, gave him an anxious smile. "Do you know where Max is?"

"She's lying down with her child," he said shortly.

"Oh, thank you." The girl turned to go, and he sighed.

"Wait, girl. Come here for a moment."

She hesitated and then joined him, folding her arms across her torso.

"Nina, is that your name?"

"Aye."

"Are you truly my half-sister?" Nicholas asked.

"I am," she said.

He stared silently at her. She had blonde hair and blue eyes like he did, but the resemblance ended there. She was small and thin and very pale, and she shivered delicately in the cold. He took off his jacket and held it out to her.

"Here."

"Oh, no. I'm fine, I don't -"

"Take it," he grunted. "You're freezing."

She took his jacket, slipping into it and buttoning it up.

"What's our father's name?" he asked suddenly.

"Emmett. Emmett McKenzie."

"Do you live with him?"

"Aye."

"Are you close to him?"

Nina hesitated. "I love him very much."

"But?" Nicholas prompted.

"He – he was disappointed when he realized I was not a Lycan," Nina said. "It pleased him very much to discover he had a son who was a Lycan."

"Does he mistreat you because you're a human?" Nicholas frowned.

"Of course not," Nina replied. "He just – he does not have a lot of spare time. He is a very busy man."

"Why is that?"

She shrugged. "He has a lot of business deals going on. Many people come to him for help with their problems."

"Do they now?" Nicky said.

"Aye," Nina said eagerly. "Our father is a very powerful and respected Lycan in the city."

When Nicky didn't reply she gave him a shy look. "You look very similar to him. He has blond hair and blue eyes like we do. He is not as big as you, but he is tall and handsome."

Nicky grunted in reply and Nina gave him a pleading look. "Will you not help us, Nicholas? I know you do not know me or our father, but I promise you, he is a good man and you will not regret your decision to come with us."

"You should not be going. The outskirts are dangerous," Nicky said.

Nina flushed. "I am not afraid."

Nicky studied her carefully. "You are. I can smell it on you, Nina."

She looked at the ground in embarrassment. "I wish I was a Lycan like you and father. Perhaps then I would be brave."

"Being a Lycan does not make you brave," Nicky said.

She stared at him in disbelief as the back door opened and

James walked toward them. Nina shrank back but James smiled kindly at her and clapped Nicholas on the back. "Are you all right, Nicky? You've been out here for nearly half an hour."

"Aye, I'm fine."

Nicky looked back at the house. "What are they talking about in there?"

James shrugged. "They are making small talk. Mama and Aunt Maya are asking the old Lycan about the city and what changes have happened to it since they last lived there."

There was a long, drawn out howl from somewhere deep within the woods. Nina jumped and made a soft cry of fear.

"It's only a wolf, girl," James said.

Nina swallowed nervously. "Are there many Lycans in the woods?"

James shook his head. "Not a Lycan. A wolf."

"Oh." She stared with trepidation at the dark trees and James cocked his head at her.

"Have you been in the country before?"

"No. I was born in the city and have spent my life there. Our father was not much for country living."

"Odd for a Lycan," James grunted.

Nicky shrugged. "Some Lycans prefer the city. You know that."

"Aye. But it still seems odd." He glanced up at the storm clouds growing in the sky before clapping Nicky on the back again. "Come, it is close to dinner and the girl is freezing."

Nicky nodded and followed James and Nina into the house.

CHAPTER 6

"Bree, will you go to Nicky's room and let Max know that dinner will be ready soon?" Avery asked.

"Aye, I can do that, Mama."

Before Bree could leave the common room, Nicky stood. "I'll do it."

He disappeared down the hallway as Avery smiled at Marian and Laura who were standing in the doorway. "I believe we'll need to eat in the common room tonight. There are too many of us to fit in the kitchen."

"I'll have Leo bring in the table." Laura eyed the roomful of people. "We may not have enough chairs."

"There should be extra in the storage room." Avery glanced at Evan who was sitting by the fire with his sketchbook and staring surreptitiously at Nina.

"Evan? Could you go to the storage room and bring the chairs to the common room?"

"Aye, Mama."

"Thank you, my love." Avery smiled at him. "Nina, do you think you could help Evan?"

Nina nodded and followed a blushing Evan from the

room. Tristan stood behind Avery and put his arms around her waist.

"You know, girl," he breathed into her ear, "you do not have to find a mate for every one of our children."

She laughed. "Please, my lord. Evan is too young for that. I am just encouraging him to make a new friend. You know how shy he is."

"Of course." Tristan squeezed her gently before turning to Doran and Marshall. "Come, we'll help Leo bring the table into the common room."

NICKY STARED AT THE SLEEPING WOMAN. SHE WAS LYING ON her back with her child curled into her side, and her arm was thrown over her eyes. He studied her mouth before his gaze dropped to her chest. Sophia's shirt was tight on her and he stared at her full breasts. He could see the outline of her nipples against the snug fabric and he took a deep breath.

He had called her thick earlier and he supposed she was heavier than the women he had slept with before, but he was already feeling guilty for insulting her. Truthfully, he thought she was lovely. Her mouth was full and lush, and she had soft skin that he was itching to touch again. He was fascinated by her different coloured eyes and he wished he could study them closer.

His eyes dropped to her chest again. Her breasts were just short of amazing. When he had walked in on her and seen them, ripe and full with nipples hard from the cool air, he could barely stop from crossing the room and touching them. She was as short as Bree but solidly built. He wouldn't have to worry about hurting her like James, undoubtedly, had to worry about with his mate.

48

He had a sudden image of Max riding him in his bed, of cupping her full breasts while she slid him deep inside of her. Sweat beaded up on his brow and he rolled his eyes. The woman was not his type. And now was not the time to be thinking with his dick. He had discovered that his birth father was looking for him, the leeches were experimenting on his kind, and he had a half-sister. Besides, he had no intention of settling down any time soon. He dated women who had the same agenda as he did – a fun time with no commitment. The woman lying in his bed had a child. He doubted she would be interested in a casual roll in the hay with him. For all he knew, she could have a husband waiting for her back at their campsite. She wore no ring so it was unlikely, but it didn't mean that she did not have a mate. Violet's father, undoubtedly.

Still, he wondered how it would feel to kiss those lush lips. What it would sound like to hear her moan as he entered her. He would not turn down the chance to –

He realized that Violet had woken and was staring at him.

"Hi, baby." He smiled at her and she smiled back.

"Hi, puppy." She sat up and stared at her mother.

"Mama sleeping." She patted Max's cheek and then lifted her arms to Nicholas. "Potty."

"Oh, um..." Nicky glanced around as Violet wiggled out from under the covers.

She stared anxiously at him. "Potty."

"Okay. Let's wake up your mama and -"

"Pee, puppy!" Violet said frantically, as if she thought he might not understand the word potty.

"Okay, baby. Come on." He lifted her out of the bed and carried her out into the hallway. Bree was just coming out of hers and James's room and he called her name with relief.

She turned and smiled when she saw Violet. "Hi, little one."

"She has to go to the bathroom and her mother is still sleeping. Do you think you could take her?" he asked as Violet pounded his back with her little fist.

"Potty!"

"Of course. Here, give her to me." Bree held out her arms and Nicky handed over Violet. "I'll take you potty, Violet." She kissed the girl's cheek.

"Potty?" Violet said hopefully.

"That's right." Bree started down the hallway toward the bathroom.

"Thank you, Bree," Nicky called after her.

She smiled at him over her shoulder. "Aye, you're welcome, Nicky."

He returned to his room and hesitated before calling Max's name. She didn't stir and he said it again, louder this time. When she didn't move, he sat beside her on the bed and shook her shoulder a bit roughly.

"Max, time to wake up," he said.

She muttered and shifted in the bed and he leaned over her and shook her again. "Max, it's time to -"

She abruptly sat up straight in the bed. Their heads connected with a solid *thud* and he grunted with pain as she fell back on the bed and grabbed at her forehead.

"The gods be damned!" she said. "Why did you do that?"

Her eyes were watering with pain, but he scowled at her. "You sat up and hit me."

"I did not!" she said indignantly.

"Aye, you did," he said. "You were sleeping and when I tried to wake you, you -"

She sat up again and he just barely avoided knocking their

heads together for a second time. "Gods, human! What are you -"

"Violet! Where's Violet?" She was looking around the bed and he could hear the panic in her voice.

"Bree took her to the bathroom. She's fine. She's safe."

She took a trembling breath and rubbed at her forehead just above her right eyebrow. "Gods, do all Lycans have heads as hard as yours?"

"Let me see it." He reached for her hand and she jerked away from him.

"It's fine."

"Let me see it." He cupped the back of her neck with his left hand before pulling her hand from her face with his other.

"Let go!" She slapped him lightly on the chest and tried to wiggle out of his grip.

"Hold still, for the gods sake," he grumbled. He leaned closer and examined her forehead. Already it was starting to swell, and he could see a dark bruise rising on her skin. He frowned. The human was more fragile than she looked.

"It's fine," she said.

"It's bruising. You might have a concussion." The pain in his forehead had already disappeared.

"I don't. I just bruise easily," she said dismissively.

He stroked his fingertips across the swelling, and she hissed with pain, her hands digging into his thighs. "Don't touch it for the gods sake!"

He stared down at her hands gripping his thighs, and she blushed and let go of his legs. She tried to tug his hand away from her neck and he tightened his grip. "Hold still, I said. I want to look at your forehead."

"You've already looked at it," she said.

"Aye, I have." He stared at her eyes. He had wanted to examine them more closely and now, with his face only

51

inches from hers, he had his chance. He stared first at the blue one and then the brown one. The blue one was very light and the brown one very dark and it made the contrast between them even more startling. As he stared at them, her pupils widened until only a thin line of colour could be seen around each of them.

"You have very pretty eyes," he said.

"Thank you." Her voice was low.

"I have never seen anything like it before."

"It's not very common." She cleared her throat nervously. "Although, I do have a cousin who has one hazel eye and one green eye. The difference is not as noticeable as mine but she still –

He stopped her mouth with a kiss.

———

MAX MOANED QUIETLY. THE LYCAN'S LIPS WERE WARM AND firm and utterly intoxicating. She kissed him back, moaning again when he bit lightly at her upper lip. He licked her bottom one and she opened her mouth, inviting his tongue in.

He slipped it into her mouth as his right arm crept around her waist and he pulled her up against him, flattening her breasts against his hard chest. He continued to kiss her as his hand rubbed and kneaded her neck before cupping the back of her skull through her short hair.

Neither of them noticed when the large candle on the table beside the bed rose into the air. It hovered a few inches from the surface as Max put her hands tentatively on Nicky's broad shoulders. She ran them down his arms, exploring his hard biceps as he deepened the kiss. The candle, spinning slowly in the air next to them, rose higher as the drawer of the bedside table inched open.

"Nicky, did you wake up -"

The sound of Leta's voice made them spring apart guiltily. Max jumped when the bedside drawer slammed shut and the candle dropped to the floor, landing on Nicky's foot. He winced and picked it up, glancing at it curiously before placing it back on the table.

Leta, carrying Violet on her hip like she was a sack of flour, stood in the doorway of Nicky's bedroom and grinned at them.

"You like the human!" she said.

"Leta, be quiet. I do not," Nicky said.

"You do too. I can smell it on you." Leta walked to the bed. She grinned at Max. "My brother likes you."

"Leta! Enough," Nicky said through clenched teeth. His cheeks were red, and Max avoided his gaze as Violet waved at her from Leta's arms.

"Hi, Mama!"

"Hi, honey."

"I went potty," Violet said.

"Good job, baby." Max held her arms out.

Violet shook her head and clung to Leta. "No, Mama. Leta."

Leta grinned happily. "I taught the baby bird to say my name. She really likes me."

She smiled at the little girl and kissed her cheek. "Do you like me, baby bird? Do you love Leta? Leta loves her baby bird." She nuzzled Violet's neck and Violet giggled loudly.

"See?" Leta said to Max.

"She does like you." Max smiled at the young Lycan.

"What happened to your head?" Leta asked

Max touched her forehead. "Oh, I bumped it."

"On what?"

"Um, your brother's forehead."

Leta looked at Nicky. "You're not supposed to hit them in the head when you're kissing a girl, Nicky."

Nicholas groaned. "Leta, be quiet."

"Here, take the baby bird," Leta said. She heaved Violet onto Nicky's lap and climbed onto the bed beside Max.

"Hold still," she said encouragingly as she reached for Max's forehead.

"Leta, don't!" Nicky said sharply but it was too late. Leta had already pressed her hands against Max's forehead. Max inhaled sharply and her eyes widened as she stared up at Leta.

"Your eyes are so pretty," Leta said. "I wish my eyes were different colours." She removed her hands from Max's forehead and peered at it. "There, all better."

Max touched her forehead, staring at Leta in silence as Leta climbed off the bed. She held her arms out to Violet. "Do you want to come with me, baby bird?"

Violet nodded and Leta pulled her from Nicky's lap with a soft grunt. She set Violet on her feet and took her chubby hand. She led her from the bedroom, and Max gasped with surprise when Nicky reached out and gripped the back of her neck again before pulling her toward him.

For one moment she thought he meant to kiss her again and her lips parted with anticipation. Instead of kissing her, he gave her a hard look and pressed his fingers into her neck. "You are not to say a word about what Leta just did. Do you understand me, human?"

"Aye," she said irritably. "We've already had this discussion, remember? I haven't told anyone about your sister's powers."

"Good. Keep it that way." His gaze dropped to her mouth and then he was releasing her and pushing away from the bed. He stalked toward the door and, feeling irritated and confused, Max scowled at his back.

"If you want your sister's powers to remain hidden, I suggest you teach her not to reveal them so willingly."

Without looking at her, he said, "Dinner is ready." He left the room, shutting the door softly behind him.

Max sighed and flopped backward onto the bed. She stared at the ceiling and traced her fingers over her forehead before touching her mouth. It was still swollen from the Lycan's kisses, and she groaned before climbing out of the bed.

CHAPTER 7

Meridan stared out the window of the common room. The snow was falling thick and fast and he couldn't see more than a few feet into the yard. Behind him, he could hear the murmuring of Nicky's family and he turned when he heard Pavina's loud laugh.

One of the Lycans, he thought his name was Doran, was standing close to her and gesturing wildly. Pavina giggled again and rested her hand on his arm. The Lycan flushed, and Meridan sighed. Pavina was a flirt. She had no wish to settle down with one Lycan and he would have to speak to her about keeping her distance from the boy. It was imperative that they did nothing to jeopardize their chances at getting Nicky to come with them. The old man wanted to meet his son and he had charged Meridan with making it happen. Before the Lycans had taken him, Emmett had strongly hinted that Meridan's debt would be paid in full if he found his son. Meridan would do whatever it took to make that happen.

You don't need his son. The Lycan is either dead already or will soon be dead. When that happens, you'll be free.

Aye, he supposed that was true. In fact, he wasn't entirely

sure why he was even bothering trying to rescue the Lycan. With Emmett gone, it would be easy to slip away in the night, to take his own path and never look back.

He looked around the room for Nina. She was sitting on the floor with Violet in her lap. Leta had discovered that Violet laughed hysterically whenever she started to shift, and she was sitting across from them and partially shifting. As her eyes glowed and hair grew on her cheeks, she growled softly at Violet before returning back to her human form. The toddler shrieked with laughter and clapped her hands.

"Again! Again, Leta!" she cried.

Meridan smiled before looking back out the window. He stayed because he knew what Ryker would do to both Nina and Max if he left. As Emmett's appointed right hand, he still held a little power over Ryker, despite the human's obvious contempt for him. Meridan knew he could convince Max to leave with him, but Nina would refuse despite her fear of Ryker. She loved her father – why, Meridan had no idea- and she was anxious to save him. He might loathe Emmett, but he had grown very fond of Nina over the years. He had, in fact, come to think of her almost as a daughter and he would do what he could to make her happy.

Tristan approached him and stared out the window. "How far away is your campsite?"

"A few miles."

"I think it would be wise for you to spend the night here. It is too cold for your horses and it will be difficult to find your way back in this blizzard."

"That is very kind of you, but we have no wish to further impose on your hospitality. It was kind of you to invite us for dinner, but I think we should take our leave now."

Avery joined them. "Listen to my husband, Meridan. It is far safer for you to stay with us for the night." She glanced at

Nina and Violet. "It will be too cold for the little ones. Let them have a night in a warm house with a soft bed. They are in for a hard journey to the outskirts."

Meridan sighed. "Aye, you are right. Thank you."

Avery looked to her sister. "Maya, will you help me figure out bed arrangements? Meridan and the others are staying the night."

Maya nodded. "Sophia? Are you and Kaden sleeping in the loft tonight?"

Sophia glanced up at Kaden who winked at her and patted her ass. She gave him a small grin. "Aye, Aunt Maya, we are."

"That leaves Sophia's room free. We can put Meridan in that room."

"Pavina can stay in my room," Doran said.

Maya smiled. "That's very kind of you, Doran. Pavina can share your room with Nina, and you can sleep on the floor in Evan's room."

A look of dismay crossed Doran's face and Dani, her arm firmly around Andric's waist, giggled loudly at her twin. He glared at her and she grinned and stuck her tongue out at him.

"That leaves Max and Violet," Avery said. "Leta could sleep in our room and they -"

"Leta can sleep with me in my room," Vivian said. "The bed is large enough for both of us, and she used to crawl into my bed as a pup anyway."

Avery smiled at Vivian. "Aye, that is true. But have you forgotten how much Leta kicks in her sleep?"

Vivian winced. "Gods, I had forgotten."

"There's the small room off the servant's quarters. The bed is small, but Max and Violet are not very big," Bree said hesitantly.

"I'll take that one." Max left her spot by the fireplace and joined them. "I don't want to kick anyone out of their room."

"That room has no fireplace and is very cold." Avery frowned. "I think it might be too cold for the baby, even with plenty of blankets."

"I'm sure it will be fine," Max assured her. "Violet does not get cold easily and -"

"Max and Violet can take my room." Nicky stood next to his mother and folded his arms across his chest. "I'll sleep in the small room."

"Thank you, sweet Nicky." Avery squeezed his arm as Max frowned.

"We'll be fine in the smaller room. You should not give up your room for us. We -"

"The room is too cold," Nicky said. "You and the baby are sleeping in my room."

He walked away before she could argue.

"Nicholas," Meridan said.

Nicky turned to look at him.

Meridan glanced around the room. It had quieted and Lycan and human alike were staring at him as he folded his hands behind his back and stepped away from the window. "I am sorry, but I need to know what your decision is. Will you come with us to rescue your father?"

Nicky stared at his mother and father. Avery crossed the room and put her arm around his waist as Tristan gave him an encouraging look. From the corner of his eye, Meridan could see Nina stand up. She had her hands folded between her tiny breasts and she was staring at Nicholas anxiously.

Nicholas looked away, his gaze falling on Max. She stared steadily at him, her body stiff with tension, and he sighed and looked at Meridan. "Aye, I will go with you."

Nina made a soft cry of delight and ran to Nicky. She hesitated and then hugged him. He patted her thin back.

"Thank you, Nicholas. You won't regret it." She smiled happily at him. "Father will be so happy to meet you."

"Aye," he said as she skipped over to Meridan and hugged him.

"We're going to get father back before he's bitten by the leeches. I can feel it in my bones, Meridan," she said.

"I hope so, Nina," Meridan said.

———

"I'm going with Nicky."

Sophia sighed. "You cannot go, James. Bree is with pup. You can't leave her. I will go with Nicky to the outskirts."

"If you're going, so am I," Kaden said.

Sophia smiled at him. "Thank you, Kaden."

"You must promise me you'll be careful." Bree reached out and took her brother's hand.

"I'll be fine, Bree." Kaden squeezed her hand.

It was just before dawn. The three oldest Williams siblings, as well as Bree and Kaden, had gathered together in the kitchen. The rest of the house was silent, and they spoke in low whispers as they sat at the table.

Nicky shook his head. "Neither you nor Kaden are coming with me, Sophia."

Sophia glared at him. "Yes, we are, Nicky. You cannot go alone, and James cannot leave Bree."

James squeezed Bree's hand. "Bree will be fine. She has Mama if anything goes wrong and… Leta."

Bree smiled at him as he lifted her hand to his mouth and kissed the knuckles gently. "I am the best one to go with Nicky. If someone gets hurt or -"

"I don't want you exposing your gift, James," Nicky said. "We don't know these people and I do not trust them. It is bad enough that the human woman knows about Leta. I don't want any of the others knowing about you or Mama or Leta."

Sophia opened her mouth to argue and Nicky shook his head. "No, Sophia. The truth of it is – every one of us will most likely die in the outskirts. I will not bring my siblings along on a suicide mission. Do you understand?"

"Yet you want us to stand idly by while you go marching to your death?" Sophia said furiously. She stood up, her chair scraping across the floor. "If you are so certain that this will result in your death, then why are you going? That Lycan is not your father, Nicky! Papa is your father. You don't need to save this Lycan. No one will think badly of you if you don't go."

She was nearly shouting now, and Kaden stood and put his arms around her. She pushed at his chest, glaring up at him with her eyes glowing bright jade, and growled. "Let go of me, human."

"No, little Lycan," Kaden replied before kissing her on the forehead.

She growled again before slumping against him and staring at her brother. "Nicky, please. Why are you doing this?"

"I need to meet him, Sophia," Nicky said. "He is my birth father and I will regret it if I don't try and save him." He looked down at his hands. "Besides, there is Nina. She obviously loves our father very much. I can't let her go to the outskirts alone."

"You just met her," Sophia said.

"She is my half-sister," Nicholas said.

Sophia tore free of Kaden's grip and knelt beside her brother. She clutched his hands. "I am your sister, Nicky. Leta is your sister. Not that silly little human girl. I know I sound cruel hearted, but I do not care. You would risk your life for a man you've never met? You are my baby brother and I love you. It will destroy me if you die. Do you understand?"

"I'm sorry, Sophia, but I'm going," Nicky said. "And I'm going alone."

"No, you're not."

The others looked up in surprise. Marshall and Doran were standing in the doorway of the kitchen and Doran glanced at his father before speaking again. "I'm going with you, Nicky."

"No, you're not, Doran."

"Aye, I am," Doran replied. "I've already spoken to Mama and Dad about it."

"Uncle Marshall," Nicky began.

Marshall shook his head. "No, Nicky. Doran will accompany you to the outskirts."

Before Nicky could reply, a low voice said. "As will I."

They turned to see Andric standing in the doorway of the kitchen. Nicky frowned at him. "Why would you go with us?"

"My entire pack was killed by the leeches. Some of my pack members, two of them my brothers, were taken. At the time, I had no idea why. Now, I understand. My brothers may still be alive."

Doran cleared his throat. "Andric, if they did take your brothers for the purpose of turning them, they would be dead by now."

Andric stared gravely at him. "Maybe, maybe not. I'm going with you – either to save my brothers or avenge their deaths and the deaths of my pack."

"And what of my daughter?" Marshall asked suddenly. "What do you think it will do to her if you die?"

"I will speak with her. I will make her understand why I need to go." Andric turned to Nicky. "When are we leaving?"

Nicky glanced at the others. "Tomorrow morning."

Andric left the room as Sophia stared anxiously at Nicky. "Nicky, I -"

"Enough, Sophia!" Nicky said. "I have made my decision."

With a growl of anger and frustration, Sophia stormed out of the kitchen.

CHAPTER 8

Nicholas sat on his bed and looked around before leaning over and burying his face in the pillow. He inhaled deeply. Max's scent was very strong on the thin fabric and he inhaled again as his cock hardened. Her scent was delicious, almost intoxicating, and he closed his eyes and pictured her naked breasts in his mind. What he wouldn't give to touch them, to hold their weight in his hands as he used his tongue to –

He cursed at himself but continued to sniff deeply at the pillow. What was wrong with him? He should be concentrating on the fact that he was about to go marching off to the outskirts on a suicide mission to save a man he had never met. His obsession with the human needed to end. His siblings had often teased him about his insatiable appetite for the opposite sex and this was living proof they were right. Even faced with the prospect of his own death, he was still acting like a horny teenage Lycan, unable or unwilling to keep it in his pants.

Max may have responded to his kisses, he may have smelled her strong desire for him, but she would not be looking for a quick roll in the hay, he reminded himself again. The smart thing to do would be to stay away from her. He fully intended to convince her to not only leave her child with his mother but that she should stay as well. She would be safe from harm and he would not have to worry about her.

He frowned slightly. Why he should care so much about a human he had just met puzzled him. He hadn't even slept with her and already he was acting like James acted with Bree. He shook his head. All his life he had maintained that his woman had the right to do as she pleased without needing either his permission or protection. He had, in fact, believed that the Lycans tendency to claim a woman, to make sure that other Lycans knew she belonged to him, had bypassed him completely. He had never felt even an inkling of desire to claim a woman as his mate and honestly believed he never would.

"What are you doing?"

He sat up abruptly, his cheeks colouring, as he stared at Max and Violet. She was standing in the doorway, still in her thin nightdress, and holding the little girl's hand.

"I came to wake you," he said as he stood up from the bed. "Breakfast will be ready soon."

"Thank you." She gave him a nervous look as Violet grinned delightedly and toddled towards him.

"Up!" she demanded.

He scooped her up and nuzzled her soft cheek. "Good morning, baby."

"I went potty," she said.

"That's a good girl." Nicholas kissed her on the cheek and gently patted her bottom.

She gave him a hopeful look. "Be a puppy?"

He grinned and closed his eyes for a moment before opening them. His eyes glowed yellow at her and she shrieked and clapped her hands with delight as a thick blond beard grew on his face.

"Puppy!" She stroked his beard and twisted to stare at her mother. "Puppy, Mama!"

Max, a small smile on her face, nodded. "I see the puppy, honey. But his name is Nicky, remember?"

"Nicky," Violet agreed happily.

She laid her head on Nicky's shoulder and rubbed his beard repeatedly as she stared at her mother.

"My puppy," she suddenly announced.

Max blushed a little. "Honey, Nicky is not your puppy."

Violet sat up in Nicholas' arms and frowned. "My puppy."

"Violet -"

"It's fine," Nicky said. "I don't mind."

Holding Violet firmly under her arms, he held her out in front of him and grinned at her as she giggled and swung her chubby legs. Without warning he tossed her high into the air. Max gasped and flinched as Violet shrieked in a combination of fear and delight. Nicky caught her easily and the toddler stared wide-eyed at him.

"Again!" she suddenly shouted.

Nicky threw her into the air again. She shrieked delight-edly as Nicky tossed her up into the air repeatedly, catching her easily each time before he suddenly turned and dropped her to the bed. He sat down beside her, lifted her nightshirt and blew a loud raspberry on her chubby, round belly. She squealed with laughter, grabbing at his beard, as he shook off her hands and did it again.

MAX BLINKED BACK THE SUDDEN TEARS. WATCHING Nicholas roughhouse with Violet shouldn't have been making her feel sad but she could feel it creeping in. Over the last three years she had often wished that Violet's father was still alive. Violet deserved a dad, someone who would play exactly like Nicky was playing with her now, and she wondered if she was doing Violet a disfavour by not finding a man who would be not only a good husband, but a good father as well.

And when exactly would you find one? You've spent the last two and a half years under Emmett's thumb and paying off your father's debt. It doesn't leave much time for dating.

She sighed to herself. Once her father's debt was paid, she would concentrate on finding a good father for Violet. Someone who was kind and loving and who could provide for her. Someone like Nicky.

She rolled her eyes. She barely knew the Lycan and just because Violet was taken with him, didn't mean he was father material. Besides, Nicholas was the only one of his older siblings without a mate and she had a feeling there was a reason for that. He did not strike her as the marrying kind or, despite Violet's instant love for him, the father type.

Leta appeared in the doorway and her eyes lit up when she saw Nicholas tickling a wildly giggling Violet.

"I'll save you, baby bird!" she shouted and shot across the room.

She launched herself at Nicky, landing on his back and clinging to him like a monkey as he stood and reached around to tickle her. She laughed and swung from his arm like it was a tree branch as Violet, still giggling, collapsed on the bed and stared at them.

"Mama sent me to find you. She wondered why it was taking you so long to wake up Max and the baby bird. I told her it was probably because you were kissing Max again," Leta said.

Nicholas dropped her to the ground with a loud thump. "Leta!" he groaned. "You did not."

"I did too," Leta replied. "It was only Mama in the kitchen, don't worry." She paused. "Oh, and Papa and Marian and Bree."

Nicky's face was red and he avoided looking at Max as he glared at Leta. "You really need to stop tattling, Leta."

"I wasn't!" she said. "Besides, Mama already knew anyway. As soon as I said you were kissing Max, she looked at Papa and laughed and he told her that fine, she was right."

She leaned around Nicholas and grinned at Max. "Lycans can smell when another Lycan likes someone. Sometimes it's hard to tell but not with Nicky. He stinks when he's around you."

"Leta!" Nicholas ground out.

"What?" She gave him a puzzled look. "Max likes you too so what's the big deal?"

She turned to Max. "Right, Max?"

"Oh, uh -"

Now it was Max's turn to blush furiously and Nicky growled under his breath before glaring at Leta. "Out, Leta. Right now."

"Sure," she said. She picked up Violet from the bed and staggered to the door with her. "Come on, baby bird. It's breakfast time."

She paused in the doorway. "Mama's waiting for you and Max, Nicky."

"Tell her we'll be there in a minute. I need to speak to Max privately."

Leta grinned saucily. "More like make out with her." She scurried out of the room with Violet as Nicky growled at her.

69

There was a moment of awkward silence and then Nicky said, "Sorry."

"It's fine," Max said. "What did you want to talk to me about?"

He cleared his throat. "I want you and Violet to stay here when we leave for the outskirts."

She shook her head immediately, frustration seeping into her belly. "No. I can't do that."

"You can," he insisted. "The outskirts is no place for a child or a defenseless woman."

"I can handle myself."

He stared at her in exasperation. "Listen, I'm all for a woman doing what she wants but going to the outskirts is too dangerous. There's a good chance all of us will die."

"I'm going, Nicholas."

He raked his hand through his short blond hair with frustration and she bit at her bottom lip nervously. She didn't want to go to the outskirts, but she couldn't very well tell the Lycan she barely knew that she had no choice. Ryker had made it clear that she was going and that if she refused, he would hurt Violet.

Fear flooded through her at the thought. Ryker was only human, but he was dangerous, and she had no doubt that he would not hesitate to hurt her child. She knew why he was insisting that she go. He believed that her powers would come in handy and had shot down her protests that she would not use them.

A shiver went down her back as she remembered the way he had grabbed her arm, squeezing tightly before rubbing his rough fingers across her mouth. "You'll use them, Max," he'd whispered. "As soon as that pretty little girl of yours is in danger, you'll do whatever it takes to protect her."

"Let go of me," she'd whispered, trying to keep the fear

from her voice.

He smiled grimly at her and pulled her closer. "Both you and Violet are coming with us. Perhaps, if you play your cards right, Emmett will be so thankful you came to rescue him that he will release you from your debt. You could be free, Max. Free to do whatever it is that you want."

He'd touched her trembling mouth again. "Of course, you might want to consider staying on even after your debt is paid. You and I could be so good together – inside the bedroom and out."

She'd pulled away from him, her entire body trembling with fear and anger, and he'd laughed delightedly when the dishes on the shelf behind her had exploded with a loud bang.

"Max? What's wrong?"

She realized that Nicky had moved until he was standing in front of her and she shook her head. "Nothing. I'm fine."

"You're not fine. You're shaking." He cupped her upper arms and she backed away from him.

"I said I was fine. I'm going to the outskirts, Nicholas. You cannot stop me."

He sighed with frustration and she retreated even further as he stalked toward her. Her ass hit the door and it shut with a quiet click as she leaned against it.

"At least leave Violet here," he said. "I promise you that my mother will take good care of her. No harm will come to her."

"I will not. I told you that Violet is safest with me," she said. He was standing very close to her now, his hard, lean body nearly touching hers, and she didn't object when he took her arms and tugged them to her sides.

Still holding her wrists, he stared at her breasts and made a low noise in his throat when her nipples strained against the thin material.

"Leta was right, you know," he said suddenly. "I do want you. Very much."

"N-no you don't," she said. "You think I'm fat."

"I think you're beautiful," he whispered before leaning in and placing a soft kiss on her throat.

He pressed his body against hers, trapping her against the door, and nuzzled her neck. "You smell delicious, Max." He breathed into her ear. "I could eat you right up."

She shivered delicately and he gave her a wide grin. "Have you been in a Lycan's bed before?"

"No," she said.

He nipped at her earlobe as his left hand came up and gripped the back of her skull. He held her firmly as he nibbled and licked the side of her neck before kissing the spot behind her ear.

"We're very thoughtful and considerate lovers," he whispered into her ear. "We spend hours tasting and exploring a woman's body. Nothing matters to us but making certain that she is pleased."

She moaned and he moved his hand to cup her breast. "I like to make sure that my woman comes at least three times before I do."

His hot breath sent shivers down her spine and she arched her back. He squeezed her breast in response and she moaned again.

"Nicholas, we – we shouldn't do this," she whispered.

"Why not?" He rubbed his thumb over her nipple, pressing his erection against her when he felt it harden beneath his touch.

She rubbed her pelvis against his and groaned under her breath. "It's – you're not what I'm looking for."

"What are you looking for?" He traced her collarbone with his tongue.

"Someone nice and -"

"I'm nice," he said. He kissed her hard on the mouth and she clutched at his broad back as he slid his tongue into her mouth and explored it roughly. His hand still gripped the back of her head and he held her steady, forcing her to open her mouth wider as he sucked on her tongue.

He released her mouth and grinned down at her red and swollen lips. "I love your mouth."

He sucked her bottom lip into his mouth, and she moaned with pleasure as he lifted her arms and pinned them against the door. He kissed her repeatedly, each brush of his mouth was weakening her defenses, and she tried desperately to hang on to her sense of control.

"I don't want a – a quickie," she murmured. "I'm looking for someone to be a father to Violet and you don't seem like the settling down type to me."

He grinned at her. "I'm not. But what's wrong with having a good time with someone? Haven't you ever slept with someone just because you wanted them?"

She shook her head. "No. I – I don't have time for that. I have a child and I -"

"You should make time for it," he said. "Join me in my bed. I'd like to show you how much fun a quickie can be."

She stared at him for a moment. Gods, she was tempted. The idea of just forgetting her worries and her fears and allowing Nicky to show her all the ways he could make her feel good was so powerful, she wasn't sure she could resist it. He was right – what was the problem with enjoying a night in his bed. They were attracted to each other and even Violet's father had not made her feel this way. If just Nicky's kisses and his touch through her nightshirt was turning her on this much, what would it be like to have him between her legs?

He was watching her face carefully and a small grin crossed his. "A bit more convincing perhaps?"

He bent his head and kissed her hard. She cried out into his mouth when he suddenly lifted her and carried her to his bed. He sat down and then laid on his back as he pulled her closer until she was straddling his lean hips. He rubbed his erection against her and stroked her warm thighs under her nightshirt.

"Take off your shirt, Max," he whispered.

She gave him a nervous look and he squeezed her thighs. "Take it off. I want to see those magnificent breasts again."

She bit at her lip and then suddenly lifted her shirt over her head. She dropped it to the bed and stared apprehensively at him. He was staring at her breasts and she watched as his eyes lightened from blue to yellow. She reached out and touched the beard on his face with tentative fingers and then gasped with pleasure when he twisted his head and captured her fingers in his mouth. He sucked heavily on them and she rocked her pelvis against him as he continued to stare at her naked breasts. With a soft pop he released her fingers.

"So beautiful," he growled.

She gave a soft squeal of surprise when he suddenly flipped her onto her back. He rubbed his fingers between her breasts, and she moaned.

"Nicky, this – this is madness. We don't even know each other and -"

"Don't think, Max." He grinned at her. "Just lie back and let me make you feel good."

Her protest died in her throat when he dipped his head and took one throbbing nipple into his mouth. He sucked hard on it before nipping lightly and she clutched his head in her hands and arched her back upward. His mouth was hot and wet, and she didn't want him to stop. When he released her nipple, she moaned in protest, but he quickly took her other nipple into his mouth and rubbed the tip of it with his tongue.

NICKY LISTENED TO MAX'S WHIMPERS AND MOANS OF pleasure beneath him as his cock swelled against his pants. She tasted as delicious as she smelled, and he pulled delicately at her nipple as she arched her back again.

He grunted with surprise when he felt something brush against his back. He lifted his head, cursing when he banged it roughly against something hard and unyielding.

"What in the gods name?"

The bed was floating in the air, so high that it was the ceiling he had banged his head against. He stared down at the woman on his bed. Her eyes were hazy and distant with pleasure and he shook her gently.

"Max? What in the gods name is happening?" he said.

She blinked rapidly and stared at the ceiling only inches from her face. "Nicky, I -"

The bed shuddered wildly beneath them. She screamed and Nicky shouted with surprise as the bed fell to the floor with a stomach-dropping thud. The frame broke apart with a *crack* and Max made a grunt of pain as the mattress hit the floor and Nicky's large body drove into hers.

There was another loud crack and the large wooden headboard teetered dangerously before falling forward. Nicky shouted again and covered Max's body, taking the brunt of the headboard on his back as it landed on them with a heavy thump.

Nicky cursed loudly and heaved the headboard off of them. It fell to the floor with a splintering crash, and he sat up and stared dazedly at the wreckage around them. As he hauled Max to a sitting position and cupped her face, staring anxiously at her, footsteps thudded down the hallway.

"Max? Are you hurt?" He shook her a bit roughly when she didn't reply. "Max!"

"I – I'm fine," she whispered. Her oddly coloured eyes were huge, and she gave him a sick look. "I'm sorry, Nicky. I didn't mean -"

The door to Nicky's room burst open and Max shrieked and dove behind his broad back. Tristan, followed by James, Avery, Bree, Sophia and Kaden, ran into the room.

They stared in surprise at Nicky and Max sitting on the remains of Nicky's bed. Broken pieces of wood and feathers from the bed surrounded them and Nicholas could almost feel the heat from Max's face burning into his back.

"The gods be damned, Nicky," James said after a moment of silence. "Are you trying to kill the poor girl?"

Nicky flushed, and Max groaned and buried her face in the soft material of his shirt as Bree and Sophia snickered.

Leta ducked into the room, surveyed the carnage before her and said, "I told you they were making out."

She ducked back out as Avery pressed her lips together in a vain attempt to stop from laughing. Even Tristan's face was twitching, and James grinned at Nicky as Max tried to reach for her nightshirt without flashing everyone in the room.

Nicky reached past her outstretched hands and snagged her nightshirt from the sheets. He handed it to her as Avery clapped her hands briskly. "Everyone out, please. Nicky, Max – breakfast is ready."

She shooed everyone out of the room as Nicky stared gratefully at her. Avery closed the door as Max slid her shirt over her head and scrambled out of the bed.

Nicky stood up and stared at the bed. "What happened?"

MAX WANTED TO VOMIT. HER STOMACH WAS ROILING, AND bile was rising in her throat and she was this close to losing it completely. "I – I don't know," she lied. "Please, this was a mistake. Can you leave, Nicholas?"

"Are you all right? Are you sure you're not hurt?" Nicky said.

"I'm fine." The tears were very close now and she blinked them back savagely. "Please, Nicky. I want to be alone. Could you go now? I just – I shouldn't have done this. Please go. Please."

He stared at her pale face and the tears swimming in her eyes and nodded. "I'm sorry, Max."

"It's not your fault," she said. "It's mine. I just – I don't want a one-night stand. I should never have pretended I did. I think we should stay away from each other, please?"

He nodded. "Aye."

"Thank you." She tried to smile at him as he left the room.

As soon as the door shut behind him, she sank to the floor and stared at her hands. She was not surprised to see them trembling badly, and as the candle on the bedside table rose and spun in in the air she moaned quietly and stared at the floor. She inhaled deeply, held it for a few seconds and then released the air in a harsh rush. She took breath after breath willing herself to calm down and after nearly five minutes, she finally glanced up. The candle was back on the table and she sighed with relief.

"It's fine," she whispered. "It's fine. No one got hurt. Everything's fine. Just stay away from him and everything will be fine."

CHAPTER 9

"You have a lovely home, Mrs. Williams." Max was standing at one of the windows of the common room. In the yard, Nicky and James were fighting with swords. A crowd had gathered around them, one that included Nina and Meridan, and she watched as the two brothers battled. Despite the cold air, both Nicky and James were shirtless, and a throb of lust went through her at the sight of the large muscles in Nicky's back flexing and rippling.

"Thank you, Max. Please, call me Avery." The Red had come up beside her and she peered out the window. James lunged at Nicky and she stared thoughtfully at Max when the woman cringed.

"Nicky is very good with the sword. Neither he nor James are in any danger," Avery said quietly.

Max looked behind her. Leta was twirling Violet in a large circle in front of the fireplace and the little girl was giggling loudly. She risked a glance at the Red, flushing a little at the look she was giving her.

"Why do your sons use swords? They are Lycans," she said.

Avery smiled. "My husband believed it would be prudent for me to learn the sword to protect myself. As our children grew, he decided they should learn it as well. Nicky proved exceptionally good at it and he has taken over the training of his siblings and his cousins."

"Do you think he would train me how to use it?"

"Aye, I believe he would," Avery replied.

There was a shout of laughter and a burst of clapping as Nicky knocked the sword from James' hand. He bowed deeply and grinned at his brother as James rolled his eyes and went to Bree. He hugged her, rubbing her belly gently before kissing her.

Avery and Max watched as Nicky approached Nina and held the sword out to her. Nina shook her head and Nicky frowned and said something too low for them to hear. Nina glanced at Meridan. He nodded his head and Nina took the sword from Nicky.

Nicky moved around her and helped her lift the sword, arranging her arm and legs until the position she was in suited him. He helped her swing the sword, speaking into her ear as he did so and Avery turned and smiled at Max.

"It looks like Nicky is going to teach Nina as well."

"Aye, I'm glad," Max said softly. "It would be good for her to learn how to defend herself."

"Especially in the outskirts," Avery replied gravely. She hesitated and then cleared her throat. "Max, would you – "

"Did you and your husband find it difficult to love Nicky like you love your other children?" Max asked abruptly. She glanced again at Violet and Leta.

"Where is Violet's father?" Avery asked in reply.

"He died before I even knew I was pregnant with Violet."

"I am sorry to hear that," Avery sighed. She stared out the

window at Nicky and Nina for a moment before smiling at Max.

"Nicky is our child. I may not have carried him in my belly and Tristan's blood may not flow in his veins, but he is ours. We love him as much as we love our other children."

Max shook her head. "It is apparent how much you love him. I'm sorry. It was a foolish question."

Avery didn't reply and Max glanced at her. "Does it bother you that Nicky wants to meet his biological father?"

"My husband believes it would serve Nicky well to meet the man who gave him life."

"Do you believe that as well?"

Avery sighed. "It isn't that I don't want him to meet him, but it's what he must do to meet him that bothers me. He is my sweet Nicky and sometimes it's difficult to see him not as the man he is now, but as the baby I rocked to sleep in my arms. The outskirts are dangerous, and I am worried for my child."

"I'm sorry," Max said.

"You have nothing to be sorry about, Max." Avery stared fondly at Leta and Violet before smiling at Max. "May I ask a favour of you?"

"Aye."

"Will you consider staying here with Violet and Nina when the others leave for the outskirts tomorrow?"

"I cannot do that," Max said.

"Why not?" Avery said.

Max bit at her lip before running her hand through her short hair. "I – I owe a debt to Nicky's father."

"One that means you must risk your life and the life of your child?" Avery raised her eyebrows at her. "What is this debt?"

"I – it was my father's debt. He died but before he did, he asked me to honour his debt to Emmett. I agreed."

Avery frowned. "I do not believe that your father wanted you to risk your life."

"Perhaps not."

"At least leave Violet with us then," Avery urged. "I promise you that no harm will come to her in our home."

Tears threatened and Max blinked them away. She wanted to do what Avery was asking her, more than anything, but she knew that if she left Violet here Ryker would be furious. He was convinced Violet was the key to her powers and Max wasn't so sure he was wrong. She would do anything to keep Violet safe. Even if it meant using the powers that she swore she would never deliberately use again.

"Max?" Avery said. She put her arm around Max and immediately a feeling of warmth and calmness filled her. Without realizing it, she leaned against Avery and rested her head on her shoulder.

Avery rubbed her arm. "Will you leave Violet with us?"

"I can't. Violet is safest with me," Max said. She wondered if Avery would find it odd if she hugged her. It felt wonderful leaning against the Red and the headache that had been starting behind her eyes had disappeared. She –

She pulled away abruptly and stared at Avery before staring at Leta. "What Leta can do – you can do as well."

"She has inherited my gift," Avery said.

"Can – do any of your other children have this gift?" Max said.

Avery didn't reply and Max shook her head. "Never mind. I imagine you don't share this knowledge with many."

"It is better – safer – for Leta and me if it remains hidden," Avery said.

"I won't tell anyone."

"Aye, I know you won't, Max," Avery said.

Max stared down at her hands. "I appreciate that you are willing to take care of Violet, but she is safest with me. I promise."

"Max, I think you should -"

"Mama!" Violet latched onto her leg and smiled up at her. "Hungry, Mama."

Max picked her up and kissed her on the cheek. "There is some bread in my bag, honey. Come, we will -"

"Don't be silly," Avery said. "You are our guests and you will eat lunch with us."

"Oh, I don't know if Meridan wants -"

"My husband has already spoken to Meridan and he has agreed to stay one more day." Avery said. "You will need all the rest you can get for your journey to the outskirts."

She reached out and took Violet from Max, cuddling the little girl close. Violet smiled at her and snuggled in as Leta put her arm around Avery's waist. "Can we have fried potatoes for lunch, Mama?"

"Aye, sweet Leta. We can." Avery took Leta's hand and, still carrying Violet, led her out of the common room.

Max glanced out the window at Nicky and Nina, her eyes lingering on Nicky's broad naked chest, before following Avery.

"YOU PROMISED ME," DANI SAID. "YOU PROMISED YOU wouldn't leave me."

She stared out her bedroom window, watching as snowflakes fell from the grey clouds. Andric crossed the room and put his arms around her. She stiffened and tried to pull away and he held her tightly against him.

"I'm sorry, Danielle. I know I am breaking my promise, but I have to go. I am certain that the leeches took my brothers to experiment on them and there may be a chance that they're still alive."

"It's been moons since they were taken," she said. "They will be dead by now, Andric."

He winced and she turned and threw her arms around his shoulders. "I am sorry. I should not have said that."

He hugged her hard and kissed the soft skin of her throat. "I do not wish to leave you, Danielle, but I need to know. Do you understand?"

She blew her breath out in a trembling sigh. "Aye, I do."

"IF YOU DIE, NICKY, I WILL NEVER FORGIVE YOU."

Nicky grinned at Sophia. "Aye, I have no doubt of that."

Her face solemn and pale, Sophia hugged him hard. "Please, Nicky. Let Kaden and I go with you."

"No, Sophia." Nicky ruffled her hair and she scowled at him before slapping him on the arm.

"Stop that."

"I will see you soon." Nicky hugged her again and Sophia kissed him on the cheek.

"I love you, baby brother."

"I love you too, Sophia."

It was early the next morning. Max watched as, one-by-one, Nicky's family said goodbye to him. She blinked back the tears when Avery, her face pale and tears shining in her eyes, cupped Nicky's face and spoke quietly to him. He nodded and then hugged her, picking her up from the floor and burying his face in her shoulder before setting her gently on her feet. She kissed him on the cheek and squeezed his face once more before stepping back and allowing Tristan to take her place.

The two men embraced, and Max turned away, unable to stop the tears from coursing down her cheeks. She searched for Violet. The little girl was inching her way to Leta who was standing by the fireplace, her usually cheerful face solemn and pale.

"Up, Leta," Violet said.

Without speaking, Leta picked her up and hugged her fiercely. Violet patted her cheek and smiled tentatively at her. "Play?"

Leta shook her head. "No, baby bird. You're leaving me now."

Violet's face crinkled and she made a short wail of anger. Leta rubbed her back. "Don't cry, baby bird."

Max stared at Violet's sweet face. What was she doing? She couldn't – *wouldn't* - take her to the outskirts.

"My lady?" Max reached out and touched Avery's arm as the Red walked by her.

"Aye?"

"Will you – if the offer still stands, I will leave Violet here with you."

"Of course. We would be happy to have her stay with us," Avery said.

Max, her stomach churning and her chest tight, took Violet from Leta and hugged her. The little girl squirmed and frowned.

"Too tight, Mama."

"Sorry, honey," Max said. She covered Violet's face with kisses and hugged her again. "You're going to stay with Leta and Avery for a little while, all right? Mama has to go away, but she'll be back soon. Will you be a good girl for Leta?"

Violet squealed excitedly. "Leta! Leta! Leta!"

She leaned out of Max's arms and Max passed her to Leta. The young Lycan kissed Violet on the cheek and smiled at her. "You're my good baby bird."

Max shrugged out of her backpack and pulled Violet's clothes from the pack as Avery knelt beside her.

"Most of Violet's stuff is at the campsite," she said. "I only have a couple changes of clothes for her and none of her toys."

"It's fine, Max." Avery rubbed her back. "We'll make do with what we have."

Max nodded and pressed her lips together before staring up at Avery. "If I – if I do not come back…"

Avery squeezed her shoulder. "You will come back to your child, but Violet will always have a place in our home. We will love her and care for her for as long as she needs us."

Max nodded and then threw her arms around Avery. She hugged her and whispered, "If I do not come back, promise me you will tell her how much I loved her."

"Aye, we will." Avery stroked her short hair. "But you will come back." She helped Max to her feet and squeezed her hand before staring at the others. "All of you."

"RYKER IS GOING TO BE ANGRY WITH YOU." NINA, HER FACE pinched with worry, said quietly.

Max continued to stare out the window of the carriage. Beside the carriage, Nicky, Doran and Andric, rode their horses in grim silence and she sighed before turning to Nina.

"I do not care."

Nina glanced at Meridan. "He will hurt her. You know he will."

Pavina growled under her breath. "Ryker would be a fool to hurt Max. We need her and he knows it."

Max shook her head. "I've already told you, Pavina. I will not use my powers. They are too dangerous, and I will never forgive myself if I hurt one of you."

"Max -"

Meridan shook his head at Pavina. "Enough, Pavina."

Pavina scowled at him as Nina peered out the window of the carriage. "Nicholas won't let Ryker hurt Max."

Max jerked in her seat. "Why do you say that?"

Nina shrugged. "He likes you. The younger Lycan told everyone that he likes you. She said she could smell it on him."

Pavina laughed. "His scent was quite strong."

Max blushed. "I'm not interested in Nicholas."

"Are you not?" Pavina gave her a considering look. "Then it wouldn't bother you if I take him to my bed?"

"I thought it was his cousin you were after," Max said.

Pavina shrugged. "Doran is sweet enough, but he is looking for a mate. I have no interest in being anyone's mate, and it is obvious that Nicky is not looking to settle down either."

She leaned over Max and stared at Nicholas through the window. "He is handsome and we'll need something to distract us from the knowledge that we are heading toward our deaths. Besides, if by some miracle we not only live but rescue Emmett and he has not been bitten, then having his son show a certain fondness toward me can only be helpful for me. If I show Nicholas a good time, perhaps Emmett will release me from my debt early if Nicky asks him to do so."

Max had to admit that the girl's plan was a good one. She had a feeling that Emmett would be more willing to bend to Nicky's will then he had ever bent to his human daughter's.

He treated the girl as though she were no more than a faithful and loyal dog and it set Max's teeth on edge. Nina deserved better than Emmett.

She swallowed her jealousy when Pavina raised one perfect eyebrow at her. "Well, Max? Would it bother you if I take Nicholas to my bed?"

"No. Why would it?" She forced herself to smile at the gorgeous Lycan. "I have no interest in Nicholas."

She looked back out the window before Pavina could see the lie on her face. Nicholas glanced toward the carriage and nodded briefly at her. She returned his nod and looked away quickly. Her stomach was in knots and already she missed Violet terribly. She bit at her lip and took a deep breath. She had made the right decision. Bringing Violet to the outskirts was madness and she didn't care what Ryker said or did to her. Protecting Violet was all that mattered.

CHAPTER 10

Nicholas dismounted and gently rubbed his horse's neck as beside him, Doran and Andric dismounted as well. Andric winced and rubbed at his thighs.

"I do not understand the humans' fascination with horses. They're slow, they smell bad and," he grabbed at his crotch and rubbed gingerly, "it's only been an hour and my balls may never be the same again."

Doran laughed and clapped him on the back. "Perhaps it would be better if you shifted to your Lycan form to travel. I shudder to think what my sister will do and say if I bring you back with a useless dick."

Andric turned red. "Shut up, Doran."

Doran laughed again. "Dani specifically told me I was to keep you safe. Apparently, she thinks you can't handle yourself in the outskirts."

"Did she now? That's interesting because she asked me to keep you safe." Andric grinned at Doran who rolled his eyes before glancing around.

There was a pack of about fifteen Lycans clustered together at the far end of the campsite. They eyed the three of them curiously before the biggest one yawned and turned away. The others followed suit and Doran grunted under his breath.

"A bit rude, don't you think?"

"We're not here to make friends, Doran," Nicky said.

"Aye, I know but -"

"I was beginning to believe you had abandoned us, Meridan." A raspy voice spoke behind them and the three Lycans turned. Nicky studied the man standing in front of one of the four tents in the campsite. He was tall and lean, and he smiled coldly at them as he walked toward them. His bald head gleamed in the cold sun and he ran his hand over his skull before holding it out to Nicholas.

"My name is Ryker. You must be Nicholas."

"Aye." Nicholas shook the man's hand before indicating to Doran and Andric. "These are my cousins, Doran and Andric."

If Andric was surprised to be referred to as Nicky's cousin, it didn't show on his face. He nodded to Ryker as Doran shook the man's hand.

Ryker looked Nicky up and down. "You look very similar to your father. I confess I had my reservations that you were actually Emmett's son, but the resemblance is undeniable."

"You work for Emmett?" Nicholas said.

"Aye. I am his," he paused, "right hand man, I guess you could say. I assist him with many of his affairs. Your father is well-regarded in the city."

"Aye, so I have heard." Nicholas glanced at Nina. The young girl was staring at Ryker with something close to hatred on her face, and she stepped closer to Max and put her arm around her waist.

The girl was afraid of Ryker, Nicky could smell it radiating from her pores, and he frowned as Max kissed Nina's cheek. Nicholas inhaled deeply. Although not as strong as Nina's scent, he could smell the fear on both Meridan and Pavina as well. Without speaking, he walked away from Ryker and stood in front of Nina and Max. He leaned forward and inhaled deeply as Max stared at him in confusion.

"What are you doing?"

Beneath the scent of Nina's fear, beneath Max's own unique scent of jasmine and vanilla, he found the faint scent of her fear. Anger swept through him instantly and he turned to stare at Ryker before turning back to Max.

"Nicky, what -"

"Why does he frighten you?" he said.

Nina jerked against Max and stared wide-eyed at Nicky.

"He doesn't," Max said.

Nicholas stared steadily at her and she swallowed and looked away.

"He is only human," Nicholas said.

"Aye," Max said.

"Why does he frighten you, Nina?" Nicholas swung his gaze to the pale, frightened girl.

"I – he doesn't," Nina said in a low voice.

"What is it you speak so quietly to your half-sister about?" Ryker approached them and cocked his eyebrow at Nicholas. "We are all friends here and there are no secrets between us."

Nicholas didn't reply and Ryker frowned at Max. "Where is your child?"

Max drew a deep breath and forced herself to look him in the eye. "I left her with Nicholas' family. She is safer with them."

Ryker stiffened and glared at Max. "You left your child with strangers? What kind of mother are you?"

Max flushed and a deep growl started in Nicky's chest.

"Watch your tongue, Ryker," he warned.

"And if I do not?" Ryker asked.

"I will rip it from your mouth."

"Aye, I am sure you would try." Ryker touched the sword that was around his waist before gazing at the sword at Nicky's side. "A Lycan with a sword. How odd. Do you carry it just for show or do you know how to use it?"

"Would you care to find out?" Nicky said.

Ryker scowled at him as Nina said, "Nicky is very good with the sword, Ryker. He is teaching me how to use one."

"Is he now?" Ryker said. "I suppose he has not yet learned what a scared little mouse you are."

Shame replaced the scent of Nina's fear, and Nicky rested his hand on the handle of his sword. "This is the last time I will warn you to watch your tongue, human. My patience grows thin."

Meridan stepped forward before Ryker could reply. "We should be leaving. The storm that delayed us at Nicholas' has abated for now, and we need to move quickly to make up lost time."

"Aye, you are right, old Lycan." Ryker turned and walked away as Nicky's hand tightened around his sword.

"Don't, Nicky," Max said. "Ryker is arrogant and a fool, but your father will be angry if you kill him."

"NICKY? MAY I SPEAK WITH YOU FOR A MOMENT?" Nicholas drove the last stake into the frozen ground and carefully tied the tent to it before standing. He stared silently at the Lycan standing before him and she flushed a little.

"I – I just wanted to apologize for my rudeness to your

mother." Pavina smiled at him. "I should not have spoken to her that way and I hope you will forgive me."

A few feet away, Max watched as Nicky studied Pavina. Her stomach dropped. Until this moment, Nicholas had paid no attention to the beautiful Lycan and she had foolishly hoped it would remain that way. She cursed herself in her head. She had known Pavina for nearly two years and what Pavina wanted, Pavina got. She had her sights set on Nicholas, and Max had no doubt that the two of them would soon be fucking like bunnies. Pavina was exactly what Nicky was looking for.

She turned and ducked into the tent she was sharing with Nina. She had rejected Nicholas, and she had no right to be angry with him if he took Pavina to his bed. She sat on the blanket and wrapped her arms around her knees. They had been riding all day and her bones ached from the jolting of the carriage. The further north they went the deeper the snow would become, and she wondered how long it would be before they would have to abandon the carriage.

She was nervous around horses and had never learned to ride. The thought of riding one for hours at a time made her cringe. It would be cold and miserable, and she was suddenly very thankful that she had left Violet behind. Nicky and Avery were right – the outskirts were no place for a small child. She suddenly missed Violet so badly her stomach was aching, and she took a wavering breath and rested her forehead on her arms.

From outside the tent came the sound of Pavina laughing. It was a warm and husky sound, meant to entice and arouse a man's interest and her stomach clenched when both Nicky and Doran laughed in response.

"I'm disappointed in you, Max." Ryker lifted the flap to her tent and ducked inside.

She sighed and looked away as he squatted next to her. "It is not like you to disobey a direct order. Emmett will be most displeased when he hears of it."

"Emmett is most likely dead, and you know it, Ryker. Besides, as cruel as he is, I do not believe even he would ask me to risk the life of my child just to save his own."

Ryker laughed. "Do you not? Then perhaps you do not know Emmett as well as you think you do. He cares little for the needs of others."

"Then perhaps we should give up this foolish rescue mission and leave him to his fate," Max said.

Ryker grabbed her arm and squeezed it until she gasped with pain. "Mind what you say about your master, Max."

"He is not my master." She tried to yank her arm free and bit back her whimper of pain when Ryker dug his fingers into the soft flesh of her arm.

"Emmett is a tough and resourceful old bastard. I have no doubt that he still lives and there will be a suitable punishment when he discovers your disobedience. Perhaps he will entrust me with it. I can think of many ways to punish you."

Her body vibrating with anger and fear, Max stared up at him. "Come anywhere near me, Ryker, and I'll kill you."

"Really? You like to think you are brave, but you are as much of a scared little mouse as that wretched creature, Nina. You don't even know how to properly use your powers. I'm beginning to believe that you will not be nearly as useful as I once thought you were."

"I told you I will not use them," Max spit out. "I won't deliberately -"

He squeezed her arm so tightly that a small moan of pain escaped from between her lips. "You would be surprised what a person will do when their life is on the line, Max. You may have left Violet behind, but I imagine you would be just as devastated to see Meridan or Nina killed because you refused to use the gift you have been given."

"Let go of me," she gritted out as Ryker leaned closer.

She could feel the power humming in her veins. It cried out to be released and she closed her eyes and concentrated fiercely on harnessing it.

Ryker laughed and planted a soft kiss on her forehead. "You were born to create chaos and destruction, Max. It is time you stopped denying your true nature."

Beside her, Nina's pack was shaking, and Max made a soft moan of dismay. Ryker grinned as the pack rose into the air.

"Perfect," he said. "Let it free, Max."

"Max? Are you joining us for dinner? It is nearly -"

Nina stuck her head into the tent and froze when she saw Ryker crouching beside Max. The pack dropped to the ground as Max yanked her arm free and scrambled to her feet. Without looking at Ryker, she ducked out of the tent and put her arm around Nina.

"Are you all right?" Nina said.

"Aye, I am fine." Max smiled shakily before leading her toward the campfire.

"I DO NOT BELIEVE YOU." PAVINA GRINNED AS SHE SAT NEXT to Nicholas.

"Aye, it is true," Doran said. "I was there when he said it."

"You actually told a human that during the full moon Lycans sprouted wings and flew?" Pavina giggled. "And he believed you?"

Nicholas smiled at her. "It is not my fault that he was an idiot."

Pavina laughed warmly and rested her hand on Nicky's thigh. She rubbed it back and forth lightly as she smiled up at him. "I suppose not."

She glanced at the others around the fire before turning back to Nicky. "Would you care to go for a run with me, my lord? It would be good to burn off some energy."

Nicky shrugged. "Aye, I could do that."

Max stared into the fire as Nicky and Pavina stood and walked into the darkness. Her face was red, and she could hear her pulse pounding in her ears. There was sudden growling and she looked up to see the pack of Lycans snarling at each other. There was a carcass of a dead deer among them and two of the larger ones began to fight over it.

Meridan stood and clapped his hands sharply. "Enough, you fools!"

They ignored him and continued to snap and snarl at each other. Meridan looked at Ryker and frowned. "Tell them to stop. They make too much noise."

Ryker shrugged. "I cannot tell them what to do. If you're so worried, then you stop them."

Meridan hesitated and then sat down beside the fire. He wrapped his coat closer around him and shook off Nina's hand when she laid it timidly on his shoulder.

"Nicky's father has some very," Andric paused as he sat down next to Max, "interesting friends."

"Aye," Max said. Meridan had told them that the Lycans were Emmett's friends when in truth they were nothing more than hired mercenaries. Emmett McKenzie had few friends who would be willing to risk their lives for him. Ryker had found the group of Lycans, how he wouldn't say, and the

Lycans were there only for the large payment that Ryker had promised them.

"What is it exactly that Emmett does?" Andric said. "These Lycans do not look like they belong in the city."

"Emmett um, he uh -"

Max didn't know how to finish her sentence.

"My father is very important," Nina said eagerly. "He is well-respected in the city."

"Is he?" Andric smiled at her. "And what does he do?"

"He, well, he helps people," Nina said. "People like Meridan, and Max's father."

"What did he do for your father, Max?" Andric turned to her.

"My father had a debt he could not pay, and Emmett loaned him the money. My father was repaying him by working for him."

"Did he do the same for you? Is that why you work for him also?" Andric said.

Max shook her head. "My father died before he could finish repaying Emmett. He asked me to honour his debt before he died, and I agreed."

"And what do you do for Emmett?"

"I help him with his paperwork."

At least she had, she silently amended to herself. Just before he was taken by the leeches, Nicholas' father had discovered her powers. He had made it clear that he expected her to use her powers in whatever way he saw fit and ignored her protests that she would not use them. She sighed heavily and stared into the fire. She wondered how Violet was doing and if she missed her mama.

"Max? What's wrong?" Nina asked.

Max stood. "I just miss Violet. I'm going to bed."

She crossed to the tent she shared with Nina as Nina

smiled tentatively at Andric. "I very much hope that your brothers are alive."

"Thank you, young human," Andric replied. "I hope so too."

Max ducked inside the tent and dropped onto her blankets.

———

MAX STARED AT THE CEILING OF THE TENT AND LISTENED TO Nina's soft and even breathing. She rolled to her side and burrowed her head under the blankets. It was cold in the tent, the ground was hard, and she had to pee. She'd been lying awake for over an hour but wouldn't admit to herself that part of her was listening for Nicholas and Pavina to return.

She sighed and threw back the covers. She would never sleep if she didn't go to the bathroom. Shivering in her thin nightshirt, she shoved her feet into her boots and shrugged into her jacket before leaving the tent.

The light snow that had been falling earlier had stopped and the stars shone brightly in the dark sky. It was bitterly cold, and she hurried past the dying campfire toward the trees. One of the Lycans on watch growled at her and she stopped, staring nervously at it.

"I'm just using the bathroom," she said.

His green eyes glowing, the Lycan regarded her for a moment before stepping back. She hurried away, breathing a sigh of relief when she stepped behind a large tree and away from its sight.

She moved a little deeper into the woods, shivering despite her jacket, and quickly squatted behind a large clump of bushes. When she was finished, she stood and shoved her nightdress down before walking slowly back to the camp.

Despite the cold air, she was reluctant to return to her tent. The thought of lying in the darkness while an all-too-vivid image of Nicky mating enthusiastically with Pavina played in her head, was an unpleasant one.

She pounded her fist against the tree and then cursed lightly at the pain before massaging her hand. She was being stupid. She had –

There was a soft growling to her left and she froze before slowly turning. A pair of yellow eyes glowed at her in the darkness, and her breath rushed out of her in a soft little whimper as they drew closer.

It was a large white Lycan and she held her hands out as she backed away. "Uh, good puppy. Stay. Stay, puppy. I'm just going to head back to my camp, and you can go and do whatever it is you Lycans do in the woods. Go on, puppy."

There was a soft pop as the Lycan transformed and she nearly sank to the ground with relief when Nicky grinned at her. "I don't mind that your child calls me puppy, but I would prefer if you didn't."

"The gods be damned, Nicky!" She scowled at him. "Are you trying to give me a heart attack?"

"Sorry," he said. "I forgot you haven't seen me in my Lycan form."

She rested her hand against her chest, feeling the runaway pounding of her heart, and glared at him again. "I thought you were with Pavina."

He shrugged. "I was. She caught the scent of a deer and wanted to hunt. I did not."

"Why not?"

"I usually only hunt during the full moon."

"That's unusual for a Lycan." She looked nervously into the darkness as Nicky moved closer.

"Perhaps. Why are you out here by yourself? It isn't safe

in the woods," he said.

"I had to pee." She could have smacked herself in the head as Nicky grinned. She blushed furiously and looked down.

It was a mistake. In her fright she had not even registered the fact that Nicholas was naked and at the sight of his large and- she drew in a sharp breath- semi-erect cock, her core dampened in response.

"Nicky?" she said as his cock hardened in front of her.

"Aye, Max?" He moved toward her and she took a few stumbling steps back until she felt the cold bark of a tree against her back.

She licked her lips and he groaned under his breath before reaching out and tracing her exposed collarbone.

She moaned and forced herself to look away from Nicky's cock. "I – I should go back to the camp."

"Not yet." He pushed open her jacket and she watched as he reached out with one long finger and traced her hardened nipple through her shirt.

"Nicky," she moaned again, "you promised you would stay away from me."

"Aye, I did. But it seems I can't resist your sweet kisses," he said.

"I'm sure Pavina helped you forget."

He blinked at her. "What are you talking about?"

"I'm not a fool, Nicky." She scowled at him. "I know what you and Pavina were doing in the forest together."

He cocked his eyebrow at her. "And what were we doing?"

"Mating, of course."

"I did not mate with Pavina."

"Of course you weren't."

"I have no interest in Pavina," Nicholas said.

"Why not? She's your type."

He traced her nipple again and she took a shuddering breath as he leaned forward and placed a light kiss on her throat. "Aye, she is. But I don't want her. I want you, Max."

She sighed and forced herself to move away from him. "Nicky, I -"

He grasped her arm and she hissed in pain and jerked away.

He frowned. "Are you hurt?"

"No, I -"

Before she could stop him, he pulled her jacket down and pushed up the sleeve of her nightshirt. He cursed when he saw the dark bruise on her upper arm. "Who did this to you?"

"It's nothing. I need to go back to the camp."

He touched the bruise. "Tell me, Max."

"It doesn't matter."

"Was it Ryker?"

She didn't reply and his face darkened. "I will kill him."

She realized with alarm that he was serious, and she snagged his arm as he turned away from her. "Nicky, no! Stop it!"

He growled and she stepped in front of him and pushed on his naked chest. "Please, Nicky. Ryker is a fool, but we need him to help rescue your father."

She hesitated and then stroked his face. "Please, Nicky."

"If he touches you again, I will rip his arm from his body," he said.

"He won't." She shrugged back into her jacket and buttoned it up. "I am cold, Nicky. I need to return to the camp. If Nina wakes and finds me gone, she will be worried."

"Aye. I will walk you back to the camp." He took her hand, linking her cold fingers with his warm ones, and led her through the trees.

CHAPTER 11

"**G**ood, Nina! You're doing very well." Nicky let his sword drop and smiled at the young girl.

Nina, her face flushed and panting heavily, gave him a pleased look before turning to Meridan. "Daddy will be so impressed when he sees how well I'm learning the sword. Don't you think, Meridan?"

"Aye, Nina. I do." Meridan smiled at her as she turned back to Nicholas.

"Shall we keep going?"

Nicky shook his head. "I think that's enough for tonight. Your arms and shoulders will be too sore to practice tomorrow if we continue."

Nina stared at him in disappointment. "I'm fine."

"Nicky is right, honey," Max said from her spot by the fire. "You have to pace yourself."

Nina dropped on to the ground beside her. "I want to be really good, Max. I want Daddy to see that -" She squinted into the dark trees around them. "What is that?"

Max followed her gaze. A small blue light was flickering in the darkness and she shook her head. "I do not know."

Pavina stood and walked over to Nicky. She smiled and rested her hand on his forearm before peering at the light. "It's pixie glow."

"Really?" Nina said. "I have never seen a pixie before."

"They're vile little pests." Ryker emerged from his tent and helped himself to an apple from the bag next to Meridan. "Although they make a satisfying crunch when I crush them under my boot heel."

Nina gave him a dirty look as Meridan glanced at the glow. "It's odd to see pixies this time of the year. They fly to warmer areas in the winter."

Doran stood and stretched. "Let's go take a look. C'mon, Nina."

He held out his hand and Nina jumped to her feet and took his offered hand.

Nicky frowned. "You shouldn't leave the safety of the fire, Doran. Besides, the pixies will be gone before you can get close."

"Pixies?" Nina said. "Do you think there is more than one?"

"Aye. They travel in packs. A pixie is rarely alone." Doran walked toward the light with Nina and, after a moment, Max stood and followed them.

She had never seen a pixie either and she was curious about what they looked like. They were notoriously shy and avoided humans and other supernatural creatures alike. There had been rumours that the Great War had completely eradicated their species but decades later, sightings of them began to emerge again.

There was a noise behind her, and she turned to see Nicky and Pavina picking their way through the trees after her. They had been traveling for nearly five days and Pavina had upped her attempts to seduce him. Although their days of travel were long, cold, and tiring, it hadn't stopped the Lycan from spending every resting moment flirting with Nicholas. Nicky's gentle rebuffs had done nothing to curb Pavina's appetite for him.

With a sick feeling in her stomach, Max wondered when Nicky would simply grow tired of rejecting Pavina and give in to her seduction.

He wants you, not her.

That might have been true, but Max had a feeling that Nicky wasn't the type to wait around for a woman to change her mind about sleeping with him. Once he realized that she meant what she had said, he would seek out Pavina's company.

It's better this way. You need to find someone who will make a good father for Violet, not a Lycan playboy who's only after a few nights of pleasure.

She hurried after Nina and Doran. It was ridiculous to be even thinking this way. They were in the outskirts, with God knows what creatures lurking in the shadows, on a suicide mission to rescue a man she loathed. She would find a good father for Violet when and if she survived this stupid rescue attempt.

Doran put his finger to his lips and Nina nodded as they crept closer to the fluttering blue light. The snow padded their footsteps and Max moved forward when she heard Nina's soft gasp. She peered over the young girl's shoulder, giving her own gasp of dismay.

The pixie froze against the fallen log and turned to stare at the three of them. Her face was twisted with pain and she grimaced at them, baring her tiny fangs, before continuing her struggle.

"The poor little thing," Nina whispered sadly.

Max moved a little closer. The pixie hissed at her and said

something in her own language before yanking at her leg again. The pixie was no larger than a tablespoon and she was completely naked. Her skin was a light shade of blue and her hair was a rich, dark blue. It cascaded down her back to her waist and her wings, the same shade as her skin, flared out from her back between the strands of thick, dark hair. Her right wing fluttered madly as she strained to free herself but her left one hung limp. Max could see a large tear in the delicate wing and when it vibrated delicately, the pixie winced and collapsed before staring in defeat at her trapped foot.

The pixie had been caught in a small crack in the fallen tree and Max wondered how long she had been struggling. She looked bone-tired and her entire body was shaking. She reached out to touch the tiny pixie and jumped in surprise when Nicky's warm hand covered hers.

"Be careful. They bite," he said.

"We can't leave her trapped like that," Max said.

"Aye, I know." He crouched down in front of the log and stared thoughtfully at the pixie. She glared at him, jabbering at him in angry tones, as he studied the fallen log and her foot. Nina knelt beside him and reached for the little pixie.

"Nina, wait," Nicky said.

"She won't bite me. Will you?"

She smiled at the pixie in a friendly way and although the pixie gave her a look of suspicion and distrust, she merely bowed her head when Nina touched the top of it with her finger. She stroked the pixie's arm and frowned at Nicky.

"She's freezing. We have to help her, Nicky."

"Aye, Nina." Nicholas reached for the pixie. Her reaction was furious and immediate. Hissing and spitting, she tried to claw at him as she twisted and squirmed madly. Her right wing was moving so quickly it was a blur and when the torn, broken left wing tried to move, the pixie gave a thin scream of anguish. Her eyes rolled up in her head and she collapsed against the log.

"Is she dead?" Nina cried out as Nicky leaned forward.

"No. I believe she's fainted."

Max watched as he held his right hand out and his fingernails lengthened into claws. He carved into the wood beside the trapped foot of the pixie and in only a few minutes, had widened the crack enough for Nina to pull the pixie free.

She held the limp, tiny body in her hands and gave Nicholas a worried look before looking around. "Where are the other pixies?"

Nicholas shrugged as Doran stood in front of her and examined the pixie carefully. "Pixies aren't known for their loyalty. No doubt when this one injured herself and could no longer fly, they abandoned her."

"That's awful." Nina stared sadly at the pixie before taking her scarf off. She carefully wrapped it around the cold little body and tucked her inside her jacket.

"You can't keep it, Nina. It's not a pet," Pavina said.

Nina glared at her. "She's injured and freezing to death. If I don't take her with me, she'll die."

"Nina," Pavina gave her an impatient look, "Ryker was right. Pixies are little pests and it's better off to just leave her. We don't need -"

"Enough, Pavina," Nicky said. "If Nina wants to take the pixie with us, we will."

"Thank you, Nicky," Nina said.

"Aye, but don't be broken hearted when the pixie wakes and immediately leaves. They don't care for humans or Lycans, even ones who save them."

MAX CRAWLED BETWEEN THE BLANKETS AND CURLED UP against Nina's warm back. "Is she awake yet?"

Nina shook her head. She had her head propped up on one hand and she was staring at the pixie lying on her pillow and still wrapped in her scarf. "She hasn't even moved. Do you think she'll live, Max?"

"I don't know, honey." Max patted the girl's bony shoulder.

Nina sighed. "I hope so. I feel like she's a good luck charm, you know? If she lives, then it means that Daddy will live too."

She glanced at Max and blushed. "It's stupid, I know."

Max smiled and brushed Nina's hair back from her face. "It's not stupid."

Nina stared at the pixie again. "I just wish that -"

The pixie stirred against her pillow. She rubbed her eyes, blinking tiredly, before looking up at Nina. Her eyes widened and she struggled out of the scarf. She tried to fly, her right wing beating madly, before wincing and collapsing on the pillow.

She stared miserably at Nina who made a soft cooing noise. "It's fine, sweet one. We won't hurt you."

She sat up slowly and poked Max's hip. "Grab some of the dried meat from my pack, will you?"

Max leaned over, shivering as the cold air hit her bare arms, and snagged Nina's pack. She handed Nina a small piece and Nina ripped off an even tinier piece and held it out to the pixie. "Here you go, sweetie. Try some, it's good."

The pixie gave her a suspicious look and sniffed delicately at the meat. She snatched it from Nina and ate it in four large bites as Nina tore off a second piece and held it out. She took that one from her and ate it quickly before sitting cross legged and examining her foot. She touched it lightly and then looked at Nina.

"Does it hurt, little one?"

The pixie didn't answer and Max, peering over Nina's shoulder, said, "I doubt she can understand us, Nina. I think pixies have their own language."

"Aye, you're probably right." Nina placed her hands on her chest and stared at the pixie. "Nina. I'm Nina." She pointed to herself. "Nina."

The pixie watched curiously as Nina pointed to Max. "This is Max. Max." She pointed at the pixie. "Your name is?"

She waited patiently and when the pixie didn't say anything, repeated the ritual. The pixie cocked her head at her before pointing at Nina.

"Nina," she said in a quiet little voice.

"That's right!" Nina made a soft squeal of excitement and the pixie grinned in response.

"What's your name?" Nina pointed at her again.

The pixie placed her hands on her naked chest and said something guttural and low.

Nina frowned. "Did you understand that, Max?"

Max shook her head. "Not really. Keela maybe?" She stared at the pixie. "Keela? Is that your name? Keela?"

The pixie frowned and touched her chest again before speaking louder.

"Kala?" Nina said.

The pixie clapped her hands together and laughed.

"Kala! Your name is Kala." Nina smiled at her and held out her first finger for the pixie to shake. "It's nice to meet you."

The pixie placed her pointer finger against Nina's and Nina giggled. "Close enough, Kala."

"The snow is too deep. There's no point in trying to drag it any further with us." Nicholas tossed the shovel to the ground and turned to look at Meridan.

"Aye, you're right." Meridan unhitched the horses from the carriage as Ryker cursed and waded through the deep snow to the pack of Lycans waiting impatiently ahead of them.

Andric stretched his shoulders and stared up at the cloudy sky. "It's going to storm tonight."

Doran shifted his pack and nodded. "Aye, I think you're right. We should find shelter before the worst of it hits."

Ryker joined them and scowled at the two Lycans. "It is only mid-afternoon. We're not stopping now. At this rate, it will take us weeks to find the leeches and we cannot afford to waste the time."

"He's right. We keep moving," Nicholas said.

Meridan shrugged out of his jacket and Max frowned at him. "What are you doing?"

"Pavina and I will shift and travel with the pack. You and Nina can ride one of the carriage horses and Ryker can ride the other."

"That's not a good idea, Meridan," Max said. "It's too far for you to travel, and the snow is deep. You're not a young Lycan."

Meridan bristled and glared at her. "I'll be fine."

"You won't be," Max said. "You know that. Do you really believe you can run for days with the other Lycans? Nina can ride with Nicky on his horse and I'll ride with you on yours."

Ryker rolled his eyes. "Are you that concerned for Meridan or is it your ridiculous fear of horses? Riding double will only tire the horses more quickly, and I'm not interested in wearing them out because you're a frightened little girl."

"Shut up, Ryker!" Max said.

His face reddened and he started toward her. "You forget yourself, Max. With Emmett gone, I am your master. Continue to speak to me so insolently and you will find yourself missing a -"

There was a low growling to her left and she turned to see Nicholas, his eyes glowing and his fangs bared, standing next to her. "Threaten her again and you will lose your head."

"You seem to enjoy threatening me, Lycan. Perhaps it's time you drew your sword and actually showed me what you think you can do," Ryker said.

"My pleasure," Nicky growled. He was reaching for his sword when Doran's hand dropped on to his arm.

"Stop it, Nicky. This isn't going to help rescue your father and we need to keep moving. The storm will be on us quickly and if we want to make any progress today, we need to go." He turned to Nina. "Can you ride a horse, Nina?"

Nina shook her head. "No. Father had no use for horses, and he said I wouldn't either."

Doran rolled his eyes. "Did he forget you're human?"

Nina flushed, and Doran shook his head. "It does not matter. Neither you nor Max weigh much, and Uncle Tristan's horses are more than capable of carrying two riders."

Andric rubbed his thighs. "Max can take my horse. I'd prefer to run anyway."

"Max, can you ride?" Doran asked.

Max shook her head. "No, I'm sorry. I was thrown from a horse as a child, and I never learned to ride after that."

Ryker snorted with disgust as Doran smiled at her. "That's fine. We'll use Andric's horse to carry the supplies from the

carriage, Nina can ride with me and you can ride with Meridan. Now, let's -"

"Max will ride with me," Nicholas said.

Max opened her mouth to protest but shut it with a snap
when Nicky stared at her.

"Fine." Doran glanced at the dark sky. "Let's get moving
before the storm hits."

CHAPTER 12

"Try and relax. You're making the horse nervous." Nicky's warm breath washed over her and Max closed her eyes.

"I am relaxed."

He snorted laughter. "No, you are not."

She sighed. "I'm sorry. I'm just very uncomfortable."

Without speaking, Nicky tightened his arm around her waist and pulled her more snugly against him.

"Better?"

"Aye," she lied. Being crammed into the saddle with Nicky's hard body against hers was making her insides a fluttering mass of nerves. His crotch was jammed against her ass, and she didn't know if she was relieved or disappointed that it seemed to have no effect on him.

"Why are you working for my father?" Nicky said.

"My father owed money that he could not pay. Emmett loaned him the money and in exchange, my father worked for him. Before Papa died, he asked me to honor his debt to Emmett. I agreed."

"How long have you worked for him?"

"A couple of years."

Nicky jerked against her. "How much money did Emmett loan to your father?"

"A great deal," Max said. "My father had a – a gambling problem."

"What do you do for Emmett?"

"I help him with the paperwork of his business. I keep track of the accounts of the people who owe him money."

Nicholas frowned. "How did my father become so successful? Where did his money come from?"

"I do not know," Max said. She had no desire to tell Nicky about his father's true nature. She was confident Nicky would not be so keen to help, despite his growing affection for Nina, if he knew how his father preyed on the weak and misfortunate.

Anxious to change the subject, she spied Kala's tiny head peering out from Nina's hair and hurriedly said, "The pixie seems to be very fond of your sister."

"Aye." Nicholas peered around her to stare at the pixie. "I'm surprised she stuck around. Although, without the ability to fly, I suppose she didn't have many options."

"It was kind of you to help free her. I know Nina appreciated it," Max said.

"Nina is a sweet girl."

"Aye, she is. She was very excited to learn she had a brother."

"Do you have any siblings?"

"No. My mother died giving birth to me and my father never remarried." She glanced at Nicky. "You are very fortunate to have so many siblings who love you."

"Aye, I am," he said. "How did Nina's mother die?"

"She hung herself in her bedroom. Nina was the one who found her."

"The gods be damned." Nicholas stared at Nina. She was riding behind Doran and she giggled softly when Kala emerged from her hair and used Nina's long braid to hoist herself upwards. She sat cross-legged on the top of Nina's head and stared with bright interest around her as Nina giggled again.

"Why did she kill herself?"

"I don't know," Max lied again.

Nicholas was quiet for a few moments before asking, "Where is Violet's father?"

"He worked for Emmett as well. One night he and a few others went to the home of some men who owed Emmett money and were not paying. The men killed Dallen and the others when they demanded payment for the loan."

"I'm sorry, Max."

"Thank you." Her face burned dully when she realized that she had leaned back against Nicholas until she was resting fully against him. Her head was tucked against his neck and her hands rested on his muscular thighs. His hand had moved from her waist to her ribcage and his thumb was brushing against the underside of her breast with every step the horse took.

"Gods. I'm sorry, Nicky," she said.

She started to pull away and Nicky's arm tightened around her. "Where are you going?"

"I'm too heavy to lean against you."

He grinned. "No, you are not. Besides, I'm cold and your body heat feels good. You're doing me a favour."

She frowned at him. "I have never heard of a Lycan being cold before."

He gave her an innocent look and shifted her more firmly against him. "Have you not? How strange. It is well-known that Lycans are always freezing."

She smiled and rolled her eyes. "Do you believe me to be dumb, Nicholas?"

"Definitely not."

He dipped his head and placed his mouth against her ear. "Truthfully," he murmured, his low voice sending shivers down her spine, "Lycans make excellent bed warmers. Are you finding it too cold in your tent, Max?"

"No," she croaked out as his warm tongue traced the shell of her ear.

"Are you sure?" He sucked on her earlobe and her glove-covered hands dug into his hard thighs. Now she could feel him, could feel his erection pushing firmly against her ass, and without meaning to she pushed back against him.

He groaned harshly into her ear and his hand tightened against her ribcage. "You could join me in my tent tonight. I know of many ways to keep you warm."

"You know I cannot, Nicky," she whispered. "I have told you repeatedly that I am not looking for a one-night stand."

"Aye, I know." He nipped her earlobe and then straightened and grinned at her. "But it does not mean I can't keep trying to convince you. Perhaps one day you'll realize how much fun fucking me will be."

She gaped at him, her cheeks going a fiery red, and he laughed so loudly at her expression that Nina craned her neck to look at them. "What's so funny, Nicky?"

"Max was just telling me a joke," he said.

"I'd like to hear it," Nina said.

Nicky grinned at Max and nudged her. "Go on, Max. Tell Nina the joke."

"I, uh, it's not an appropriate joke for someone your age, Nina."

"Oh." Nina shrugged and turned away as Nicholas snickered.

"Well done, Max," he said.

She elbowed him lightly in the stomach "You're incorrigible, Nicholas."

"I know," he said cheerfully.

"THE GODS BE DAMNED!" NINA MUTTERED AS SHE BURROWED deeper under the blankets. "It's so cold tonight."

Max curled up closer to her. "Aye. We'll be lucky if we don't freeze to death in the night."

She shivered and listened to the wind howling fiercely outside of their tent as Kala climbed onto Nina's pillow and crawled under the blankets. She rested her tiny body against Nina's neck and kissed it affectionately before closing her eyes.

"I think you've made a friend for life," Max said.

"Aye, I hope so. I am very fond of her," Nina replied without opening her eyes. She yawned and buried her face into her arm.

"Good night, Nina," Max said.

"Good night."

DORAN STOMPED HIS FEET AND BLEW ON HIS HANDS BEFORE tucking them into the pockets of his jacket. He leaned against a tree and watched as Nicholas lifted his head to the air and sniffed deeply.

"Do you smell something, cousin?"

Nicky shook his head. "I'm not sure."

He inhaled again before running his hand through his hair. Although the wind had finally abated, the snow was falling hard and fast and Doran could hardly make out the tents erected among the trees. The pack of Lycans were sleeping snow-covered lumps, and Doran frowned.

"I do not know how they can sleep like that."

Nicholas grinned. "You have grown too accustomed to your warm bed, Doran. Many Lycans still prefer to sleep in the outdoors in their wolf forms."

Doran rolled his eyes. "They're fools."

"Perhaps." Nicky was staring at Max's tent and Doran touched his shoulder.

"What's going on with you and the chubby human?"

"She's not chubby." Nicky scowled at him.

"Chubbier than you normally like." Doran pointed out. "Not to mention her situation."

"What do you mean?"

"She has a child, Nicky. She's also intelligent and remarkably level-headed. Everything you dislike in a woman."

"That isn't true," Nicky said.

"Is it not? I have never seen you attracted to any woman who has an IQ higher than a rock."

"There was Jillian! She was very clever," Nicholas said.

"Aye because she was a sociopath. I have never met a Lycan as mad as her. Remember how she stalked you for months? Uncle Tristan finally had to speak to her father after he found her hiding in your closet, wearing your pants on her head."

Nicholas flushed. "That was not my fault."

"Perhaps not. Whatever happened to mad Jillian, anyway?" Doran asked with amusement.

"Her father moved their family to Westmore," Nicky said.

"Aye, that's right," Doran said. "I had forgotten."

He straightened and looked around the trees before

persisting with his question. "Are you planning on fucking the chubby human?"

"Call her chubby one more time, cousin, and you'll feel my boot in your ass. Do you understand?" Nicholas said.

"Okay, calm down," Doran said. "I'm just wondering why you're suddenly so interested in a woman with a child. You've told me time and time again you have no wish to settle down."

"Aye, and that hasn't changed. My interest in Max is purely physical. I want to fuck her and nothing more," Nicholas said. "Besides, who wouldn't want to mate with her? She's beautiful."

"That is true," Doran replied. "Those eyes of hers – I have never seen anything like them before. I like a woman with curves, and she seems to be an excellent mother. Her body could bear many healthy Lycan pups."

Nicholas growled and glared at Doran. "You will stay away from her, cousin. Do you hear me? I know you are anxious to find a mate, but it will not be Max. If I see you anywhere near her, I will -"

Doran laughed and punched Nicholas on the shoulder. "Gods, Nicky, you make this too easy."

Nicholas flushed as Doran laughed again. "You have no idea how amusing it is to watch you finally meet a woman who you cannot charm your way into her pants."

"Aye, very amusing." Nicholas turned away from Doran and glanced up at the dark sky. "Where are the other Lycans? Our shift is over. They should be -"

There was a rustling in the trees to their left and the Lycans turned, growling deep in their throats. There was an answering growl and two men, both of them naked, emerged from the trees.

"You're late," Nicholas said.

They didn't reply and Nicky frowned at them. "Keep careful watch."

One of the Lycans shifted to his wolf form as the other shrugged. "The night is not fit for man nor beast. Nothing will happen."

"Keep your eyes open for trouble," Nicky said. "Not all creatures find the cold as troublesome as you."

The Lycan bared his teeth at him before shifting. Nicholas stared silently at him until the Lycan turned away and then clapped Doran on the back.

"Good night, cousin. I will see you in the morning."

THE DYING LYCAN'S SCREAM WOKE MAX FROM HER SLEEP. She sat up straight, every hair on her body trying to stand on end, as howling split the air outside the tent.

Nina, her face white and her eyes large in her thin face, sat up and stared with fright at her. "Max? What is happening?"

Kala clung to her neck and Nina made a loud cry when there was another howl of pain. "Max? What's going on?"

"Nina, stay here!" Max struggled out of the blankets and crawled to the front of the tent. "Do not leave this tent, Nina. No matter what you hear. Do you understand?"

"Max! You can't go out there!" Nina said. "Please, don't leave me!"

"They may need my help." Max had to shout to be heard above the growls and howling. "Stay here, Nina!"

She darted out of the tent, the cold snow burning her bare feet, and stared in horror at the sight in front of her. The snow was still falling thick and fast, and she screamed and ducked back when a body came hurtling toward her. It fell to her feet with a harsh thump and she stared wide-eyed at the dead faerie. Half its skull was missing, and black blood was pouring from its open mouth. Its muddy brown eyes stared blankly at her, and she stumbled away as more faeries flew down in droves from the dark sky.

They were hooting and hollering loudly, jabbing their spears into the night sky as they attacked the Lycans. She watched in horror as one of them ducked into Pavina's tent. It backed out of the tent, dragging a struggling Pavina by one blanket-wrapped leg. The Lycan was already beginning to shift, her eyes glowing dark yellow as she snarled and growled at the faerie. It shrieked laughter and raised its spear into the air. Before it could thrust its spear into the wildly twisting Lycan, a dark brown wolf was leaping onto its back. It tore into the faerie, its teeth snapping and its claws digging deep into its wings. The faerie screamed in agony, and Max whimpered with revulsion and fear when the Lycan tore the faerie's spine from its flesh.

The wolf howled loudly in triumph as Pavina shifted fully. She slipped gracefully from the blanket and joined the other Lycans in the fight. Max took a few staggering steps forward. Her mind was numb with panic and fear and she watched as Ryker, his sword flashing in the falling snow, beheaded a faerie.

"C'mon then, you filthy faeries!" he shouted. "Is that the best you can do?"

A faerie swooped down, hissing at Ryker as he hurtled his spear at him. Ryker dodged it easily and bellowed laughter into the cold air before thrusting his sword into the chest of the faerie. He pulled it free, the faerie's black blood splattered across the snow, and raced toward a group of faeries who were jabbing their swords into a fallen Lycan. The Lycan howled miserably as one of the faeries reached down and tore a large chunk of flesh from his heaving side.

The shrill scream of a faerie drew Max's gaze across the campsite. Nicky, his white fur splattered black with faerie blood, launched his body into the air. He caught one of the faeries by the leg and with a loud crunch, severed it from its body. It shrieked with pain as blood poured out of the stump. It flew jerkily for a few feet before crashing into one of the snow-covered trees. It fell to the ground with a heavy thud and Meridan, his silver fur gleaming in the snow, fell on it and tore its throat out.

Max realized with horror that despite their ferociousness and their bravery, the Lycans were losing. The faeries were everywhere, and they had already killed over three quarters of the Lycans that Ryker had hired. There was a loud cackling behind her, and Max spun around to see a faerie reaching for the flap to hers and Nina's tent.

"Nina!" she screamed.

The faerie turned and grinned at her. "Hello, human!"

Its large leathery wings flapping, it rose into the air and flew toward her. "You'll make a nice tasty snack, won't you? I can't wait to -"

It flinched when a rock hit it in the back. It whirled in the air and stared in disbelief at the trees behind it. The wind was picking up, the trees were creaking and swaying, and the faerie screamed and raised its hands to shield its face as a hailstorm of rocks and fallen branches came shooting out of the trees.

There was a loud groaning noise and a boulder, buried deep within the ground, shuddered its way free and hovered in the air. It rose high into the air and the faerie dropped its hands and stared at it with a cocked head.

"What sorcery is this?" it muttered in a screechy little voice. "Who can control the -"

The boulder was hurtling down toward him and he raised his hands and screamed as the rock fell on him. It flattened him to the ground with a wet splat, and one moss-covered hand twitched wildly for a moment before going limp.

———

SNARLING, NICKY SUNK HIS TEETH INTO THE THROAT OF THE faerie that was attacking Andric and ripped the flesh open. Faerie blood filled his mouth and he spat out the vile liquid before barking at Andric. The Lycan staggered to its feet and barked in reply, shaking his head to clear it.

Nicholas whirled around when he heard Ryker shout, "That's right, Max! Show them what you're made of, you crazy little bitch!"

Nicky froze as he stared in disbelief at the scene in front of him. Max, looking very pale and small, was standing in the middle of the campsite. Her short hair stood on end and her night shirt was blowing madly about as the snow danced and floated around her body in a small tornado of wind.

He barked a warning, his blood freezing in his veins, as a faerie flew up behind her. Before the creature could grab her, a stone came flying out of the darkness and hit the faerie directly in the forehead. It embedded itself deep into the faerie's filthy skin and the faerie dropped to the ground, blood pouring out from the hole in its forehead.

More rocks and branches were flying out of the darkness. They whipped through the air, striking Lycan and faerie alike as Max raised her arms and closed her eyes. A hard, deep shudder went through her and a boulder, bigger than the carriage, flew past her and into a large group of faeries. They shrieked with pain as they were bowled over, and Nicky could hear their limbs breaking as they struggled to escape the path of the boulder.

He flinched when a large branch slammed into his face and he dropped to his belly as Doran, still in his Lycan form, crawled toward him. Doran barked and Nicky glanced at him before starting to worm his way toward Max. The air was filled with rocks and branches and he watched in amazement as a large thick branch broke from one of the trees with a loud cracking noise and flew past Max, just barely missing her.

The faeries, screeching with fear, were retreating into the trees. Their wings flapped roughly against the wind and some of them were clinging to the madly swaying trees, using them to claw their way into the dark forest.

Max was nearly invisible in the snow that whirled around her and she didn't open her eyes when Meridan shifted to his human form and shouted, "Max! Enough! Control it, Max! You'll kill us all! Do you hear me? Stop!"

Pavina launched herself at the old Lycan, knocking him to the ground just as a large rock hurtled toward him. It hit the tree behind them, and the tree broke in half with a loud snap.

"Max!" Meridan shouted again. "Stop it! Stop it now!"

Max's eyes fluttered open and she stared at Meridan.

"Meridan?" she whispered.

"Stop, Max," he pleaded.

Blinking in confusion, Max stared around the campsite.

"No!" She moaned and dropped her arms. The wind was dying down and Andric yelped in pain when a thick branch fell across his back and knocked him to the ground.

Doran yanked the branch off of him and, as Andric shifted, helped him to his feet. "Are you all right?"

"Aye." Andric nodded grimly as he rubbed his back.

"What have I done?" Max moaned again as Nicky shifted and bounced to his feet.

"Max?" he said.

"Nicky." She turned to him and his heart ached at the look of shame and despair on her face. "I'm sorry, I -"

"Max! Look out!" Nicholas shouted.

A rock the size of his fist slammed into the side of Max's head. Her eyes rolled up into her head and she dropped to the ground as, all around them, rocks and other bits of the forest fell to the ground with loud thud.

The remaining humans and Lycans stared at each other cautiously through the falling snow. The howling wind had died completely, and Nicky's ears were ringing in the sudden silence.

"What in the gods name was that?" Doran asked. "Was that – did Max do that?"

Meridan struggled to his feet as Ryker laughed and kicked at the body of a dead faerie. "I knew the little bitch would come in handy."

"Shut up, Ryker!" Meridan said. "Keep your mouth -"

There was a sudden loud shriek of laughter and Nicky watched with horror as a faerie dropped out of the darkness and landed on Max. Before anyone could move, the faerie grabbed Max under her arms and, wings flapping loudly, flew upward and disappeared into the trees.

Nicky howled with rage and shifted before bounding into the trees after them.

CHAPTER 13

The faerie looked around furtively before dropping the woman. She landed face first in the soft snow and the faerie glided down next to her and flipped her onto her back.

He grinned, his teeth black and rotting, and clapped his hands together as his wings flapped lightly behind him.

"Pretty, tasty, pretty, tasty." It sang in a tuneless little mutter. "Pretty, tasty snack for me!"

He suddenly threw his hands in the air and danced a demented jig around the unconscious woman. The snow continued to fall thickly, blanketing the trees and the ground, and the faerie clapped his hands again before straddling her body. He reached out and tenderly wiped the snow from her face before leaning over her. He stared at her mouth.

"Tasty, pretty." He giggled and clutched her head tightly between his grimy hands before placing his mouth just above hers.

"All mine," he cackled. He started to inhale, licking his lips at the taste of the grey mist rising from the woman's parted lips.

The faerie stiffened and looked away from the woman, breaking their connection as a low growling started. He twisted his head to the left and the right, squinting through the snow and the trees. His leathery wings vibrated, and he twisted his body to look behind him.

The growling was growing louder, and the faerie glanced down at the woman, making a soft mewl of hunger and need, before starting to rise. He looked to the left, his eyes widening with horror as the giant white wolf appeared. It leaped at him, its teeth flashing in the darkness, and the faerie made one panicked squeal before the Lycan was on him.

***

"MAX, WAKE UP. OPEN YOUR EYES, SWEETHEART."

Nicky's low and raspy voice pulled Max from the darkness. She blinked, staring hazily up at him, as he cupped her face and rubbed her cheekbone with his thumb.

"Hello, sweetheart."

"What happened?" she groaned.

She struggled to sit up, her entire body was freezing, and he wrapped his warm hand around the back of her neck and helped her into a sitting position. She looked around at the trees that surrounded them.

"Where are the others?" she said.

"Back at the campsite. You were knocked out and a faerie took you." Nicky ran his fingers through her short hair, and she winced as he touched the tender spot where the rock had hit her. He frowned at the blood on his fingers.

"Are Meridan and Nina all right?"

"Aye, they are. Hold still." He parted her hair and examined the wound carefully. "The wound is shallow and starting to clot. How do you feel? Are you dizzy? Nauseous?"

She shook her head gingerly. "No, but I'm freezing."

He stood and hooked his hands into her armpits before lifting to her feet. She swayed unsteadily as her ears started to ring and he put his arms around her. She leaned into his warmth. Her body was shaking violently, and he searched the area around them as she rested her head against his shoulder.

"Can you walk, Max? We need to find shelter before you freeze to death."

"Should we not go back to the others?" she said.

"No. The faerie carried you many miles before growing tired. You'll freeze before we get back to camp, even if I carry you on my back. Come on, sweetheart. We need to get moving."

"R-right," she said. Her bare feet were burning in the snow and, holding Nicky's hand tightly, she took a few stumbling steps forward. He glanced at her feet and muttered a curse before picking her up.

"I can walk," she said. "You can't carry me, Nicky."

"Just relax, sweetheart." He rubbed her back as he strode through the trees.

"Where are we going?"

"I passed a small cave not too far back. We'll shelter there for the night and return to the others in the morning."

She nodded and closed her eyes, burying her face into his thick neck and clinging tightly to him. After about fifteen minutes, Nicky stopped, and she raised her head wearily and stared at the dark cave in front of them. It was small, even she would have to crawl into it, and she gave Nicky a nervous look.

"What if there's something in there already?"

He placed her gently on her feet. "Stay here for a minute." He approached the cave and crouched down next to it, inhaling deeply for a second or two.

"It's empty." He held his hand out to her and she dropped to her knees beside him and took it. They crawled into the cave. It was too dark for her to see and it smelled musty, but she breathed a sigh of relief at being out of the snow and the cold. She raised her hands and felt blindly for the ceiling of the cave. She realized that she could sit without hitting her head and she dropped onto her ass and raised her knees, clasping her arms around them as shivers racked her body.

"How did you find me?" she said.

"I followed your scent."

"Oh." She hesitated and then reached out, searching for his hand. He clasped it gently and she squeezed it hard. "Thank you for rescuing me, Nicky."

"Aye, you're welcome." He squeezed her hand again before dropping it. "We should try and get some sleep."

"Aye." Max curled up in a small ball. The ground was hard, and she squirmed around trying to find a more comfortable position. Behind her, she could hear Nicky lying down and she tried to keep herself from shivering violently. The thin nightshirt she wore did nothing to keep her warm and when her teeth began to chatter, Nicky cursed and crawled over to her. He pressed his body up against hers and she jerked and looked behind her.

"What are you doing?"

"Keeping you from freezing to death. Turn around."

She squirmed over to face him and he pulled her into his embrace, wrapping his arms around her waist. She buried her cold face into his throat and rested her numb feet against his legs. She sighed with relief. Despite the coldness of the cave and his nakedness, Nicky was unbelievably warm, and she squirmed even closer to him.

"Gods, you're so warm," she said.

"Aye, all Lycans are." He stroked her back through her shirt. "Try and get some sleep."

"Are you afraid of me?" she said.

He rubbed the back of her neck. "Why would you ask me that?"

"You've seen what I can do, and how badly I can hurt people. Even the ones I – I care about," she said.

"I'm not afraid of you, Max," he said. "We'll talk more tomorrow. You need to rest."

She clung to him as he rubbed her back and she closed her eyes.

WHEN SHE WOKE, IT WAS MORNING AND LIGHT ENOUGH IN THE cave for her to see his hand cupping her breast through her shirt. She had turned in her sleep and the thick, hard length of his cock was pressed against her ass.

As she watched, his hand tightened and then his thumb searched for her nipple. It hardened immediately under his touch, and she gasped as he placed a warm kiss on the back of her neck. His right arm was under her head, cushioning it from the hard ground, and she blinked in surprise when his left hand unbuttoned her shirt.

"Nicholas!"

"Aye?"

"What – what are you doing?"

"What does it look like I'm doing?" He nuzzled her neck as his hand slipped into the opening of her shirt and cupped her naked breast.

"It – ohhh," she moaned when he rolled her erect nipple between his finger and his thumb.

131

She arched her back, her ass pressing against his erection and he muttered a curse before pulling his hand free of her shirt. Disappointment coursed through her, but it quickly turned to surprise when he yanked the back of her shirt up and pulled her panties down past her knees.

"Nicholas!" She gasped again as he pushed his cock between her ass cheeks and pulled her back against him with one hard hand on her hip.

"Aye, Max?" He slid his hand up her shirt and cupped her left breast, squeezing and kneading firmly as he rubbed his erection against her.

"You shouldn't be doing this," she moaned, even as her back was arching again.

"You started it." He traced her ear with the tip of his tongue and nipped her earlobe.

"What?" She twisted her head to look at him as, behind Nicky's back, a rock from the floor of the cave hovered in the air.

"I said, you started it."

"I did not," she protested as he trailed a path of hot kisses down her neck.

"You did. I woke up to find you rubbing your ass against my cock. It was a particularly nice way to wake up."

"I was sleeping." She moaned when his fingers moved to her right breast and pinched her nipple.

"How was I to know that?" He squeezed her breast and licked her neck. Behind him, another rock joined the first still hovering in the air.

"I was – ohhh…"

She moaned again when he rocked his pelvis against her, and his cock rubbed firmly against her ass.

"All I knew was that you were pushing your sweet, firm

ass against my cock. No Lycan alive would turn down an invitation like that."

She turned her head to stare at him. "I wasn't inviting you to do anything. I told you, I was -"

He cut her off by kissing her. He traced her lips with his tongue and, feeling like she was descending into madness, she opened her mouth so he could slip his tongue between her lips. She kissed him hungrily and moaned into his mouth when he moved his hand to her firm thigh and stroked it.

"Open your legs, Max," he said against her mouth.

"Nicky -"

"Open them." He pulled on her leg and she allowed him to pull it back and over his hip. He skimmed his hand down her flat belly, and she tensed when he ran his fingers through the curls between her legs.

"Nicky, I -"

He pressed his fingers between the lips of her pussy and found her clit. He stroked it lightly and her entire body jerked against him in surprise.

"Gods be damned! Nicky, that – that feels so nice," she said and then blushed at how stupid she sounded.

He laughed, and her blush deepened. "I'm glad it feels nice, Max." His hot breath blew against the sensitive skin of her neck and she shuddered against him.

"Let's see if we can make it feel a little better than just nice." She could hear the grin in his voice, and she closed her eyes in embarrassment.

"I'm sorry. I just – I've never..."

The thought was lost when Nicky rubbed her clit in slow, firm circles. It swelled under his touch and she shuddered again and stared at the rock wall in front of her. It was cold in the cave, she could see her breath, but the warmth from

Nicky's body surrounded her and was heating her up. It was making her breath catch in her throat and her legs weak.

As an unfamiliar aching throb began in her belly, she moved her legs restlessly and stared at the wall in front of her again. Tiny cracks were beginning to appear in the wall, and as she watched they widened with a low groaning noise.

Nicky gripped her leg and pulled it even further over his hip before continuing to rub her clit. "I want you to come for me, Max."

She was very wet, and he rubbed some of the moisture down toward her tight opening. He slipped one thick finger into her and she cried out and arched her hips against him. Vaguely, through her haze of pleasure, she could hear the cave creaking, and dust and small chips of rock were falling from the ceiling to settle on the ground in front of her.

She could feel her body tightening around Nicky's finger, trying to push out the unfamiliar digit, and Nicky made a soft, soothing noise. "Relax and let me in, sweetheart."

She took a deep breath, forcing herself to relax, and moaned again when Nicky's finger pushed fully into her.

"Gods!" She cried out when his thumb found her clit and circled it roughly.

"That's right," he murmured into her ear. "Don't hold back, sweetheart."

He sped up the motion of his finger within her and the pressure of his thumb against her clit. The ache grew in her belly and she pressed her hand against Nicky's.

"Nicky, please!" She begged as she thrust her pelvis against him. "Please, oh please, oh…"

She had no idea what was happening to her. She couldn't breathe, she couldn't think, she couldn't feel anything but Nicky's fingers rubbing and stroking and his lips against the column of her throat. As the pleasure built to an unbearable fevered pitch, she screamed and arched her body. Her orgasm burst through her in a sweet, hot rush of warmth and indescribable pleasure, and she screamed again.

Her scream was drowned out by a loud, sharp crack, and Nicky shouted in surprise and fear when large jagged cracks appeared in the walls of the cave and a chunk of the ceiling landed beside his head with a hard bang.

"Max!" he shouted and then he was crawling forward and dragging her from the cave as it collapsed around them. Dust and rocks rained down around them and Nicky cursed when a large chunk of the cave landed on his right shoulder. Max, her legs shaking, and her underwear still tangled around her knees, stumbled and fell onto her stomach. Nicky hauled her back to her knees and, half-carrying, half-dragging her, he yanked her from the cave and into the early morning light.

They collapsed a few feet from the cave and Max, coughing and choking on dust, tugged up her panties as Nicky staggered to his feet and stared in disbelief at the collapsed cave.

"The gods be damned," he breathed and then coughed.

Max climbed to her feet and lurched her way to Nicky. His shoulder was trickling blood and she made a small moan of dismay at the bruising and cut that was on his shoulder.

Nicky turned and grabbed her by the shoulders. He looked her up and down before touching her head and face. "Max, are you hurt? Did you get hit by the falling rock?"

She shook her head. "No. But you're hurt, Nicky. I'm so sorry," she said hoarsely.

"It's nothing," he said dismissively. He eyed her trembling body. "Are you sure you're not hurt?"

"Aye," she said.

He turned to stare at the collapsed cave again. "How in

the gods name did that happen? Why would it just start to cave in like that? What would -"

He stopped and Max made a soft moan of dismay when he turned and stared at her.

"It was you," he said. "When you came, your powers destroyed the cave."

"I'm sorry, Nicky," she said. "I'm so sorry. I didn't mean -"

"You could have warned me for the gods sake, Max," he said as he rubbed at his shoulder. "We could have died in that cave."

"I – I didn't know that would happen," she said.

He gave her a dry look. "You have a child. You're not exactly a blushing virgin. How have you not learned to control your powers when you -"

"I'm sorry!" she said. "I didn't know, I swear! I've never -"

She stopped abruptly and looked down at the ground, wrapping her arms around her shaking body as her bare feet burned in the snow.

She closed her eyes when Nicky cupped her head and tipped it up.

"Look at me, Max," he demanded.

She shook her head and he squeezed her face lightly. "Look at me."

She opened her eyes, they were swimming with tears of humiliation, and swallowed thickly. "Nicky, I -"

"How many men have you slept with?"

"Just Violet's dad."

"How many times did you have sex?"

"Just the once," she said.

He frowned. "Did you come?"

136

She closed her eyes in embarrassment and refused to answer. Nicky squeezed her face again.

"Answer me, Max. Did he make you come?"

Another wave of embarrassment flooded through her and she yanked away from his grip. She stumbled on her feet but hissed angrily at him when he tried to steady her. "That's none of your business, Nicholas!"

"Considering that you nearly killed me in that cave, I think you can share a little more with me, sweetheart," he said.

"No! He didn't make me come. It was – was very quick and painful and I was afraid to try it again. A week later he was dead. Two months after that, I found out I was pregnant with Violet."

Tears were starting down her cheeks and she brushed them away. "I didn't know this would happen, Nicholas."

"Why have you not learned to control your powers?" he said. "Do you have any idea how dangerous it is to not -"

"I'm not talking with you about this!" she shouted. "My powers are none of your business!"

"None of my business?" He stared at her in disbelief. "You almost killed us, Max. You – you broke my bed and -"

"I'm so sorry about your bed," she said sarcastically. "Why don't you tell your father about it? He'll buy you a new one and he can add the cost to the debt I owe him."

He flushed. "Your powers go haywire whenever I touch you, and you should have been honest with me about them. I would not have been so keen to bed you if I knew you had no control over your abilities."

"I have control over them!" she shouted again. "I saved your furry ass from the faeries, did I not?"

"No, you don't!" he shouted back. "You may have killed the faeries, but you nearly killed your friends in the process.

You knocked yourself out with your own damn powers! That doesn't sound like someone who has control over them."

He cupped her arms and shook her gently. "You need to learn to control them before you seriously harm or kill someone you care about, Max. How would you feel if you -"

Her face completely bloodless, she yanked herself away from him. She stumbled and fell to her knees but when he tried to help her up, she snarled at him and shoved his hands away. There was a creaking, groaning noise and the pile of rocks blocking the front of the cave shifted. Four of them rose in the air and Nicky stared at Max in alarm.

"Calm down, Max. It's all right." He backed up a few steps.

"Please don't be afraid of me," she moaned before she made a high-pitched keening noise and buried her face in her hands. She rocked back and forth, muttering softly to herself. "Everything's fine. Everything's fine. Just relax. Everything's fine."

After a few moments, the rocks fell to the ground with a soft thump and she heard Nicky release his breath in a harsh breath. "Max?"

She dropped her hands and stared at him. "I'm fine," she said in a toneless little voice.

"Max -"

"We should get going." She struggled to her feet and started to walk through the trees.

"Wait," he said. She stopped but didn't turn around. "You'll have frostbite on your feet before we make it back to the campsite. It'll be faster and easier if you ride on my back."

"Perhaps," she said in the same toneless voice, "but you have made it perfectly clear that you don't want me touching you. I will walk quickly."

"That isn't what I meant, Max," he growled. "You will ride on my back and there will be no arguing."

He shifted before she could reply and barked sharply at her. When he laid down beside her, she curled her fingers into his thick shaggy fur and climbed onto his back. He barked again and she held onto his fur as he moved swiftly through the trees.

CHAPTER 14

"Max! Oh, Max!" Nina ran to Max and nearly pulled her from Nicky's back. She hugged her and Max wiped the tears from her cheeks.

"Don't cry, Nina. I'm fine, honey."

"We wanted to go after you, both Meridan and I did, but they wouldn't let us." Nina gave Doran and Andric a wounded look as Max shook her head.

"They were right not to let you, Nina." She touched Nina's hair and then smiled a little when Kala poked her head out from the golden strands.

"Hello, Kala."

"Max," Kala replied in her low voice before disappearing back into Nina's hair.

"I guess." Nina looked down at Max's bare feet. "Come, you must be freezing."

As Max followed Nina to their tent, Nicholas shifted to his human form. He took the pants Doran offered him with a nod of thanks and tugged them on before shoving his feet into his boots.

"Welcome back, Lycan," Ryker said. "Thank you for

fetching our weapon for us. I imagine you now understand why Max needed to come with us."

Ignoring him completely, Nicholas stalked over to where Meridan was crouched next to the fire. "We need to talk, Meridan. Right now."

Without waiting to see if Meridan would follow, he stormed off into the trees.

"Why has Max not learned to control her powers?" Nicky said when Meridan joined him.

Max stared silently at him.

"Meridan," Nicky said. "Why can Max not control them?"

"It's complicated."

"It is not," Nicky said. "How long has she had them?"

"Jordan – Max's father – said she's had them since she was a toddler."

"Gods!" Nicky cursed under his breath. "Did her father have the same abilities?"

Meridan shook his head. "No. But he believes that his aunt did. His uncle moved her to the country after there was an incident involving their neighbour, and Jordan never saw her again."

"Max nearly killed us and herself yesterday. Her powers are dangerous. How could her father not realize that she needed to be taught to control them? Sooner or later she's going to kill someone and -"

He studied Meridan. The old Lycan had paled and he swallowed heavily before staring at the ground.

"She's killed someone, hasn't she?" Nicky said.

"Nicholas, I don't believe it's my place to share what happened. Max doesn't want -"

"Enough!" Nicky roared. "You will tell me what I want to

know, Meridan, or the gods help me, I will go back to my home and leave all of you to your fate."

Meridan's mouth compressed into a thin line and a low growl radiated from his chest. Nicholas crossed his arms over his chest and waited. After a moment, Meridan slumped against the tree and rubbed a hand over his beard.

"I was not close to Jordan. He kept to himself most of the time, but one night I stumbled on to him in the common room of your father's home. He was drunk and feeling sorry for himself over the debt he owed to Emmett. We got to talking and he told me about Max's powers."

"Go on," Nicky said.

"Jordan had a gambling problem – it was why he owed Emmett money – but at one point he was quite wealthy. Max went to one of the best schools in the city and she had everything she wanted. Jordan admitted to spoiling the girl, perhaps in an effort to make up for her dead mother, but she was always sweet to everyone, despite that."

Meridan sighed and rubbed at his beard again. "When she was seven, she killed a boy at her school."

Nicky's mouth dropped open. "The gods be damned," he said. "Are you sure?"

"Aye. Apparently, there were some boys, teenagers, at Max's school who were – well - Jordan called them troubled. There was one in particular who enjoyed tormenting the girls. From what Jordan tells me, Max stumbled in on him in the bathroom hurting one of the older girls. He was trying to," Max paused, his tanned face pale and sick looking, "rape her."

Nicky's stomach was rolling with nausea, but he nodded at Meridan to continue. "What happened next?"

"I guess Max tried to stop him, but she was just a little girl. The boy hit her hard – Jordan said she had a cracked rib and bruising all up and down her side – and went back to attacking the older girl. Max was scared," Meridan paused again, "but more importantly, she was angry."

"Angry enough to kill him," Nicky said.

"Jordan didn't give me the details. He just said that Max lost control of her powers and killed the boy."

"And the lawmen just let Max go? Was there not an inquiry into it? Did the boy's parents not want to know why their child was dead?"

Meridan shrugged. "I do not know the particulars. Jordan didn't share them with me. I imagine it was a combination of his money and the boy's parents not wanting his image tarnished. They had already lost their son. I suppose they did not want his memory tarnished by the attempted rape as well."

Nicky didn't reply and Meridan gave him a pleading look. "She was only seven, Nicky. Murder is an automatic banishment to the outskirts. Max would have died a slow and painful death. It was an accident. She didn't mean to kill him, and he would have seriously hurt or killed her."

"Aye, I know," Nicky said. He could feel a strange ache in his chest at the thought of a seven-year-old Max being forced into a life and death situation.

"She would never hurt someone unless she was forced to," Meridan said.

"I'm not judging her," Nicky said. "She did what she had to. But I still don't see why Jordan didn't help her learn to control them. Especially after killing that boy. He should have seen how dangerous it was for her to not -"

"He tried," Meridan said. "Max was so traumatized by what she had done that she refused to even talk about her powers after that. She shoved them down deep inside of her and Jordan said he hadn't seen her use them since. He said she pretended that she was normal, and that she learned to control her fear and her anger instead of learning to control her powers."

He glanced over at the campsite. Max was still in the tent with Nina and most of the others were gathered around the fire. He lowered his voice anyway. "There were rumours at the school, of course. Max was shunned at school. The other children were afraid of her and eventually Jordan pulled her out of school and hired a private tutor for her."

"She had another incident with her powers after I rescued her," Nicky said. "She begged me not to be afraid of her."

Meridan sighed deeply. "She won't admit it but she's terrified that she'll be rejected by us. She's worried that someone will think she's a danger to Violet and try to take her away from her."

"The gods help anyone who tries," Nicky said.

"Aye," Meridan said.

"Does my father know about her powers?"

"He does. Max had kept them hidden but one night Emmett took Nina and Max to the theatre. Ryker was with them as well. After the show, they were crossing the street and a man lost control of his carriage. Nina froze in the middle of the street and would have been crushed by the horses had Max not shoved her out of the way. She wasn't anywhere near the girl, but she used her powers to push Nina to safety. She tried to deny doing it, but your father is not a stupid man."

Meridan glanced at Nicholas. "Shortly after that, Emmett was taken by the leeches. Ryker forced Max to come with us, believing that her powers would be useful even though she insisted she would not use them. He used both Nina and Violet as leverage. It was why he was so angry when Max left Violet with your family."

"Has he hurt her?" Nicholas said.

"No. Ryker isn't afraid of Max, but he isn't stupid either. He sees her as a weapon that can be used against the leeches and Emmett's enemies."

"He should be afraid of her," Nicholas said.

"Nicholas – Max isn't dangerous. I promise you that she -"

"She is dangerous," Nicky said. "We both know it. Her lack of control over her powers makes her dangerous."

Meridan didn't reply and Nicky rubbed at his forehead before glancing at the older Lycan. "We need to teach Max how to control her powers."

"She will refuse. She is afraid to -"

"She needs to learn to accept her powers," Nicky said. "She'll kill herself or someone she cares about if she doesn't. I will help her learn to control and use her powers."

"She will not let you," Meridan said.

"She will," Nicky said, "or I will send her back to my home today."

"Ryker will not allow that to happen and besides, Max will not leave Nina in danger. She loves the girl."

"Ryker has no say in it," Nicholas said. "And I am not above using Nina as a way to force Max to accept her powers."

Without waiting for Meridan's reply, he pushed away from the tree and strode back into the campsite and toward Max's tent.

"MAX? ARE YOU ALL RIGHT?" NINA SAID.

"Aye, I am only tired, Nina."

"You should eat something. I imagine we'll be leaving

soon." Nina touched her back. "I could bring you some soup."

"I am not hungry." Max continued to stare at the side of the tent as Nina sighed.

"Max -"

The flap to the tent opened and Nicholas stuck his head in. He glanced at Max and Nina before smiling at the young girl.

"Nina, can you give us a moment? I wish to speak with Max in private."

"Aye, I can do that." Nina squeezed Max's arm before sliding past Nicholas.

Nicky sat down on the blankets and stared silently at Max. The minutes ticked by and finally Max said, "Go away, Nicholas. I am tired and we have a long day of travelling."

"We need to talk, Max."

"No, we don't."

"Aye, we do. You're going to learn to control your powers and I'm going to help you."

She shook her head. "I will not, Nicholas. You have no idea how dangerous they are. How badly I can -"

"I know what happened to that boy at your school," Nicky said.

Max sat up and twisted around to stare at him. Her mouth trembling, she cringed back when Nicky tried to touch her. "How do you know?"

"Meridan told me. Your father confided in him."

Max scowled at him. "Meridan had no right to tell you."

Nicky inched closer and Max held her hand out. "Stay away from me, Nicky."

He shook his head. "If you do not allow me to help you, I will send you back to my home."

"You can't do that," she said.

"I can and I will. Do you really want to leave Nina? You and I both know the danger she's in. I will do my best to protect her but there are many creatures in the outskirts."

"You would use Nina like this?" she said. "I thought you were a good man."

"I am. I care about you and Nina and want to protect you both."

"You don't," she said. "You wish to use me as a weapon like Ryker does. You are no better than him."

She flinched when Nicholas quickly reached out and pulled her into his lap. "Let go of me!"

He shook his head and pinned her arms behind her back with one hand before cupping her face with the other. He stared down at her with his eyes glowing yellow and said, "I am nothing like him. Do you honestly believe me to be?"

She hesitated and then slumped against him before shaking her head. "No. I'm sorry I said that. I did not mean it."

He stroked her short hair before massaging the back of her neck. "I wish only to help you, Max. Your powers are a gift and you must learn how to use them. I know you are afraid you will hurt someone, but I promise that this is the best way to prevent that. You know it is."

"Aye," Max said. "But if I cannot learn to control them? Then what, Nicky? What if using my – my powers only makes them grow stronger. What if I can't keep them under control?"

"You will, Max."

She pushed free of his arms and huddled on her bed, wrapping her arms around her knees before resting her forehead on them.

"Fine," she said. "I will attempt to learn how to control them."

"This is a good thing, Max," Nicky said.

"Maybe, maybe not." She lifted her head. "But if you're wrong, if I – I start to hurt someone innocent and cannot be stopped, you must promise to kill me, Nicky. I can't stand the thought of killing another again."

He shook his head. "It won't come to that."

"It might," she said. "Will you leave me now? I am very tired and would like to get some rest before we leave."

He touched her back. "Aye. It'll be fine, sweetheart. I promise you."

CHAPTER 15

"Come with me, Max." Nicholas held his hand out.

Meridan stood. "Nicholas, it's been a long day of travel. Max is tired and she needs her rest after what happened yesterday. You can start tomorrow night."

Nicholas shook his head. "No. We start tonight."

"Nicholas -"

"Enough, Meridan!" Nicholas glanced around the campfire at the remaining humans and Lycans. "We lost most of my father's Lycans to the faeries yesterday. If we are attacked again, we have no chance without Max's powers. She must learn how to use them as quickly as possible."

Meridan opened his mouth to protest and Max shook her head at him. "He is right, Meridan. You know he is."

She stood and crossed to Nicky's side but didn't take his outstretched hand. "Where are we going?"

"Into the forest. It'll be easier for you without distractions." Nicholas headed into the trees and with a final glance at Meridan and Nina, she followed him.

"THIS IS FAR ENOUGH."

Nicolas stopped in a small clearing. Although the trees blocked the moon, the snow on the ground reflected light and Max watched as he crossed to a fallen log. He dug through the snow and found three medium-sized rocks to place on the log.

"When you were a child, did you have any control over them?" he said as he returned to her side.

"I do not remember."

"Think back on it," Nicky said.

She closed her eyes. After a few minutes, a faint smile crossed her face. "I remember when I was about five or six, we were coming back from shopping. I was still in the carriage. My father's hands were full, and he was struggling to open the door of our house. I opened it for him without leaving the carriage."

"Good. Do you remember how you made the door open?"

She frowned. "Not really. I remember that my father was going to drop the bag that had my new dress, and I didn't want it to get dirty, so I opened the door."

Nicholas nodded. "Good. I want you to try and move the rocks, Max."

She sighed. "I don't even know where to begin, Nicholas."

"Concentrate on the rocks. Think about wanting to move them," he said.

She took a deep breath and stared at the rocks. They stayed planted firmly on the log and after a few minutes she snorted with frustration. "It's not going to work, Nicholas."

"Keep trying," he said. "It's only been a minute or two."

She shook her head. "It's pointless and this was a dumb idea. I don't even know how to make it work. I'm tired and I'm cold and I want to go back to the camp."

"We're not leaving until you make the rocks move." He folded his arms across his chest.

"I'm a grown woman! You can't tell me what to do."

"I can and I will," he said.

She gaped at him. "Let's make something perfectly clear, Nicholas. I've been around enough Lycans to know they have some weird bullshit idea that their women belong to them. Just because I made out with you a couple of times, doesn't mean I'm your – your mate and you can just order me around."

He grinned at her. "My mate? You're already talking about being my mate? Is this a human female thing? A few kisses and groping and you're ready for a ring and a lifetime commitment? No wonder human males seem so miserable. Or is it because I gave you your first orgasm?"

She blushed hotly and he knew his grin only infuriated her more. "That isn't what I meant, and you know it. I have no desire to be your mate, Nicholas. You would be a terrible husband."

He laughed and she scowled at him.

"Besides, it wasn't my first one," she said.

"We both know that isn't true, Max." He grinned again at her.

"Frankly, it wasn't that great," she said. "I couldn't imagine being your mate if that's the best you can do in bed."

He winked at her. "Sweetheart, that's only a fraction of what I'll do to you in bed. And if it wasn't that great, what was with all the begging?"

She clenched her hands into fists. "I didn't beg!"

"Aye, you did. And such sweet begging it was." He stepped closer and mimicked her in a low voice. "Please, Nicky, oh please, oh please -"

"You bastard!" She swung at him. He dodged it easily and caught her wrist.

"Let go of me!" she said. "Let go of me right now or the gods help you, Nicholas! I'll -"

"Max, look!" He turned her toward the fallen log. The three rocks were spinning and rotating in the air and she stared blankly at them as Nicholas moved behind her.

He slid his arm around her waist and lowered his mouth to her ear. "Good. Move them higher, Max."

"I can't," she said.

"You can. Concentrate," he said.

She stared at the slowly spinning rocks and after a moment, Nicholas felt that hum of energy. Max shivered in Nicky's arms and they watched as all three rocks rose higher into the night sky.

"Good," he said. "Now lower them."

The rocks lowered until they were nearly touching the log. Max was staring intently at them, her entire body vibrating, and unable to stop himself he pressed a gentle kiss against her throat.

It had been pure torture riding with Max today. He had kept his erection under control, but just barely, and now he couldn't resist tasting her soft skin. He licked her throat, sliding his tongue along the smoothness of her skin, and Max moaned quietly. The stones rocketed upwards as she pressed herself against Nicky's hard body.

He nipped at her throat, his hand squeezing around her hip, and she inhaled sharply as there was a loud cracking noise. A thick branch broke off from the tree to their right and fell to the ground with a soft thud. The stones dropped and bounced off the log into the snow as Max tore herself away from Nicky.

"I'm sorry," she said.

"It's fine. You did very well. Tomorrow you can practice with smaller stones while we're riding."

"Aye, whatever," she said. "Can we go back now? I really am very tired."

He nodded and held out his hand. She shook her head and, leaving a few feet between them, walked back toward their campsite.

"THAT IS SO COOL," NINA SAID. SHE WAS RIDING WITH Doran and she poked him lightly in the back. "Do you see that?"

Doran nodded. "Aye, very impressive, Max."

"Thank you," Max said. She was staring at the five small stones that floated in front of her. They hovered above the broad head of Nicky's horse and Max frowned deeply and raised her hand. The stones rose higher, spinning lazily in the air, as Doran slowed his horse until they were riding beside Nicky and Max.

"You've learned how to do that in just one night?" Doran whistled appreciatively.

"She's doing very well," Nicky said.

Max snorted and the rocks dipped lower. "Hardly. Moving five stones no bigger than marbles is not impressive."

"It is," Nina said as Kala crawled out from her hair and eyed the floating stones with bright interest. "You should be proud of yourself."

Max didn't reply as Nicky put his arm around her hips and shifted her in the saddle. It pressed her ass more firmly against him and she took a shaky breath. His fingers stroked the firm flesh of her leg and she twitched when she felt his erection press into her ass.

"Max? Are you all right? Your face is red," Nina said.

Nicky laughed softly and Max shuddered all over when he let his glove-covered fingers linger on the inside of her thigh. The stones were spinning crazily now, and she gasped when the one closest to Doran suddenly flew toward him and hit him in the arm.

"Ouch!" Doran rubbed his stinging arm. "Careful, Max."

The rest of the stones dropped out of the air and Nicky caught them easily.

"I'm so sorry, Doran! I did not mean to hurt you," Max said.

"It's fine. Do not trouble yourself over it," Doran said.

"Try again, Max." Nicholas held the stones out to her, and she shook her head.

"No, I am tired. I'll try again later."

"Keep practicing," Nicky said.

Max gave him a dirty look and he squeezed her thigh roughly. "You know I am right."

She sighed but didn't take the rocks from him. Instead she turned her gaze to Kala who was riding cross-legged on Nina's shoulder. Max shivered against Nicky, and then Kala was slowly rising off of Nina's shoulder.

Nina made a gasp of surprise as Kala floated in front of her. After a moment, the pixie grinned broadly and unfurled her right wing. She flapped it gently, wincing when her torn left one tried to join it, and blew a kiss to Nina.

Max moved the pixie toward her. Kala hovered in front of her and blew her a kiss. Max grinned as Nina said, "You're flying again, Kala."

"Fly," Kala said in her low voice. A look of sorrow crossed her face. "Kala, no fly."

Max's chest tightened at the pain and misery in the pixie's voice and she quickly moved Kala back to Nina. She made a small grunt of concentration as she lowered Kala to Nina's shoulder.

Kala landed with a quiet thump and gave Max a sweet look tinged with sorrow. "You thank, Max."

"Thank you," Nina corrected quietly before gathering the pixie in her hands. She kissed the top of her head. "I'll find a way to make you fly again, Kala. I promise."

Ryker rode up beside them. "The moment the little pest is able to fly again, she'll leave you, Nina. She's only using you."

"I don't care," Nina said. "Pixie's are meant to fly. I'll find a way to help her, even if it means never seeing her again."

CHAPTER 16

Max concentrated and the large rock rose in the air in front of her. There was a soft noise behind her, and she frowned when she felt the hot breath of Nicky on the sensitive skin of her neck. The rock hovering in front of her fell to the ground with a loud thump. "Don't do that."

"Don't do what?" Nicky stepped closer, and she stiffened when his arm slid around her waist. He gripped her hip and pressed his growing erection against her ass.

"Stop it," she said. "You're distracting me."

"That's the point, Max." He cupped her breast and squeezed it. "Keep going."

"I can't," she said.

"No?" He squeezed her chin and turned her head to show her the rocks that were slowly rising and spinning in front of them.

She moaned with dismay and Nicky kissed her cheek. "Don't fight it."

"I can't do this," she said.

"You can."

"I can't. Not with you touching me. It – it makes it harder."

Nicky smiled a bit smugly. "My touch does seem to make your powers increase, does it not?"

She flushed but nodded her agreement. "That's why you need to stop."

"Actually, is it not better for me to keep going? If my touch makes it more difficult, than this is the perfect way for you to practice. You need to learn to control it when you're frightened, or surprised, or, "he paused and then licked her neck, "aroused."

His left hand joined his right in squeezing and cupping her breasts and she moaned as a branch from small tree to their right cracked.

"Control it, Max. Concentrate," Nicky said.

"I'm trying," she said.

His thumbs were circling her nipples and she tried to think past the pleasure and focus on the power she could feel rippling through her. She stared at the rocks that were hovering in front of them, and Nicky watched as three of them rose higher than the others and moved to the right. The other rocks fell to the ground with a soft thud and Max made a low grunt of concentration. The rock in the middle rose a few feet higher while the other two continued to hover where they were.

"Good," Nicky said. He suddenly pinched her nipples and then yanked her to the ground when the rock flew toward them. It just missed their heads and it, and the other two fell to the ground as Max stared at him.

"I'm so sorry," she said.

"It's fine." He rolled her on to her back and brushed his hand across her cheek. "You're doing very well."

"I just about brained the both of us with a rock," she said.

"Keep trying." He pulled her to her feet and turned her around. "Go on, Max."

Max shivered when he rubbed his erection against her ass before unbuttoning her jacket. His hands cupped her breasts through her shirt, and she moaned. "Nicky, I -"

"I want you so much, Max," Nicky rasped. "It's driving me crazy that you can resist me so easily."

"It's not easy," she said.

"Is it not?" He unbuttoned her shirt and she gasped when the cold air hit her naked breasts.

"No." She arched her back into his warm hands as the rocks began to hover again.

He tugged and pulled at her nipples until they were dark red and throbbing. She made another soft groan of need when he slipped his hand down the front of her pants. He cupped her pussy and bit her neck gently when he felt the wetness that coated her.

"Nicky, wait," she said.

He made a harsh grunt of frustration and pulled his hand out from her pants. He took a step back and she turned to look at him. His face was a mixture of frustration and need.

"Maybe you're right. Maybe if I can learn to control my powers when you're touching me, it'll be easier to – to use them when I'm um, frightened."

His nostrils flared and he stepped closer. "I think it's worth trying."

"Aye, I suppose you do. But, Nicky, I'm only doing this because it might help me with my powers. Do you under-stand? When all of this is over, we need to go back to the way things were. I need to concentrate on Violet and – and finding her a good dad, someone who's interested in settling down. All right?"

He nodded as he pressed his body against hers and reached around to squeeze her ass. "Aye, I understand."

He pulled her jacket off her body and placed it on the fallen tree. "Do you understand what I want, Max?"

"You want to fuck me," she said.

"That's right. I do," he said. "I need to be inside of you. You have no idea how much I need that. Once we start, there will be no stopping, no changing your mind or worrying about what will happen."

He leaned forward and licked her trembling lower lip. "I'm going to fuck you hard and fast, and you're going to control your powers when you come."

His hot words sent a sharp stab of desire through her pelvis and she nodded as he reached for the button on her pants. He tugged her pants and her underwear to her knees before lifting her and sitting her on her jacket. He yanked her clothing from one leg and let it dangle from the other before stepping between her parted legs.

The fallen tree was the perfect height and she moaned when his fabric-covered erection pressed against her naked core. The air was cold, but her desire and Nicky's body heat drove the chill away.

He reached between them and unbuttoned his pants before tugging his cock free through the opening. She stared wide-eyed at it before he grabbed her naked hips and pulled her closer. The head of his cock rubbed against her clit and she moaned as rocks rose in the air around them.

"So wet already, Max," he said teasingly.

He dipped his head and sucked on one throbbing nipple. His mouth was deliciously hot and wet, and she arched her back, threading her fingers through his short hair. He rubbed his thick beard across her nipple, and she moaned loudly.

"Be quiet, Max," he whispered into her ear. "Do you want the others to hear?"

She shook her head as he grabbed her thighs and pulled them apart. He glanced at the rocks spinning crazily around them. "Concentrate, Max."

"I am," she groaned.

"You're not," he said. He guided his cock to her wet entrance and pushed his cock deep inside of her warmth.

Max cried out and Nicky ducked as a rock went flying past his head.

"Max!" he said sharply. "Open your eyes."

Her eyelids fluttered open and she stared at him pleadingly. "Please, Nicky."

"Not yet. Concentrate first," he said hoarsely.

"I'm trying!" She pouted at him and he shook his head.

"Try harder. I'll stop if you don't."

He ducked again as another rock went whizzing past his head.

"Max, I'm not moving until you control it," he said through gritted teeth.

She moaned with need and frustration and stared grimly at the rocks. After a moment, the stones fell to the snow with a soft thump and he thrust into her. She gasped and clung to him as he cupped her breast and rubbed her nipple with his thumb.

They kissed hotly, their tongues sliding and licking as Nicky plunged in and out of her. "You feel so good, Max."

She bit his bottom lip and he growled deep in his throat as his eyes turned a dark yellow. Around them the trees were bending and swaying, and the fallen tree shifted beneath her. She jerked, her pussy tightening around him, and he groaned before thrusting back and forth rapidly.

"Oh, oh, oh," she repeated breathlessly. A branch fell

from the tree closest to them and she made another soft moan as Nicky reached between them.

He rubbed her wet clit, pinching and tugging it lightly, and she made a breathless cry of need as her fingers dug into his broad shoulders. "Nicky, I -"

She stopped and arched her back as her pussy squeezed around him. He clamped his hand over her mouth as her orgasm rushed through her and she screamed. He thrust into her and, as a tree next to them tore free from the ground with a loud, splintering moan and crashed to the ground, he came hard inside of her.

The log she was sitting on cracked in two and they spilled to the ground. He landed on her with a heavy thud and she winced as the cold snow touched her bare ass and legs. Branches, heavy with snow, continued to fall around them and he touched her face gingerly.

"Max? Are you all right?"

"Aye. My ass is freezing."

He snorted laughter and pulled out of her before standing and helping her to her feet. Standing awkwardly on one foot, she pulled her pants and underwear back over her boot and up her legs as Nicky buttoned his own pants. He snagged her jacket from the snow and handed it to her as she buttoned her shirt.

She stared around them. The log had cracked in half and the ground was littered with branches. The tree that had uprooted lay on the ground, and she sighed.

"What's wrong?" Nicky took her hand.

"I didn't handle my powers very well."

He pulled her into his embrace. "You're wrong, Max. You did very well."

She snorted. "Have you looked around us, Nicky?"

"Aye. But considering that the last time I made you come,

you nearly killed us both, I'd say this is an improvement." He winked at her and she blushed.

"Besides," he bent his head and nuzzled her throat, "we can keep practicing until you have full control."

"Did you – did you enjoy it, Nicky?"

A broad grin crossed his face. "Aye, very much, Max. Although I would have preferred to have you in a warm, soft bed where I could take my time."

She swallowed thickly as he buttoned her jacket. "We should get back to the others before they come looking for us. I'm surprised they didn't come running when the tree fell over."

He took her hand and led her back to the campsite.

"WHAT HAPPENED OUT THERE?" NINA LEFT THE CAMPFIRE and joined them. She took Max's hand and scanned her face anxiously. "Are you all right?"

"Aye, I'm fine," Max said. "I was just practicing."

Pavina joined them and she frowned before inhaling deeply. She stared first at Max and then at Nicky and a look of disappointment flickered across her face. Max blushed furiously as Nicky walked to Doran and Andric and grins crossed their faces. Doran winked at her and she blushed again as Pavina sighed loudly.

"Well, there goes my chance."

Nina frowned at her. "What are you talking about, Pavina?"

Pavina shrugged. "Max and Nicholas had -"

"Hold your tongue, Pavina!" Max said. She grabbed Nina's arm and tugged her to the campfire. "Stay close to the fire, Nina. It's cold out tonight."

She sat on the blanket next to Nina, as Meridan crouched down beside her.

"Do you know what you're doing, Max?" he said in a low voice.

"Aye."

"Are you sure? Emmett will not be happy when he finds out you are sleeping with his son. You know how he feels about humans."

"I don't care," she said. "Besides, I only do it as a way to help me practice controlling my powers."

Meridan snorted. "Is that why?"

"Aye," she said. "Although who I choose to spend my time with is none of your business, Meridan."

He stared at her with a hurt look on his face. "I don't want you getting hurt, Max. Nicky seems like a decent Lycan, but you must remember who his father is."

"He is nothing like Emmett!" Max said.

"Perhaps not," Meridan said as Ryker approached Nicholas and the others.

"We are getting low on supplies. There is a town not far from here called Morden. We can stop there, pick up some supplies, and spend the night. Sleep in a real bed." He rubbed his hand along his bald skull.

"Morden is no place for them." Andric glanced at Nina and Max.

"It's fine," Ryker said impatiently. "I have been to Morden many times."

"Aye, as have I," Andric said. "It is full of nothing but thieves and murderers."

"And which are you, then?" Ryker asked. "A murderer or a thief?"

Andric made a low growl and Nicky rested his hand on his arm. "Easy, cousin. Do not let him get to you."

"We have no choice," Ryker said. "We cannot make it to the leech's colony on the supplies we have left. Besides, we do not even know where exactly the colony is. Someone in Morden will know."

Nicholas glanced at Andric and Doran. "He is right. We need to stop there. Perhaps we could leave Nina and Max with Meridan and Pavina just outside of the town."

Ryker sighed. "We are not leaving our weapon behind. We may need her in Morden."

"Your desire to use a woman to protect yourself leaves me wondering how much of a coward you really are, Ryker," Nicky said.

Ryker bristled. "I am no coward, Nicholas." His hand drifted to his sword and caressed the handle. "Believe me when I say I am more capable of bloodshed then you can imagine. Push me again and you'll find out for yourself."

Doran shook his head. "The gods be damned! Perhaps the two of you should just pull out your dicks and do a size measure right now."

Andric snorted laughter as both Nicholas and Ryker flushed.

"I get that the two of you hate each other but frankly, I don't care. It's getting tiring," Doran said. "You both want the same thing – to save Nicholas' birth father. The sooner we do that, the sooner the two of you can part ways."

Nicholas studied his cousin carefully. It wasn't like Doran to be so short-tempered and as Ryker stalked away, Nicky squeezed Doran's shoulder.

"Are you all right, cousin?"

"Aye." Doran rubbed his forehead. "I am fine, Nicky. Just tired and anxious to return home."

Nicholas gave him a guilty look. "I am sorry, Doran. I should not have asked -"

"You didn't," Doran said. "I volunteered, remember? Do not trouble yourself, cousin. I'll be fine."

He turned to Andric. "How much further to Morden?"

"If we leave early tomorrow morning, half a day's ride. We could find lodging there for the night," Andric said.

"Aye, it will be good to sleep in a bed again." Doran rubbed his neck before glancing at Nicholas. "Although I do not think you'll be using your bed for sleep."

Andric snorted softly and Nicholas shrugged. "I told you the ladies love me."

He glanced behind him at Max. She was sitting on a blanket next to Nina and staring into the fire. Already he wanted her again. Their time in the forest had been way too brief, and he was anxious to find a soft bed in which to take her properly. He could strip her naked and spend hours touching and exploring her warm body.

Doran gave him a thoughtful look. "You need to be careful, Nicky."

"Aye, I know."

"Max isn't like other women," Doran said. "She's not the love them and leave them type and I'd hate to see what she would do to you with those powers of hers, if you make her angry."

Nicky shook his head. "I'm not going to make her angry. Besides, she agreed to it only as a way to help control her powers, not because she has any type of feelings for me."

"Is that right?" Doran glanced at Andric who shrugged.

"Aye, it is." Nicholas glanced at Max again. "Good night, cousins."

"It is still early." Doran frowned.

"Aye, but I am on watch with Meridan later." Nicky disappeared into his tent.

CHAPTER 17

Nicholas pulled Max away from the others who had congregated outside the door of the only hotel in Morden. He motioned for Nina to join them. "The two of you are to stay close to me or my cousins at all times. Do you understand?"

Nina nodded as Max glanced around. They were standing in the main street of Morden and despite the dinner hour, it was bustling with activity. Although most of the people walking past them looked human, Max had a feeling that there were more Lycans and other creatures than it appeared.

As if to prove her point, a short and wiry man, his face covered in a thick, bushy black beard, slowed to a near stop as he walked past them. He inhaled deeply, his eyes turning a dark yellow as he stared at Nina.

Nicholas stiffened and turned to stare at the Lycan. A low growl radiated from his chest and he bared his teeth at the man. "You would be wise to keep moving."

The Lycan seemed to shrink under Nicky's fierce gaze and he grinned half-heartedly before continuing down the street.

"Is there a restaurant?" Pavina asked Andric.

Andric shook his head. "There's that. It has some food."

He pointed further down the street and Max squinted at the large hand-written sign propped on the sidewalk. The letters were faded, and she shook her head when Nina asked her if she could read it.

"No. The letters are too faded."

Nina took a few steps forward, stopping when Nicky placed his hand on her arm. "I cannot read it either."

"It's called 'Sal's Bar'," Andric said.

"Is it safe?" Nina said.

"No place in Morden is safe. You would be wise to remember that, young human," Andric said.

"Let's go," Ryker said. "I'm hungry."

Without waiting for the others, he strode down the street and toward the bar. Max held out her hand to Nina and smiled encouragingly at her. "It will be fine, Nina."

NICHOLAS AND MERIDAN SAT ACROSS FROM THE ANCIENT Lycan. They stared quietly at him for a moment. The Lycan's eyes were milky with age and his beard hung nearly to his waist. He had deep wrinkles in his forehead and around his eyes, and an air of weary resignation clung to him.

"What do you want?" The Lycan's voice was gravelly and he took another drink of beer before staring mistrustfully at Nicky and Meridan.

"The barman says you know where the leech colony is," Meridan said.

The Lycan eyed him shrewdly. "Aye, I might."

"We want to know where it is," Nicholas said.

The Lycan's gaze swung to him. "Do you now? You wish for death, do you?"

"Will you tell us where the colony is?" Nicky said.

"Why should I? What's in it for me?" The Lycan took another drink and wiped at the beer that dribbled into his beard. "Ain't doin' nothin' for free."

Nicholas sighed as Meridan reached into the coin purse that hung around his belt. He pulled out a gold coin and showed it to the Lycan. The Lycan's eyes gleamed and he sat up straight, smoothing his shirt and drinking the last of his beer.

"Tell us where the colony is, and this is yours." Meridan placed the coin on the table in front of him. It glowed in the light and the old Lycan reached for it eagerly. He growled in surprise when Nicky's hand dropped on to his wrist.

"Let go of me!" he snarled.

"Tell us where the colony is," Nicky said.

He glanced behind him as he waited for the old Lycan to speak. The rest of their group was sitting at the bar. Max was sitting next to Nina and encouraging her to eat. Nina was picking at a salad, but Max's sat untouched in front of her. Nicky frowned. He had ordered the salad for her, even though she insisted she wasn't hungry, and it worried him that she wasn't eating.

"Why do you want to go to the colony, anyway?" the Lycan asked.

Nicholas turned back to face him. "That's none of your business."

The Lycan bared his teeth at him. "Perhaps I have forgotten the way to the colony. I am an old man now."

Nicholas growled at him and Meridan placed a hand on his arm. "Be calm, Nicholas." He smiled at the Lycan. "I'm sure you have not forgotten the way."

The Lycan grunted. "You could save yourself a gold coin and just stay here for a few weeks. They'll come for you. They've picked off most of us, one-by-one."

"How many of our kind have they taken?" Meridan said.

The Lycan shrugged. "Plenty. This town used to be teeming with Lycans. The last I heard, there was only a dozen or so of us left. All rotten to the core, of course."

He sneered at Nicholas. "Nothing at all like you, pretty boy."

"And how have you escaped their clutches?" Nicholas said.

The Lycan barked sharp laughter. "I'm too old. They don't want me." He glanced around the crowded bar and lowered his voice. "The leeches are experimentin' on us. They say the leeches have found a way to walk in the sun."

"Who are 'they'?" Meridan frowned.

"You know 'they'." The old Lycan waved his hand vaguely.

"Have you seen a leech walk in the sun, old man?" Nicholas said.

"Not personally. But they say -"

Nicky snorted. "You're a fool."

"I ain't!" The Lycan growled again. "The rumour is true! They're taking the Lycans."

"Aye, we know," Meridan said. "We believe you. They've taken a friend of ours and we want to get him back."

"It'll be too late. Your friend is either dead or a half-breed leech."

Meridan shook his head. "The leeches have not been successful in their effort to walk in the sun. There is still a chance our friend is alive."

"How do you know they have failed?" the Lycan said.

"Because if they have created a race of half-Lycan, half-leech, we'd all be dead or turned by now," Meridan answered. "Now, will you tell us where the colony is, or should I put my gold coin back in my pocket?"

"YOU NEED TO EAT SOME MORE, NINA." MAX PUSHED THE plate toward her, and Nina shook her head.

"The lettuce tastes funny."

Max eyed her own salad before sighing. "Aye, it does. I still have some dried meat in my pack back at the hotel room. We can eat some of that."

Nina nodded and Max gave her an anxious look. The young girl's face was pale, and her mouth was trembling. "Are you all right, Nina?"

"Aye." Nina glanced around the bar. "Just afraid, I guess. I hate that I'm not brave like you or Nicky."

"You're plenty brave." Max put her arm around her shoulders and hugged her. "Besides, once you have mastered the sword, you'll be the fiercest woman I know."

Nina smiled faintly. "Aye, perhaps."

Kala stuck her face out from her hair and peered around.

"Stay hidden, Kala," Nina said. "This is not the place for pixies."

She jumped and nearly fell off the bar stool when a dirty and scarred hand touched her soft blonde hair. She peered up at the man standing next to her.

"You're a pretty little thing." He grinned at her and she grimaced at the sight of his stained, yellow teeth.

"I ain't seen anything as pretty as you in a long time. Why don't you come have a drink with me, pretty little thing?"

"No, thank you." Nina's entire body was vibrating and

Max, swallowing down her own fear, reached over and pushed his hand away from Nina.

"Don't touch her."

The man scanned her up and down before looking at Nina. "Is she your mama?"

Nina shook her head and the man grinned again. "Then she ain't got the right to tell me what to do. Now, are you coming with me like a good little girl, or am I gonna have to carry you off?"

He took Nina's arm and Max slid off the stool. Before she could approach the man, Doran and Andric were standing beside him.

"Take your hand off my young friend," Doran said.

"And if I don't?" The man was both taller and heavier than the two Lycans and he stared down at them in annoyance. "What are you two going to do about it?"

Andric and Doran snarled in unison, their eyes glowing as their teeth lengthened into fangs.

The man scoffed. "I ain't afraid of your kind. I've killed more than my fair share. In fact, my bed is lined with Lycan pelts. Bigger and stronger Lycans than you."

"Let her go," Doran repeated.

Pavina joined them, resting her hand protectively on Nina's back, before making a low growl at the man.

He eyed her body with interest. "The gods be damned. Welcome to the party."

Pavina tugged lightly on Nina's shoulder and the man dropped his hand. He continued to stare at Pavina. "I ain't never been interested in fucking a Lycan before but for you, I'd make an exception."

"I'd rather fuck a leech," Pavina said. She inhaled deeply, her nose wrinkling in disgust. "At least they smell better."

"Bitch! I'll kill you for that!" The man tried to lunge past

Nina to get at Pavina, and Doran and Andric shoved him backwards.

"Let him go," Pavina snarled. "I'll tear the stupid human apart limb by limb."

"Pavina, be quiet!" Doran said as she moved in front of Nina.

Max turned to look behind her. Nicholas and Meridan were deep in conversation with an old Lycan and had taken no notice of them. She twisted to the left and stared at Ryker and the remaining four hired Lycans.

"Help them!" she said. She could feel her power humming through her system, and she concentrated fiercely on controlling it. She had no desire to test her new control in a crowded bar of humans and Lycans. If she couldn't control it…she shuddered at the thought.

Ryker rolled his eyes but stood and ambled toward Doran and Andric. He rested his hand on the butt of his sword as the four Lycans spread out in a tight circle around the man. He had pulled a large, sharp dagger from his belt and his fingers tightened around it. He stared at the Lycans that surrounded him, a look of unease crossing his face for the first time, before holding his hands up.

"The gods be damned! Can't a man pay a woman a compliment?"

When no one replied, he shrugged and backed up. "I think it's time for me to go."

"Wise choice, my friend," Doran growled.

The man turned away and Pavina laughed before snorting derisively, "Pussy."

She turned to face Nina as the other Lycans relaxed. "Did he scare you, Nina? Did he -"

"Pavina! Look out!" Nina shouted. She shoved Pavina to the side and Max watched as her thin body twitched and she made a soft gasping cry. The man who had insulted them was standing a few feet away, his body tense and his arm extended in front of him. Max stared curiously at his odd position before Nina staggered around to face her.

"Max?" she said. Her face was white, and Max stared horrified at the dagger sticking out of her chest.

"Hurts," Nina whispered. Her fingers grasped at the handle of the dagger.

"Nina! No! Don't!" Max shouted as Nina yanked the dagger free.

Blood spurted out of the wound, coating Max's shirt and hands and she made a harsh cry and caught Nina as she collapsed. She sank to the ground with the young girl and pressed her hands against the wound. Blood continued to gush from it, and she made another harsh cry of fear.

"Nina! Nina, stay with me, honey!"

"Can't breathe," Nina whispered.

Max could hear a horrible whistling noise with every breath that Nina laboured to draw in and she started to cry as Nicholas dropped to his knees beside her.

"What do we do?" she shouted at him.

There was a loud howl and Meridan shoved his way past Doran and Andric.

"NINA!" He howled again and fell to the floor beside her. He cradled her head in his hands and kissed her pale, sweaty forehead.

"Be still, my love. It will be all right," he said.

Nina didn't reply. Blood was starting to soak into the floorboards beneath her and she drew in gasp after gasp of ragged breath.

"Nicky, tell us what to do," Max said.

Nicholas, his face ashen and his hands trembling, took Nina's hand in his own. "There is nothing we can do."

Max stared at him in horror as above them, the glasses stacked neatly in shelves behind the bar exploded one after the other. The bar stools tipped over and someone behind them cried out with fear when the mirror behind the bar cracked with a jagged, coughing noise.

"Stop, Max!" Nicky shouted. "Stop right now!"

Panting, Max struggled to harness in the power that was screaming to be free as Nicky bent over Nina.

He kissed her forehead and gave her a trembling smile. "It'll be all right, sweet one."

There was movement in Nina's hair and Kala crawled free of the golden strands. She kissed Nina's cheek and marched across the young girl's chest. She pushed at Max's hands still pressing against the wound in Nina's chest and glared at her before muttering something in her own language.

"Kala, get out of the way!" Max cried. She was still struggling to control her powers and another glass exploded as Meridan howled in sorrow.

Max hissed and snatched her hands back when Kala bit her hard with her needle-sharp teeth. She stared in shock as the little pixie stood in the river of blood flowing down Nina's chest and rhythmically clapped her hands.

"What's she doing?" Max said.

"I do not know," Nicky said.

The pixie was glowing now with a bright blue light. Max squinted as Kala chanted in her native tongue. Her right wing was flapping so quickly it was a blur and the pixie winced when the left one fluttered. The glow surrounding the pixie grew brighter as Kala clapped harder and faster.

"The gods be damned," Nicky whispered when bright blue dust fell from Kala's clapping hands. It coated Nina's wound until nothing could be seen but a thick layer of softly glowing pixie dust.

"What did she do to her?" Meridan stared at her in confusion when the small pixie suddenly stopped clapping and staggered backward. Her glow cut out abruptly and she fell to her knees on Nina's sternum, panting harshly with her head lowered.

Max studied Nina. Her face was still pale but as she watched, her cheeks turned a soft pink. "Nina?"

They all jumped when Nina drew in a harsh gasping breath and coughed. She blinked up at them, her eyes hazy with confusion, before staring at her chest. It was still covered in pixie dust and before anyone could stop her, she brushed it away, grimacing when she touched the blood-soaked dust beneath the top layer. "What is this?"

Max's mouth dropped open and Nicky made a loud grunt of surprise. The wound in Nina's chest was gone. There was a tear in her shirt and her front was covered in blood and pixie dust, but Max couldn't see any fresh blood.

"Nina, hold still!" She unbuttoned Nina's shirt and stared in disbelief at the smooth skin.

"Max, stop it!" Nina, blushing furiously, pulled her shirt together and struggled to sit up. "I'm fine."

Kala, still kneeling on her sternum rolled limply from Nina's body and Nina caught her neatly. "Kala!"

She held the little pixie close and stroked her back. "Kala, are you all right?"

The pixie laid in Nina's hands and nodded wearily. "Kala all right."

She closed her eyes as Nina made a soft cry. "Is she dying?"

Nicky leaned in and studied the little pixie. "I think she's all right, Nina. She's just tired."

He stood as Meridan pulled Nina to her feet and hugged her. "Oh, Nina."

"I'm fine, Meridan," Nina said. "I feel great, actually."

Tears dripping down his face, Meridan laughed raggedly and hugged her again. "Thank the gods, Nina. Thank the gods."

"Thank the pixie is more like it," Doran said. He stared at Kala still cupped in Nina's hands. "How is that possible?"

"I don't know," Nicky said. He glanced around the bar. Most of its patrons had fled when the glasses started to explode, but the ones who were left were staring at them with barely hidden fear.

"It's time to go." He took Max's hand and pulled her toward the door as the others followed them.

"Where is he?" Max asked as she scanned the bar.

"Who?"

"The man who tried to kill Nina." A chair tipped over as she walked by it.

Nicky shook his head. "I imagine he's hiding in some far corner of the town by now."

"I want to find him!" she spat. "I want to find him and -"

"Kill him?" Nicholas raised his eyebrows at her. "Is that what you wish to do, Max?"

The power still humming through her body disappeared in an instant and she gave Nicky a sick look. "I... no, I don't want... I mean..."

He squeezed her hand. "He will pay for what he did. I promise you."

CHAPTER 18

"Nina?" Max touched the young girl's back.

Nina didn't look up. She had made a nest out of her sweater and had tucked the still-sleeping Kala into it. "Aye?"

"Are you sure you're all right?"

"I'm perfectly fine."

Max glanced quickly at Pavina. The three of them were sharing a room and the Lycan was stretched out on the other bed. She shrugged at Max and stared up at the ceiling.

"Nina, you should probably talk about what happened," Max said.

Nina shook her head. "I don't want to, Max. I'm fine, really. I'm just worried about Kala."

"She'll be fine." Max sat next to Nina on the bed. "What she did, well, it most likely took a lot of her energy."

"Aye," Nina said. A tear dropped on the quilt on the bed and she wiped roughly at her face. "If I had done what the others told me, if I had left her to her fate back in the forest, I would be dead, Max."

"I know, honey." Max stroked her back as Nina sniffed and wiped at her face.

"Why hasn't she healed herself?" she said. "If she could heal me, why hasn't she fixed her wing?"

"I don't know. Perhaps it doesn't work that way. Perhaps her abilities only work on others."

"Maybe." Nina crawled into the bed. She closed her eyes as she cupped her hand around her sweater. "Good night, Max."

"Good night, honey."

Max stood and crossed to the window. She stared out into the darkness. It had been nearly three hours since they had left the bar and she was feeling restless and anxious. She sighed and shifted from foot to foot. She wanted to go to Nicky, and she was tired of trying to deny it. She leaned her head against the glass of the window and waited patiently for Pavina and Nina to fall asleep.

SHE STOOD IN THE HALLWAY AND STARED AT THE CLOSED door for a moment before knocking quickly. There was no answer and she tried the doorknob. It turned easily under her hand and she opened the door and slipped into the room.

She shivered. The window was wide open, and it was cold in his room. Nicky was standing naked at the far end of the room in front of a basin resting on the dresser. His back was to her and she studied his ass for a moment as desire trickled through her. He bent and she heard the splashing of water.

"Hello, Max."

"Hello, Nicky. Your door was open."

"I left it open for you," he said.

She closed the window and walked toward him. She placed her hand on his naked back and when he didn't turn, she stepped to his side. "Nicky, what…"

She stared at the blood that covered his hands, chest and face. "Are you hurt?"

"It's not my blood."

He continued to scrub at his chest and face as Max swallowed. "Nicky? Whose blood is it?"

He didn't reply and her eyes widened as understanding washed over her. "Did you kill him?"

"He shouldn't have tried to hurt her," Nicky said.

Max took a step back and Nicky sighed. "Are you afraid of me now, Max?"

She shook her head before reaching for a cloth. "No, of course not."

She dipped the cloth into the water and wiped the blood from Nicky's face before dipping the cloth back into the water. It turned a pale pink and she dumped it out the window before pouring fresh water from the jug.

"Hold still, honey." She scrubbed the blood from his hands and chest before drying him with the towel. "There. Much better."

He reached out and cupped the back of her neck. He rested his forehead against hers and sighed again. "I want you so much, Max. I should be concentrating on how to free my birth father from the leeches but you're all I can think about. I can't sleep, and I feel like I'm going crazy."

She could hear the frustration in his voice as he said, "I don't know how to get you out of my head. I can't stop -"

"Shh." She pressed her mouth against his. "I want you too, Nicky. I'm tired of denying it."

"Aye, to help you practice with your powers," he said with a tinge of bitterness.

183

She shook her head. "No, that's not the reason."

"Is it not?"

"No."

He didn't reply and she kissed him lightly on the mouth and took his hand. "Come to bed, Nicky."

He followed her to the bed and watched as she reached for the buttons on her shirt. He tugged her hands away. "No, let me."

He undressed her slowly and when she was finally standing naked in front of him, his cock was huge and standing proudly from his body. She took him in her hand, stroking him as his eyes drifted shut and he moaned.

"Lie down on the bed, Max," he said.

She did what he asked and licked her lips with anticipation when he stretched out between her thighs. He kissed her inner thigh, licking the sensitive skin and rubbing his thick beard across it and she moaned loudly and spread her thighs wide.

"Please, Nicky." She was shameless in her need and she reached between her thighs and pushed on the back of his head. "Please."

He stared at her exposed, glistening sex and a small grin crossed his face. "You're so wet already, Max."

Without a shred of embarrassment, she nodded eagerly. "Aye, you do that to me. Hurry, Nicky."

He shook his head. "Not this time, sweetheart."

Her groan of frustration turned into a gasp of need when Nicky licked her with an agonizingly slow stroke of his tongue. Her hips arched off the bed and she cried out when his tongue brushed against her throbbing clit.

"Gods be damned!" she nearly shouted. "Please."

"I love hearing you beg, Max." He licked her clit again. "You taste so sweet."

Her fingers dug into his scalp and she pushed. He grinned and began a slow, sensual assault with his lips and tongue. She moaned and gasped, thrusting her pelvis against him as he drove her need higher and higher.

"The bed, Max," Nicky said.

Her eyes popped open and she studied the approaching ceiling for a moment before closing her eyes. The bed lowered gently to the floor and she took a deep breath. "I'm sorry."

"It's fine," he said. "But perhaps I should stop eating your sweet pussy."

"What? No! Don't you dare stop, Nicky! I can control it. I swear to the gods." Her fingers tightened in his hair, preventing him from moving, and he laughed.

"Have you had your sweet pussy eaten before, Max?"

"You know I haven't," she moaned.

The candles on the table beside the bed rose in the air, spinning slowly, and Max made a harsh noise of frustration before staring at them. They lowered back to the table and Nicky rose to his knees and leaned over her. He blew the candles out and winked at her. "Just in case."

"Aye," she said. "Keep going."

He grinned. "What was I doing again?"

"You know what you were doing. Please, Nicky."

He leaned down and licked her mouth. She could taste herself on his lips and it sent another throbbing bite of lust through her body.

"I have a poor memory," he teased.

She pulled his head to hers and nipped his bottom lip. He twitched against her before sucking on her bottom lip in return.

"Bad girl," he growled.

She bit him again before pushing on his shoulders. "Nicky!"

With another teasing grin he kissed his way down her body. He stopped at her breasts and took his time in kissing and licking her nipples. He pulled lightly on them with his teeth and she arched her back and clutched at his head. When they were throbbing heavily and she was panting and moaning, he continued downward. He kissed her flat stomach and each hipbone before settling himself between her thighs again. At the feel of his warm breath on her pussy, the bed jerked beneath them, and he stared up at her.

"Control, sweetheart."

"I know," she panted.

He bent his head and licked her clit again. He slid two fingers deep inside of her, thrusting back and forth as he licked and sucked at her swollen, pink nub. She cried out with pleasure and her hips rose up from the bed. She made a final, harsh cry and wetness flooded his face as her pussy clamped down around his fingers. He licked her clean as she moaned and twisted beneath him and the bed rose into the air.

"Nicky!" She gasped and he slid up her body, positioning his cock at her tight entrance. The bed returned to the floor with another soft thump.

"Ready, sweetheart?"

"Aye, so ready," she moaned.

She hooked her legs around his hips as he slid into her with one deep thrust. He plunged in and out as she gripped his hard biceps. He kissed her deeply on the mouth, tasting and exploring its warmth, as he slid in and out of her.

He slowed his pace and she squeezed his arms in dismay. "Don't stop, Nicky."

"Three times, remember, Max?" He murmured into her ear. He licked the curve of her ear before working his hand between them. His fingers found her swollen clit and she moaned again as he rubbed it roughly.

"Gods!" He cried out when her pussy clamped around him and her entire body shook. The candles fell from the nightstand and the bed jerked and shivered beneath them as she came again, her tight core rippling around Nicky's thick cock.

"Control," Nicky groaned when the nightstand hovered in the air.

"I'm trying!"

He thrust deeply into her and she hooked her feet together in the small of his back and urged him on with soft moans and cries. He thrust harder as she moaned his name repeatedly.

The pictures were vibrating on the walls, as he dipped his head and growled into her ear, "Mine, Max. You're mine."

He pinned her arms to the bed and lowered his mouth to her throat. His fangs were out, and he pressed them against her neck, pinning her to the bed with his hands and mouth. She arched into him, almost hoping he would bite her, claim her, show everyone that she belonged to him and only him.

She made a final harsh cry and jerked against him, her pussy tightening around his cock as he thrust one last time. The bed lurched beneath them and the nightstand crashed to the floor. Nicky howled against her throat as he came deep within her.

He collapsed against her soft body and released her throat. He stared at her neck. She reached up and touched her throat. There was no blood, he hadn't broken the skin, but she could feel the deep indents in her flesh. He pushed her hand away and licked her throat as she shuddered beneath him.

"I'm sorry," he said.

She stroked his short blond hair. "For what?"

"I nearly bit you."

"It isn't a full moon."

"I should have had better control." He licked her neck again and she caressed his naked back.

"I guess I'm not the only one who needs to practice." She smiled at him and he kissed her full mouth before easing to her side.

"I think you did very well. The bed is still in one piece," he said.

"Aye, but the nightstand is not." She leaned over him and frowned.

The nightstand was lying on its side with two of its legs broken off.

"You did very well," he repeated. He pulled her into his embrace and stroked the back of her neck. "Will you stay with me tonight, Max?"

"Aye," she said. "I'd like that."

"As would I." He rubbed her back as she curled into him and slung her thigh over his hips.

CHAPTER 19

"This can't be right," Ryker said

Meridan shrugged. "The old Lycan said this was the place."

Max leaned around the tree she was hiding behind and stared at the small cabin situated in the field just beyond the trees. Calling it a cabin was generous, she decided. It was nothing more than a run-down shack.

She glanced at Nicky. He, along with Andric, were tying the horses to the trees and she studied him carefully. She had spent the night with him before sneaking back to her room in the early morning of dawn. Her legs and pelvis muscles were aching and sore and she stretched them gingerly.

"Do you smell that?" Doran asked Andric in a low voice.

"Aye," Andric said.

"Leeches?" Nina whispered.

Meridan shook his head. "No. Gogmagogs."

Ryker stared at the empty field. "Where are they?"

"The better question is - why would we smell them?" Doran said. "Gogs hate leeches."

"Maybe they were just in the area but are gone now?" Nina said.

Nicholas began to strip off his clothing. "We need to check the cabin. If what the old Lycan said is true, then this is the leech colony."

Ryker snorted. "Ridiculous. The colony is very large. Do you believe they're crammed inside?"

Nicky ignored him as he took off his shirt. "We stay together. Stick close to each other and stay alert."

He glanced at Nina. "Stay close to Max. Do you understand?"

Nina nodded. Meridan smiled at the young girl and kissed her on the forehead.

"It will be fine, Nina. We will find your father and take him home. I promise."

"Thank you, Meridan." Nina hugged him and Meridan kissed her forehead again before stepping back.

Nina took Max's hand and Max squeezed it reassuringly as the rest of the Lycans stripped and shifted. Nicholas barked softly and the group crept from the trees toward the dilapidated cabin.

Max, her heart racing and her legs shaking, followed Andric closely. Nicky was in the lead, followed by Doran, Ryker and Andric. The hired Lycans were behind her and Nina, and Pavina and Meridan were bringing up the rear.

The sun was reflecting off the snow and she squinted at the cabin as they grew nearer. No birds sang in the forest behind them and she could feel her unease growing. Something wasn't right, something –

There was a soft thump just behind them and she whirled around as Pavina snarled and Meridan gave a strangled yelp. She froze, staring in shock and disbelief at the Gogmagogs rising from the ground.

She realized with horror that the Gogs had been hidden in chambers beneath the ground and she screamed a warning as, all around them, the snow rippled and heaved as the Gogs threw back the heavy wooden doors buried beneath the snow and emerged into the bright sunlight. There were at least twenty of the giant beasts and they grinned viciously as they attacked the small group.

Max stared wide-eyed at the Gogs. She had never seen one before and she couldn't get over the sheer size of them. The smallest of them was still over ten feet tall and they towered over the Lycans and the humans. Their thick, muscular bodies were covered in a layer of dark hair beneath the pelts they wore.

Nina, her entire body trembling like a live wire, shrieked Meridan's name and darted toward him. The Gog who had grabbed the old Lycan roared with pain as Meridan sunk his fangs deep into his wrist.

"Meridan!"

Nina screamed again as the Gog wrapped one meaty hand around Meridan's throat and the other around one madly flailing back leg. With a scream of triumph, he tore the old Lycan in half.

Pavina, howling in shock and anger, leaped onto the Gog. She scrambled up his back, her claws digging into the wolf hide he wore as the Gog dropped Meridan's body and reached behind him. Before he could pull Pavina away, her mouth was at his throat. She sunk her fangs in and blood flew from his throat in a thick spray. He screamed and dropped to his knees as Pavina tore his throat open.

Nicky snarled and Max turned to see him taking down a Gog that had Doran by the front leg. There was a sharp crack and Doran howled with agony as the Gog dropped him to the ground.

Andric, growling fiercely, bit the Gogmagog in the face. The Gog screamed as Andric's teeth punctured his eye and Nicky's fangs tore away his lower jaw. There was movement to her left and Max cringed in horror as she watched two of the Gogmagogs simply stomp one of the hired Lycans into the ground. Blood and brains splattered across the bright snow as they crushed the Lycan's head beneath their boots.

The remaining hired Lycans turned and fled into the forest as Ryker screamed hoarsely. With a wild look of fierce determination on his face, he swung his sword and sliced off the left leg of the Gog in front of him. As the Gog screeched and fell to the ground, Ryker swung his sword again and chopped its head from its body.

"Max!" He shouted as another Gog approached him. "Do something, you stupid bitch!"

There was a loud keening noise as Nina knelt beside Meridan's body.

"Meridan, no! Please, no!" She begged to the dead Lycan. "Oh, Meridan." She moaned and wept, her body shaking with her sobs.

A Gog appeared behind the young girl, his face breaking into a grin to reveal his stained yellow teeth.

"Pretty human," it said and reached for Nina.

"No," Max said.

Her entire body was vibrating, and she could feel the power soaring through her. It throbbed and pulsed within her, begging to be released, and with a small, strange smile, she set it free.

NICKY, HIS SIDES HEAVING, AND HIS FACE AND CHEST covered in blood, looked up from the Gog he had just killed as the wind began to blow. Andric barked sharply and Nicky followed his gaze. Max, her hair standing on end and the wind rippling her clothing, raised her hand toward the Gog about to take Nina.

The Gog had time for one brief look of confusion before he was lifted into the air and flung across the field. He crashed into a tree head-first with a wet smacking sound, his large body shuddering once before he slumped to the ground.

Three of the Gogs charged at Max. She turned to face them, a bitter grin on her face, and shook her head. "No."

She flicked her hand at them, and a brief whine of shock escaped Nicky's throat as the three giants burst apart. Blood and guts rained down on the snow as the remaining Gogs roared with surprise.

Max looked at Nicky and his fur rippled and snapped with energy as her gaze fell on him. "Behind you, Nicky," she said in a soft, dreamy voice.

He whirled to see a Gog reaching for him. Before it could grab him, he felt another weird ripple of energy and the Gog exploded. He was immediately drenched in blood, his white fur stained red, and he shook the hot liquid from his eyes before staring at Max.

Andric had shifted and he stared at Nicky in fear. "What in the gods name?" he shouted hoarsely over the rising wind.

Nicky shifted, wiping the blood from his face as he stared in disbelief. The Lycans and humans watched as Max, with almost lazy gestures and flicks of her hands, destroyed the suddenly terrified Gogmagogs, one by one. When there was nothing left of them but shreds of clothing and bits of bone and guts, and the snow was stained with their blood, she dropped her hands. The howling, raging wind died down, and the group stared silently at the woman standing in the midst of the carnage.

193

"Max?" Nicky approached her cautiously but when he reached out to touch her, she shook her head warningly.

"Look at me, sweetheart," Nicky said.

She raised her head and he took an involuntary step back. Her different coloured eyes were glowing with a strange light and she gave him a wide, vacant smile that chilled him to the bone.

"You shouldn't touch me, Nicholas. It isn't safe," she said.

Nina wailed loudly. She was still cradling Meridan's dead body but instead of going to the young girl, Max turned and walked toward the cabin.

"Where are you going?" Nicky said.

"To find your father."

Nicky crossed to Nina and crouched beside her. "Nina, I'm sorry, little one. We must keep going."

"Meridan?" She gave Nicky a look of anguish as Kala peeked out from her hair and stroked her cheek anxiously.

"He's gone, my love. I'm sorry."

She wailed again and Nicky hugged her before lifting her to her feet. "We must keep going, Nina."

"Aye." She turned to look at Meridan's body and Nicky shook his head.

"No, little one. Do not look again."

Pavina approached and she licked Nina's hand consolingly before shifting. "I'm sorry, Nina."

"Keep her with you," Nicky said, and she nodded before putting her arm around Nina's shoulders.

"How badly are you injured, cousin?" Nicky knelt next to Doran.

Cradling his left arm, Doran winced as Andric heaved him to his feet. "It's only a broken arm but when I shift, I won't be able to walk on it."

Nicky squeezed his shoulder. "Aye, stay in your human form. We will protect you."

"You or her?" Doran looked over his shoulder. Max, Ryker following closely, was nearly at the door of the cabin. "What she just did – what she's capable of – I don't know if it's safe for us to be around her."

"We have no choice, Doran," Nicholas said. He headed toward Max and Ryker and, after a moment, Andric and Doran followed.

"I TOLD YOU THEY WEREN'T HERE. IT WAS NOTHING BUT A trap," Ryker said.

They had gathered in the cabin. There was a large worn rug on the floor and a few broken pieces of furniture but nothing else, and Ryker stared in disgust at the beams of sunlight that shone through the boarded-up windows.

"We can smell the leeches. This is the place," Andric said.

Ryker rolled his eyes. "There isn't -"

He stopped as Nicky pushed past him and shoved the rug back. There was a trap door hidden in the floor beneath it and Nicky grabbed the thick iron ring attached to the door.

"Nicky, wait," Pavina said. "There aren't enough of us. We should go back and -"

"No. They're down there and, if he is still alive, so is my birth father. This is what we came to do," Nicky said. "We don't turn back now."

He pulled on the ring. The door opened with a harsh squealing noise and Nina cringed back as Nicky peered into the darkness below. He glanced at Max. She had wandered away from the rest of them and was staring between the boards of one of the windows with the same soft and dreamy look on her face.

"Max?"

"Aye?" She didn't turn around.

"Are you ready?"

"I am." She crossed the room and, without hesitating, sat at the edge of the trapdoor and dropped into the darkness.

Nicky stared at the others. "Let's go. Stay behind Max."

THE SMALL BAND OF HUMANS AND LYCANS FOLLOWED MAX down the narrow path beneath the shack. They were descending deeper into the earth and despite the total darkness, Max moved forward quickly and confidently.

After nearly five minutes of walking, the path widened into a large cavern. Max paused at the opening as Nicky inhaled deeply. The air was damp and humid, and the stench of leech was overpowering. He heard Pavina make a soft gagging noise as she placed her hand over her nose and mouth.

"Where are they?" Andric said as the group stepped into the cavern. "I can smell them but where in the gods names are they?"

Without speaking, Max pointed upward. As one, the group looked up and Nicky heard Nina take a deep wavering breath. The girl was going to scream, he was sure of it, and he pushed past Andric and Doran and clamped a hard hand over her mouth.

"Stay calm, Nina," he breathed into her ear.

She nodded and he released her mouth as Max wandered deeper into the cavern. He glanced upward again, feeling sick to his stomach, as he stared at the leeches hanging upside down from the rocky ceiling. The cavern was filled with the filthy bloodsuckers and he squeezed Nina's hand when her cold fingers wrapped around his.

"Why are they not killing us?" she breathed into his ear.

"They're in their daysleep," he said. "They will not wake until the sun goes down. Do not worry, baby sister."

He hoped he was telling her the truth. Much of what he knew about the leeches came from stories and with over a hundred leeches hanging from the ceiling like overgrown bats, they didn't have a chance. The leeches would destroy them in minutes.

Max had crossed the cavern and was standing at a large, thick wooden door. She traced the carvings on it before squinting at the carvings in the stone wall next to it. She moved closer, her foot dislodged a stone and it clattered down a small dip in the ground. The rest of the group froze, staring wide-eyed at the leeches above them, but Max took no notice. She continued to study the wall as Doran leaned closer to Nicky.

"The gods be damned, Nicky. Did they – did they build this?"

"They must have," Nicky said. "Come on."

He dropped Nina's hand and, moving slowly, crossed the large cavern. The cavern was not particularly high, and he ducked carefully past a low-hanging leech. The scent of humid earth and putrid leech was making him nauseous, and he covered his nose and mouth as he moved toward the wooden door.

When the entire group had gathered at the door, Nicky pulled the handle gingerly. It opened easily enough and all of them winced when it squealed. They stared upward in fear but not a single leech moved, and Nicky nodded to the others before stepping through the doorway. They clustered together just beyond the door and Nicky gave them a quick glance, frowning when he didn't see Max.

He called her name softly and when she didn't appear, shouldered past the others. Before he could get to the door, Nina had darted back into the cavern.

"Nina!" He growled her name in frustration.

She reappeared, holding Max by the hand, and gave him a timid smile. "I have her. She's fine. Let's -"

Nicky snarled in surprise when a leech, its eyes glowing red and its fangs dripping with saliva, dropped in front of the two women. It stared unblinkingly at Nicky, its eyes widening with surprise, before it bared its fangs and hissed. Its long, pale fingers gripped the door and Nicky leaped forward as the vampire slammed the door shut. His body hit the door with a hard thud and he howled with rage and fear, slamming his fists against the door as he heard the soft thuds of the leeches dropping to the ground and Nina screaming.

CHAPTER 20

Growling and snarling, Nicky slammed his body repeatedly into the thick door. Nina screamed again and he hammered frantically on the door when the scream was abruptly cut short.

"NINA! MAX!" He howled as his body rippled and the shift started to happen. He turned and nearly tore Andric's head off when the younger Lycan gripped his shoulder.

"Nicholas! Stop! Let me help you!" Andric shouted.

Panting harshly, Nicholas nodded, and the two of them rushed the door. They slammed into it with their bodies, both growling with anger when the door didn't budge. They repeatedly hit the door until, with a grunt of frustration, Nicholas kicked below the door handle, making another growl of rage when nothing happened.

"Leave them!" Ryker shouted. "It's too late and you know it. We must find another way out of here before the leeches open the door and kill us all!"

"I won't leave them, you coward!" Nicholas snarled. "Do you hear me? I won't leave them!"

"Quiet!" Pavina shouted. "Listen!"

The group quieted. They could hear the wind howling, and shrieking and pleas of mercy from the leeches, and they jumped when the door suddenly shook in its frame. The shrieks and moans died out and Nicholas touched the door. "Max?"

The door swung open with a quiet click and Nicholas sprinted into the room. All the breath escaped from his lungs and he stared in horror at Max. She was standing in the middle of the room, drenched in bright red blood and grey ash. The ground was a river of blood and ash and as Max lowered her arms and stared into the distance, he took a step toward her.

"Nicky!"

Nina was standing flat against the wall with Kala clinging grimly to her neck. Both the young girl and the pixie were splattered with blood and Nina wiped at the blood on her face with a small grimace.

Pavina hugged Nina. "What happened?"

"She killed them," Nina said. "She killed them all."

Nicky stood in front of Max. She stared through him and a shiver went down his spine.

"Max?"

"Aye, Nicky?" she said.

"Are you hurt? Have you been bitten?"

She grinned. Her teeth looked very white against her red-stained skin and another shudder went down his spine.

"No. I have not been bitten."

He reached out to touch her and she flinched and stepped back. "Keep your distance, Nicky."

"You're covered in blood, sweetheart. Let me clean it off."

She stared down at her soaked clothing. "So much blood.

She took another step back when Nicky reached for her again.

"No!" she said. "Do not, Nicky."

"Max -"

"I can feel it, you know." Her voice had gone back to that dreamy quality. "I can feel it humming through my veins. It wants to be free again. It wants to hurt and destroy – it likes it. It's what I was made for."

"No, don't say that."

"It's true."

"It's not, sweetheart."

"You should kill me, Nicky," she said. "Kill me before it's too late. It doesn't want to be controlled anymore and I – I don't want to control it."

"No!" His heart thumped wildly in his chest and he stepped forward and wrapped his arms around her. She stiffened and every hair on his body stood up as a tingle of energy went through him.

"You can control it, sweetheart. I know you can. Violet needs you. Don't leave her alone," he said.

At the mention of Violet, she moaned and slumped against him. He rubbed her back and tilted her face up. He kissed her on the mouth, ignoring the leech blood that covered her, and she wrapped her arms around his waist and clung to him.

"Everything's fine, sweetheart. Everything's fine," he said.

"It isn't." Her voice was filled with despair and he tightened his hold on her before stroking her short hair.

"It is. I promise you."

She backed out of his embrace. "We need to go."

She started toward the door and he breathed a sigh of

relief when he reached for her hand and she took it willingly enough.

As they walked by Nina, the young girl reached out and touched Max's arm. "Thank you, Max."

Max nodded. "Aye, you're welcome, Nina."

The small and battered group left the cavern and walked quickly down the earth-lined corridor. After only a few minutes, there was a bend in the path, and they turned it to discover another thick, wooden door.

Ryker tried the handle. "It's locked."

Nicky, still holding Max's hand, felt a shiver go through her and the door opened with a quiet click. The group crowded into the narrow hallway.

"The Gods be damned!" Pavina made a gagging noise and Nina clapped her hand over her nose. They were in a long hallway with wooden doors built into the earth on either side of them. Each door had a narrow window with thick silver bars, and the stench of death and decay was overpowering.

Doran peered into the window of the first door and made a low groan before turning away. His face was white, and he shook his head at Pavina when she started toward the door.

"Do not look in there. The Lycan is dead."

Ryker strode down the hallway. "Emmett!" he shouted. "Emmett, are you here?"

A chorus of moans and cries for help suddenly filled the dank air.

"Get these doors opened." Nicky looked into one of the cells and yanked on the door handle. "We need to get them out of here. All of them."

Max raised her hands and the doors clicked open. Andric, his face pale and his hands trembling, started down the hallway.

"Ragan! Jackar!" he shouted. "Answer me!"

There were more soft moans for help and then a voice drifted from one of the cells. "Andric?"

Andric bolted for the cell. He stared into the cell, his heart beating frantically in his chest.

"Jackar!" He ran forward and fell to his knees beside the young Lycan chained to the wall with a silver collar around his neck. "Brother!"

"Andric? Did I finally die? Am I in hell?"

"No, brother. You are safe now." Andric touched his face with shaking fingers as Nicky joined them. He tried not to let his horror show at the condition of Andric's brother. Jackar was so thin he was skeletal looking, and he was covered in dirt and blood.

Andric kissed his brother's forehead. "Where is Ragan?"

Jackar shook his head as tears dripped down his cheeks. "He is dead. He has been dead for weeks. The leeches bit him almost immediately. He was so strong. He – he lasted nearly two moons before he died. I'm so sorry, Andric."

He began to weep, and Andric pulled him into his embrace. "Do not apologize, Jackar. There was nothing you could do. At least you are alive."

Jackar licked his chapped lips. "Not for long. The leeches bit me last week. They waited because I was not as strong as some of the others, but I think they were getting desperate."

He laughed weakly before pulling his shirt open. Nicky sucked in his breath. A large bite, festering and oozing, was just below his collarbone and Jackar moaned with pain when Andric brushed it with his fingers.

"Is Mama alive?" Jackar whispered. "She was in the house with Freya and Royce. Did they survive?"

Andric shook his head. "No. There is no one left but you and me."

Jackar wept harder and Andric hugged him hard. "Shh, Jackar."

Nicky studied the silver collar around Jackar's neck. It had long silver prongs on the inside and he could see the way they pressed against Jackar's neck. He studied the lock on it. They would need to find a key. It was solid silver and impossible to break.

"Some of the Lycans chose to die," Jackar said. "Some of them simply shifted and allowed the silver to kill them. I – I wanted to do the same, but Ragan made me promise before he died. He made me promise that I wouldn't. He said that you would find me."

Tears flowed down Andric's cheeks. "I'm sorry it took so long, brother."

"You are here now. I can see you before I die," Jackar said.

"You are not going to die!" Andric said. "Do you hear me, Jackar? You're not going to die. I can save you."

"There is no cure," Jackar said. "Every Lycan they bite dies."

"You won't die," Andric said. "Trust me, brother."

He squeezed Jackar before staring at Nicky. "We need to find a key for the collar around his neck."

"Aye," Nicky said.

Andric cupped Jackar's face. "I will return shortly and we will leave this wretched place together. I promise you."

There was a soft click and he stared in confusion as the collar opened around Jackar's neck. Nicky glanced behind him. Max was standing in the doorway and she gave him a small nod before lowering her hands and leaving. Andric gingerly pulled the collar from Jackar's neck and lifted him to his feet before wrapping his arm around his waist.

"You'll be fine, Jackar," he said.

Nicky stepped out into the hallway, studying Ryker as he walked past the cells.

"Emmett!" Ryker shouted again. "Where are you?"

He peered into the final cell and inhaled sharply before turning and staring at Nina.

"Daddy?" Nina whispered.

She ran toward Ryker and skidded to a stop beside him before staring into the cell.

"Daddy!" She screamed and ran into the cell.

Nicholas, his pulse pounding, stepped into the small space. Weeping steadily, Nina was kneeling beside a pale and sweating Lycan.

"Oh, Daddy," she whispered.

"Nina," he said. He touched her face as Ryker knelt beside them.

"Emmett? Have you been bitten?"

"Aye. Nearly a moon ago," the Lycan said.

"Daddy, we found Nicky," Nina said. "He's here, Daddy."

Emmett blinked at her in confusion. "Nicholas?"

"Aye." Nina smiled at him through her tears before glancing behind her. "Nicky, come closer so that Daddy can see you."

Nicholas crouched next to Nina and stared at his birth father. The resemblance between them was remarkable and he took the Lycan's hand when he held it out.

"Nicholas." Emmett squeezed his hand. "You're really here."

"Hello, Emmett," Nicky said.

"I am glad to see you before I die." The Lycan coughed, and Nina shook her head.

"You're not going to die, Daddy. You're so strong."

Emmett ignored her. "Have you had a good life, Nicky? Did the man who took you from me treat you well?"

"Aye. He treats me like his own son."

A faint line creased Emmett's brow. "You are my son. Never forget that."

Nicholas didn't reply as Nina stroked her father's face anxiously. "Daddy, I love you. I've missed you so much."

"Aye, I know, Nina." Emmett glanced at Ryker. "Where is Meridan?"

"Dead," Ryker said. "Torn apart by the Gogs."

Nina made a soft, gasping sob before dissolving into tears. She rested her head on her father's chest and he made a soft noise of impatience before pushing on her head. "Enough, girl."

Nina raised her head and wiped at her face. "Sorry, Daddy."

She tugged at the silver collar around his neck. "We're going to take you home. You'll be just fine, you'll see. A few days of rest and -"

"Nina, leave. I wish to speak to Nicholas alone," Emmett said.

Nina shook her head. "Daddy, no. I want to stay with you. I have been -"

"Go, Nina." Even in his weakened state, Nicholas could hear the edge in Emmett's voice and Nina immediately stood.

"Sorry, Daddy," she said. Nicholas caught her hand and squeezed it before smiling reassuringly at her. She smiled faintly in return and left the cell.

"Nicholas, if I had known of your existence, I would have taken you into my home. Do you understand?" Emmett said hoarsely.

"Aye, I do."

"Your mother never told me. I swear to the Gods, she didn't." Emmett clutched at Nicky's wrist. "Do you believe me?"

"Aye," Nicky said.

"Good." Emmett sagged against the wall and glanced briefly at Ryker before returning his gaze to Nicholas.

"I'm dying, son. I can feel the leech infection running through my veins and every day I grow a little weaker. I want you to have my home in the city and my business. Ryker knows the details of what I do. He will help you run it. You can trust him – he's a good man."

Nicholas frowned. "You ask me to live in the city?"

"Aye, I do. Everything I have will belong to you after my death. It is my gift to you. You are my son and with this gift, you will never want for anything again. You are all that matters to me."

He glanced again at Ryker. "You are a witness to everything that I have said. You will tell the others that Nicholas is my successor. Am I clear?"

"Of course, Emmett." Ryker said with a small nod.

Emmett sighed wearily and squeezed Nicky's hand again. "You are all that matters," he repeated.

"What of Nina?" Nicky said.

Emmett stared blankly at him and Nicholas arched his eyebrows at him. "What of your daughter? Are you not worried about what will happen to her once you're dead?"

Emmett smiled faintly. "I assume you will look after your sister. Do not judge her for being only human, Nicholas. She is a good enough girl."

Before Nicky could reply, Emmett began to cough. He gagged and retched, and Ryker and Nicholas turned him on to his side as blood and mucus sprayed from his mouth. With a groaning sigh, the Lycan's eyes rolled up in his head and he slumped against the wall he was chained to, breathing harshly.

Nina skittered into the cell and dropped to the floor beside them. "Is he dead?"

Nicky shook his head. "No, he has fainted."

He looked up as Max, Doran and Pavina crowded into the cell.

"Unlock his collar," Ryker said to Max.

She didn't move and Nina made a soft sound of hurt. "Max, please."

Max closed her eyes and the collar clicked open. Emmett tipped to the side and Ryker caught him neatly. The Lycan's breathing was harsh and irregular and Nina sobbed quietly as she stroked her father's hair.

Nicholas picked up the silver collar, staring thoughtfully at it as Doran knelt next to him. He cradled his broken arm as he glanced at Nicky. "What is it, cousin?"

"These collars are the same ones used by Draken to keep the half-breeds as his slaves."

Pavina appeared in the doorway of the cell. "We need to leave this wretched place."

"Aye," Nicholas said. He glanced at Ryker. "Help me carry Emmett."

"He's dying, Nicholas," Max said. "We might as well leave him."

"Max!" Nina gave her a look of shock.

"We're taking him back to my home." Nicky said to Nina. "He'll be fine, Nina."

Nina wiped away the tears as Nicholas and Ryker carried Emmett from the cell.

"WILL YOUR FATHER EVEN SURVIVE THE TRIP BACK?" DORAN asked Nicholas in a low voice. He was still cradling his arm against his chest and Nicky squeezed his shoulder.

"How is your arm, cousin?"

"Sore as hell," Doran said. "But I believe it's starting to heal."

Nicky glanced around the campsite. They had left the leech colony and travelled deep into the woods. He had wanted to go further but Emmett's breathing had taken a turn for the worse and Nina had begged them to stop for the night. His birth father had fallen into unconsciousness and his entire body was burning up with fever.

"Nicholas? Will he live?" Doran repeated.

Nicholas rubbed his bearded face. "I do not know. He was bit nearly a moon ago and, if the weather cooperates, it'll be at least another eight days' journey back. Two of the others have died already."

There had been ten survivors in the leech prison. Four of them had been bitten, his father and Jackar and two other female Lycans. The females had died only hours after they left the underground prison. Although Nicholas had invited the remaining six survivors to join them, they had gone their separate ways. They had been nervous and thin and had shifted immediately to their Lycan forms before scattering into the forest. There had been no sign of them since.

"Will you ask your mother to heal him?" Doran said in a low voice.

"Aye, if he lives that long," Nicholas said. "Nina will be devastated if he dies."

"Do you think she can heal him?"

"I don't know. But if she cannot, I will ask James to try."

"Leta could probably -"

"No." Nicholas shook his head immediately before

glancing around the camp. "We do not reveal her powers, even if it means Emmett dies." He rubbed his face again. "How is Andric's brother?"

"Jackar? He's not as bad as Emmett but he is smaller and thinner. I don't believe he will last as long. If he is to have any chance, we need to get him to your mother quickly."

"Aye." Nicky stood and clapped Doran on the back. "You should get some rest, cousin."

"Where are you going?"

"I want to check on Max. She's still acting strangely."

"Be careful, Nicky," Doran said.

"She will not hurt me."

"Are you certain?"

"Aye," Nicky said but he could hear the doubt in his voice.

He left Doran by the fire and crossed to Max's tent. Max was lying on her bedroll and she continued to stare at the wall of the tent as Nicky sat cross-legged at the foot of her blankets.

"Max? You need to eat something."

"I'm not hungry. Did Nina eat?"

"Aye, a little."

"Good. Is she still with Emmett?"

"Aye. I believe she will spend the night with him."

Max nodded as Nicky reached out and touched her blanket-covered leg. She pulled it away from him and curled into a smaller ball.

"Are you all right, Max? Do you feel tired?"

"I feel fine."

"We should talk about what happened with the Gogs and the leeches."

"No." She burrowed deeper under the blankets. "I do not wish to talk of it."

"Max -"

"If your father survives the journey home, will you ask Leta to heal him?"

"Not Leta," he said. "No one is to know of her powers, Max. I will not risk her safety to save the life of a Lycan I barely know."

"Fair enough," she said. "But you will ask your mother."

"Why would you say that?"

"I am not stupid, Nicholas. Leta's inherited your mother's powers. Will your mother be able to help him?"

"I do not know. But I need to try – for Nina."

"Nina would be better off without him," Max said.

"What do you mean?"

"Nothing," she sighed and closed her eyes. "Will you leave, Nicholas? I'd like to get some sleep."

"I can stay with you in your tent," Nicky said. "You will be cold, and I can -"

"Be my bed warmer?"

"Aye," he said.

"Our time together is done, Nicholas," she said. "We did this only to help practice my powers so that I could save your father. I have done that. There is no point in us continuing to," she hesitated, "warm each other's beds."

Hurt ran through Nicholas and he squeezed the blanket as Max sat up. "Have I hurt your feelings, Nicholas?"

"No," he lied.

"I have and I'm sorry. But we both knew this was only temporary. I needed to practice my powers and you wanted…"

"What did I want, Max?"

"You wanted a roll in the hay. We both got what we wanted and I'm sure you're anxious to move on to your next conquest. Pavina, perhaps?"

He scowled at her. "Max, what is wrong with you? Do you honestly believe that I would hop from your bed to Pavina's?"

She shrugged. "I really know nothing about you, Nicky. Do I? And the only thing you know about me is that I'm dangerous."

"I'm not afraid of you, Max."

"Aye, that's good." She laid down again. "Thank you, Nicky. I really enjoyed our – our time together."

Nicholas growled with frustration. "Max -"

"Please, I do not wish to speak about this further. You should be concentrating on Nina and your father."

"Max, I don't -"

"Good night, Nicholas."

He sighed harshly before standing at the opening to the tent. "Good night, Max."

***

MAX STARED AT THE WALL OF HER TENT AS NICKY LEFT. HER throat was aching, and her eyes were burning, and she had come dangerously close to bursting into tears while Nicky was in the tent. More than anything, she had wanted to pull Nicky into the blankets with her and lose herself in his touch. She sighed as the tears slipped down her cheeks. She was a fool. Nicholas had made it perfectly clear what he was interested in. She was happy when he had come to her tent, when he had told her he was not afraid of her despite what she was capable of, but she forced herself to reject him. There was no future for them.

She shifted onto her back, feeling the hot tears running down her cheeks and pooling into her ears. When they were back at Nicky's home, she would take Violet and leave. She had made her father a promise, but she could no longer keep it. If Emmett survived, he would want her to do terrible things with her powers, she knew that without a doubt, and if he didn't survive Ryker would never let her go. She would sneak away with Violet and she would never see Nicky or his family again.

The thought filled her with sorrow, and she turned onto her side and wept bitterly into her pillow.

CHAPTER 21

"Evan, you raise your sword too high," James said patiently. "It leaves an opening for your enemy to slide his sword into your belly. Keep your blade lower."

Evan dropped his blade lower. "Aye, let's try again."

"Remember, you need to -" James stopped as Kaden and Sophia emerged from the barn. "You're late."

"Sorry, baby brother. Something came up," Sophia said with a cheeky grin.

Bree snickered and James said, "Do not encourage her."

"Of course not, my love," Bree said.

"If Kaden is to learn the sword, he must practice," James said.

Sophia pulled her sword from the sheath around her waist. "Aye, I know. Are you ready, human?"

"Aye, little Lycan." Kaden pulled his own sword free. "The real question is – are you ready?"

Sophia lifted her head and inhaled deeply before turning to James. "Do you smell him?"

"Aye," James said.

Evan dropped his sword and ran toward the front of the

house. The rest of them chased after him and Sophia made a hoarse cry. Nicholas and the others were riding up to the house in a wagon and Nicholas pulled the wagon to a stop and hopped down.

Sophia threw herself at him. He caught her and she kissed him on the cheek before hugging him hard.

"Oh, Nicky," she said.

She studied him carefully. He was thinner and there were dark hollows under his eyes. She touched his thick beard and rested her forehead against his. "Are you all right, baby brother?"

"I'm fine, Sophia," Nicky said. He hugged her again before setting her on her feet and allowing James to embrace him. He winced a little. "Careful, James."

"Sorry, Nicky." James, grinning ear to ear, hugged him again before Evan was pushing between them.

"Did you find him? Did you find your real father?" Evan asked as Nicholas hugged him and ruffled his hair.

"Aye, Evan. We did."

The front door opened, and Tristan emerged. He was followed by Avery and Maya, and Nicky hugged his mother as Maya ran toward Doran.

"Hello, Mama." Doran grinned at a crying Maya who wrapped her arms around him.

"I am so glad you're home, dearest," she said.

Danielle ran out of the house. She threw her arms around Andric, kissing his face repeatedly before he buried his face into her neck.

"You look tired, sweet Nicky." Avery stroked Nicky's face and he smiled at her.

"I am looking forward to my own bed." He hugged Tristan as Max climbed out of the wagon and tugged on Avery's arm.

"My lady? Violet, is she…?"

"She's fine, Max," Avery said. "She is playing with Leta in her room. She has missed her mama and will be so happy to see you."

Max turned toward the house. Marshall and Vivian were coming out the front door and she smiled distractedly at them.

"Look, baby bird. Your mama is home." Leta, carrying Violet on her hip, stepped out of the house and grinned at Max.

"Violet," Max said.

Violet screamed with delight and squirmed in Leta's arms. Leta set her down and the toddler ran toward Max.

"Mama! Mama!" She tripped over her own feet and Max, crying loudly, caught her before she could fall.

Nicky watched, his throat tight and an ache in his chest as Max hugged Violet hard. She kissed Violet's face as Violet squealed and giggled and placed wet and sloppy kisses on Max's face.

"Hi, Mama!" She patted Max's face and Max kissed her again.

"Hello, Violet. I've missed you, honey."

Violet threw her arms around her neck and rested her head on her shoulder as Max swayed back and forth, pressing kisses on the top of her head.

"Hi, Nicky!" Leta wrapped her arms around his waist.

Nicky lifted her and kissed her on the cheek. "Hi, Leta."

"I'm glad you're home."

"Me too."

"Where is Meridan?" Vivian asked.

"He was killed by the Gogs." Pavina's voice was hoarse and she blinked back tears. Maya, standing closest to her, hesitated and then pulled the Lycan into her embrace. Pavina twitched in surprise before resting her head on Maya's shoulder. Maya rubbed her back as Nicky lifted Nina from the back of the wagon.

Nina had started to sob at the mention of Meridan and Vivian stepped toward her. "Come here, girl,"

Nina, her head bowed and her shoulders shaking, stood in front of Vivian. Vivian tilted her head up and wiped roughly at the tears on Nina's face. "I am sorry for your loss."

Nina didn't reply and with a soft sigh, Vivian hugged her. "There, there," she said. "It'll be fine. Stop your crying, girl."

"Did you find him, Nicky?" Tristan asked.

"Aye, we did." Nicky pointed to the back of the wagon and Tristan and Avery peered into it. Avery inhaled sharply as Tristan cursed under his breath.

They stared at Jackar and Emmett who were lying in the back of the wagon under a thick layer of blankets. Jackar's cheeks were bright red with fever. He was breathing harshly and as they watched he coughed and then moaned weakly.

Andric appeared on the other side of the wagon and he reached in and stroked the Lycan's hair. "It's all right, Jackar."

He stared pleadingly at Avery. "My brother needs your help, my lady."

Nicky watched as Tristan glanced behind him. Ryker was standing a few feet away, watching them with a bored indifference, and Tristan nodded to him.

"That is Ryker," Nicky said in a low voice meant only for Tristan. "He is my father's right-hand man and is not to be trusted."

Tristan turned to Kaden and Evan. "Can the two of you help Andric carry his brother into the house?"

As Evan and Kaden climbed into the back of the wagon, Tristan took Avery's hand. "Would you accompany them, girl? I am sure Andric's brother would appreciate the soothing touch of a mother."

"Of course, my lord," Avery replied. As Evan, Andric and Kaden carried Jackar into the house, she squeezed Tristan's hand and followed them.

Tristan turned back to Emmett lying in the wagon. He was completely white, and his breathing was sporadic and shallow. Nicky leaned over the wagon and touched Emmett's face. It was cold and he gave Nina a quick glance as Ryker joined them.

"It is too late for your father," Ryker said.

Behind them, Nina burst into fresh sobs and Vivian patted her back.

"We will take him to Sophia's room and make him comfortable." Tristan motioned for James to join them. "Help us carry him into the house, James."

"Aye, Dad."

As James climbed into the wagon, Nicky looked for Max. Still holding Violet closely, she walked into the house without looking at him or the others. He ignored his urge to chase after her and hoisted himself into the wagon.

"HOW ARE THEY?" NICHOLAS ENTERED THE KITCHEN AND SAT down at the table beside Tristan.

He had bathed and shaved, and Tristan reached out and cupped his head affectionately. "You are too thin, Nicky."

"Aye. A few days of Marian's cooking and I'll be back to normal." Nicholas grinned at Marian who was coming out of the pantry.

She hugged him hard. "It is good to have you home, Nicky."

He kissed her cheek. "It is good to be back."

She brushed away the tears and cleared her throat. "Your father is right. You are much too thin."

He watched as she carefully ladled out a bowl of thick stew and set it in front of him.

"It smells delicious. Thank you, Marian."

"Aye, you're welcome, Nicky. Eat up. The others have already eaten their fill but there's plenty left."

As Marian left the kitchen, Nicky stared at his father. "How are they?" he repeated before spooning the rich stew into his mouth.

"Your mother is lying with Andric's brother. I checked in on them and she believes it is working."

Nicholas paused. "Is she sure?"

Tristan nodded. "Aye. But your brother is not so certain about your birth father. He thinks it might be too late, Nicky."

Nicholas stared into his stew. "Aye, I was afraid of that."

"I'm sorry, son." Tristan squeezed his arm. "We could try with Leta if -"

"No." Nicholas said. "We keep Leta away from them. No one is to know of her powers. Not Emmett or Ryker. Especially not Ryker."

"She is more powerful than -"

"I know," Nicky said. "But I will not risk exposing her powers in order to save a man I barely know. I would rather Emmett die than risk Leta. Do you understand, Dad?"

"Aye, I do."

"We must speak with Leta. We must make her understand that she cannot use her powers around anyone but us. We can't risk -"

"Your mother and I have already spoken with Leta. She understands the importance of keeping what she can do a secret," Tristan said.

"Leta is young and impulsive."

"Aye, that is true. But I believe she understands the serious risks of revealing her powers. She will keep them a secret."

Tristan studied him. "Was Emmett lucid when you found him? Did you have a chance to speak with him?"

"Aye. He lapsed into the sleep shortly after we found him."

"What did you think of him?"

"I don't know, really. He was happy to see me, and he told me that his estate and his business belonged to me once he was dead."

"That was kind of him."

"Aye. He wants me to live in the city in his home and run his business."

"Is that what you want?"

"You know I don't. I could never live in the city," Nicky said.

He ate another spoonful of stew before staring at Tristan. "He didn't say anything about Nina."

"What do you mean?"

"I mean, he never once asked me to take care of her or even seemed worried what would happen to her once he was gone. He was very," Nicky paused as he searched for the right word, "cold to her."

"Some men value sons more than daughters," Tristan said. "I do not understand it, but I've seen it."

"Aye, perhaps."

Nicky stirred his stew, staring into it until Tristan touched his arm. "I want you to tell me everything that happened, Nicholas. Are you up to it?"

Nicholas nodded. "Aye, I am."

JACKAR SNUGGLED CLOSER TO HIS MOTHER. HER BODY WAS warm and soft, and she stroked his back soothingly as he put his arm around her waist. His skull-splitting headache had finally abated, and he no longer felt like he was burning up from the inside out.

"Mama," he sighed again. "I had the most terrible dream."

"Do not fear, my love," his mother whispered.

"You and father were dead, and I had been taken by the leeches," he said before burying his face into her throat. "It was awful, Mama. I was so afraid."

"Shh, my love. Go back to sleep. You need your rest."

"Aye," he said. "I am very tired, Mama."

"I know you are. Go to sleep. You're safe." She kissed the top of his head and he made a whine of protest when she eased away from him.

His eyelids were extremely heavy, but he forced them open. He stared in blurry confusion at the woman sitting on the edge of the bed. Her back was to him and he watched as she slipped a nightshirt over her head and smoothed her long, red hair. There was a knock on the door, and he squinted at the woman. Already it was nearly impossible to keep his eyes open and he reached out weakly as the woman stood.

"Mama?" he said.

ANDRIC KNOCKED AND HURRIED INTO THE ROOM. DANIELLE was right behind him and she followed him to the bed as his brother whispered, "Mama?"

He sat on the bed next to him and took his hand. "You're safe, brother. Go to sleep."

Jackar closed his eyes as Andric rested his hand on his forehead. "The fever is gone."

"That is good news." Dani hugged him before turning to Avery. "Aunt Avery? Are you all right?"

"Aye," Avery said. "Just very tired."

She staggered as she took a step forward and Dani put her arm around her waist. "Come, Aunt Avery. I will lie with you in your bed."

"That's sweet of you, Danielle," Avery replied as she rubbed at her forehead.

The door opened and Sophia peered into the room. She hurried to her mother's side and slipped her arm around her waist, just above Dani's.

"Mama?" She stared at Avery in alarm. "You're very pale."

"I'm fine." Avery rested her head on Sophia's shoulder. "I just need to lie down."

"I was going to lie with her for a bit," Danielle said as they guided Avery to the door.

"We both will," Sophia said. "It will be better for her."

"I will come back later, Andric." Danielle said.

"Aye." Andric stroked his brother's hair before staring at Avery. "Thank you, my lady. I will spend the rest of my life in your debt."

"You're welcome, Andric," Avery said as Sophia and Dani helped her from the room.

CHAPTER 22

"It has been three days, brother," Nicky said.

James was lying in bed with Emmett. He sat up and studied the sleeping Lycan. "Aye, I know. His breathing is easier."

"But he has not woken." Nicky rubbed his face as James climbed out of the bed and slipped into his pants.

"Nina will be here soon to see him. I'm going to go to Bree for a while."

"Thank you, brother. I know this has been draining for you."

James squeezed Nicky's shoulder and left the room.

Nicholas stared at Emmett. James was right, his breathing was better, and colour had returned to his face. He shifted in his chair as his thoughts drifted to Max. He had barely seen or spoken to her since they returned, and he missed her. She was deliberately avoiding him, and he couldn't help but be hurt by it.

The door opened and Nina slipped into the room. "Good morning, Nicky."

"Hello, Nina."

She gazed down at her father before stroking his cheek. "He looks better. I believe he is going to wake soon."

"Aye, perhaps."

"Andric's brother has beaten the leech infection. There is still hope for Daddy," she said.

"I believe you are right," Nicky said. "It is a good sign that he -"

Emmett groaned and Nina turned to him eagerly as his eyes fluttered open.

"Nina?" he said hoarsely.

"Hi, Daddy." Nina kissed his forehead and sat down on the side of the bed. "How are you feeling?"

"Better. Where am I?"

"You're in Nicky's home. We brought you here."

"Where is Nicholas?" Emmett started to sit up and Nina pressed gently on his chest.

"You need to rest."

He frowned at her. The frown turned to a look of relief when Nicholas appeared beside her.

"Nicholas. Hello, son."

"Hello, Emmett."

Another frown crossed Emmett's face before he smiled at him. "Thank you for rescuing me."

"You're welcome."

"I'm so happy you're feeling better." Nina squeezed Emmett's hand. "Do you think you could eat something?"

"Aye. Bring me some soup," he said.

"Of course." Nina kissed his cheek and nearly skipped out of the room as Emmett turned his gaze to Nicky.

"I do not understand why I still live."

Nicholas shrugged. "It would seem your body was strong enough to fight off the leech infection."

"Aye, perhaps. Help me sit up, would you?"

Nicky helped him into a sitting position, tucking the pillows behind his back as Emmett sighed wearily and glanced around the room. "Whose room is this?"

"My sister Sophia. She is staying with her mate."

"I remember her. She was a very strong-willed and opinionated child."

"She still is."

"Aye, I have no doubt. Your mother was very opinionated herself. It's what led to her death. Do you remember her at all?"

Nicholas shook his head and Emmett sighed. "That is a pity. A child should not have to grow up without a mother."

"I have a mother," Nicky replied. "Her name is Avery and you will meet her soon."

"Is she Lycan?"

"No. She is human."

"The Lycan who took you from me married a human?" There was distaste in Emmett's voice and Nicholas frowned at him.

"Nina's mother was human."

"Aye, she was." Emmett gave him a thoughtful look. "You should know that I did not love Nina's mother. She was a human who worked in my household and seduced me one evening when I was drunk. She was a very cunning and sly human."

He stared out the window for a moment. "I fear that Nina is very similar to her mother."

"Nina does not strike me as either sly or cunning," Nicholas replied. "She is a sweet girl."

"Aye, she does well at hiding her true nature," Emmett said. "Still, she is my daughter and it is my duty to care for her despite her shortcomings."

Before Nicholas could reply, Nina returned carrying a tray

with soup and bread. She placed the tray on Emmett's lap and smiled at him. "Try and eat it all. You need to regain your strength."

She turned her smile to Nicholas. "I told you Daddy was strong, didn't I? I can't wait until he's feeling well enough to return home. Will you come with us to the city, Nicky? I know you were raised in the country, but the city is so lovely. I think you would enjoy it. Plus, you could meet my friends – my best friend is Sanda and she's so sweet – and I can show you my room and take you to my school. Oh, and we could go to the theatre! I love the theatre! Have you ever been to the theatre?"

Nicky shook his head and Nina clapped her hands excitedly. "Then we must go together! We always dress up and go to dinner beforehand. Daddy, we should take him to the restaurant where -"

"Enough, Nina!" Emmett dropped his spoon into his bowl and scowled at her. "Your silly chattering is giving me a headache."

Nina shrank back on the bed before giving her father a chastised look. "I'm sorry. I'm just so happy to see you feeling better and excited that we are together as a family. Nicky has -"

"Nina, leave," Emmett said.

"Please don't send me away, Daddy. I – I'll be quiet, I promise."

"You will not. You cannot keep your mouth closed for more than five minutes at a time," Emmett said. "I require peace and quiet to finish healing. Go on, girl."

"I'll come back later this afternoon and visit with you," Nina said.

"Aye, go on." Emmett flapped his hand irritably at her

and without another word, Nina slid off the bed and left the room.

Emmett sighed with relief. "The girl never shuts up. Just like her mother." He rolled his eyes before biting into a piece of bread. "Come, Nicholas. Tell me about your life. I would hear all of it."

"HELLO, NINA." TRISTAN PEERED INTO THE EMPTY STALL.

Nina stood and swiped the tears from her face as Kala scurried off her shoulder and back into her hair. "Hello, lord Williams."

"Call me Tristan." Tristan stepped into the stall beside Nina's and rubbed the broad nose of the giant black stallion. He pulled a piece of carrot from his pocket and handed it to the horse before beginning to brush his smooth coat.

"I've never seen a pixie so attached to a human before," he said.

"She saved my life," Nina said.

"Aye, Nicky told me." He smiled at her. "I hear your father is awake and doing well."

"Aye. He's feeling much better." Nina leaned against the stall and watched Tristan as he worked.

"That is good news." He glanced over his shoulder at her. "I'm surprised you are not with him."

"I was," Nina said quickly. "I was there when he woke this morning and I went back after lunch, but he is very tired. He needs his rest."

Tristan didn't respond and Nina cleared her throat. "May I ask you a question, lord Williams?"

"Aye."

"Why do you have so many horses? My father says Lycans who use horses are lazy."

Tristan snorted soft laughter as Nina, realizing what she said, gasped in horror. "I am sorry, lord Williams. I did not mean to offend."

"It's fine, Nina. I have so many horses because I like them," he said. "I have been very fond of them since I was a boy."

"I like them too."

"Do you ride often?"

"I don't know how to ride." She paused. "I'm not afraid of them. I – my father didn't believe it was necessary for me to learn."

Tristan reached into the leather bag hanging on the side of the stall and pulled out a second brush. "Would you like to help me?"

"Aye," Nina said. She joined him in the stall and patted the horse's thick neck before brushing him gently. "What's his name?"

"Samson."

"Hello, Samson." She petted his neck again and smiled when the horse snuffed at her hair.

"My best friend, Sanda, has many horses. She is human like me. One time I was at her home and she tried to teach me to ride on one of her older ponies. He bit me right on the calf while I was climbing into the saddle, and I had a big bruise that went nearly to my knee. I told Daddy that I fell out of Sanda's treehouse. He was angry that I was so careless, but I was worried if he found out that I was trying to learn how to ride, he wouldn't let me go to Sanda's anymore. Another time I was petting her horse, Sable, and she -"

She suddenly stopped and stared at him apologetically. "I'm sorry, lord Williams."

"Sorry for what?"

"I have a tendency to talk too much," she said.

Tristan laughed. "You have not yet spent enough time with Leta if you believe that you are talking too much. Go on, girl. Finish your story."

"Are – are you sure?"

"Aye, little Nina, I am sure."

"PUPPY!" VIOLET, FOLLOWED BY LETA, TORE DOWN THE hallway toward Nicholas.

He grinned and picked her up, tossing her into the air, before holding her closely and kissing her soft cheek.

"Hi, baby. Did you miss me?" He tickled her belly before inhaling her sweet smell. Violet had been clinging to Max since they arrived home, and this was the first time he'd gotten a chance to see the little girl.

"Where's Mama?" she said before patting his face.

"She's in Nicky's room." Leta stood on Nicky's feet and put her arms around her waist. "I was just going to take the baby bird there."

She cocked her head as Avery's voice drifted out of the kitchen. "Leta? Could you come into the kitchen, please?"

"Aye, Mama!" Leta hollered. She bounced up and down on Nicholas' feet, grinning when he winced. "Will you take the baby bird to Max?"

Nicky nodded and kissed Violet's cheek again before carrying her toward his bedroom. He had insisted that Max and Violet continue to stay in his room while he slept in the room off the servant's quarters. The bed was small, and the room was cold but the thought of Max sleeping in his bed comforted him.

He knocked on the door and opened it. "Max? I've brought - what are you doing?"

Max, in the middle of stuffing clothes into a large leather bag, froze and stared guiltily at him. "I – um, nothing." She dropped the bag on to the floor at the end of the bed as Violet squirmed out of Nicky's arms.

"Hi, Mama."

"Hi, honey." She picked up Violet. "Were you a good girl for Leta?"

"Aye!" the little girl said.

Max laughed as Nicholas drifted closer to them.

"How have you been?" he asked.

"Fine." She shifted Violet in her arms until she was between her and Nicky. "I hear that your father is awake."

"He is."

"Down, Mama!" Violet said.

She set Violet down and the little girl grabbed Nicky's hands. He lifted her and swung her back and forth by her arms as she giggled.

"Emmett is a lucky man," Max said.

He was puzzled by the bitterness in her voice but before he could question her further, Bree stuck her head into the room. "It's almost dinner."

"Thank you, Bree." Max scooped up Violet and carried her toward the door. Nicholas glanced at the bag on the floor before following her.

———

NICKY PICKED UP THE DISHTOWEL AND BEGAN TO DRY THE dishes. Avery, elbow deep in warm, sudsy water, gave him a grateful smile. "Thank you, my love."

"Aye, you're welcome, Mama."

"Marian is not feeling well this evening and has gone to bed. I wanted to lie down with her for a bit, but she would not let me. She insists that I need to rest after what I did for Jackar. If she's not feeling better by tomorrow, I will force her to sit with me."

"Do you feel all right, Mama?" Nicky said.

"Aye, sweet Nicky, I feel perfectly fine. Sophia and Dani both rested with me, and later that night your father -"

She paused, her pale cheeks flushing. "Never mind, my sweet."

Nicky grinned good-naturedly at her as a burst of laughter came from the common room.

The others had gathered in the common room after dinner and Avery smiled as more laughter drifted through the kitchen doorway. "It is so good to have all of my loved ones home again."

Nicky dried the bowl and set it on the counter. He reached for a glass and Avery touched his hand. "How are you feeling, my love? I've scarcely had a chance to speak to you since you returned home."

"I feel fine. A few good nights of sleep and Marian's cooking has restored me."

"That is not what I mean," she said.

Nicholas picked up another glass to dry. "I don't know, Mama. Meridan and Nina spent so much time telling me what a good man my birth father was that I expected something different, I suppose."

"What do you mean?" Avery said.

"He's so cold to Nina, Mama. She is his daughter and he treats her like she is a thorn in his side that he must endure. He speaks rudely to her and dismisses her."

"People are often different when they're not feeling well," Avery said.

"Aye, I know. But he is feeling better now and his attitude toward her has not changed. She is a sweet girl. I do not know why he harbors such resentment for her. It is not her fault that her mother was human or that she seduced her father. Emmett says she is sly and not to be trusted."

Avery frowned. "Nina does not strike me as untrustworthy. A little uncertain and immature, perhaps, but not untrustworthy."

"Aye," Nicky said.

"She seems to have taken a liking to your father." There was a grin on Avery's face and Nicholas grinned in return.

"Aye. When I left the common room, she was nearly sitting on his lap and talking a mile a minute to him."

Avery laughed. "Tristan is a kind man and a wonderful father. If what you say is true about Emmett being distant with Nina, it is not surprising that she would attach herself to Tristan."

They washed the dishes in silence for a few moments before Avery glanced at Nicky. "Is everything all right between you and Max?"

Nicholas leaned against the counter and stared moodily out the window at the falling snow. "She is avoiding me."

"Aye, that is obvious. But your father tells me that your scents indicate your attraction to each other."

"I do not know what to do. For the first time in my life, I desire something more with a woman and she will have nothing to do with me."

Avery smiled a little. "I do not believe she will be able to resist you for long. You must convince her of your love for her."

Nicky gave her a startled look. "I do not love her, Mama."

"Do you not?" Avery said.

"No. I care for her very much and I am very fond of both her and Violet, but I am not in love with her."

"My mistake, then." Avery smiled and Nicholas flushed before grabbing a dish to dry.

"She is going to run," he said.

"Do you think so?"

"Aye, I know she is. She is afraid that she'll hurt one of us."

Avery pursed her lips. "I thought she was learning to control her powers."

"She is. But she doesn't believe she is strong enough to ever truly control them. Honestly, I'm not certain she's wrong. What she can do, Mama," he paused, "the way she destroyed both the Gogs and the leeches, I have never seen anything like it. If it had not been for her, we would all be dead."

Avery squeezed his hand. "Are you afraid of her?"

"No. But I'm afraid she will leave, and I'll never see her again."

"Then convince her to stay," Avery said.

Leta bounced into the room. "Mama! Jeffrey just asked Rene to marry him! In front of everyone!"

Avery laughed and dried her hands. "Did she say yes?"

Leta rolled her eyes. "I think so. She was crying so hard it was difficult to tell."

Avery laughed again and held her hands out to her children. "Come, let us go and celebrate with them."

CHAPTER 23

Max crept down the hallway. It was close to midnight and the house was quiet and still. Violet, asleep in the carrier on her back, snorted softly and muttered in her sleep. Max stroked her soft hair before adjusting the heavy leather bag slung across her chest.

She headed toward the front door, grimly ignoring the voice in her head that was screaming at her to stop.

"It is late to be going out."

She just barely kept in her scream of surprise. She whipped around, Violet made a sleepy protest, and Max stared wide-eyed at Nicky.

"What are you doing here?" she said.

He arched his eyebrow at her. "I live here."

"Why are you not in bed?"

"Why are you taking your child out in the bitter cold in the middle of the night?"

"I wasn't. I was just, uh…"

Violet lifted her head and made a sleepy little wail.

"Hush, Violet. It's okay, honey," she said.

"Tired, mama. It's sleepy time," Violet whined. She

squirmed in the carrier and tugged at the straps that bound her to her mother. "Dark is sleepy time."

"I know, honey. Just close your eyes and go to sleep, all right?" Max said.

Violet made another unhappy whine and hitched in her breath. Max flinched. Violet was a bear when she was woken from her sleep. If past experience was any indication, the little girl's cries would be loud enough to wake the entire house.

Before Violet could begin crying, Nicky was unbuckling the straps from the carrier and pulling the little girl free. He rested her against his chest, rubbing her back, and she put her arms around his neck before burying her face in his neck.

"Sleepy time, puppy," she said before her body slumped against Nicky's and she lapsed into soft snoring again. He turned and carried her down the hall.

"Nicholas, bring her back," Max said in a low voice.

"No. It is too cold for the baby out there." He disappeared into the darkness.

She shut the door of his bedroom as Nicholas laid Violet on the small bed in the corner of the room. While they were gone, Tristan had brought Leta's toddler bed from the storage room for Violet to use. He had moved it from his and Avery's room to Nicky's, the day they returned.

Nicholas carefully eased Violet out of her coat and boots before pulling off the knitted cap and mittens she wore. He tucked her into the bed, kissing her forehead as she curled into a ball and snored loudly.

He straightened and grinned at Max. "How do you sleep with her snoring away like that?"

"You get used to it." Max took a step back when he reached for her scarf. "Nicky, I have to leave."

"No, you don't." He unwrapped her scarf and dropped it

to the floor before unbuttoning her jacket. "You can stay here with me."

He bent his head and nuzzled the soft skin of her throat. Max moaned as her jacket joined her scarf.

"This isn't a good idea," she said.

He licked her throat. "I've missed you."

"I've missed you too," she said.

He kissed her, pulling her up against his warm, hard body as his tongue traced her lips. She parted her lips and he explored her mouth with soft, coaxing strokes.

"I don't want you to leave," he said against her mouth. "Please stay."

"I'm not looking for just a good time," she said. "You know that, Nicky. It won't work out and I need to leave before I become too – too attached to you."

He slid his arms around her waist. "I want more, Max. I want you to belong to me. I want to take care of you and Violet."

She stared at him in surprise and he nodded. "It's true. I swear it."

"Nicky, I – I don't know what to say."

"Tell me that you'll stay. Give it a chance. Give *us* a chance," he said.

"I don't know if I can. It isn't just this. Your father -"

"I will speak to Emmett," Nicky said. "You saved his life, Max. He will free you of your father's debt."

She didn't reply. It wasn't the debt but the knowledge that Emmett would use her power to make her do terrible things. And if she refused, he would use Violet against her. She knew that as well as she knew her own name.

She couldn't tell Nicky that. She couldn't tell him that his birth father was a horrible monster who stopped at nothing to get what he wanted. Nicholas obviously wanted a relationship with him. Why else would he have brought him back here and asked his mother to save his life.

She sighed as Nicky kneaded the back of her neck with his warm hand. She wanted to stay with Nicky. She wanted to take what he was offering, but sooner or later Emmett would demand her to use her power and she couldn't do that. Every time she unleashed it, the power became harder to control, more difficult to harness back in, and she was terribly afraid that eventually it would become impossible.

Images of the young boy in the bathroom, images of the Gogs bursting apart like wet balloons and the leeches simply disintegrating into blood and ash, flickered through her mind and she shuddered violently.

"What's wrong?" Nicholas pulled her closer and kissed her forehead.

"Nothing," she whispered. "I will stay with you, Nicky."

He smiled happily at her and kissed her on the mouth. "You won't regret it, Max."

As he led her toward his bed, she ignored the knot of anxiety growing in her belly. If Emmett did not release her of her debt, if he tried to make her use her powers, she would leave. It didn't matter how she felt about Nicky. She couldn't let Emmett use her powers for his own dark needs.

Nicholas was unbuttoning her shirt and she made a soft moan of need when he licked her collarbone. He tugged off her shirt and dropped it to the floor as his hands reached for the buttons on her pants. She helped him remove his shirt, her mouth going dry at the sight of his broad chest and flat abdomen, and then traced his abs with one finger. He inhaled sharply before nearly tearing at her pants.

"I've missed you so much," he said.

"I've missed you too." She kissed his thick neck, tasting his skin with her tongue as he groaned and pulled her against him. He ground his erection against her pelvis, and she reached into his pants and wrapped her fingers around his cock. He groaned again and then froze guiltily when Violet made a soft, snorting cry.

"Max, perhaps we should…"

His voice trailed off as she rubbed him firmly, circling her thumb around the broad head of his cock and nipping at his neck.

"Should what, Nicky?" she whispered into his ear.

"I'm not sure we should do this. If Violet wakes -"

"She will not wake," Max said.

"I do not want her to -"

"She won't wake up," Max repeated. "That is, if you can keep your moans and groans to a quieter level."

She grinned at him before giving his cock a firm squeeze. He arched his hips into her hand and bit back his groan of pleasure. "I will if you will."

She laughed softly and they quickly helped each other finish undressing before slipping into the bed. Nicky lay on his side next to her and he propped himself up on one elbow before cupping her breast.

"You're so beautiful, Max."

"Thank you." She threaded her fingers through his hair when he dipped his head and sucked firmly on her nipple. It hardened in his mouth and when he pulled gently on it with his teeth, she had to press her lips together to quiet her loud groan.

"Lie back, Nicholas."

He shifted to his back and she pressed soft, wet kisses across his chest. He sighed and stroked her short hair as she kissed her way down his body. When he felt her breath on his cock, he arched his pelvis and she placed a soft kiss on the head of it. He moaned and she grinned up at him.

"Quiet, Nicky."

"Aye, quiet," he muttered. "Please, Max."

"Please, what?" She licked his cock and he shuddered deeply.

He pressed on her head, trying to move her mouth down over his cock, and she laughed quietly. "Tell me what you want, Nicholas."

"Suck my cock," he said.

A hard throb of lust exploded in her belly. She took him into her mouth, sucking firmly, and he made a strangled gasp of need as his hands tightened in her hair. He watched as she licked and sucked, varying the pressure of her mouth, and he groaned with frustration when she stopped.

"Am I doing this right, Nicky?" she said sweetly. "I've never done this before."

"Aye, it feels so good."

"Are you sure?" she teased. "I can stop if it isn't right."

"Max!" He glared at her. "You're driving me crazy. Do not stop."

She licked his cock again in reply, her fingers tracing small circles on his inner thighs, until he was gasping and shaking beneath her gentle touch. She sucked lightly on just the head, tracing it with her tongue, as she stroked the shaft with her hand.

"Max," he moaned.

She sat up and threw her leg over his thighs before moving forward until she was straddling him.

"Don't stop!" he begged, and she placed her finger across his lips.

"You are too loud, Nicky. I cannot continue."

He cursed under his breath and she could barely stop the smile from crossing her face. She rubbed her core against him, a delicious tingle going through her body when his cock dragged across her clit, and his hands tightened around her thighs.

"Gods be damned, Max! You're killing me," he growled.

His eyes were glowing now and with one quick motion, she grasped his cock and guided it into her warmth. He arched his hips and she rested her hands on his chest as the pillow next to them rose into the air.

She stared at it and it dropped back to the bed as Nicky thrust his pelvis against her. She shuddered with need as his thick cock rubbed against her walls and she rode him hard for a few minutes. He rubbed and kneaded her breasts, pulling firmly on her nipples before reaching for her hand and guiding it to her clit.

"Touch yourself, Max," he breathed.

She rubbed her swollen clit, her breath catching in her throat as Nicholas watched her.

"I love watching you touch yourself, sweetheart," he murmured. He continued to thrust into her as she rubbed and circled her clit.

"Make yourself come. I want to see it," he demanded.

She barely heard him. Her entire body was filled with a sweet undeniable pleasure and she rubbed faster. There was a thick grating noise as the bed shifted beneath them and she muttered a curse and concentrated, her fingers still stroking rapidly between her thighs. Nicholas was swelling within her, his breath coming in harsh pants, as his fingers dug into her hips and he made soft, low growls of lust.

The bed settled back to the floor with a soft thump as her orgasm consumed her. She threw her hand over her mouth, stifling her cry, as Nicholas' back arched and warmth flooded through her. He shook and thrust beneath her before collapsing back against the bed. She rolled off of him, lying on her back next to him and staring up at the ceiling.

Nicky's face appeared above her. He stroked her short hair before cupping the back of her neck. "Are you all right, Max?"

"Aye," she whispered. "Are you?"

His face broke out into a grin. "Never better, sweetheart.

CHAPTER 24

"Where are you going, Papa?" Leta waded through the deep snow after Nina and Tristan.

"I'm teaching Nina how to ride," Tristan said.

"You don't know how to ride? How old are you?" Leta frowned at Nina.

Nina blushed and Tristan tapped Leta lightly on the butt. "Leta, be polite."

"I am," Leta said. "It's odd that she does not know how to ride, Papa."

"Not everyone is as lucky as you," Tristan said.

"I guess." Leta shrugged and took his hand before peering around him at Nina. "Are you nervous about riding a horse?"

"Oh no!" Nina said. "I love horses and I have always wanted to learn how to ride."

"Then why didn't you?" Leta said.

"My father didn't – oh!"

Slipping on a patch of ice under the snow, Nina clutched at Tristan's arm. He kept her from falling but her flailing feet kicked snow all over his pants and boots. Gasping in horror,

Nina brushed frantically at the snow on his pants. "I'm so sorry, lord Williams."

"It's fine, Nina. It's only a little snow." He patted her back as she stared at him in embarrassment.

"I'm so clumsy. Daddy says if I held my tongue while I was walking, I wouldn't fall so much."

Tristan frowned. "I do not think you're clumsy, Nina."

She didn't reply and Leta leaned around Tristan again. "I talk all the time and I never fall down. Perhaps you need to practice by talking more while you're walking."

Tristan laughed as Nina blushed again and brushed at the snow that still clung to Tristan's pants. "I really am sorry, lord Tristan."

"Why do you keep apologizing? It's just snow. Papa loves the snow. Don't you, Papa?" Leta said.

He turned to face her and bellowed in surprise when the snowball hit him in the face. Leta giggled wildly as Tristan wiped the snow from his face and growled at her. Nina watched wide-eyed as Leta, her eyes dancing with glee, backed up and Tristan stalked her through the deep snow.

"It's only a little snow, Papa." She grinned saucily at him and he growled again as she scooped up more snow.

She gave him a cheeky look and threw the second snow-ball at him. It hit him in the chest, and she shrieked and turned to run as he reached for her. He picked her up and tossed her into the deep snow. Laughing so hard she could barely breathe, Leta struggled to her feet and launched herself at her father's legs. She clung to him, trying to knock him off his feet, as he reached down and tickled her.

"Nina! Help me!" Leta hollered as she pulled at Tristan's leg. Her face breaking out into a wide grin, Nina charged through the snow and tackled Tristan. He staggered on his feet and Leta shrieked in victory when he fell backward into the snow. The two girls pounced on him, both of them laughing and squealing loudly.

"NINA WILL CATCH A COLD PLAYING IN THAT SNOW," MAYA said. She and Avery were standing at the window of the common room, watching as Tristan wrestled with the two young girls. "She's so thin and fragile."

"Aye, she could use a bit more meat on her bones," Avery said. "Do not worry, Maya. Tristan will not keep them in the snow for very long. Besides, I believe this is the most fun Nina has had in moons."

"You are right." Maya smiled at her sister and Avery blinked in surprise when the pixie's face poked out from Maya's blonde hair.

"I see you've made a new friend."

Maya laughed as Kala crawled onto her shoulder and peered out the window at Tristan and the girls. "Nina told Kala she needed to stay with someone while she was learning to ride. I was more surprised than anyone when Kala chose me."

She touched the pixie's foot gently. "I think she chose me because of the blonde hair."

"Do you think she would let me hold her?" Avery studied Kala's torn wing.

Maya glanced around the room. It was empty, but she lowered her voice anyway. "Do you think you can heal her wing, Avery? Nina says it has been this way for a long time."

"I do not know. But it wouldn't hurt to try." She held her hand out to Kala. "Will you sit with me for a while, Kala?"

The pixie stared mistrustfully at her for a moment before stepping off of Maya's shoulder and into Avery's hand.

Moving slowly, Avery brought her to her chest and cupped both hands around her. "Be very still, Kala."

She closed her eyes as Maya waited patiently. After a few minutes, Avery opened her hands and frowned with disappointment. The little pixie's wing was still torn and lay flat against her back.

"It's been too long," Maya said.

"What's been too long?" Bree asked as she and James entered the common room, Tia at their heels.

"Avery is trying to heal the pixie's wing," Maya said. "It isn't working."

"James should try." Bree smiled at the little pixie and held out her hand. "Kala, will you let James hold you for a moment?"

Kala stepped willingly into Bree's hand but when James reached for her, she bared her fangs at him and hissed.

"It's all right, Kala," Bree said. "He's trying to help you."

She jabbered at them in her own language before frowning at James. Bree glanced at him. "I don't think she understands, James."

"Aye, it doesn't appear so." James held both his hands out in front of Kala. "I'm friendly. I swear it."

Bree laughed. "She does not believe you."

James grinned at her and kissed Bree's forehead before stroking her round belly. "Well, I do not speak pixie so until she learns more of our language, I cannot -"

He stopped as Kala, studying the way he touched Bree's belly so gently, leaped from Bree's hand to her shoulder. She moved cautiously to James' arm and didn't flinch when he slowly reached up and cupped his hand around her.

Only her head stuck out and she stared at him as the minutes ticked by. When he opened his hand, Bree sighed with disappointment. "It didn't work."

"Sorry, little pixie," James said as Kala climbed his arm to his shoulder. She touched his red hair before smelling it.

Bree grinned when she held onto James' ear and licked his hair with her tongue.

"What is she doing?" James said.

Bree snorted laughter. "She's licking your hair."

James rolled his eyes as Kala moved down his arm. Maya held out her hand and Kala jumped onto it before climbing her arm and disappearing into her hair.

"DON'T BE NERVOUS, MAX. MY FAMILY LIKES YOU, AND they'll be happy that we are together," Nicky stood outside the common room, carrying Violet and holding Max's hand.

"I'm not nervous," she said.

He leaned down and kissed her cheek, making Violet giggle. "Puppy kiss Mama."

Nicholas grinned at her before leading Max into the common room.

Avery smiled at them, "Good morning."

"Good morning, Mama." Nicholas kissed Violet's soft cheek before placing her on the ground. Tia, her tail wagging furiously, stood on her hind legs and licked the little girl's face.

Violet giggled and patted the small dog before staring at Avery.

"Up?" she said hopefully.

Avery picked her up and kissed the top of her head. "Are you hungry, Violet? Would you like a biscuit with honey?"

"Aye!" Violet shouted.

Avery carried Violet from the room as James turned to Nicholas. "How is Emmett feeling today?"

"I do not know. I have not talked with him this morning," Nicky said. "I was going to -"

He stopped as Ryker and Emmett entered the common room. The Lycan, although thin, looked much better and he shook off Ryker's hand when he tried to take his elbow.

"I told you, Ryker. I feel fine," he said.

He nodded to the others in the room. "Good morning."

"Good morning, Emmett. You look well," Nicholas said.

"Hello, son." Emmett smiled at Nicky. "I am starting to feel like myself again."

He gazed at Nicky's and Max's clasped hands before staring at Max. "I hear you are to be thanked for saving me."

Max didn't reply and Nicholas glanced at her when he felt her tremble.

"Max? What's wrong?"

"Nothing," she said. "I believe I will go and check on Violet." She squeezed his hand before nodding stiffly at Emmett. "I am glad you're feeling better, Emmett."

"Thank you, Max." Emmett sat down in the armchair closest to the fire as Max left the room.

"Emmett, this is my brother James and his mate Bree, and this is my aunt Maya." Nicholas joined Emmett by the fire.

Emmett studied James' red hair. "I have never met a Red Lycan before."

"We are a rarity," James said.

Maya shook Emmett's hand. "It is nice to meet you, Emmett."

He kissed the top of her hand. "It's nice to meet you as well. It has been a long time since I've seen someone as lovely as you."

"Thank you, my lord. Are you hungry? I could bring you something from the kitchen, if you'd like?" Maya said.

"I would like that." Emmett smiled again at her.

Bree joined them and extended her hand to Emmett. "Hello, lord McKenzie."

"Please, call me Emmett." He kissed her hand as well and held it. "Aren't you the sweetest little thing? How old are you, girl?"

"Nineteen, my lord."

"I remember that age well." His thumb stroked her hand and Nicholas could smell Bree's discomfort.

James appeared beside Bree. He put his large arm around her waist and drew her away from Emmett. "Will you do me a favour and make me a cup of tea, Bree? It is chilly this morning."

"Aye, my love. I will make us both a cup."

"Thank you, little one. I will join you in the kitchen shortly."

The front door slammed and Nina and Leta's excited chattering filled the hallway.

"We should let her ride Bella, Papa! I can show her what to do."

"We will teach Nina on Rosie, Leta. She's the smallest and the gentlest," Tristan said.

"She's boring," Leta huffed.

"It's probably best if I start with the small boring one." Nina laughed. "I am not so sure that I will not fall off."

They were stopped outside of the common room now, and Nicky grinned to himself. The girls were covered in snow and Nina and Leta both clung to Tristan's hands. Nina's usual pale cheeks were flush with colour and her eyes sparkled with happiness as she leaned against Tristan.

"Both of you need to go and change your clothes before you catch colds. We will teach Nina to ride after lunch." Tristan squeezed their hands and winked at Leta. "I bet your mama would make you some hot cocoa if you say please."

Leta squealed excitedly. "Mama makes the best cocoa, Nina! Come, we will -"

She peered into the common room and Tristan and Nina followed her gaze. At the sight of her father sitting in the chair, Nina quickly dropped Tristan's hand and gave Emmett a guilty smile.

"Hello, Daddy!" She crossed the room and hugged him.

He patted her back before pushing her away. "Hello, Nina. You're soaking wet."

"Sorry." She stood next to his chair and took his hand. "We were playing in the snow."

"I can see that." He rose from the chair and held out his hand as Tristan entered the room.

"It is nice to meet you, lord Williams."

Tristan shook his hand. "You as well, lord McKenzie."

There was a moment of awkward silence that Nina broke nervously. "Lord Williams is going to teach me to ride a horse, Daddy."

"I'm sure lord Williams has more important things to do than teach you to ride, Nina. Perhaps you could make yourself useful by helping around the household. We do, after all, owe lord Williams a great debt."

"That won't be necessary. I am happy to teach Nina how to ride," Tristan said.

"That's very kind of you. I should warn you that my girl is on the clumsy side." Emmett laughed as Nina blushed. "You may find it more difficult than you think."

Leta stood next to her father and frowned at Emmett. "Nina isn't clumsy."

Tristan squeezed her shoulder gently. "This is my youngest daughter. Leta, say hello to lord McKenzie."

"Hello, lord McKenzie." Leta held her hand out to Nina. "Come to my room and play with me, Nina." She giggled when Tia scratched at her legs and quickly scooped the little dog into her arms. "I'll show you all the tricks I've taught Tia."

"Sure." Nina stared anxiously at her father. "Would that be all right, Daddy?"

He shook his head. "Maya is being kind enough to bring me some food. Why don't you help her? I'm sure she would appreciate it."

"Not at all," Maya said. "I do not need her help. Go and have some fun, Nina." She patted Nina's arm and smiled when Kala slid out from her hair and ran down her arm and onto Nina. The pixie kissed Nina's cheek affectionately as Emmett grunted in surprise.

"Since when did you have a pixie as a pet?"

"I saved her, Daddy. Well, Nicky helped me save her. She was trapped in a log and we freed her. She has a broken wing and cannot fly," Nina said. "And then, when we were in Morden, she saved my life. I was stabbed by a man who -"

Emmett held up his hand. "Enough, girl. No one is interested in your mindless chatter."

Nina flushed miserably as Leta scowled at Emmett. "You're rude."

"Leta!" Tristan said. "You will mind your manners or find yourself without riding privileges."

"Sorry, Papa," Leta muttered. She stared mistrustfully at Emmett. "My apologies, lord McKenzie."

He smiled thinly at her as she reached for Nina's hand again. "Come to my room, Nina."

"Aye, Leta." Nina kissed her father's cheek. "I will see you later, Daddy."

He nodded as Leta, still holding Tia, led Nina from the room. He glanced at Tristan. "She reminds me of Sophia. She was very strong-willed."

"Aye, and she still is," Tristan said.

"I am not surprised. As I recall, her mother indulged her behaviour on many occasions. Children at that age do better with a firm hand to guide them. Wouldn't you agree, lord Tristan?"

Before Tristan could answer, Maya cleared her throat. "I will return shortly with some soup for you, Emmett."

She looped her arm around Bree's and the two women left the room as Tristan crossed to the armchair opposite of Emmett's.

Ryker cleared his throat. "Emmett, unless you need me, I'm going to return to my room to rest for a while."

"That's fine, Ryker," Emmett said absently.

James clapped Nicky on the back. "Well, as much as I'm enjoying this awkwardness, I believe I will join Bree in the kitchen."

He grinned at his brother before leaving. Nicky joined Tristan and Emmett in front of the fire as Emmett crossed his legs and folded his hands across his midsection.

"I owe you a great debt, lord Williams. There are few men who would take in a child that does not belong to them and raise them as their own son."

"Nicholas has made both his mother and me very proud," Tristan said. "We could not imagine our lives without him."

Aye, I am very impressed with the Lycan he has become." Emmett smiled at Nicholas before looking around the room. "You seem to have done well for yourself. What is it that you do, lord Williams?"

"I breed horses."

"Really? An odd profession for a Lycan, is it not?"

Tristan shrugged. "Some believe so, aye."

"And your sons help you with this?"

"They do. Although, I know they may eventually choose a different path."

"Do you enjoy your work, Nicholas?" Emmett asked.

"Aye," Nicky said.

"I own a very successful business in the city," Emmett said to Tristan. "I imagine it will not surprise you to learn that I am eager for Nicholas to join me in that business. I have always wanted a son and was very pleased to learn of his existence."

When Tristan didn't reply, Emmett leaned forward. "I'm asking that you allow Nicholas to travel with me to the city. He can see my home and learn about my business. He may find that he enjoys it as much as he enjoys breeding horses."

There was a thin thread of condescension in his tone and Nicky frowned as Tristan said, "Nicky is a grown man. He is free to make his own choices and does not require my permission."

"Aye, that is true," Emmett said. "What do you say, Nicholas? Will you join me in the city?"

"I am not fond of city living," Nicholas said.

"How do you know? You have spent your entire life in the country. You may find that you enjoy it."

"Unlikely," Nicholas said.

Frustration crossed Emmett's face. "I see that you are quite fond of Max. She is under my employment and will be returning with me to the city. Perhaps she can convince you to join us."

"Actually, I wanted to speak with you about Max. She is responsible for saving your life."

"I know," Emmett said. "Ryker shared the details. I knew of the girl's powers before I was taken by the leeches, of course, but I had no idea what she was capable of. Her powers are truly remarkable."

255

"If it had not been for her, you would have died in that cell," Nicky said.

"I am aware of that," Emmett said. "I am grateful to her and will express my gratitude more succinctly the next time I speak with her."

"That is kind of you, Emmett, but I want you to release her of her father's debt."

Emmett blinked at him. "Are you serious, Nicholas? Her father owed me a great deal of money and it is not even halfway paid. Max promised him on his death bed that she would honor his debt to me."

"She also saved your life. Do you not think that is worth more than the money her father owes? My understanding is that you're a very wealthy man. Would it be such a hardship to grant Max her freedom of her father's debt? Especially when she risked her own life to save yours?"

"I did not become wealthy by allowing the people who owe me money to simply walk away from it," Emmett said.

Nicholas sat forward. "Are you really that selfish, Emmett? Does money mean that much to you? I have no wish to get to know you if all you care about is how much money lines your pockets."

He stood up from his chair. "Max deserves to live her own life. She deserves to be free of her father's debt and to make her own choices about what she wants. I cannot believe you even have to consider returning her freedom. What kind of Lycan are you?"

"Nicholas," Tristan said.

Nicholas glared at him. "What?"

Tristan stared silently at him and Nicholas took a deep breath. "Sorry, Dad." He sat back in his chair. "Forgive me for my rudeness, Emmett."

"I will give Max her freedom," Emmett said after a

moment. "You are right – she deserves it. But will you do me a favour, Nicholas? Will you at least consider traveling to the city with your sister and me? Nina would be thrilled, and I believe it would be good for you to spend some time with us."

"I will consider it," Nicholas said.

"Good." Emmett sat up in the chair as Maya, carrying a tray with soup and bread, entered the common room. Marshall followed her.

"Lord McKenzie, this is my husband, Marshall. He is Tristan's brother," Mia said.

"It is nice to meet you, Marshall."

"You as well, Lord McKenzie." Marshall and Maya sat down on the couch as Emmett ate a spoonful of soup.

Emmett turned to Tristan. "So, how long have you been in the horse breeding business, lord Williams?

CHAPTER 25

"Do you have a dog?" Leta asked.

They were sitting on the floor of her room and she watched as Nina rubbed Tia's belly gently.

"No, I do not have any pets."

"Why not? I have two cats as well. They live in the barn. Kaden gave them to me as a gift. Well, actually one belongs to my sister Sophia, but Hudson is mine."

"Daddy doesn't like animals in the house." Nina continued to stroke Tia's belly as Leta rolled her eyes.

"He's a Lycan. That makes him an animal and he lives in the house."

There was a loud snicker from the doorway, and they turned to see Evan standing there holding his sketch book. "What are you two doing?"

"Nothing," Leta said. "Just playing with Tia. Papa's teaching Nina how to ride after lunch."

Evan sat down beside Nina. "I did not know you couldn't ride. I would have taught you."

Leta made a face and flopped onto her back on the floor as Nina blushed and stared at the floor. "Thank you, Evan."

"Thank you, Evan." Leta mimicked her in a high-pitched voice and Evan punched her in the leg when Nina flushed even brighter.

"Don't be a dork, Leta."

Leta rubbed her leg and growled at him. "I'm telling Mama you punched me."

"Go ahead," Evan said. "I'll tell her you were making fun of Nina."

"I wasn't!" Leta said. "I was making fun of you. I know you like Nina."

"Shut up, Leta!"

"You shut up!" She turned to Nina. "Boys are so gross. I'm never dating one."

"You'll change your mind," Evan said.

"No, I won't. I'm only going to date girls," Leta said. "They're way more fun than boys."

Evan laughed. "Mama and Dad won't let you date girls."

"They will too!" Leta gave him a wounded look. "I already told Mama I am going to date girls when I grow up and she said that was fine."

Nina pointed to Evan's sketchbook. "What is that, Evan?"

"I like to draw. Would you like to see?" he said.

"Aye, I would." Nina smiled as he handed her the book. She flipped through the pages. "These are really good."

"Thank you. I practice a lot," Evan said.

"He practices all the time. He's always drawing pictures of the girls he moons over. He had like a thousand pictures of Bree before she married James." Leta sat up and grabbed the sketchbook from Nina. "I bet he has pictures of you in here."

"Leta, give that back!" Evan glared at her as she flipped to the very back and squealed in triumph.

"See, told you so!" She dodged Evan's flailing hands and threw the book at Nina.

Nina stared at the sketch. "I really like it. You've made me look so pretty."

"You are pretty," Evan said.

She shook her head. "I know I'm not. I'm too pale and too thin. Daddy says I'll never find a husband looking the way I do. He says not even a human will be interested in me."

"Your papa is mean," Leta said.

"Leta," Evan said warningly.

"What? He is," Leta said. "If he was my papa, I'd bite him in the leg." She half-shifted, baring her fangs at Nina and growling playfully under her breath, as Nina snickered.

"I don't have fangs, remember? I'm only human."

"Evan and I are half-human," Leta replied. "Our mama is human, and she found a husband. You will too. Maybe even a Lycan or a half-Lycan."

She looked meaningfully at Evan who scowled at her and then flushed when Nina smiled sweetly at him. "You really are good at drawing, Evan."

"Thank you. Do you like to draw?"

"I've never really tried," she said.

"Here, you should try now." He pulled a pencil from his back pocket before flipping to a clean page in the sketchbook.

"Oh, I don't know. I'm not - I mean - I don't even know what I would draw."

"Draw me!" Leta sat up straight and smoothed her hair down as Evan scooted closer to Nina. He handed her the pencil.

"You shouldn't start with faces. They're difficult to do. But you could try drawing one of Leta's toys." He pointed at a wooden horse that was sitting on the floor by her bed. "Try drawing that."

"I'd better not. I don't want to waste your paper," Nina said.

"It's not a waste," he said. "Besides, you won't know if you can draw unless you try, right? If you're bad at it, it's no big deal. I'm the only one in our family who can draw."

He smiled encouragingly at her and Nina took a deep breath before studying the wooden horse. "I'll try."

"Good!" Evan moved closer until his shoulder was brushing against hers. "What you want to do is -"

He twitched when Kala's face peeked out of Nina's hair and she hissed at him.

"Kala, no," Nina said. "Evan is a friend."

She said something in her language and Nina reached into her hair and gently pulled her free of the golden strands. "Friend, Kala. Evan is a friend."

"Friend," Kala said.

"That's right," Nina said.

"I've never seen a pixie before," Evan said.

"Would you like to hold her?"

"I'd better not. She doesn't seem to like me."

"It's fine. She just needs to get to know you. Hold your hand out."

Evan held his hand out and Nina placed the pixie in his hand. He studied her as she returned his look solemnly.

"Hello, Kala." He smiled at her.

"Can you say Evan, Kala?" Nina said.

"Evan," Kala said.

"What happened to her wing?" Evan said.

"I don't know. It was like that when we found her. She saved my life, you know," Nina said as Kala jumped on to Evan's knee and then slid down to the floor.

"Really? How?"

"I was stabbed right in the chest by this awful man in a bar. She used pixie dust to heal my wound."

"The gods be damned," Evan said. "I didn't know pixies could do that."

"Me either. I don't know why she doesn't try and heal her own wing. Max believes that perhaps her healing powers do not work on her own body," Nina said.

Leta held out her hand to the pixie standing on the floor in front of her. "C'mon, Kala. Let me hold you. I'm as nice as Nina," the little girl coaxed.

Evan's eyes widened and he whipped his head around as Kala hopped obligingly onto the palm of Leta's hand. The little girl grinned with delight and cupped her hands around her.

"Leta! No! Do not -"

"What's wrong with her?" Nina cried as Kala, only her head sticking out from Leta's closed hands, suddenly made a loud, keening wail. "Leta! You are holding her too tightly."

"I'm not," Leta said. "I swear I am being gentle. I didn't hurt her."

She opened her hands and Evan groaned in dismay. Nina gasped and stared wide-eyed at the pixie standing in the palm of Leta's hand.

Leta, her bottom lip trembling, stared at Evan. "I'm sorry, Evan. I forgot."

"It's okay." He tried to smile at her as Kala, her small face beaming, unfolded her perfect wings and flapped them gently. She rose into the air, hovering just above Leta's hand, and babbled excitedly at Nina in her own language.

"The gods be damned," Nina whispered. "Her wing – how…"

Squeaking and muttering, Kala zipped around the room. She dive-bombed at Tia, smacking the dog on the backside and laughing hysterically when Tia jumped and barked.

"Leta, you – you did that," Nina said.

"No, I didn't!" Leta stared at Evan with fear. "It wasn't me!"

"It was." Nina stared at Evan. "I know it was, Evan."

"Nina, you can't say anything," Evan said. "Leta has – well, she has healing powers. But you have to promise not to tell anyone. No one else can know. Promise me."

"I promise," Nina said. "You healed Daddy and that other boy, didn't you?"

Neither Leta nor Evan replied, and Nina shook her head. "You must have. No other Lycan has survived a leech bite."

She leaned forward and hugged Leta. "Thank you," she whispered before kissing her cheek.

Leta stared guiltily at Evan over Nina's shoulder and Evan shook his head. "Nina, it is very important that you don't say anything. Do you understand? If people find out what Leta can do -"

He stopped and inhaled deeply as a look of alarm crossed his face. He turned to look behind him at the open door. "Who's out there?"

Ryker appeared in the doorway and Evan scowled at him. "Do you always spy on people, human?"

"Watch your tongue, little boy," Ryker said. "I was merely on my way to my own room."

He twitched in surprise when Kala flew at his face. She hovered in front of him and made a rude gesture with her hand before flying back across the room.

"What in the gods name?" he said. "How is this possible?"

He stared at Nina. "Nina, answer me. How is the little pest's wing healed?"

Nina glanced at Evan. "She healed it using pixie dust."

"Did she now? Odd that it would take her so long to heal herself," he said.

Nina didn't answer and Ryker stared steadily at her for a long moment before stepping back into the hallway and disappearing.

Nina blew out her breath. "I do not think he believed me."

"I will tell Papa what happened," Evan said.

"No! Evan, you can't! If they find out what I did, they'll be angry with me," Leta said.

Evan shook his head. "It was an accident, Leta. They won't be angry."

"They will," Leta said. "Please, Evan. We will tell them that Kala healed herself. Please, please, please, Evan!"

"All right, Leta."

Nina stood and walked toward the window. Kala had flown to the windowsill and was looking longingly outside.

"What are you doing?" Leta said as Nina pushed the window open.

"Giving Kala her freedom." She stroked the pixie's back. "She only stayed with me because she was injured. I will not force her to continue to do so now that she can be with her own kind again."

She smiled at Kala and stroked her naked back again. "Goodbye, Kala. Thank you for saving my life. I love you."

Kala glanced briefly at her before flying out the open window. Blinking back tears, Nina leaned against Evan when he joined her and put his arm around her shoulders.

"I'm sorry, Nina."

"I'm not," she said. "I'm glad she can fly again. She missed it so."

Evan led her away from the window as Leta stood up and held out her hand. "Come, Nina. We will ask Mama to make us hot cocoa. She makes the best hot cocoa and it will make you feel better."

Nina took her hand before slipping her other hand into

Evan's. As the three of them started toward the door, there was a tiny squeal behind them. Nina gasped when Kala flew back through the open window and landed on her shoulder. She kissed Nina's cheek before scurrying into her hair.

Nina grinned happily at Evan. "She came back!"

"Aye, I am not surprised," Evan said as he returned to the window and closed it. "Come on, Leta's right. Mama does make the best hot cocoa."

CHAPTER 26

"Did you actually see the Lycan heal the pixie?" Emmett, sitting on the edge of his bed, asked Ryker.

"No," Ryker said. "But I heard Nina say that she did, and I saw the pest's wing myself. It's healed."

Emmett rubbed his forehead. "You said the pixie saved Nina's life with pixie dust. She probably healed herself."

"She didn't," Ryker said. "If she could use her own dust to heal herself, she would have done so long before now. The young Lycan healed her. And I believe she healed you and that other Lycan as well."

Emmett frowned at him. "My Lycan healing -"

"No." Ryker paced back and forth in Emmett's bedroom. "You were dying, Emmett. You don't remember but by the time we arrived back here, you were only hours from death. I thought it to be a miracle that you survived but now…"

He stared into the flames. "It was the young Lycan who saved you. I know it. Powers like hers would come in very handy."

Emmett nodded. "Aye, they would. If they even exist.

Bring me proof of their existence and we'll discuss the next step."

"Discuss the next step?" Ryker arched his eyebrow at him. "Has your time with the leeches made you weak? The Emmett I knew took what he wanted and did not allow anyone to stop him."

"We must tread carefully, Ryker," Emmett said. "Nicholas and the Lycans he calls a family do not trust me yet. I need to earn their trust if I am to have him join me. He does not yet think of me as his father, and he will side with lord Williams if pushed. I cannot simply take the snotty little Lycan like a thief in the night. These Lycans are a powerful group, the giant Red one could snap you in half easily."

"Bullshit!" Ryker said. "The Red is an idiot. One only needs to look at him to know that. I would burn him and his Red witch mother if you would let me."

Emmett sighed impatiently. "Aye, because that would help me gain Nicholas' trust."

"Have you considered that you may never win his trust? He is obviously loyal to these Lycans, and he and Max are fucking. If she tells him what you're really like…"

"And what am I really like?" Emmett, his face red, stood up from the bed and glowered at Ryker as his body rippled and hair grew on his cheeks. "Are you saying I'm a monster?"

"Of course not," Ryker said. "But this lord Williams has instilled a sense of ridiculous pride and pleasure in helping others into Nicholas. Do you really think he wants to take over a business that preys on the weak?"

"Preys on the weak?" Emmett said. "I do what I can to help the less fortunate. Is it my fault that they cannot pay me back and must find other ways to relieve their debt to me? If I didn't help them, they would be worse off."

He was growling now, his fangs lengthening as his fingers turned to claws and Ryker held his hands up.

"Calm yourself, Emmett. Would you really kill your most loyal friend over a son who doesn't even think of you as his father?"

Emmett looked away and drew in a few deep breaths before returning his gaze to Ryker. "Bring me proof of the Lycan's powers."

⸻

THE NEXT MORNING NINA KNOCKED LIGHTLY ON EMMETT'S door. At his gruff "come in", she peeked her head into the room.

"Good morning, Daddy."

"Hello, Nina."

"How do you feel today?"

"Better." Emmett buttoned his shirt as Ryker joined them.

"I'm glad you're feeling better." Nina smiled at her father. "I thought perhaps you could watch me ride this morning. I had my first lesson yesterday and lord Tristan says that I am a natural. He said it was fine if you wanted to come to the barn and watch me ride."

Emmett shook his head. "I have other business to take care of today."

Nina's face fell. "Are you sure you could not watch me ride for just a few minutes? You do not have to stay long. I would like it very much if you -"

"Nina, enough!" Emmett shouted. "The gods be damned, girl! I did not come back from the brink of death to listen to you nattering at me all day long. I have told you that I am busy."

"I'm sorry," Nina said.

"Aye, you're always sorry, aren't you?" Emmett said. "You're just like your mother. Always whining and crying and carrying on like a spoiled little child. Do you know I actually believed after she killed herself that I would finally have a moment's peace? If I had known that you would take up her mantle of constant badgering, I would have sent you to the outskirts the day you found your mother hanging in the closet."

Nina made a harsh sobbing cough as Emmett strode forward and shook her roughly. "I have had all I can take of you, girl. If you are wise, you will leave my sight now and -"

"Get away from her."

Emmett dropped Nina's arm and looked up at Nicholas standing in the doorway.

"This does not concern you, Nicholas."

"She is my sister. It concerns me," Nicky said. He put his arm around Nina and hugged her to his side. "What is wrong with you? What type of Lycan would treat his own flesh and blood so poorly?"

"Nicholas, your sister knows that I -"

"Enough!" Nicholas roared. "You are a vile excuse for a Lycan, and I want you to leave my home. Now."

Nina gasped. "Nicholas, you cannot mean that."

"I do." Nicholas stared at Ryker. "Take your human and go. Nina will be staying here."

He yanked his arm back when Emmett tried to take it. "Nicholas, please. I beg you, do not -'

"Get out," Nicholas growled.

There were footsteps in the hallway and James stuck his head into the room. "Nicky? What is wrong?"

"Nothing, James," Nicholas said. "Emmett and Ryker were just leaving. Can you get their wagon ready?"

"Aye. I can do that." James disappeared down the hallway as Nicky snarled under his breath.

"What are you waiting for? Get out."

"Nicholas," Emmett said. Tears ran down his face, and he staggered to the chair by the fireplace and collapsed in it.

Nina tried to run to him, but Nicky held her back. "Stay here, Nina."

Ryker stared at Emmett in alarm. "Emmett, are you all right?"

"Aye. Just feeling a bit weak," he said.

"Bullshit," Nicky said.

"Nicholas, please listen to me," Emmett said. "You're right. I am a terrible Lycan. I've treated Nina horribly over the years, but you have to understand that I do not know any other way to be. My father was hard on me, harder than I am on Nina, and I believed that was the way a father must act if he wanted his child to be strong."

Nicholas snorted and Emmett wiped at the tears on his face. "It is true, Nicholas. I swear it. I love Nina in my own way, of course I do, and I know that I must learn to control my temper and be more patient with her."

He staggered to his feet and approached them. "I am so sorry for the way I have treated you over the years, my sweet Nina. I want you to know that I did not mean it. The things I said to you were born of an anger with your mother. I know that is not your fault and I feel terrible for what I have said and done to you. Will you give me the chance to make it up to you?"

"Why should she believe you?" Nicky said. "The cruel things you have said to her have shown what type of Lycan you really are. And it is not one I care to know."

"I will change. I swear it. Lying in that cell, knowing that I was dying, it changed me, Nicholas. I vowed to be a better father to Nina, to be a better person, and I am sorry that I have broken that vow already. If you, if Nina, would only give me another chance, I will prove it to you," Emmett said.

He turned to Nina. "Please, Nina. I am truly sorry. Will you forgive me?"

"Of course, I will, Daddy." Nina pulled away from Nicholas. She hugged Emmett as he patted her back and kissed her smooth cheek. "I love you."

"I love you too, Nina, very much," Emmett said.

"Please, Nicky," Nina said, "give Daddy another chance. For me?"

"You have a week," Nicky said. "One week to prove to us that you have changed. If I see you treating Nina with disrespect or cruelty, I will throw you out of this house. Do you understand?"

"Aye, I do. Thank you, Nicholas," Emmett said.

"You won't regret this, Nicky," Nina said.

"That remains to be seen," Nicky said. "Come, it is almost breakfast and I must speak to James."

He held out his hand and Nina took it willingly enough. "Daddy, are you joining us?"

"Aye, just give me a moment, sweet Nina." Emmett wiped at the tears on his face. "And if you still want me to, I will watch you ride later."

"I do," Nina said. She squeezed Nicky's hand and smiled happily at him as they left Emmett's room.

Ryker closed the door behind them and leaned against it before studying Emmett. "That was quite the performance."

"I could have a career in the theatre. Could I not?" Emmett said.

"Aye, you could."

Emmett paced in front of the small fireplace. "We must watch everything we say and do, Ryker. Nicholas belongs with me in the city, not here. If that means I must suppress my true nature for a while, I will do so."

"For a while?" Ryker arched his eyebrow at him. "You cannot be so foolish as to think that Nicholas will ever accept you for who you are. The idiot he calls father has raised him to be weak. You would be better off molding Nina into the successor of your business. She, at least, believes every word out of your mouth."

"Aye, you may be right about my son," Emmett said. "In truth, I am more interested in finding out if what you say about that bratty little Lycan is true. If she does have healing powers, then she would be very useful to me in the city."

"And how do you propose to get her to the city?" Ryker said. "You would have to kill the lot of them in order to take her. They may be idiots but there are more of them than us."

Emmett shrugged. "There are always Lycans to be hired for this type of work. Just think, Ryker. If I had both Max and this Leta in my household, the power I would have would be incredible."

"You released Max of her debt, remember?"

"If you think I meant that, then you are as foolish as Nicholas. I will not leave this place without Max."

Ryker shook his head. "You do not understand what she can do, Emmett. She could kill us both with a flick of her hand. There is no way we can take her."

Emmett stared into the flames. "There is always a way."

CHAPTER 27

"You're quiet today."

"Am I?" Max smiled at Nicolas when he put his arms around her waist and kissed her neck.

"Aye. What's wrong?"

"Nothing," Max said. "I'm a little tired. Violet woke up a few times in the night."

"Aye, I heard." Nicholas grinned at her.

"I'm sorry. She isn't always the best sleeper. I could move back into the small room if -"

"Don't be silly." He kissed her mouth. "I don't mind. And I can take my turn with her in the night."

"That's very kind of you but I'm sure you don't want to be half-shifting in the middle of the night to placate my grumpy child."

Nicholas laughed. "She does seem to be obsessed with the shifting, does she not?"

"Aye. Leta spent most of yesterday afternoon shifting back and forth just to amuse her."

"Where is Violet?" Nicholas asked as Leta, wearing her dress from Bree's wedding, skipped into the common room.

"Nina took her to the barn to see the horses."

"Look at my dress, Max. Don't I look pretty?" Leta twirled in front of them. The small stones caught the afternoon sun flooding through the window and Max smiled at the way the little girl seemed to sparkle.

"It's beautiful, Leta."

"Thanks. I wore it for Bree's wedding. I was her flower girl. It's a really important job." Leta continued to twirl as Sophia stuck her head into the room.

"Leta, have you seen Kaden?" She nodded to Max and Nicholas.

Max tried not to let her immediate nervousness show. In the two weeks since they'd returned, she didn't think it was her imagination that Sophia was cool with her. The Lycan female intimidated her and she had no idea how to break through the barrier that Sophia seemed to have toward her.

"Aye. He was going to the barn, he said," Leta said.

"Thanks." Sophia disappeared and Leta turned back to Nicholas and Max.

"I hope it doesn't snow today. Papa, Nina and I are going riding this afternoon. We haven't been able to go all week. The lord McKenzie has been taking up all of Nina's time."

"That's a good thing, Leta. Emmett is making an effort with Nina and that makes Nina very happy," Nicholas said.

"Aye, I guess," Leta said. "I still don't like him."

She stared guiltily at Nicholas. "Sorry, Nicky. I know he's your real papa."

Nicholas winked at her as Kala flew into the room and landed on Leta's head. Leta giggled. "Hi, Kala."

"Leta," Kala said before flying off her head and hovering in front of her face. She blew a kiss to Leta before zipping from the room.

"Wait for me!" Leta chased after her.

"Do you believe Evan, Nina and Leta's story that the pixie healed herself?" Max said.

"No. Leta healed her, I'm almost sure of it," Nicholas said.

"Aye." Max said.

"What is it?" Nicholas said.

Gods, she hated how well he could read her already.

"Emmett seems to be really trying," she said.

"Aye, he does. It's been a week since I told him to leave and he's been a completely different Lycan with Nina and with the rest of us."

"That's true."

"You still don't like him." It was a statement not a question and she gave him a nervous smile.

"I'm sorry, Nicky."

"You don't have to apologize or explain. Emmett was not a good man – that was plain to see. I wish you and Meridan would have told me the truth about him."

"Would you have gone with us to rescue him, had you known?" Max said. "You were on the fence as it was. If we had told you how he really was, you would never have gone with us. Nina was desperate to save her father and Meridan believed that rescuing him would give Emmett a reason to release him of his debt."

"Did you believe the same?"

"No. Honestly, I still can't quite believe that you convinced him to release me of my debt."

Nicholas grinned at her. "Now that you share my bed every night, you have forgotten how determined I can be when I want something."

Max laughed. "Perhaps I should deny you for a night or two – give you the chance to work on your skills of persuasion."

He growled at her before slapping her playfully on the ass. "We both know you cannot resist me."

She poked him in the chest. "Is that a challenge?"

He cupped her breast and rubbed her hardening nipple as he placed a path of kisses down her throat. "Every night after you fall asleep, you rub your ass against my cock until I'm so hard I can't sleep. It doesn't matter how many times I made you come earlier. You're shameless."

She turned bright red and stared at him. "I do not."

"Aye, you do," he said. "It is all I can do not to wake you up for more."

"You could try turning your back to me."

"Aye, I could," he said as his hand slipped inside of her shirt. "But what fun is that? Shall we go back to our bedroom, Max? Violet is with Nina and it seems a shame to waste our alone time."

He reached behind her and squeezed her ass. Max smiled up at him. "I thought you'd never ask."

He took her hand and led her toward the door. "I told you. You can't resist me at all."

She scowled at him. "Keep it up, mister, and you'll see exactly how strong my willpower -"

They both froze when they heard the terrified shout coming from outside.

"FIRE!" Leo bellowed again. He was racing across the yard toward the smaller barn, followed by Jeffrey and Evan.

Max's heart beat fiercely in her chest at she stared out the window at the black smoke rising from the back of the barn. Already she could see flames licking their way across the roof of it and she squeezed Nicholas' hand.

"Violet," she whispered. She could almost feel the blood draining from her face and her entire body trembled wildly as a vase on the mantle above the fireplace fell to the floor and shattered. Nicholas cursed and raced outside. Her legs like blocks of wood, Max stumbled after him.

"THE LAKE! WE NEED WATER FROM THE LAKE!" JEFFREY shouted.

"It's frozen solid." Nicholas started toward the barn and Leo grabbed his arm.

"No, Nicky. It is too dangerous!"

Nicky shoved him away. "Violet and Nina are in there!" The barn was nearly engulfed in flames now and he flinched when a piece of the roof caved in with a loud bang.

Avery appeared beside him. Her face was pale, and fear was etched into her features. "Your father and Marshall have gone in. They will find the girls."

"Sophia and Kaden are in there as well." Nicholas shook off his mother's hand. "I need to get in there, Mama."

He ran toward the barn as James joined him. "We need to be quick, Nicky. The barn is going to collapse any moment."

"Aye, I know," Nicholas said.

They were almost to the barn now. The heat from the flames was tremendous, and Nicholas' eyes watered, and the harsh, acrid smoke filled his lungs. There was a piercing whistle and James yanked him out of the way as horses stampeded from the barn.

They were foaming at the mouth, neighing and rearing with fear as they ran past the Lycans and into the forest surrounding the house.

"Leo! Jeffrey! Go after them!" James shouted as more horses stampeded past them.

Nicky, holding his shirt over his mouth, flinched when a wet blanket was dropped around his shoulders. Maya threw a second blanket over James. Holding them over their heads, water running in cold streams down their faces, the brothers inched forward into the smoke and flames. They heard Marshall shouting and a final horse ran from the barn, its eyes rolling wildly in their sockets as it joined the others in the forest.

A figure appeared in the smoke. Coughing and gagging on the thick smoke, Marshall stumbled out of the barn and collapsed a few feet away. He laid on his back, coughing harshly, as Maya, Doran and Dani surrounded him.

Tristan with Nina in his arms, ran out from the barn. Kaden followed carrying Violet, and Nicky breathed a sigh of relief when Sophia, holding the yowling, struggling Hudson and Piper by the scruffs of their necks, appeared behind Kaden.

"Dad!" Nicky dropped the wet blanket and grabbed his father's arm. "Are you hurt? Is Nina all right?"

"Aye, we're both fine." Tristan coughed as Emmett appeared beside him.

"Nina!" He pulled the young girl from Tristan's arms and cradled her. "Are you all right, my sweet Nina?"

Coughing steadily, Nina choked out, "Violet! Where is Violet? I couldn't find her in the smoke. I couldn't find her!"

She burst into sobs. Emmett sat down in the snow and held her on his lap. "Hush now. She's all right. They have the baby, Nina."

Nicholas followed Kaden as he carried the baby away from the barn. The big man's face was white, and he looked sick to his stomach. Avery threw her coat on the ground and he placed Violet on it as Max fell to her knees beside her.

"Violet? Baby, open your eyes." She rubbed Violet's arms and chest and kissed her face. "Please baby, breathe."

Avery dropped down beside her and rested her hands on Violet's chest before kissing the baby on the mouth.

"C'mon, Violet," she whispered before shouting James' name.

James knelt across from them and joined his mother in touching and stroking Violet's chest and arms as Max stared wide-eyed at her limp body.

"Violet?" Max said as James stared grimly at Avery before lowering his head to the baby's chest.

"I cannot hear a heartbeat," he said.

Max shoved him away from Violet. "You lie!"

She gathered Violet into her arms and rocked her back and forth as she kissed her small face. "Wake up, Violet. Wake up right now! Stop scaring Mama and open your eyes!"

Nicholas knelt beside her. He made a harsh sobbing groan before touching Max's back. "Honey, she's gone. I'm so sorry."

Max raised her face to the sky and screamed. Her body trembling, she placed Violet on Avery's jacket and staggered to her feet. She backed away, her face a combination of shock and grief, and Nicky winced when she reached up and tore at her short hair.

She screamed again. The wind was picking up, the trees swaying, and the flames and smoke from the burning barn were being driven directly toward them. The wagon sitting in the side yard suddenly exploded in a splintering crash, and chunks of wood and metal were sent flying into the air as the others ducked and cringed. Behind them, every window in the house exploded with a sound like a jagged cough. Shards of glass spun crazily in the wind and Dani cried out in pain when a large piece of glass embedded itself in her leg.

Andric pushed her to the ground and covered her body with his as Jackar knelt beside them.

"Andric! What is happening?"

"Lie down and cover your head, Jackar!" Andric shouted as another chunk of wood flew over their heads. Marshall, still coughing and wheezing, yanked Maya off her feet and into the snow as the seat to the wagon whipped by her.

"Bree!" James ran across the yard, stepping in front of her just as a wheel from the wagon bounced toward her. It hit him in the back with a bone-jarring thud that dropped him to his knees. He grunted with pain as Bree cried his name and crouched before him.

"I'm fine!" He drew her into his embrace. He used his large body to shelter her from the branches and stones that were flying through the air, and he made another loud grunt of pain when a board peeled away from the house and slammed into his side.

The wind continued to howl as there were thunderous crashes from the forest. The trees were being uprooted as though an invisible giant simply plucked them like flowers. Max, her body shaking like a live wire, screamed repeatedly as Nicholas fought against the wind to get close to her.

"Nicholas! No! She'll rip you apart!" Doran shouted.

He ignored his cousin and moved in front of Max. "Max, stop! You have to control it, honey! Control it!"

She stared at him and he shuddered at the look of madness in her eyes. The air was suddenly closing in around him. His ears were ringing and the hair on his body stood on end as electricity crackled around him. He could feel his body starting to swell from the pressure, it felt like his eyes would simply pop from their sockets.

He was about to die.

Max was gone, lost to her power, and he stared wide-eyed at her as the pressure intensified.

"I love you," he said.

For one brief, terrifying moment the pressure and pain became unbearable and he howled in agony before Max tore her gaze from his face and stared at the burning barn. It exploded with a deafening bang and the others ran for cover as fire rained down around them.

Max turned to the forest, raising her hands above her head and shrieking Violet's name. The wind shrieked back, becoming a blustering, moaning, unstoppable force, and all the trees within a ten-foot radius flattened to the ground with a ground-shaking *whomp*.

A burning board slammed into Nicky's back, knocking him to the ground. He scrambled to his feet, barely noticing the pain in his back. Max collapsed to her knees in the snow and sobbed into her hands.

The wind died down in an instant and the others climbed cautiously to their feet, staring at each other with shell-shocked gazes as Nicky approached Max. "Max?"

"Don't cry, Max." Leta appeared beside Nicky. She rested her hand on Max's head for a moment. "The baby bird is only sleeping."

She drifted through the deep snow. Her dress, the stones reflecting off the snow so brightly they created a halo of light around her, made her look nearly ethereal. She knelt next to Violet as Max lifted her head and stared numbly at the young girl.

"It's time to wake up now, baby bird," Leta crooned. She gathered Violet into her arms and kissed her mouth.

When Violet's body continued to hang limply in her arms, Leta cradled her closer and cupped the back of her head before kissing the baby's mouth again. "Can you hear me, baby bird? Open your eyes."

Max made a harsh, keening cry when Violet's body

twitched in Leta's arms and she coughed weakly before opening her eyes and staring at Leta. "Want Mama."

"She's right here." Leta kissed her forehead and stood up, holding Violet close.

Max staggered to her feet and stumbled forward. "Violet?"

"Mama." Violet held her arms out and Max took her into her arms.

"Hi, Mama."

"Hi, Violet." Sobbing, Max covered her pale face with kisses as Nicholas joined them.

"Puppy." Violet grinned at him and he touched her soft hair with a shaking hand.

"Hi, baby."

Tristan lifted up Leta and kissed her cheek before taking Avery's hand.

"I'm sorry, Papa," Leta said. "I know I shouldn't have done that."

She glanced at the others. Ryker was standing next to Emmett and Nina, and both he and Emmett were staring at her.

"I'm sorry." She stared anxiously at Avery and Tristan.

"Shh, Leta," Avery said as Tristan rubbed Leta's back. "You did the right thing."

Leta wrapped her arms around Tristan's neck and hugged him. Still standing with Max and Violet, Nicholas glanced at Avery. Dread was etched into her face and she was staring at Emmett and Ryker. Tristan squeezed her hand until she looked at him.

"Do not worry, my love. I will keep her safe," he said.

"Aye, I know," Avery said, but Nicholas could hear the fear in her voice.

CHAPTER 28

"Max? May I come in?" Avery knocked on the bedroom door before opening it.

Violet was asleep in the bed and Max was packing their clothes into her leather bag.

"How is Violet?" Avery approached the bed.

It was cold in the room. Marshall, Doran, Andric and Jackar were placing plastic or boards over each of the broken windows, she could hear the soft pounding of their hammers from the other side of the house, but even with the plastic covering the window the cold wind was seeping into the room.

"She is – is good." Max continued to shove clothes into the bag. "She had a bite to eat and then we cuddled, and she fell asleep."

She glanced at Avery. "How is everyone else? Are they – is anyone seriously hurt?"

"Mostly just bumps and bruises. Vivian's arm was broken by a board and the glass in Dani's leg was fairly large but -"

Max moaned in dismay and Avery shook her head. "They

are all fine now. Leta went around to everyone and," she hesitated, "helped them."

Tears were slipping down Max's face and she brushed them away angrily.

"How are you?" Avery said.

Max laughed, the note of hysterics in it made Avery nervous. "I'm just great. I mean, my child died today and was brought back to life, I tried to destroy your house, hurt your loved ones, and nearly murdered the man I love but I -"

She made a hoarse, barking sob and buried her face in her hands. Her body shook, and she sagged against Avery when the Avery put her arms around her. She stroked Max's hair and crooned soft words of comfort as Max sobbed.

After a few moments, Max straightened and wiped the tears from her face. "I'm so sorry."

"It's fine. You needed to get it out." Avery took her hands and squeezed them. "Why are you packing your things, my love?"

"Why?" Max stared at her. "I nearly killed your child and I almost destroyed your home. I am a danger to you and your family, and you cannot possibly wish that I stay."

"We all understand why it happened and no one blames you," Avery said.

"You cannot mean that, my lady."

"I do," Avery said. "If you leave, it will destroy Nicky."

"How do you know that? Have you spoken with him? I came within seconds of killing him. Why would he ever want me to stay?"

"I have not spoken with him," Avery said. "He has been helping his father and Kaden round up the horses from the forest and move them into the other barn. But I do not need to speak with him to know that he does not want you to leave."

She gave Max a small smile. "I know my Nicky and if

you leave – he will go after you. He has chosen you as his mate. You know that, do you not?"

Her bottom lip trembling, Max shook her head. "With time he will forget about me and find another mate. Someone who -"

"I did not take you for a fool, Max."

"Why are you being so kind?"

"Why would I not?" She took Max's hands. "You are focusing on what almost happened instead of what actually happened."

"What do you mean?"

Avery squeezed her hands. "During the worst moment of your life, you controlled your powers."

Max blinked at her, opened her mouth, and then closed it again. Avery kissed her on the forehead. "You controlled them, Max. I know it was close and I know right now you feel terrible, but I believe you need to give it a few days before you make any rash decisions about leaving."

"I told you, my lady, I do not believe that Nicky will want -"

"At least wait and speak with him, Max. I think you will be surprised by what Nicholas wants. Will you speak with him first?"

"Aye, I can do that." Max said.

Avery hugged her hard. "Good. Now, I'm going to bring you some food and you're going to eat every bit of it and then crawl into bed with Violet. You need to rest, my love."

"IS THAT THE LAST OF THEM?" JAMES ASKED AS KADEN AND Nicholas led the two cold and shivering horses into the larger barn.

"Aye. We got lucky and found nearly all of them in the same area." Kaden led Rosie into the last empty stall and threw a blanket over her shivering body before rubbing her nose.

"Do you know where your sister is?" He left the stall and latched it.

"I'm right here." Sophia emerged from the back of the barn. She hooked her arm around Kaden's waist as he leaned down and kissed her on the mouth.

"How do you feel?" he said.

"Fine." She smiled at him. "Nothing a hug from Leta couldn't fix."

She squeezed his waist. "You lost all of your belongings in the fire, Kaden. I'm sorry."

"They're only things, little Lycan. What matters is that no one is hurt and -"

He yelped in pain when Piper came flying out of nowhere and attacked his leg.

"The gods be damned!" He grabbed Piper by the scruff of the neck and pulled him off his leg.

"You could try being a bit more grateful, you rotten cat," he said as Piper hissed at him.

He dropped him gently to the ground and Piper hissed again before disappearing into an empty stall. They could hear him growling softly and Hudson's answering growl, and Kaden rolled his eyes. "I don't regret climbing into the hayloft and risking my life to save his, at all."

Sophia grinned at him. "He's just upset. He'll calm down in a few days and be back to the loving Piper we all know."

James snorted as Sophia kissed Kaden on the cheek. "Thank you for saving my rotten cat, human."

"Aye, you're welcome." He tugged lightly on her braid.

She turned toward Nicholas. He was standing apart from them, staring silently at the horses, and Sophia went to him.

"Baby brother? Are you all right?"

"Aye, I'm fine. Why?"

Sophia cupped his face. "You almost died today, Nicky. Max nearly killed you."

"No, she didn't."

She sighed before glancing at James. "She did and we all know it. Nicky, I know you care for her, but she is dangerous."

Nicholas glared at her and she cupped his face again. "She does not mean to be, I know that. But the power she wields – it is a danger to us all. What if she hadn't stopped today? She would have killed you, that is certain, and possibly the rest of us as well."

"Her daughter was dead! Do you blame her for reacting the way she did?" Nicky said.

"No. I do not," Sophia said. "But I love you, Nicky, and I have no desire to see you or the rest of my loved ones be in danger. I do not think she should stay with us any longer."

Nicholas pulled away from her. "She is my mate, Sophia. If she leaves, so will I."

"Nicky -"

"No! I will not discuss this any longer." Nicholas pulled away from her and stalked out of the barn.

Sophia stared helplessly at James. "I am not trying to upset him, James. I just – I'm worried about him."

"Aye, I know," James said. "But if you continue to push him about this, he will leave with her. You know he will."

Sophia rubbed at her forehead. "What are we supposed to do then?"

"I don't know," James said.

"ARE YOU CERTAIN THAT NO ONE SAW YOU?"

"Aye, I told you that," Ryker said. "The only ones in the barn were Nina and Violet and neither of them saw me start the blaze."

"Good." Emmett stared into the fire. "It turned out better than I thought it would. The demonstration of both Max's and Leta's powers was beyond my wildest imagination."

He stroked his chin. "Do you remember Teagen?"

"Aye, the blacksmith."

"Tomorrow morning you leave for the city. You will go straight to Teagen and give him a description of the silver collars the leeches used to hold us prisoner. We will need at least a dozen of them. While he is making the collars, you are to go to the south side of the city and speak with Jonathan. He will arrange for as many Lycans as we need."

Ryker frowned at Emmett. "One – why would Teagen ever make collars that would trap his own kind and two – there will be a hefty price for the number of Lycans we require. Jonathan does not provide his services cheaply."

"I realize that. Do you think me a fool?" Emmett said. "The cost does not matter. I will do and pay whatever it takes to get my hands on that girl."

"There is still the matter of Teagen -"

"The gods be damned, Ryker! Must you question everything? You will tell Teagen that the collars will be considered payment of his debt. That will erase any lingering misgivings he may have about making them."

"Fine!" Ryker said. "I will return to the city and do what you ask. I grow tired of the country and this ridiculous family, anyway. But before I go, would you mind telling me how you think you're going to stop Max? She'll rip us apart if we give her the chance."

Emmett smiled bitterly at him. "I have one more errand for you, Ryker. You are to go to Darven's and purchase some pine nettle syrup."

"And will it be you who gets close enough to use it on her?"

"We will figure out a way."

"Aye," Ryker said, "of course we will. And do you believe it will stop her from using her powers to destroy us?"

"She cannot destroy us if she cannot see us," Emmett said.

There was a knock on the door and Emmett called, "Come in."

He smiled when Nicholas and Tristan entered the room. "Nicholas! How are you feeling, son?"

"Fine," Nicky said.

"Good, I am glad to hear it. And the others? I was just on my way downstairs to check on your sister."

"We were very lucky." Nicholas glanced at Tristan. "There is a matter that we must speak with you about."

"You are here to ask me to keep the young Lycan's powers a secret." Emmett said.

"Aye, we are," Tristan said. "It is a matter of great importance that no one outside of this family knows what she is capable of. She is my child and I will do whatever is necessary to protect her. Do the both of you understand what I am saying?"

Emmett held his hands up. "My lord Williams, of course we do. You forget, I am the father of a young girl and I understand perfectly your desire to protect her."

He gave them a wide smile. "Nicholas is my son and I would never do anything that would jeopardize or put his adopted family in harm's way. What Leta can do will never be revealed by either me or Ryker."

"Do I have your word on that?" Tristan said.

"Of course." Emmett held his hand out and Tristan shook it.

"Now," Emmett clasped his hands behind his back and smiled at Nicky, "I don't suppose you are interested in traveling back to the city with me in the next day or so?"

"Nicholas shook his head. "I will be staying to help Dad and the others rebuild the barn."

"That's what I thought." Emmett cleared his throat. "I have been away from my business for too long, but I would very much like to stay with you for a little longer, if that is agreeable to you. I would, of course, gladly help with the clean-up and the rebuilding of the barn."

"That is very kind of you, lord McKenzie, but if your business requires your attention, we have more than enough hands to help us rebuild," Tristan said.

"Nonsense!" Emmett said. "You can always use more people for this kind of thing. I've already decided to send Ryker to the city on my behalf. He is more than familiar with the business, and he will let my associates know that I have escaped the leeches' clutches and will be returning soon."

"Very well." Tristan gave Emmett a strained smile and he and Nicholas left the room.

MAX CAUGHT HER BREATH AND HER HEART QUICKENED WHEN the door to the bedroom opened. It was late evening. She had not seen Nicky since she had nearly killed him this morning. She'd been hiding in his room like an embarrassed child, and she had no idea what he would say or do. Frankly, despite her earlier talk with Avery, she was shocked he was even in here.

Perhaps he is here to tell you to leave his home and never come back.

She bit back her sob and stared down at Violet's sweet face. The little girl was in Nicky's bed with her. She had told herself she was doing it because it was still cold in the room despite the flames radiating warmth from the fireplace, but in truth she hadn't had the heart to move her into her own bed. She had almost lost Violet forever and she needed desperately to feel her child's warmth and touch her soft skin as reassurance that she was all right.

If Nicholas asked her to leave, she would do so. It didn't matter that she loved him. She had nearly killed him, and he would have to be insane to want her after today. She would not beg or plead for a second chance. She would accept his decision and move on. Violet was all that mattered, she reminded herself, not her own heart's desire.

She jerked in surprise when Nicholas slid into the bed behind her. He put his arm around her waist and rested his chin on her shoulder as he stared at Violet. "How is she?"

"Fine," she said. "She's acting perfectly normal."

"That's good." He kissed her shoulder through her shirt. "How are you?"

"Nicky, I…" She twisted around to face him. He stroked her face from her jaw to her temple, his warm fingers sending shivers down her spine.

"Why are you here?" she said.

A small smile crossed his face. "This is my bed."

"No, that isn't what I meant. I mean -"

"I know what you mean, sweetheart." He studied her face in the dim light of the candle before pressing his mouth against hers in a gentle kiss. "I'm here because I love you."

She choked back her soft sob as tears ran down her face. "I almost killed you today."

"You didn't."

"But I -"

"You didn't." He kissed her again and stroked her back. "I love you, Max. I love you and I love Violet, and I want to be your mate and Violet's father. I want to spend the rest of my life with you, and I will do whatever it takes to make you and Violet happy."

"You aren't looking for a relationship," she said. "You just want a – a quickie."

He laughed so loudly that Violet made a soft snort of displeasure and rolled away from them. She curled into a ball and muttered, "bad puppy" before lapsing into loud snoring.

"You made me see the light, sweetheart. And now you're stuck with me forever."

She threw her arms around him and hugged him. "I'm sorry, Nicky. I'm so sorry. I was out of my mind and I lost control, but I swear I never meant to hurt you. I won't lose control like that again. I promise you. I know that doesn't mean much but -"

"Stop," he said. "It's all right, my love."

"I do not deserve you."

He frowned at her. "That isn't true. Do not say that again, Max."

She kissed him and hugged him again. He returned her hug before giving her a nervous look. "Do you – that is – do you have feelings for me?"

She stared blankly at him and he said, "It is understandable if you do not uh, feel as strongly for me as I do for you. I know we haven't known each other long and I -"

"Nicholas, I love you," she said quickly. "Why would you think I do not?"

"You've never said it." The look of relief on his face was oddly adorable. "I'm not trying to push you into anything, Max. If you need more time I'll understand, but I'm not letting you go. I can't."

"I love you, I love you, I love you," she whispered before cupping his face and pressing kisses across his face. "I love you."

He laughed and she said, "Technically I've said it more times than you now."

He gave her a wicked grin and cupped her breast. "I prefer showing you how much I love you, sweetheart."

She made a soft moan of approval when he pinched her nipple lightly, before glancing at Violet sleeping next to her. She bit at her lip. She wanted Nicholas but her desire to keep Violet close was overriding her desire for Nicky.

"Nicholas, I'm sorry, I -"

"Do not apologize. Violet comes first."

She smiled gratefully at him and turned on to her side. Nicholas spooned her as she reached out and stroked Violet's warm back before tucking the covers more firmly around her. "Did you know that Leta could – could bring back the dead?"

His warm breath washed over the back of her neck. "We suspected it. She saved Dad's life the day he was shot with that arrow, but we weren't entirely sure if he had actually died and Leta brought him back or if she healed him before he died."

Guilt flooded through her. She needed to tell Nicholas that it was Ryker who had tried to kill Tristan, but she was afraid. Afraid of what would happen when he found out the truth. Nicholas would go after him and Ryker and Emmett were dangerous. Emmett might be pretending that he was a changed man, but she doubted that he could keep up the pretense for much longer.

And if Nicky finds out that it was Ryker? What do you think he'll say and do to you when he discovers you knew all along?

She shoved the voice out of her head. She was a coward, she knew that, but deep down she secretly hoped that Emmett would be unable to continue to deny his true nature and that Nicky would simply banish both him and Ryker from his home.

Emmett will never let you go. And now that he knows about Leta, he's even more dangerous.

"I – I'm worried now that Emmett knows about Leta," she said. "I know he's trying to change but I'm not certain that he can ever truly become a good person."

"He released you of your father's debt," he said.

"Aye, he did."

He kissed the back of her head. "Dad and I spoke to Emmett and Ryker about keeping Leta's secret. They promised not to reveal it."

"Do you believe them?"

She felt him shrug behind her. "I don't know. But they would be wise to stay true to their word. My father is very," he paused, "protective of his loved ones. He will do what is necessary to keep them safe from men like Ryker and Lycans like Emmett."

"You mean he would kill Ryker and Emmett," she said.

"Aye." He didn't hesitate. "He would."

She twisted her head to study his face. "Even though Emmett is your birth father?"

"Aye."

"How do you feel about that?" It was a stupid question, but she couldn't think of any other way to put it.

"I don't know. Does it make me a fool to just hope that it does not come to that?"

She shook her head. "No. I don't think so."

He sighed again and she took a good look at him. There were dark circles under his eyes and tiny lines of weariness etched around his mouth. He needed rest and she was babbling away to him. She raised his hand to her mouth and kissed his knuckles gently. "I think we should try and get some sleep. Do you mind if Violet sleeps in the bed with us tonight?"

"No." He blew the candle out before nuzzling her neck affectionately. "I love you."

She smiled into the darkness. "I love you, Nicky."

CHAPTER 29

M ax stared nervously at Sophia. In the month since the fire she'd been shocked by how quickly Nicky's family had accepted her. Despite the destruction she had caused, despite the fact that she had come within seconds of simply obliterating Nicky, they'd been nothing but kind to her and Violet.

The only two that were distant toward her were Sophia and Vivian, and she had a feeling that Vivian was distant with almost everyone. Nicky's grandmother made her nervous and one afternoon she had shared that with Bree.

Bree had grinned at her and nodded. "Aye, I know exactly what you mean. When I first arrived at James' home, I was terrified of her." She glanced around before leaning closer. "Truthfully, I still am a little."

She hooked her arm through Max's and grinned again at her. "Mama says that deep down Vivian is actually very soft hearted and that we would know if she didn't like us."

Max gave her a doubtful look, but the topic of their conversation walked into the room at that very moment. Vivian, Andric at her side, was grinning at the sandy-haired

Lycan, and Max blinked in surprise when Andric said something too low for her to hear and a soft blush crossed the old Lycan's face.

"Perhaps," Bree murmured to her, "we should take lessons in charm from Andric. He has her wrapped around his finger and has from the moment she met him."

Bree snickered and Vivian arched her eyebrows at her as Dani and Jackar joined them in the room. "Something funny, little Bree?"

"No, my lady," Bree said sweetly. "Max and I were just going to the kitchen to get some tea. Would you like some?"

"Aye, that's kind of you." Vivian sat down with a soft thud in the chair by the fireplace and Bree had taken Max's arm and led her from the room.

Now, Max waited patiently as Sophia continued to speak to Marian.

"Honestly, Marian. You need to go. You haven't been to town in forever and you deserve the break. We're perfectly capable of cooking our own meals."

"It is not just me that would be leaving," Marian fretted. "Nadine and Laura are going as well. There's the laundry and the housework and -"

Sophia laughed. "It is two days, Marian. Renee will want your help in picking out her wedding dress and besides, Uncle Marshall and Aunt Maya are returning home tomorrow. Grandmamma is going with them and so is Pavina and Andric and Jackar. We will be fine for a couple of days without you. I promise."

"I don't know," Marian said. "It doesn't feel right to just be -"

Sophia shook her head. "Marian, I love you, but if you do not go, I will tie you up and throw you in the wagon myself."

Marian giggled like a schoolgirl. "Aye, I imagine you

would. Fine, I will go. It would be nice to pick out a new dress for Jeffrey and Renee's wedding."

"Good!" Sophia pushed her gently toward the hallway. "Now go and pack your things. I will finish the lunch dishes. Jeffrey said you would be leaving at first light tomorrow."

"You're a sweet girl, Sophia." Marian kissed the Lycan's cheek and waved to Max before starting down the hallway. "Hello, Max."

"Hi, Marian." Max cleared her throat.

Sophia plunged her hands into the sink of dishes. Max picked up a dishtowel and stood next to her.

They washed and dried the dishes in silence for a few minutes until Max gave Sophia a tentative smile. "How are you today, Sophia?"

"I'm well, and you?"

"Good, thank you." She placed the bowl she had just dried in the cupboard and grabbed a glass. "I wondered if I could speak with you about your brother."

"Go ahead."

Max took a deep breath. Part of her had been certain that Sophia would simply deny her request and for a moment she had no idea what to say.

"I – I love him," she blurted out.

"Aye, that is obvious," Sophia said.

"I just wanted you to know that I would never hurt him, and I understand why you do not like me, but I promise you I will treat him well." She groaned at how foolish she sounded.

"Max, it is not that I don't like you. I know I am coming across that way but truly, it has nothing to do with whether I like you or not," Sophia said.

When Max didn't reply, she scrubbed at a plate for a moment before continuing. "Did you know that Nicky nearly died when he was a baby?"

Max gave her a surprised look and Sophia nodded. "Aye, it is true. He was a very sick baby. He could not keep milk down and he coughed and wheezed nearly all the time. After our mother was taken by the leeches, I remember thinking that now I was the one responsible for him. Not that our mother took very good care of him, she didn't, but I was so frightened at the thought that Nicholas would die. My mother's cousin told me that my father was coming for me, but that Nicky would be sent to the orphanage. When Papa arrived, I took Nicholas and hid in the attic of our house. Although I was worried that Nicky would die because of something I did or didn't do, I was more terrified that Papa would take me away from him and he would die alone."

"How old were you?" Max said.

"Seven."

Max gave her a sympathetic look. "That is a heavy burden for a child."

"Aye, I suppose," Sophia said.

She rinsed the plate before staring out the window in front of her. "It did not take long for Papa to find us in the attic. I could hear his footsteps on the stairs, they were so loud and heavy, and I was terrified. He opened the door and I remember I had to crane my neck to look at him. He was the biggest Lycan I'd ever seen."

She smiled faintly. "He crouched and stared at me so solemnly. I was holding Nicky in my arms and he was wheezing and starting to cry, and I tried to quiet him. I knew if I were to have any chance at keeping Nicky with me that I would have to convince Papa that he wasn't a bad baby. Papa asked if I knew who he was and I just looked at him and," she paused and her smile widened, "I blurted out that I would not leave Nicky behind. I told Papa I would kill him if he tried to stop me from bringing Nicky with us. My fear was starting the shift, at that time I did not have much control over it, and Nicholas was outright screaming by that point."

"What did Tristan do?" Max said.

"He simply nodded and told me that of course we would bring Nicholas with us. A rush of relief went through me, it was so strong I thought my knees would buckle, but when Papa reached for Nicky, I growled at him and tried to bite him."

She shook her head at the memory. "Papa didn't even flinch. He promised me that no one would hurt Nicky or me and that we would not leave the city without him. I had no reason to believe him. I had no memory of him and no way to tell if he was lying to appease me. But I knew he was not. There was something in his face that, even as a child, made me understand that he could be trusted. He held out his hands for Nicky and I passed him over. He held him gently and tried to soothe him before taking my hand and leading me out of the attic. We left for his home the very next day."

"Did Nicholas get well on his own or did Avery heal him?" Max said.

Sophia gave her a startled look. "You know about Mama?"

Before Max could reply, she shook her head. "Of course, you do. Nicky would have told you."

"He didn't, actually," Max said. "I discovered it on my own. I knew about Leta of course, and then your mother hugged me and, well…"

"Aye, it is not difficult to figure out that she is different once she touches you. Papa tries to stop her from touching people as often as he can, but Mama is a hugger." Sophia laughed.

Max smiled as Sophia continued. "Mama healed Nicholas. He would have died had it not been for her. We didn't know at the time that she had done it, she had been bought by my father to work in the household and she was keeping her powers a secret from us, but we discovered the truth fairly quickly."

She sighed. "I love Nicholas deeply, Max. He will always be my baby brother and perhaps because I was responsible for him when he was a baby, I am overly protective of him. I know he is a grown man and I know how much he loves you, but I am finding it difficult to not worry. Do you understand?"

"Aye, I do," Max said. "I promise I won't hurt him, Sophia."

"And I promise to stop being such a bitch."

Max gaped at her as Sophia grinned.

"You weren't a – a bitch." Max tried to make it sound like the truth and Sophia's grin widened.

"You're a terrible liar, Max." She handed her a bowl to dry. "Now, do you think my cousin Doran has a chance with Pavina? He's quite smitten with her no matter how much he denies it."

EARLY THE NEXT MORNING, MAX WATCHED AS NICHOLAS AND his family said their goodbyes. She smiled at Pavina and hugged her when the Lycan threw her arms around her.

"I will see you in a couple of weeks, Max," Pavina said.

Max nodded. "I am surprised that Emmett agreed to let you go. You are still under his employment."

"Aye, I was surprised as well. I had barely gotten the request out before he was agreeing to it."

Pavina turned to look at Emmett. He was standing off to the side, holding Nina's hand and smiling down at her as she talked animatedly to him.

"Perhaps he really has changed," Pavina said.

"He has not," Max said. "Do not let him fool you into thinking he has. No doubt this will cost you something."

Pavina's face fell and Max immediately felt guilt. "I'm sorry, Pavina. That was rude of me. Go and have a wonderful time with Doran and his family."

"Aye, I will." Pavina glanced quickly at Doran. "I like him, Max."

She blushed as Max grinned and squeezed her waist. "I'm glad."

"I mean, he talks entirely too much about our future and he acts as though I have already agreed to be his mate, but I have never felt this way before."

Max laughed. "Try not to be married to Doran before you return to us."

Pavina stared at her with horror. "Bite your tongue, Max!"

Max laughed as Pavina hurried away to Doran. Violet's delighted squeal brought a smile to her face. Nicky was throwing her up in the air and the little girl shrieked again as he caught her and tickled her round belly before hugging Maya goodbye.

The last month had been the happiest time of her life. Violet was happy and growing more attached to Nicholas with each passing day, and she knew that Nicky loved both her and Violet. If it wasn't for her lingering doubt that Emmett would try and use her power and Leta's power for his own gain, she would have no worries at all. She glanced over at Emmett and Nina.

Emmett was staring at her, there was something cold and calculating about his gaze, and a shiver wracked her body. She stood a little straighter and returned his gaze defiantly. After a moment, he smiled and nodded at her and she nodded back stiffly before turning to join Nicky and Violet.

"This feels weird," Leta said.

"What does, my love?" Avery passed her a bowl of potatoes.

"There's hardly anyone here. It's too quiet." Leta stared around the dinner table as Tristan ruffled her hair.

"It has been a long time since we've had so few visitors," he said.

"I agree with Leta. It's weird," Sophia said.

Tristan laughed. "Jeffrey, Leo and the others will be back the day after tomorrow, and I'm sure it will not be long before Maya and Marshall return. They do have to bring Mother back at some point."

"Aye, you are right." Avery smiled at Emmett. "Help yourself to more venison, Emmett."

"Thank you, my lady. The food is as delicious as Marian's." He piled more meat onto his plate.

"Do you know when Ryker will be returning?" Avery said.

"I imagine any day now. I'm surprised he's been gone this long," Emmett said.

"Will we be returning to the city soon, Daddy?" Nina said.

"Missing your friends, are you?" Emmett said with a smile.

Nina shrugged before glancing at Evan. "No. I've decided I like country living."

"Have you now?" Emmett laughed. "My little city girl has been influenced by her big brother."

Nina flushed. "It's very pretty here."

"Aye that it is. But we cannot overstay our welcome," Emmett said. "The lord Williams has been very gracious in allowing us to stay for so long, but we will have to return to the city soon."

He glanced at Nicky. "Perhaps you will join us for a visit."

"Perhaps," Nicky said. 'Would you care to see the city again, Max?"

Max paused in cutting up the meat on Violet's plate. "It does not matter to me. I enjoy country living and the city holds many bad memories."

"I imagine it does," Emmett said with a brittle smile. "Still, you should not deny Nicholas the chance to make his own opinions on the city."

"I wouldn't dream of it." Her own smile was strained. "If Nicky wants to go to the city, I will not stop him."

She could feel the tension like a thick cloud between her and Emmett. She had spent the last month doing her best to avoid him but with the household less crowded now, she had a feeling it was about to become more difficult."

She breathed a sigh of relief when Violet broke the awkward silence. "I have to potty, Mama."

"Okay, honey. I'll take you."

"No." The little girl shook her head. "Puppy take me."

"Honey, Nicky is eating. Mama will take you to the potty," Max said, but Nicholas was already standing.

"Come here, baby." He lifted Violet into his arms and kissed her soft cheek.

"I have to poop, puppy," she said.

James laughed as Max pushed back her chair. "Here, you don't need to be a part of that joyous occasion."

Nicholas shrugged. "It's fine. I don't mind."

He carried Violet from the room as James snickered again.

Bree elbowed him lightly. "Laugh it up, my love. It will be your turn soon enough."

"I thought we agreed that the diapers would be best handled by you, little one," James said.

Bree rolled her eyes. "You suggested it. I did not agree to it."

Evan, sitting on the other side of James, poked him good naturedly. "Your hands are so large and clumsy, there's no way you're not getting poop on them when you change a diaper."

"Evan," Avery chastised. "We're at the dinner table."

"Sorry, mama." Evan grinned at her. "But James started it."

"Technically, Violet started it," James said.

"She's three, James!" Bree laughed as he leaned down and kissed her forehead.

Max couldn't stop the smile from crossing her face. She had always longed for a big family and as she stared at Nicky's family, she sighed happily. She had finally found what she was looking for.

CHAPTER 30

"It's about time." Emmett leaned against the house and glared at Ryker. "It's been over a moon."

Ryker shrugged. "It took time to get what you asked for, Emmett. Where are the others?"

"That Red bitch is in the kitchen with the little blonde woman. The rest of them are working in the barn. We got lucky. Marshall and Maya returned home yesterday, and the slaves are in town. It will be easier than we thought."

Ryker grunted as Emmett stared into the trees. "Did you get the Lycans I asked for?"

"Aye, they're in the woods. We have ten minutes before they show themselves."

"Good. I will draw Leta toward me. You will -"

"Have you thought about how we're going to handle Max?" Ryker said. "I have the pine nettle syrup but if she sees me coming, she'll kill me before I get the chance to -"

"Your timing is perfect," Emmett said. "Max and her child are napping in Nicholas' room. Get up there before she wakes."

"Fine," Ryker snarled. "But if this doesn't work, Emmett,

if it doesn't stop her, we're all dead. You know that, do you not?"

"Of course, I do. It will work," Emmett growled. "But only if you go now."

Ryker, his face pale and grim, headed into the house as Emmett withdrew a dagger from his belt. Nina was just leaving the half-built barn and he swiped the dagger across his arm. He hissed as blood appeared from the deep cut and dripped down his arm.

Holding his arm, he walked quickly around the side of the house as Nina waved at him.

"Hi, Daddy! Are you going to watch me ride today? I'm going to try riding Bella and -"

She stopped, her eyes widening at the blood dripping into the snow. "Daddy! What happened?"

"It's nothing, Nina. Do not worry." He grimaced and staggered a little on his feet. "It will heal in a day or two."

"It's really bleeding." She gave him a worried look. "Maybe I should get Leta. She would heal you. I know she would."

"Do not trouble the poor girl." He winced as more blood dripped down his arm. "I do not wish to be a burden."

"It's not!" She started toward the house. "Stay right here. I'll bring Leta to you."

"Thank you, my sweet Nina." He waited nervously, scanning the trees every few minutes for signs of the other Lycans. "The gods be damned! Where is she?"

"Daddy!" Nina came around the corner of the house with Leta on her heels. "I found Leta."

"Thank you, my love." He glanced into the woods again.

Leta stared at him with obvious mistrust before reaching out and placing her hand on the cut. A tingling warmth when through him and he twitched a little before she pulled her hand back. He stared at the smooth skin and wiped away the blood as Leta used the snow to scrub his blood from her hand.

"Thank you, Leta. You are very kind to help me."

"Aye, you're welcome."

He held his hand out and smiled encouragingly at her. After a moment she took his hand and shook it. She frowned when his hand tightened around hers. "Let go of me."

Without replying, he yanked the little girl toward him and whipped her around. He held his dagger to her chest as she snarled and swelled in his arms.

"If you shift, I'll plunge this dagger into your heart. Do you hear me, you little brat?"

She stiffened in his arms as Nina stared at him. "Daddy? Daddy – what are you doing?"

"Be quiet, Nina." He glared at her as over thirty Lycans loped silently out from the trees. They leaped over the fallen trees gracefully and he nodded to the largest one. It carried a leather bag around its neck and as the Lycans stopped in front of him, it shifted and dropped the leather bag to the ground.

"There are two women in the kitchen. Bring them to me alive."

The Lycan nodded to five of the wolves and they slunk toward the house. Nina, her face white, backed away. "You – you can't do this, Daddy."

"Nina, get over here and keep your mouth shut or I will kill Leta. Do you hear me?" He growled at her.

She nodded as tears dripped down her cheeks. "It'll be all right, Leta," she said. "Just – just do what he says, okay?"

The little girl growled before snapping her teeth at Emmett. He shook her roughly and pressed the dagger against her chest. "Enough!"

She slumped against him. "My papa will kill you."

"I'm going to kill your papa and your mama if you don't shut your mouth," Emmett said.

Leta's face paled and she began to cry as Emmett turned her to face the barn. He nodded to the biggest Lycan. "Give me one of the collars."

The Lycan opened the leather bag and pulled out a silver collar. It gleamed in the sun and Leta whimpered when he locked it around her neck. She touched the silver prongs on the inside of the collar and Emmett grinned at her.

"You won't want to shift, Leta. You know what the silver will do to you if you shift to your Lycan form."

The barn door suddenly swung open and Emmett stiffened. "Here we go."

Tristan ran from the barn. He was followed by Evan, Nicholas, Sophia, James, and Kaden, and they all skidded to a stop and stared at the group of Lycans standing in the yard.

"Good morning!" Emmett called as the Lycans began to growl.

"Let her go," Tristan said. His body swelling and Emmett shook his head.

"Do not shift, Lycan. If you do, I'll kill the little brat." He pressed the dagger against Leta's chest before cocking his head. "Do you think she'll die or will she heal herself? I confess, I'm curious."

"You're not going to kill her. You want her powers." Tristan stalked toward them.

Emmett laughed. "Do you care to find out if I will? Is it worth risking the life of your child?"

"Daddy," Nina whispered. "Please don't. This isn't right. She saved your life and you cannot -"

"Shut up, Nina!" Emmett turned and backhanded her across the face.

She fell to the ground, knocked unconscious from the blow, and Nicholas snarled at him.

Emmett shook his head. "Do not shift, Nicholas. I'll kill both Leta and Nina if you do."

"She's your child!" Nicholas shouted. "Are you mad?"

Emmett shrugged. "Perhaps."

He nodded to the Lycan standing beside him and the Lycan bent and pulled more collars from the leather bag at his feet.

"My friends are going to put these collars around your necks and you," he stared at Tristan and the others, "are going to stay perfectly still while they do. Is that clear?"

Tristan snapped his teeth at him as the beard thickened on his face and Sophia rested her hand on his arm. "Papa, do not. He'll kill her. I can smell his madness."

She closed her eyes, keeping her hands at her side, as a Lycan locked a collar around her throat. He caressed her arm and leaned in closer. "You're a pretty one."

Kaden made an inarticulate sound of rage and punched the Lycan in the face. The Lycan's head snapped back and he wiped at the blood on his mouth before leaping at Kaden. The big man caught him and threw him to the ground before falling on him and punching him repeatedly in the face.

"Kaden, no!" Sophia cried as three other Lycans pulled him off their bleeding, unconscious companion, and pinned him to the ground. One of them, his fingernails turned to razor sharp claws, swiped his hand across Kaden's chest, tearing through his shirt and slicing into the skin beneath it.

"Kaden!" Sophia screamed again and lunged for the Lycans.

Two other Lycans dragged her back and she struggled against them as Emmett whistled piercingly. "Enough!"

The Lycans holding Kaden down glared at him. "He's human and useless. Let us kill him."

Emmett shook his head. "No. Not yet."

The Lycans snarled and he bared his fangs at them. "I said, no."

"Do we collar him?" One of the Lycans grunted.

"No. Don't waste a collar or the silver chains on the human. Bind his hands with rope," Emmett said

The rest of the Lycans quickly locked collars around Tristan, Evan, James and Nicholas.

"Take them into the barn and chain them to the wall," Emmett said.

"Papa!" Leta cried

"It will be fine, my love. Do what he tells you to do and do not shift. Promise me you will not shift," Tristan said.

"I – I promise, Papa," she whispered.

The Lycans dragged him and the others toward the barn. Leta started to cry, and Emmett shook her roughly.

"Stop your blubbering."

He glanced at Nina's unconscious body before turning to the Lycan still standing next to him. "Bring her into the house."

The Lycan nodded and heaved Nina over his shoulder before following Emmett into the house.

"MAMA, DO YOU NEED HELP?" BREE, HOLDING HER SWORD IN one hand, walked into the kitchen and peered into the walk-in pantry.

Avery shook her head. "No, little one. I'm just looking for some flour."

Bree leaned her sword against the wall of the pantry

before standing on her tiptoes and plucking out an apple from the basket on the top shelf. She caught a shadow from the corner of her eye and peered into the kitchen for a moment.

"What is it?" Avery said.

"Nothing, I guess." Bree shrugged. "I thought I saw something."

"Are you doing some sword training today?" Avery moved a bag of sugar and peered behind it.

"Aye. Nicholas is training both Nina and me today. Do you know that Nina is already better at the sword than I am? It's embarrassing how bad I am."

Avery smiled at her. "You will get better, Bree. It just takes time."

"Aye." Bree said as she walked out of the pantry. "But I -"

Bree gasped and Avery said, "Bree, what's wrong?"

When there was no reply she turned and stuck her head into the kitchen. "Bree? Are you…"

She stared at the two men standing in the kitchen. One of them was holding Bree by the arm and he grinned at her, revealing large white fangs. "Hello, m'lady."

"Who are you?" Avery, her heart pounding and adrenaline shooting through her veins, reached behind her for the sword Bree had left in the pantry. She stepped out of the small room, holding the sword behind her back with her right hand. "You would be wise to leave my home, Lycan."

The two Lycans glanced at each other and laughed before the second one held his hand out. "Come closer, m'lady. I promise I will not harm you if you obey me."

Avery shook her head. "Let go of her and leave. This is your last chance."

The Lycan laughed again and studied her red hair. "I've never seen a Red before. The humans say you are witches. Are you going to cast a spell on me, m'lady?"

"Come closer and you'll see what spells I cast," Avery said.

"Aye, it would be my pleasure," the Lycan said.

He lunged at her, his hands reaching to grab her shoulders, and the Lycan holding Bree frowned when a sword, its tip drenched in blood, appeared through the back of the second Lycan's shirt. The Lycan made a soft gurgling whine as he dropped his hands to his sides.

Avery, her cheeks flushed and her breath coming in short, hard gasps, wrenched the sword free of his chest. He stared down at her dumbly for a moment before his gaze fell to his chest. Blood blossomed on the fabric of his shirt and he touched it, staring at the blood on his fingers before he turned. He held his hand out, showing his companion the blood, before collapsing face-first on the floor with a thud that made the dishes rattle.

From outside came the faint sound of Sophia screaming Kaden's name and Bree made a low sound of fear. The first Lycan stared disbelievingly at Avery. She raised her sword, it was coated with blood, and grinned fiercely at him.

"Shall I take your heart next, Lycan?"

"You bitch," the Lycan said. He tossed Bree to the side and charged at Avery.

"Run Bree!" Avery shouted.

Bree turned and fled as Avery swung her sword at the Lycan. It sliced off his right ear and he howled with pain before batting the sword from Avery's hand. He slammed her up against the counter and wrapped one meaty hand around her throat as blood sprayed from the hole where his ear had been.

"I'll kill you, you stupid red whore!" he shouted as his hand tightened around her throat.

"Ranan! Enough!" A low voice growled. Ranan, blood

coating the side of his head, ignored it and squeezed tighter. Her face red, Avery pulled uselessly at his hands before thrusting her thumb into the Lycan's left eye.

He shrieked in shock and pain and dropped her to the floor as hard hands pulled him away.

"Outside, now!" A Lycan with olive-coloured skin and dark eyes, shoved him from the kitchen.

Coughing and gasping, Avery stared up at the Lycan through watering eyes.

"You're a feisty one then, aren't you?" the Lycan said before hoisting her to her feet with one hard hand under her arm.

Behind them, two more Lycans were standing in the doorway. They had Bree between them.

"I'm sorry, mama. They – they were waiting for me in the hallway," she said.

"It's all right." Avery coughed harshly. The front of her shirt was covered in Ranan's blood and she pulled the sticky material away from her body as the Lycans led her and Bree out of the kitchen.

***

RYKER MELTED INTO THE SHADOWS OF THE COMMON ROOM when he heard Bree walking toward the kitchen. She passed by him, swinging her sword idly, and he listened to her greet Avery before he slipped down the hallway toward the bedrooms.

He paused outside of Nicky's door and rested his head against the wood, straining to hear for noise from the room. It was silent and he eased the door open, wincing when the hinges squealed softly, and stepped into the room.

His heart was pounding, and adrenaline was making his

limbs shake as he stared at Max. She was sleeping on her back and he quickly checked the small bed close to the fireplace. He could see the top of Violet's head just poking out from the covers and, licking his lips nervously, he crept to Max's bed.

He was very aware of the sound of his own heartbeat and his bladder was suddenly, painfully full. He was not a man who frightened easily but as he stared down at the sleeping Max, he realized he was terrified. If she woke before he could use the syrup on her, she would tear him apart limb by limb.

He took a deep, calming breath and stared at his right hand until it stopped trembling. He reached into his pocket, pulled the small green bottle from his pocket and uncorked the top. Pine nettle syrup had a bitter smell and his nose wrinkled as he held the bottle over Max's face. Quickly, before the smell could wake her, he clamped his left hand over her mouth and nose. Her eyes popped open and he poured the liquid directly into them.

Her reaction was immediate and intense. As faint wisps of smoke rose into the air, she bucked her body wildly. He staggered backward, wincing when Max screamed piercingly and rubbed at her eyes. She screamed again and again as, behind him, Violet made a startled cry.

Ryker felt a surge of electricity in the air and he flinched when the water pitcher and bowl shattered, and small cracks appeared in the walls of the room. The closet door flew open and shut, and the bed rose into the air as Max shrieked again before her entire body stiffened and she fainted.

The bed fell to the floor with a harsh thump and Ryker, his pulse pounding and sweat pouring down his face, approached the bed cautiously. He prodded Max's limp body with his foot and breathed a sigh of relief when she didn't move.

"Mama?" Violet whimpered behind him. She was sitting up in the bed, her hair sticking up and her small face pale, and she held her hands up and scooted backward as he walked toward her.

"Bad man," she whispered as tears streaked down her face. "Bad man."

CHAPTER 31

"Mama!"

The front door opened and Emmett, holding Leta by the arm, entered the house. Leta tore away from him and ran to Avery. She wrapped her arms around her waist and buried her face against her.

"They have Papa and everyone, and they hurt Kaden," she sobbed.

"I know, my love," Avery said. She touched the collar around Leta's neck before stroking her dark hair. "Do not fear. Everything will be fine."

She stared at the Lycan carrying Nina over his shoulder. "What have you done to Nina?"

"She'll be fine." Emmett turned to the Lycan holding Nina. "Take her to the third room down the hallway on the right, along with this one, and lock them in. You are to stand guard outside the door. Do you understand?"

The Lycan grunted in reply. He reached for Leta and she snarled at him, baring her fangs as hair started to appear on her cheeks.

"Leta!" Avery squeezed the young girl's arms. "Do not shift, my love."

"Mama, don't let them take me away," she moaned.

"Shh, it will be fine." She bent and kissed Leta's pale face before stroking her hair back. "I promise you. Go with Nina and take care of her."

"Aye, Mama," Leta said.

The Lycan took Leta's arm and led her down the hallway. Ryker, carrying a crying, squirming Violet, passed them without speaking and shoved the baby into Bree's arms. "Take this one and shut it up."

Bree cuddled Violet closely as the little girl clung to her.

"Mama!" she wailed as Bree rubbed her back.

"Shh, Violet. You're all right, sweet one. Shh." Bree rocked her back and forth.

"Did it work?" Emmett asked Ryker.

"I'm standing here, aren't I?" Ryker said.

Emmett scowled at him. "Where is she?"

"She passed out from the pain. I've tied her to a chair. You'd better hope that when she wakes, she has enough control over her powers that they don't go haywire."

Emmett glanced at Bree and Violet. "Put these two in the room with her. She's more apt to stay calm if her baby is in the room."

"What did you do to Max?" Avery said.

Emmett shrugged. "Nothing your child won't be able to cure, I'm certain."

"What did you do to her?" Avery repeated.

He rolled his eyes. "Have you heard of pine nettle syrup, my lady?"

"Aye." Avery said. "It is used to keep the nettle weed from overpowering a garden."

"Aye, that is true. It's very powerful and it burns quite

badly if you touch it with bare flesh. Can you imagine what it does to a person's eyes, my lady? Can you imagine how it must hurt?"

"The gods be damned. You blinded her with the pine nettle syrup." Avery's voice was filled with horror.

"Aye, I did," Emmett said. "Quite genius of me, was it not? It won't kill her," he paused and smiled faintly, "at least I do not believe it will, but the pain and her blindness will stop her from using her powers."

He smiled cheerfully at her. "Come. Let's have a chat with your husband, shall we?"

"AVERY!" TRISTAN GAVE HER A FRANTIC LOOK WHEN Emmett led her into the barn. They Lycans had driven thick metal hoops into the walls of the barn and had chained Tristan and the others by their collars to the hoops. Their hands were bound behind their backs with silver chains and Tristan snarled at Emmett and pulled uselessly at his chains.

"I'm not hurt, my love. It is not my blood," Avery said.

"Aye, your mate has spirit." Emmett laughed. "She killed one of my Lycans and took another's ear. Not bad for a female human."

"Mama, where is Bree?" James said.

"She's fine. She is in the house with Max and Violet."

"Are they hurt?" Nicholas stared with smoking hatred at Emmett.

"Nicky, do not look at me like that. Of course they're not hurt. I am not the monster you think I am," Emmett said.

"He blinded Max with pine nettle syrup so she could not use her powers," Avery said.

"You bastard!" Nicholas growled, his eyes glowing a dark yellow, and Emmett held up his hands.

"Careful, Nicholas. You know what will happen if you shift." He crouched and examined the collar around Sophia's neck.

"These collars are quite something, are they not? If the leeches hadn't used them against me, I would have applauded them for their creativity."

"I will kill you for what you've done to Max!" Nicholas snarled at him.

"Enough, Nicholas," Emmett said. "She'll be fine. Once Max realizes that she has no choice, that I will kill everyone she ever cared for if she does not use her powers in the manner that I need, I will use Leta to heal her. Of course, that might take some time and some convincing. I can't, after all, have her making promises not to use her powers against me and then do so. I do hope that I won't have to do something drastic to make her understand that she has no choice but to obey me."

He cocked his head and studied Nicholas. "It would be a shame if I have to kill the man she loves."

"You would kill your own son?" Tristan said.

"Nicholas is no more my son than he is yours!" Emmett said. "My blood may run in his veins, but you destroyed that which would have made him useful to me, when you took him!"

He drew in a deep breath as Ryker joined them in the barn. Nicholas stared at the bow and arrows slung across his back, their bright blue feathers blowing gently in the breeze, and Ryker grinned at him.

"That's right, Lycan. It was my arrow that pierced your father's heart. I imagine you are not surprised by that."

He crouched in front of Tristan. "The real question is –

where did that little brat's power come from? Her mother or her father? Did you heal yourself, Lycan, or did your daughter heal you? She was with you when you fell, was she not?"

Tristan didn't reply and Ryker took his sword and placed it against Tristan's heart. "There is only one way to find out, I suppose."

"It's me," Avery said. "Leta got her powers from me."

Tristan stared at her. "Avery, do not -"

"Hush, my love." Avery stared unblinkingly at Ryker. "I can heal as well."

Emmett clapped his hands together. "How marvelous. You must tell me, my lady, which of your other children have this power as well."

"There is no other," Avery said. "Only Leta."

"Surely one of your other children has inherited your remarkable power. Now, we know it's not Nicholas and we know it's not Sophia." Emmett winked at Sophia and she bared her teeth at him in a silent snarl.

"That leaves just this young lad," he ruffled Evan's hair and Evan jerked away from him, wincing when the collar dug into his neck, "or the Red."

He turned to Ryker. "My money's on the Red. What do you think?"

"Aye, I agree." Ryker moved to Evan and pointed his sword at him. "Again, there is an easy way to find out which it is. I think -"

"It's me," James said.

Emmett laughed. "Oh, Nicholas, your family is delightful. So willing to save each other no matter what the cost."

He studied the chained Lycans. "Both Ryker and I saw the way the two Reds were touching the baby after the fire. We are neither blind nor stupid, but we do appreciate the honesty.

Still, neither of you were able to bring her back like Leta did. Either you are lying to me or Leta's powers have evolved."

"They've evolved," Avery said. "We can heal but not as quickly as Leta, nor can we bring back the dead."

"You'll understand if I don't just take your word for it." Emmett turned to one of the Lycans standing in the barn. "Unchain the Red's hands."

He quickly unchained James' hands and stepped back as James flexed his arms.

"Don't try anything foolish," Emmett said, "or I will have Ryker kill the boy." He tapped Evan lightly on the top of the head before pointing at Kaden who was sitting on the ground next to James. The front of his shirt was soaked in blood and it was pooling on the ground around him. Kaden's face was pale, and his body shook lightly from shock.

"Go on. Heal him."

James placed his hands onto Kaden's chest. Kaden winced before stiffening and closing his eyes. After a few moments, James sat back and clapped Kaden on the shoulder.

"Better?"

"Aye, thank you." Kaden gave Sophia a brief smile and she breathed a sigh of relief.

As the Lycan re-chained James' hands, Emmett studied Kaden's chest through the rips in his shirt.

"Remarkable," he said before standing and returning to Avery and Evan.

"Your turn, my lady." He withdrew a dagger from his belt and quickly slashed Evan across the cheek.

Evan yelped in shock and pain. Tristan growled angrily as blood welled up from the slash and poured down his face. Avery dropped to her knees and pressed her hands against Evan's cheek before placing soft kisses on his forehead and mouth.

"Close your eyes, my sweet," she said.

Evan closed his eyes obediently and she continued to press kisses across his face before resting her forehead against his. After nearly five minutes, Emmett prodded her in the back.

"Get up."

Avery wiped away the blood on Evan's cheek before kissing him again and rising to her feet. Emmett peered at Evan's smooth cheek before chuckling.

"You know," he said, "I used to believe that humans were useless. Detested them, in fact. Even more so after I was seduced by that dreadful bitch Nina called a mother. Ryker is human, of course, but I believed he was an anomaly of his kind. He certainly has the courage of a Lycan, and his abilities with various weapons and his absolute lack of compassion and remorse for his fellow humans has come in handy on many occasions."

He paced back and forth in the barn. "But then I found Max and her incredible power and now," he reached out and touched Avery's cheek gently, "you and your children."

He looked Avery up and down. "It is a shame you are past your child-bearing years, my lady. It would serve me well to have children with your powers. Although, perhaps you may still possess the ability to bear children. There's only one way to find out."

Tristan growled and lunged forward. The collar around his neck snapped him back, and Avery cried out when he fell to his knees coughing and choking.

"Tristan, do not!" she said when he lifted his head and she saw his eyes glowing brightly.

"Look at me!" she shouted. Tristan turned his gaze to hers after a moment.

"Be calm, my love," she said.

"If you touch her, I will rip you apart," Tristan said to Emmett.

Emmett smiled and stared upward. The roof of the barn had not been completed yet and he studied the clear sky for a moment.

"It will be a cold night," He glanced at Sophia. "Do you think your human mate will last the night?"

"Take him inside," Sophia said. "You can keep him captive just as easily in the house."

"Aye, I could," Emmett said before beckoning to Ryker. "Come, we have much to discuss."

He pointed to the Lycan standing near the door. "Keep watch. If they try to escape, you have my permission to kill them." He stared at James. "Except for the Red, of course. I want him kept alive."

CHAPTER 32

"Max? Can you hear me?"

The soft voice drifted into the darkness. Max groaned quietly. She had been floating in the darkness, plagued by neither pain nor bad dreams, and as her head began to throb with a nauseating pain, she tried to sink back into the black.

"Max? Squeeze my hand."

She ignored the voice. Her entire head was throbbing now, the pain pulsing out from her eyes in slow waves, and she was terrified of how it would feel if she allowed herself to fully wake. She wanted to drift forever, she wanted to –

"Mama?"

It was Violet's voice, full of fear and misery, and with a low groan Max forced herself to wake fully. The pain clawed at her face and she made a harsh cry of fear.

"Max, it's all right."

"Bree?"

"Aye. I'm here."

She opened her eyes and felt panic blossom in her chest when the darkness didn't disappear. She blinked rapidly. Each movement of her eyelids felt like razors scraping across her eyes. When nothing happened, she moaned in panic.

"Bree, I cannot see! What's wrong with me? What's happening?"

The power surged within her and she struggled to control it as she heard the jagged cough of breaking glass.

"Max! Stop!"

There was panic in Bree's voice and it drove Max's fear higher. The chair she was sitting on began to shake beneath her and she tried to move her hands, her heart thrumming like a frightened bird when she realized she was tied down.

"Bree! What's happening?"

"Calm down, Max! Please!" Bree shouted. "Violet is in the room. You must calm down!"

Max took breath after breath, ignoring the pain and the fear, and concentrated on the rhythm of her breathing. After five minutes, she raised her head.

"Violet?"

"Mama."

She heard Bree make a soft grunt and then Violet was sitting on her lap, her small hands patting her face anxiously, and Max couldn't stop the tears from sliding down her cheeks. It made her eyes burn even more and she bit back her groan of pain.

"Hello, baby." She tried to smile, and Violet whimpered before kissing her cheek.

"Bad man, Mama. Bad man."

She buried her head into Max's chest as Bree squeezed Max's leg. "Do you remember what happened?"

"No. Violet was having a nap and I was tired, so I laid down for a bit. That's the last thing I remember. What is happening, Bree? Why – why can't I see?"

Bree squeezed her hand again. "Ryker used pine nettle

syrup to blind you. He and Emmett have – have taken over the house. Ryker returned with a group of Lycans and they used silver collars to capture James and the others. They are holding them in the barn."

"Nicky? Is Nicky all right?" Max said.

"I believe so. I have not seen them. Emmett and Ryker took Mama to the barn with the others. Leta and Nina are locked in another room."

"Emmett wants Leta's powers," Max said.

"Aye, and yours as well," Bree said.

"This is all my fault," Max said. "I knew that Emmett was a monster and I should have told Nicky, but I couldn't. There was a part of me that thought maybe Emmett really was trying to change, and I wanted that for Nina and for Nicky."

"This isn't your fault, Max." Bree stroked Max's hair. "How is the pain?"

"It's bad," Max said. "I can hardly think past it."

"I'm sorry," Bree said.

"We need to get out of here."

"Aye, we do. Can you use your powers to defeat Emmett and the others?"

"I cannot see," Max said. "How can I use them to defeat an enemy I cannot see?"

Bree didn't reply and Max slumped against the chair. She kissed the top of Violet's head. "I am sorry, Bree."

"What if I described it to you?" Bree said. "If I told you what was happening could you perhaps use them to…"

Max shook her head. "I don't think so."

"Let's try." Bree stood and moved behind Max. "There is a nightstand to your left next to the bed. Can you move it?"

Max turned her head and tried to picture the nightstand in her mind. After a moment, the power hummed within her and, focusing past the pain roaring through her face and head, she tried to move the nightstand.

There was a loud bang and the sound of glass breaking and Violet cried out before clinging to Max.

"It's all right, my love," Bree said.

"What happened? Did it move?" Max said.

"No." There was disappointment in Bree's voice. "The mirror fell off the wall."

Max rested her face against Violet's soft hair. "I'm sorry."

"It's fine." Bree stroked her short hair again. "Try and get some rest, Max."

"WAKE UP, NINA."

Nina's eyes popped open and she stared at Leta. The young girl was leaning over her and stroking her forehead. Kala was hovering beside her, her tiny face pinched with worry.

"Hi, Nina," Leta said.

"Hi, Leta."

Nina sat up and looked around as Kala landed on her shoulder and kissed her cheek repeatedly.

"Nina." She stroked Nina's hair.

"I'm okay, Kala." They were in her bedroom and Nina slid off the bed and hurried to the door.

"It's locked," Leta said. "And there is a Lycan standing outside."

Nina buried her face in her hands as Leta patted her back. "I'm so sorry, Leta."

"What for? It's not your fault your papa is a – a bastard."

The little girl covered her mouth with her hands. "Do not tell Papa I swore."

"I won't," Nina said. "Where are the others?"

"Papa and Nicky and the other Lycans are in the barn." She gave Nina a sick look. "They hurt Kaden. He was bleeding very badly. I need to get to the barn and help him."

"He'll be okay." Nina tried to smile reassuringly. "What about Max?"

"I don't know. Your papa has Mama and Bree, and Ryker was carrying Violet. I don't know what they did to Max. Do you – do you think they killed her?" Leta's eyes were welling up with tears. "She would have used her powers by now if they hadn't."

Nina shook her head. The little girl had voiced the fear in her heart, and she tried to shake off the paralyzing panic that was threatening to take over. "I am sure they did not. Daddy wants her power like he wants yours. I am sure of it."

Leta started to cry and Nina hugged her. "It will be all right, Leta. We will rescue the others."

Leta frowned up at her. "How? I'm only a little girl and you're just a human."

Nina moved to the bed and crouched beside it. She reached under the bed and drew out a sword. "I have this."

"You're not good enough yet. You've only been training for a little while," Leta said. "There are too many Lycans."

Nina stared out the window of her bedroom. "We are not far from the barn. The sun is starting to set. When it's dark, I will sneak over there and release your father and the others," she said quietly, glancing at the closed door of the bedroom.

Leta took her hand. "I'm going with you."

"No, Leta. It is too dangerous."

"I'm going!" Leta said. "I won't stay here by myself. Please don't make me."

Nina hugged her. "All right. We go together."

EMMETT RAISED HIS GLASS OF WINE TO RYKER. "TO SUCCESS and the beginning of a new world."

Ryker stared into the fire. "We have not succeeded yet, Emmett. If you believe that Max will simply use her powers to do your bidding, you're a fool."

"Watch your tongue, Ryker," Emmett said. "Remember who you work for."

Ryker didn't reply and Emmett took a drink of wine. "It may take some time, but Max will do exactly what I tell her to do. I have her daughter and the Lycan she loves, remember?"

"Aye, I remember."

"Tomorrow when the Lycan's slaves return, we'll kill them. They're not needed, and it will show the others what I am capable of," Emmett said.

"You should kill the lord Williams and the others as well. They are too dangerous to keep alive," Ryker said.

"We will keep them alive for a while longer. Leta will be more inclined to help us if we have her family to use against her."

"We don't need all of them. Keep her mother and the other Red alive and kill the rest," Ryker said. "You're only asking for trouble by keeping them alive."

"I heard you the first time, Ryker," Emmett said.

"And what of Nina and the Red's mate?" Ryker said.

"She carries the Red's pup in her belly. We will keep her alive. If the pup she carries has healing powers, it will come in useful."

"And Nina?"

"What about her?" Emmett said. "She is a useless, scared little mouse. I will allow her to live as long as she obeys me.

If she does not, I will do what I should have done years ago and abandon her in the outskirts."

There was a knock on the door and a Lycan entered the room. "Lord McKenzie, may I speak with you?"

"Aye. What is your name?" Emmett said.

"Bran, my lord."

"What is it, Bran?"

"Ranan seeks revenge."

Emmett frowned at Ryker. "What is he talking about?"

"The Red killed a Lycan and took Ranan's ear," Ryker said.

"The Lycan she killed was Ranan's brother. He wants his revenge," Bran said.

"Does he?" Emmett said. "And does this Ranan know that I am the one in charge?"

"Aye. But there are many of us and only two of you."

"Are you threatening me, Bran?" Emmett said.

"No, my lord. Only stating the facts. Ranan wants revenge and we believe he should have it."

Emmett smiled. "Does he want me to lop off the Red's ear and give it to him as a gift?"

Bran didn't return his smile. "No, my lord. He is calling for her death. He wants the Red witch to burn."

"Very well," Emmett said. "Build your wooden pyre and tonight we will watch the witch burn."

Bran nodded. "I will tell Ranan and the others."

He left the room as Ryker stared at Emmett. "Have you gone mad? She has healing powers. We can use her. Allowing the Lycans to burn her is madness!"

"You forget, Ryker, that we have her daughter. We'll appease the Lycans need for revenge by burning her alive. Then, we'll simply have Leta bring her back," Emmett said.

"Must you question everything I say or do? I grow weary of your constant doubt."

"Forgive me, lord Emmett," Ryker said. "Perhaps I do not share your faith that the Lycan brat will be able to bring back a body burned beyond recognition."

Emmett sat back in his chair, a smile crossing his face. "It will be a true test of Leta's powers."

CHAPTER 33

"What are they building out there?" Sophia said.

Nicholas shook his head. "I do not know." He tensed his muscles and, arms bulging, strained at the chains that bound his wrists. They didn't break and he snarled in frustration.

"Easy, Nicky. You will not break them that way. You know that," James said.

"He has Max! He has Mama and Leta and Bree! Do you expect me to just sit here and do nothing like you are?" Nicky said.

"At least I am smart enough to know that I should not waste my energy trying to break silver chains," James said.

"Aye, you're the smart one." Nicholas rolled his eyes and James glared at him.

"What are you saying? Do you believe me to be stupid? Is that what you -"

"Enough! Both of you!" Tristan growled at them. "Your petty arguing will not help us save anyone. For the gods sake, quiet your tongues and let me think."

A Lycan strode into the barn. There was a white bandage

covering the side of his head and he spoke briefly to the Lycan guarding them before moving toward the captured Lycans.

He studied them one by one before his gaze swung back to Tristan. "You are the mate of the Red, are you not?"

"Aye, I am," Tristan said.

The Lycan crouched in front of him. "Your mate killed my brother and took my ear with her sword."

He looked around at the others before returning his gaze to Tristan. "You disgust me. A Lycan taking a human as his mate - breeding with her – you are a disgrace to the Lycans. You must think you were so clever to teach your weak human how to fight with a sword."

Tristan didn't answer and the Lycan leaned closer. "You were wrong to teach her to fight. She killed my brother and now, she will burn for what she has done."

Tristan's nostrils flared and his eyes turned jade as a low growling began in his throat.

Ranan grinned at him. "No doubt you will hear her screams, but do you think you will smell her burning flesh from in here? I think you will."

Tristan, his eyes glowing with a mad light, stared steadily at Ranan. "You will be the first to die. Your pack will watch as I take your head and give it to my mate as a gift."

"You're nothing more than a chained dog." Ranan left the barn.

"Papa? Are you all right?" Sophia said.

He didn't reply. He was staring down at the floor, breathing harshly as his entire body trembled.

"Papa? Please talk to me. Please -"

"Sophia, leave him be," Kaden said. He rubbed his wrists together again. The rope had dug into his flesh and the friction had ripped the skin open. Blood had soaked into the rope and dripped down his hands.

"Stop, Kaden," Sophia said. "The ropes are too thick. You will not break them."

"Aye, I know, little Lycan," he replied before stealing a glance at the Lycan who stood guard at the door. His back was to them and Kaden, wincing a little, rubbed faster.

Nicholas knew Kaden believed the blood might help him slip free of the rope and he hoped Kaden was right.

Sophia stared at Tristan. "We will save her, Papa. I swear it."

He didn't reply and with a soft sigh, she leaned her head against the wall behind her and closed her eyes.

———

"ARE YOU READY, LETA?" NINA SAID.

Leta nodded and Nina squeezed her hand. Moving quickly, Nina climbed out the window and helped Leta crawl out after her. Darkness had fallen and she leaned down and whispered in the young Lycan's ear. "I cannot see in the dark. You will have to lead the way."

Keeping their backs flush against the house, they moved to the corner of it. They peered around the edge of the house. They Lycans had gathered in the yard and a few of them were digging a hole in the frozen ground. Beside them, a large wooden pole lay in the snow and Leta put her mouth to Nina's ear.

"What are they doing?" she breathed.

"I do not know," Nina whispered. "Come, we must hurry. It is only a few feet to the woodpile. Stay low to the ground, Leta."

Holding hands and with Leta in the lead, the two girls

scurried from the safety of the house across the yard to the large woodpile. They hid behind it, their breaths escaping in frightened little puffs of steam as they stared at each other.

They could hear the laughter of the Lycans as one of them cursed loudly. "The gods be damned, Dre! That was my foot you just tried to dig up. Have you gone blind?"

"Shut up. If you weren't so clumsy, my shovel would have been nowhere near your foot. I swear to the gods, you are the most useless Lycan ever born!"

Leta's eyes widened and she clutched at Nina's hand as the sounds of a fight began. The Lycans cheered as the two Lycans growled and snarled and snapped their teeth. Nina peeked over the woodpile. The Lycans were on the ground, rolling and wrestling and snarling at each other as the other Lycans cheered them on.

"Now is our chance," she said to Leta.

Holding Nina's hand in a death grip, Leta ran for the barn. Nina, feeling like every step would be her last, resisted the urge to look behind her at the Lycans and concentrated on the dark shadow of the barn looming ahead of them. Her sword bumped comfortingly against her leg as she ran, and she breathed a sigh of relief when they reached the barn and slipped out of the Lycans' sight. She collapsed on the ground next to Leta, leaning against the barn and shivering violently.

"Are you hurt?" Leta whispered.

"No, just cold."

Leta hugged her. Nina buried her cold face in Leta's warm neck and took a few deep breaths before slipping out of her embrace.

"Kala, are you ready?" she said.

The little pixie slipped free of her hair and hovered in front of her. She nodded solemnly and Nina said, "Be careful, Kala. He will be quick. Do not let him catch you."

Kala nodded again and buzzed forward to place a gentle kiss on Nina's nose. "Kala loves Nina."

"I love you too, Kala." Nina pulled her sword free of its sheath and gripped it. "Stay here, Leta. We won't be long."

JAMES NUDGED NICHOLAS. "LOOK," HE MUTTERED BEFORE jerking his head upward.

Nicholas frowned. Kala, her wings fluttering rapidly, had just flown in from the open ceiling. He watched as she flew gracefully downward toward the Lycan standing guard at the door. The Lycan was staring out the open door, watching his pack, and Nicholas frowned again when Kala lit up with a bright blue light.

"What is she doing?" Evan whispered.

"I do not know," James said. "But she's going to get herself killed."

Kala darted forward and bit the Lycan on the ear. He grunted with surprise and clapped his hand against his ear before looking around. Kala, hovering just out of his reach, grinned at him before sticking her tongue out.

"A pixie?" The Lycan stared at her in puzzlement. "What in the gods name is a pixie doing here?"

Kala zipped forward and bit him hard on the end of his nose before flying away. The Lycan snarled with pain and swiped at her, his fingernails extended into claws.

"You little pest!" he growled. "Do that again and I'll crush you under my boot."

Kala stuck her tongue out at him again and dive bombed his head. She yanked hard on his hair, laughing and jabbering in her own language as he snapped his teeth and grabbed at her. She fluttered out of his reach, darting and

341

dipping in dizzying circles as he swung his arms futilely at her.

"Stop it!" he growled. "I swear, I will -"

"Excuse me?"

Nicholas' blood froze in his vein at the sound of Nina's voice.

The Lycan swung around, his eyes widening with shock when he felt the sword slide into his belly. He stared in numb disbelief at Nina standing in front of him. Her face pale and her mouth trembling, she pulled the sword from his stomach and stepped back as blood spilled onto the ground.

"I'm sorry," she whispered.

He fell to his knees, holding his hands against his abdomen as she skittered around him. "Nicky!"

"Nina, are you hurt?" Nicholas said.

"No, I'm fine. I just -"

"Look out!" Evan said.

Nina turned, a frightened squeak emerging from her throat. The Lycan she had stabbed was swaying before her and she moaned when he grinned at her. Blood coated his teeth and he spat a mouthful of the red liquid onto the floor of the barn.

"Always stab a Lycan in the heart, girl. Didn't they teach you that?"

Blood was still dripping from the wound in his stomach, but he paid no attention to it. Nina raised her sword as he lunged forward. He knocked it easily from her hands and dragged her toward him as Nicholas snarled with anger and fear. Nina stared mesmerized at the Lycan as his jaw cracked and lengthened and his teeth turned to long, sharp fangs.

"I'm going to enjoy this, girl," he said.

"No!" Nicholas shouted as the Lycan bent his head to Nina's throat. Kala zipped forward, biting and clawing at the

Lycan's face but he ignored the tiny pixie. Before he could rip Nina's flesh apart, there was a hoarse growl and he gasped with pain. Leta, her claws out and her fangs gleaming in the dark, was clinging to his leg and with another hoarse growl she bit him hard on the leg again.

He growled, tossing Nina to the side as he reached down and yanked Leta off his leg. She snapped at him, her eyes glowing fiercely, and kicked at his legs as he lifted her by the front of her shirt and glared at her.

"You little bitch! It's time you were taught some manners."

Leta kicked at him again and he winced when her flailing foot caught him in the groin. He groaned and threw her to the ground.

"I'll kill you for that!" he wheezed.

He snarled with pain when Kala bit him hard on the ear and he reached up to crush her tiny body. She darted away and Nicholas shouted again as the Lycan suddenly froze, his back arching, and stared down at his chest. The blood-soaked blade of a sword was sticking out of his chest and he touched it gingerly before it was ripped free.

"What?" He collapsed to the ground. He stared up at Nina standing over him before dying.

Panting harshly, Nina helped Leta to her feet. "Are you all right, Leta?"

"I'm fine." Leta batted her hands away and ran to Tristan. She threw her arms around him and hugged him.

"Oh, Papa." She started to cry as he rubbed his face against her hair.

"It's all right, my sweet," he said. "You were very brave."

"They have Mama," she sobbed.

"I know. We'll get her back," he soothed.

Nina crouched in front of Nicholas as Kala landed on her shoulder. She hugged him and he kissed her soft cheek.

"That was incredibly foolish of you, Nina," he said. "You were nearly killed."

She blinked back the tears. "This is my fault. I convinced you to let Daddy stay. I wanted him to be good, Nicky. I thought he could be good."

"It's not your fault," Nicholas said. "I'm going to kill him for what's he done, Nina. You know that, do you not?"

"Aye," she said. "I do."

She returned to the fallen Lycan and quickly searched the pockets of his pants. "There is no key."

Kaden sat forward. "Use your sword to cut the rope, Nina."

She did as he asked, and he gingerly rubbed his bleeding wrists before crouching in front of Sophia. He kissed her before plucking hairpins from her braided hair. Moving quickly, he opened the lock on the collar, tossing it to the ground, before working on the lock of the chains around her wrists. Within a few minutes, she was free, and she threw her arms around him and hugged him. He returned her hug and then she eased her way to the open door of the barn as he crouched in front of Evan.

"What do you see, Sophia?" James said.

"They have the pole in the ground." She gave her father a sick look. "They're putting wood and branches around it.

Kaden finished unwinding the chain from around Evan's wrists and squeezed his shoulder before handing him two of the hairpins. "Like I taught you, Evan. Take your time."

Evan nodded and knelt before his father as Kaden moved to Nicholas. Within a few minutes, they had freed the others from the collars and chains. Tristan picked up Leta, holding her and rubbing her back as she buried her face in his throat.

They gathered in a tight circle and Tristan stared at each of them. "There are too many of them for us to defeat. We need Max. I will take Leta to the house. Once she has healed Max, she will -"

There were sudden cheers from outside and Sophia crept to the door of the barn. She turned to the others, her face pale, and her mouth trembling. "They're bringing Mama out."

Tristan cursed under his breath as Nicholas took his arm. "I will take Leta to the house. We have the element of surprise. You can save Mama and then you and the others must hold them off while Leta is healing Max."

"We will need your help, Nicky," James said.

Tristan cupped Evan's head. "Evan, I need you to take your sister and Nina to the house and find Max. Can you do that? Can you keep them safe?"

"Aye, I can," Evan said.

"Good." Tristan kissed his forehead and then set Leta on her feet. "You must go with Evan, my sweet."

"No, Papa. I don't want to leave you." She clung to him.

He hugged her close. "I need you to be brave for just a little longer, Leta. You must heal Max. Evan will not let anyone harm you. All right?"

"Aye, Papa," Leta said.

"That's my good girl."

He hugged Evan and then Nina before walking them to the door. Evan took Nina and Leta's hands and Tristan stared gravely at Evan. "Be careful. Do not let them see you."

"I won't, Papa."

The three of them disappeared into the darkness.

Tristan stared into the yard. Avery, dressed in her white nightshirt with her long red hair unbound and flowing down her back, was being led toward the wooden pole erected in the yard. Her face was pale but composed, and he clenched his hands into fists as the one named Ranan leaned closer and whispered something into her ear.

"Easy, Dad." James rested his hand on his shoulder as Tristan began to growl.

"He is mine. No one else touches him," Tristan said.

"Aye, we know."

They watched silently as Avery was lashed to the pole. Behind him, Tristan could hear the soft sound of James, Nicky and Sophia shifting to their wolf forms. Kaden, an axe in one hand and a sword in the other, stood next to him.

"Are you ready?"

Tristan nodded, with his gaze fixated on Avery's long red hair. "Aye, I am."

CHAPTER 34

Holding hands, Leta and Nina leaned against the woodpile. Nina's heart was pounding from their frantic scramble through the deep snow and she stared back at the barn as Evan peered around the woodpile.

"We do the same thing," he said in a low voice. "Stay low to the ground and stay quiet. It's only a few more feet to the house. Are you ready?"

"Aye," Nina whispered.

Leta peeked past the woodpile at the crowd of Lycans.

"Mama?" she whispered. "What are they doing to Mama? Why are they tying her to that pole?"

Her eyes widened and she began to tremble. "They have a torch, Evan! They're going to burn Mama!"

She tried to dart past Evan and he pinned her to the ground, clamping his hand over her mouth as she started to scream.

"Hush, Leta! Papa will save her! We have to go to the house!"

After a moment, her struggles ceased, and she stared at

him with tears in her eyes. He released her mouth cautiously and she whispered, "Do you promise Papa will save her?"

"Aye, you know he will." Evan tried to give her a reassuring smile, but Nina could see his mouth trembling. He lifted her to her feet and held her hand before taking Nina's. "Come, we must hurry."

EMMETT WATCHED AS RANAN AND BRAN TIED AVERY TO THE pole. He stepped forward and smiled at the Red.

"Do you have any last words, my lady?"

Avery stared at him. She was trembling from the cold and her lips were turning blue. Her face was calm, but he could see the fear in her eyes.

"Perhaps if you beg Ranan for forgiveness and apologize for killing his brother, he'll let you live," Emmett said.

"I will not," Ranan grunted. He finished lashing her arms to the pole and touched her long red hair. "Tell my brother I said hello when you see him in hell."

"You'll tell him yourself and soon. I have no doubt of that," Avery said.

Ranan barked laughter and slapped her across the face. "I cannot wait to watch you burn."

He and Bran stepped back and he took the torch that Ryker held out to him. He stood in front of Avery, staring at her as Ryker joined Emmett.

"Quite the show, is it not?" Emmett grinned at the human.

Ryker snorted irritably. "Tell them to get on with it."

"Let them have their fun," Emmett said. "It's always good to keep your hired Lycans happy." He stretched, cracking his knuckles before glancing at Ryker. "I think Nina and that little brat should see this. It will help remind them that I am in charge."

He glanced at the Lycan standing nearest to him. "Bring out my daughter and the Lycan bitch."

The Lycan nodded and moved toward the house as Ranan waved the torch in front of the sticks and branches at the base of the pole, grinning tauntingly at Avery as he did so.

"Get on with it!" a Lycan yelled. Ranan frowned at the group of Lycans before returning his gaze to Avery.

"Do you think your mate will shift when he hears your screams of agony? I think he will. I do not think he'll be able to control it." He grinned. "He'll die as you die."

"My mate is going to kill you," Avery said.

Ranan laughed. "Aye, he mentioned that."

He bent and held the torch to the paper stuffed between the branches and woods. As they slowly caught fire and the flames licked at the wood, he stepped back and smiled at Avery again.

"Goodbye, Red witch."

BREE MADE A LOW CRY OF DISTRESS AND MAX TURNED HER head toward the sound. "What's wrong, Bree? What's happening?"

Bree clutched the windowsill and made another low cry. "They're going to burn Mama."

Max pulled at the ropes that bound her to the chair. "Bree, find something to cut me loose! I must help her."

Bree searched the room frantically. Violet, asleep on the bed, snorted loudly when Bree knocked over the nightstand.

"There is nothing!" She was nearly crying with panic and

she ripped open the drawer of the nightstand and pawed frantically through its contents. "I can't find anything."

"The mirror! Use the broken mirror," Max said.

Bree gasped in surprise, her hand pressing against her stomach, when Evan appeared in the window. He lifted the pane and crawled into the room.

"What? Who is it?" Max said.

"Evan!" Bree ran across the room and hugged the teenager. Leta and Nina slipped through the window behind him and Nina ran to Max. She made a harsh cry of pain at the sight of Max's eyes.

"Oh, Max." She dropped to her knees and rested her head on Max's lap.

"Evan – where is James? Is he all right? What about Kaden?" Bree said.

"Aye, he's fine. They both are. Nina and Leta freed us from the silver but they're about to burn Mama at the stake. There are too many of them for us to defeat. We need Max's help."

Evan crossed the room and used the sword to slice through the ropes on Max's arms.

Max rubbed her wrists before reaching up to touch her face. Nina pulled her hands away. "No, Max. Don't touch your eyes."

"Is it bad?" Max said.

"Aye," Nina said.

"Hi, Max." Leta's voice was in front of Max.

"Hi, Leta." Max tried to smile at the little girl as she felt her lean forward.

"Don't move." Leta's hands touched her face and she felt Leta's warm breath on her lips before the young Lycan pressed her mouth against hers. There was a warmth and tingling through her face and Max made a soft cry when the warmth became a blinding sharp pain in her eyes. Leta squeezed her face before stepping back.

"Open your eyes, Max," she said.

Max released her breath in a hard rush and opened her eyes. Leta was standing before her and Nina brushed past her and threw her arms around Max.

"Thank the gods," she said.

Max stood and picked up Leta. She hugged her and kissed her cheek. "Thank you, Leta."

"You have to save Mama now," Leta said as the door to the bedroom swung open and two Lycans stepped into the room.

They stared in surprise at the small group. "What in the gods name?"

Evan snapped his teeth at them as his body swelled and hair sprouted on his face. The Lycans snarled in return as their own bodies began to swell.

"Enough," Max said. She waved her hand at the Lycan closest to her. He yelped in surprise when he flew back through the open doorway and slammed into the wall. The other Lycan rushed forward and Max raised her hand. He stopped as suddenly as if he had hit a wall and his face tightened in shock as Max lifted him into the air.

"No, do not," he begged as a large fragment of broken mirror rose from the floor and hovered in front of him. "Please, do not -"

He made a harsh gurgling noise as the mirror fragment sliced across his throat. His head slid from his body and landed on the floor with a wet thud as Bree made a soft cry of disgust and turned away.

The Lycan on the floor in the hallway stared dazedly at them as Max, still holding Leta, took a few steps forward.

She flicked her hand and the Lycan's head twisted sharply to the left, his neck breaking with a sickening crack.

Leta whimpered and Max kissed her cheek before setting her next to Bree. "Stay here with Leta and Nina and Violet. We will not be long."

Leta jerked against Bree when the loud howling came through the open window. "Papa?"

Bree sat down on the bed and gathered the little girl close. "It's all right, Leta. Max will help them."

Leta climbed into her lap and Bree rocked her gently as Max and Evan started toward the door.

"I'm coming with you." Nina joined them at the doorway and Max studied her before nodding.

"Let's go then."

EMMETT STEPPED BACK FROM THE HEAT AS THE FIRE GREW. He could barely see Avery through the smoke and the flames, and he glanced at Ryker. The human was staring at the fire with a small grin on his face and the grin widened when Ranan tossed the torch into the flames and laughed.

"I'm starting to enjoy country life. How about you?" Emmett said with a laugh.

Before Ryker could reply, there was a loud snarling and a giant white wolf appeared out of the darkness. He leaped onto Bran and the Lycan's startled cry was cut off when the wolf tore his throat open.

Emmett staggered back, his eyes widening with shock, as more wolves materialized in the light of the flames. They were followed by the human mate of Sophia and he tightened his grip on the axe and sword he carried as the wolves fanned out in a circle in front of the rapidly growing blaze.

Tristan, his face grim, strode through the smoke toward Ranan. Ranan stared at him with a numb look of curiosity. "How -"

Without speaking, Tristan grabbed him by the hair and yanked his head back. As Ranan started to shift, Tristan raised his hand. His nails had turned to claws and he sliced easily through Ranan's neck. Ranan's body fell to the ground as Tristan raised the Lycan's head high into the air. Blood poured from the neck to splatter onto the white snow and Tristan lifted his face to the dark sky and howled in triumph.

"No!" Emmett screamed as Tristan dropped Ranan's head and, ignoring the flames, climbed the wood surrounding the pole. He cut through the ropes binding Avery to the pole with one swipe of his claws before lifting her into his arms and leaping to the ground. He set her on her feet and touched her face before shifting to his Lycan form and standing in front of her.

There was a moment of silence and then Emmett screamed again. "Kill them! Kill them all!"

His pack of Lycans shifted and, snarling and growling, rushed toward Tristan and the others.

A Lycan, a faded scar across its nose, leaped for Sophia. Kaden swung his axe, decapitating the wolf, and its body fell to the ground with a loud thump. Sophia barked and lunged for the throat of the Lycan behind him. Snarling loudly, she tore its throat out as it whimpered helplessly.

Nicholas, his white fur gleaming in the fire, launched his body at a Lycan about to sink his teeth into the back of James' neck. He hit the Lycan with a hard thud that drove it into the snow, and they wrestled in the deep snow, snarling and growling loudly, until Nicky pinned it and sunk his teeth into its throat.

He backed away, his snout covered in blood, and howled.

There was a soft whooshing sound and he yelped in pain, collapsing to the ground when the arrow pierced through his thick fur.

He shifted to his human form as Ryker, his eyes dancing in the light of the fire, lowered his bow and stalked toward him. He stared at the arrow sticking out from Nicky's chest and grinned as Nicky made a low whine of pain. "Your sister is not here to save you like she saved your father."

Nicky whined again and Ryker crouched next to him before tapping him lightly on the face with a second arrow. "Your entire family is going to die tonight, Lycan."

He glanced around at the chaos before staring down at Nicky once more. "Must you take so long to die? Max will undoubtedly be heartbroken to hear of your suffering. Perhaps she will ask me to soothe her pain. I know of many ways to help her forget you."

He leaned closer, studying the arrow in Nicky's chest. "Can you feel your heart slowing, Lycan? Do you have anything you wish to say to Max? I will gladly pass it on."

Nicky made a soft wheezing noise and Ryker bent his head. "What was that? I did not hear you."

Ryker jerked in surprise when Nicky yanked the arrow from his chest and dropped it into the snow before wrapping his hand around the back of Ryker's neck.

"I said, you missed," he whispered as Ryker's eyes widened.

"No, do not -"

With a soft snarl, Nicky sank his fangs into the flesh of his throat and ripped it wide open. Ryker clutched at his throat, blood pouring between his fingers, as he stared at Nicholas. Nicky, his mouth and teeth stained with Ryker's blood, howled as Ryker collapsed face first into the snow.

Nicky staggered to his feet, yelping as pain shot through

his chest and ribs, and he collapsed again. He could hear the snarls and cries of the Lycans, and he tried to struggle to his feet.

Panting harshly, holding one hand to his bleeding chest, he growled at the small black Lycan who was stalking toward him. Before the Lycan could attack him, the wind picked up and the Lycan made a startled whine as he was lifted and tossed into the flames. He screamed as his fur caught on fire and he scrambled out of the fire, his entire body ablaze. Howling and screaming he turned and fled toward the forest, collapsing just inside the tree line.

"Max," Nicky said.

Her face serene, Max strode toward him. "Hello, Nicky. Everything will be fine now."

He watched as she turned her back to him and raised her hands. The wind howled and snow filled the air as Max smiled and flicked her hand at the Lycan who had Kaden pinned to the ground.

The Lycan burst apart in a shower of blood and guts and Kaden winced and threw his hands up to shield his face as the Lycan's insides rained down on him. A Lycan leaped at Max and she flicked her hand again. The Lycan tore in half, its intestines sliding out of it and onto the soft snow in a bloody heap as the remaining Lycans howled in fear.

They were backing away from Max and the others and Nicky groaned when James, still in his Lycan form, dropped his heavy body on top of his. He pinned Nicky to the ground and chuffed softly at him as Max turned to face the suddenly terrified Lycans.

One of them shifted to his human form and fell to his knees in the snow. "Mercy! Have mercy on us!"

"You will have no mercy from me," Max said. She held her hands out to them. There was a loud humming sound

355

and she smiled again when the Lycans simultaneously exploded.

Max lowered her hands and stared silently at Emmett. He was pressed against the house, his eyes wide and his lips speckled with spit, as he held his hands up. "Please, Max."

She didn't reply and he took a cautious step forward, smiling uneasily at Nina who had knelt next to Nicky.

Nicky pushed at James and his brother eased his body from his before joining Sophia and Kaden. Nicholas examined the healing wound in his chest. He took Nina's hand and she helped him to his feet.

"Nina, honey, I'm your father," Emmett said. "Do not let her kill me. You would watch your own father die?"

"You're not my father," Nina said. "You never were."

"Nicholas, I will leave and never come back. I swear it," Emmett said. "Neither you nor Nina will ever hear from me again."

Nicky glanced at Tristan and Avery. He studied the burns on his father's arms and legs and the singe marks on Avery's nightshirt before turning back to Emmett.

"You do not deserve to live," he said.

Emmett's eyes widened as Max took a step toward him. "Max, I treated you well for many years. I saved your father's life when he was going to be killed for his debt. Does that not mean anything to you? I promise you, I will not -"

"You're boring me," Max said. "Goodbye, Emmett."

"Max! No, I -"

There was a wet, ripping sound and Emmett staggered back before staring wide-eyed at the bloody slab of meat hovering in front of him. His fingers brushed against the hole in his chest and he whimpered before crumpling to the ground. Max lowered her hand and his heart, still twisting and turning in the air above him, thumped to the ground.

She bent her head and closed her eyes, breathing deeply.

Nicholas touched her back. "Max?"

She took another deep breath before opening her eyes. "Hello, Nicky."

"Hi." He reached for her and she wrapped her arms around his waist, burying her face in his throat as he hugged her.

"I love you, Max."

"I love you too."

EPILOGUE

"I should be in there with her." James paced back and forth in the common room as Nicholas stared at him in amusement.

"She is fine, James. Mama is with her. If they need you or Leta, they'll tell you."

"How can you be so calm?" James said.

"Women birth babies every day. She's healthy and strong. She'll be just fine. Tell him, Dad."

"Aye, she will be." Tristan smiled at James but there was worry in his eyes.

"I still think I should -"

He stopped as Bree entered the common room, carrying a chubby-cheeked, blonde-haired baby in her arms. "Here, my love. Take your daughter. I'll go and check on Sophia."

The baby grinned and made a sharp cry of excitement before holding her arms out to James. He took the baby and kissed her soft cheek before holding her against his chest.

"Hello, Maddie." He kissed her cheek again and the baby giggled before grabbing his nose in her tiny hands.

Bree laughed and stood on her tiptoes to kiss James' cheek. "I'll be right back."

She left the common room as James jiggled Maddie before lifting her up and nuzzling her belly. She giggled again and yanked on his hair, making him wince, before he nestled her against his chest again.

"I cannot believe she is eight moons already." Tristan grinned at the baby. She cooed at him before resting her head against James' chest.

"Aye, I know," James said.

He resumed his pacing as Violet poked her head into the common room. She was followed by Tia and Leta, and she ran to Nicholas as Leta climbed into Tristan's lap.

"Hi, Papa." Violet smiled at him as Nicky picked her up.

"Hi, baby. Where's your Mama?"

"In the kitchen with Grandma Vivian." Violet slung her chubby arm around his neck and then wrinkled her nose. "What's that smell?"

James held Maddie out and made a face. "The gods be damned, Maddie. For such a little thing, you make a terrible smell."

Nicholas snorted laughter and James arched his eyebrow at him. "It will be your turn soon enough, big brother."

"Aye, that's true," Nicky said before tickling Violet. "Your baby brother or sister will be here soon, Violet."

"Tomorrow?" Violet said.

Leta rolled her eyes as she leaned against Tristan. "Try another five moons. It's not soon at all, Nicky."

There were shouts of laughter from outside and Leta twisted on Tristan's lap to look out the window. Evan and Nina were practicing with their swords and she watched them for a few minutes before sliding off Tristan's lap. "I'm going to go outside with Evan and Nina."

Tristan caught her arm. "Do not tease your brother about liking Nina. Do you understand?"

Leta gave him an innocent look. "I don't tease him."

"Do you not?" Tristan said.

Leta shrugged. "It's not my fault I caught them kissing behind the barn when they were supposed to be practicing their sword fighting."

Tristan pulled her into his arms and kissed her forehead. "No teasing, Leta. I mean it."

"All right, Papa." Leta grinned at him and then held her hand out to Violet. "Do you want to come with me, baby bird?"

Violet shook her head. "No, I stay with Papa."

Leta shrugged before whistling for Tia. "Come on, Tia. Let's go see Evan and Nina."

They left the common room as James carried Maddie to the couch and changed her. Max poked her head into the common room and wrinkled her nose. "Whew! That's some smell."

"Aye, I know." James laughed as Max crossed the room to Violet and Nicky. Nicky rubbed her belly as she kissed him on the mouth and smiled at Violet.

"Are you getting hungry, Violet?"

"Aye, Mama," Violet said. "I want potatoes."

"Then potatoes it is," Max said. "Come, we will -"

She stopped as Avery entered the room. Tristan stood and stared anxiously at her. "Is she all right, my love?"

"Aye, she's fine. She's a little tired."

"What did she have?" Max said.

"A boy. Both she and Kaden are thrilled." Avery grinned at them and Tristan hugged her hard.

"What did they name him?"

"Ian," Avery said.

361

"It is a good name." Tristan's voice was hoarse.

"Aye, my love. It is." She rubbed his back.

"I'm hungry, Mama," Violet said to Max.

"Aye, I remember. Come to the kitchen and we'll make you some potatoes." Max squeezed Nicky's hand and the three of them left the common room.

James picked up Maddie. "Is Bree still upstairs?"

"Aye. She's going to stay with Sophia for a bit. She said if you wanted to take Maddie home, she would meet you there."

James shook his head. "I will wait for her. I don't like her walking alone."

Avery smiled at him. "It is a three minute walk to your house, James. She will be fine."

"I know, Mama." James grinned at her. "But I will wait."

He kissed Maddie's cheek again. "Come, little one. We will go to the kitchen and wait for your mama."

As he left the room, Tristan wrapped his arms around Avery's waist and nuzzled her throat affectionately. "Is she all right, my love?"

"Aye, she is. Do not worry, Tristan. Everything went smoothly and you will meet your grandson soon."

Tristan squeezed her hard and she smiled up at him before kissing him on the mouth. He deepened the kiss, stroking his tongue against hers as he cupped her breast in his hand.

"Perhaps we should find something else to occupy our time while I'm waiting to meet him," he whispered into her ear.

She laughed. "Leo and Jeffrey said the fence in the west field needs mending again. Perhaps we should ride out there and fix it."

He growled and nipped at her neck. "I can think of a much better use for my hands and yours."

"Aye, I imagine you can," she said.

362

He stroked her hair as she stared up at him again. "Are you happy, Tristan?"

"Aye."

"As am I." She kissed him and he stroked her soft hair again.

"I love you, girl."

"I love you, Tristan."

WILLOW AND THE WOLF EXCERPT

THE SHIFTERS SERIES, BOOK ONE

"I love your car." Willow smoothed her hand over the dashboard.

"Thanks," Mal said.

He opened the window and had to restrain from sticking his head out into the breeze. Willow's scent was everywhere, and he could barely concentrate on his driving. Her scent would cling to him for the rest of the day and drive his wolf absolutely mad with need.

"Maybe I could drive on the way back?" Willow said.

"No."

"Why not?"

"Because you're too little to handle this type of power."

She laughed and rolled her eyes. "Please, I've been driving cars like this since I was sixteen."

"Really?"

"Yup. My dad was a mechanic and a collector of fast cars." She stared out the window. "He taught me how to drive when I was twelve."

"Twelve?" He couldn't keep the disbelief out of his voice.

"Yes. Mama wasn't very happy about that. She gave him the biggest lecture when she found out. She was worried I'd get in an accident. Of course, it was fine. Daddy was a very safe driver and he taught me to be safe as well."

He grunted in reply and she smiled at him again. "So, what do you say? Can I drive on the way back?"

"No."

She wrinkled her nose at him. "Meanie."

"Did you just call me meanie?"

"Yes. What? Is everyone too afraid of the big bad wolf to tell him the truth about his personality?"

"I'm not a meanie," he protested.

"Well you're definitely a grumpy," she said.

"You don't know anything about me," he said.

"That's true. But whose fault is that? Not mine. I've been trying to get to know you over the last month," Willow replied.

"You don't need to know anything about me. You're my employee, nothing else."

"That doesn't mean we can't be friends."

She pouted adorably and he had to clench his hands around the steering wheel to stop himself from pulling the car over and kissing away the pout. "It sort of does."

"Ridiculous," she snorted. "I think you just dislike humans."

"I don't dislike humans," he said.

"No? Then it's just me?"

"Ms. Tanner, I don't -"

"You know what I think? I think you just don't know enough about me. Once you get to know me, you won't be able to resist me, Mal." She wiggled her eyebrows at him, and he almost groaned out loud when she wet her bottom lip with her small, pink tongue.

"So, here are the facts about Willow Blossom Tanner. I'm twenty-five, I -"

"Your middle name is not Blossom," he said.

"It totally is. My parents were hippies. Did I forget to mention that?" She giggled.

He didn't reply and she continued. "As I was saying, I'm twenty-five, single – but you already know that – and my best friend is Ava. What was up with Bishop and the sniffing, by the way?"

"Uh…" He didn't know how to respond.

"He certainly seemed to like her smell. Is that a bear shifter thing or a shifter thing in general?"

"Most shifters have an excellent sense of smell. They use it to figure out all sorts of things about other paranormals and humans."

"Like what?"

He shrugged. "Where they live, what they do for a living, how old they are, their emotions at the time."

"Really? How old they are?"

He nodded. He was suddenly sweating, and he hoped she wouldn't notice. Most shifters could tell from a single sniff if a person was hungry or happy, or frightened or – he swallowed thickly – aroused.

"That is so cool," she said thoughtfully. "Paranormals are so lucky. Imagine being able to sniff someone and know instantly if they were happy."

"Not all paranormals can do it," he reminded her. "Some have better senses than others."

"I suppose something like a penguin shifter wouldn't be able to smell your happiness," she replied.

"There is no such thing as a penguin shifter."

"How do you know?" She countered immediately. "Just because you've never seen one doesn't mean they don't exist. They wouldn't live here, would they? It's much too warm for them."

"Penguin shifters do not exist," he said through gritted teeth.

"Do you believe in spirits?"

He blinked at the abrupt change in topic. "What?"

"Spirits? Do you believe in them?"

"You mean ghosts?"

"Ghosts, spirits, ethereal beings – whatever you want to call them." She shrugged.

"There is no such thing as ghosts."

She frowned at him. "You know, for being a paranormal you have an awfully restricted view of the world."

He rolled his eyes. "I'm just not prone to ridiculous thoughts and ideas, Ms. Tanner."

"You think I'm ridiculous?" She gave him a hurt look.

"I didn't say that. I'm just implying that you have ridiculous *ideas*."

She mulled that over. "I suppose you have a point. To the unbeliever I would come across as ridiculous."

"The unbeliever?"

"Yes. You know, someone like you. You're much too practical for your own good, Mal. You have to open your heart and your head to the possibility that there are things in this world that can't be explained."

"I prefer to be seen as normal, thanks. It's better for business."

She laughed. "True. I blame your upbringing."

"You know nothing about my upbringing," he replied.

"I know your parents aren't hippies like mine were."

"Were?" He glanced at her.

For the first time since he'd met her, the cheerful look on her face dropped away. "My parents died two years ago in that plane crash. You know the one."

He nodded. It had been all over the news. One hundred and twenty-five humans and forty paranormals were killed instantly when the plane they were in had crashed into the ocean. "I'm sorry."

"Thanks. I miss them terribly. I'm an only child and neither of my parents' siblings are still alive."

She stared out the window for a moment. "It gets pretty lonely, you know? Thank God for Ava."

She fidgeted with the buttons on her shirt. "I thought maybe I would see them again. Thought that maybe they would make an appearance just to say they loved me but that never happened. I shouldn't be surprised. Both my parents were extremely happy people. There was nothing left to keep them in this world. Still... I hoped they would want to see me one last time."

"What are you talking about?" Just when he thought she was normal, she threw out random crap like that.

"Nothing," she said cryptically. "Where was I? Oh yes, we were telling each other about our personal lives. It's your turn now."

He shook his head. "We weren't talking about our personal lives - you were talking about your personal life."

"Oh c'mon," she wheedled. "Throw me a bone, would you? I want to know something about the big bad wolf."

He snorted and she grinned at him. "Maybe I can guess."

She studied him for so long that he could feel a blush creeping up his neck. "Stop staring at me."

"I'm just trying to figure you out."

"It's rude to stare."

"I suppose it is. Maybe I should sniff you instead."

Before he could stop her, she had leaned over and nearly buried her face in his neck. She inhaled deeply and he stiffened and leaned away.

"It's even ruder to smell someone without their invitation," he snapped.

"Man, I've got a lot to learn about shifters. I thought shifters would be cool with the sniffing."

She sat back in her seat. "That didn't tell me anything, anyway. Other than you wear really great cologne."

He blushed and she clapped her hands with unrestrained glee. "I made you blush!"

"No, you didn't!" he snapped again.

"Of course not. Your natural colour is bright red," she replied.

He stopped the car at a red light, and she grinned impishly. "Maybe you should smell me."

"Definitely not," he growled.

"Oh c'mon…it'll be fun!"

She unclicked her seat belt and leaned in until he could feel her small breasts pressing against his arm. He stared at her in panic as she tilted her head up.

"Go on, Mal. Sniff me," she said.

"Ms. Tanner, this isn't -"

"Are you a chicken?" She smacked him playfully on one broad thigh. "I've never seen you in your wolf form. Maybe you're actually a chicken shifter."

He growled angrily and pressed his face into her soft throat. He inhaled deeply, his cock hardening against the worn fabric of his jeans as her scent washed over him. He inhaled again and again as Willow waited patiently.

"Well? What can you tell about me?" she asked.

"You showered this morning."

"Obviously. I shower every morning. C'mon, wolf boy, tell me something you couldn't possibly know."

"You had strawberries and wine last night for dinner. You wear vanilla body lotion but not this morning, you were excited by something last night and you're twenty-six, not twenty-five."

She leaned back a little and stared at him in wide-eyed wonderment. "That's amazing! I did totally lie about my age!"

He could feel a grin creeping across his face and her eyes sparkled happily in response. "Do me again, Mal!"

"I – what?" he croaked out. He couldn't stop the immediate mental image of yanking up Willow's skirt, tearing off her panties and making her straddle him while he fucked her senseless.

"Sniff me again! Tell me something else!"

"Uh, no, I don't think -"

He groaned out loud when she shoved her throat eagerly into his face. This time she rested one warm hand on his thigh, and he was helpless to stop from cupping the back of her head and holding her steady while he breathed in. His traitorous tongue licked her soft skin, his balls tightening when she moaned softly in response. Her hand clenched on his leg as he licked her again.

"Does – does taste tell you something as well?" she squeaked out.

"Yes," he muttered. Her arousal was strong and overpowering in the small car, and his wolf howled with delight when he nipped her neck.

"Oh!" She jerked against him and he gripped her neck and forced her head to the side before licking from the hollow of her throat to her earlobe.

"What does it tell you?" she asked breathlessly.

"That you taste good," he whispered.

"Why do I get the feeling that the big bad wolf wants to eat me right up?" She laughed nervously.

He sucked on her earlobe. "Oh, he does, Willow. He wants to eat your sweet pussy until you're begging him for mercy. Until you've come so many times you can't -"

The loud blaring of a car horn had them jerking apart. The light had turned green and as the horn blasted again, he waved in apology and stepped on the gas.

He didn't dare look at Willow. His wolf was begging to be free, begging for him to pull over the car and take the little human who so obviously wanted him to. He controlled it fiercely, breathing in shallow breaths to try and avoid the smell of her need.

"So, um, that got a little weird, yeah?" Willow said.

"I'm sorry," he said hoarsely. "That was incredibly inappropriate of me and I -"

"Don't worry about it," she said. "It was my fault anyway. I was the one who practically sat on your lap and forced you to sniff me."

He shook his head. "I want you to know that I understand how this must make me look and I promise you, I'm not the employer who – who hits on his staff."

"I know," she said. "Listen, if you keep my actual age a secret, I'll keep your inappropriate licking a secret. Deal?"

He stole a quick glance at her. She was acting calm, but he could still smell her excitement and see her flushed skin. If he wanted to, he could take her right now. She was wet and more than ready for him.

He growled and slammed his fist against the steering wheel.

"Hey, don't do that!" There was a thin thread of alarm in her voice and she patted him on one broad shoulder. "Seriously, it's fine. I'm not going to sue you for harassment or anything like that."

He blew his breath out. He had licked Willow and, even worse, talked about eating her pussy. He didn't know what the hell he was thinking. He wasn't – that was the problem. His dick was doing all the thinking. Christ, he was in trouble. Willow said she would keep it quiet, but the girl never stopped talking. Kat and Bishop were going to find out and he'd never live it down.

"Hey, Mal?" Willow's hand touched his tentatively and he jerked it away.

"Yeah?"

"I meant it when I said I wouldn't say anything. I know I talk a lot, but I can keep a secret, sometimes," she said.

"Yeah, I know. It won't happen again, I promise you."

ABOUT THE AUTHOR

Elizabeth Kelly was born and raised in Ontario, Canada. She moved west as a teenager and now lives in Alberta with her husband and a menagerie of pets. She firmly believes that a person can survive solely on sushi and coffee, and only her husband's mad cooking skills prevents her from proving that theory.

For more information about Elizabeth, check out her website at

www.elizabethkelly.ca

facebook.com/EKellyBooks

twitter.com/ElizabethKBooks

instagram.com/elizabethkelly_author

amazon.com/Elizabeth-Kelly/e/B00EOHZ0MS

bookbub.com/authors/elizabeth-kelly

ALSO BY ELIZABETH KELLY

Tempted Series

Tempted

Twice Tempted

Forever Tempted

Breathless

Tempted Trilogy (Books 1-3)

Red Moon Series

Red Moon

Red Moon Rising

Dark Moon

Alpha Moon

Pale Moon

Red Moon Bundle Books 1 – 3

Red Moon Bundle Books 4 – 5

The Recruit Series

The Recruit (Book One)

The Recruit (Book Two)

The Recruit (Book Three)

The Recruit (Book Four)

The Recruit (Book Five)

The Recruit Series Bundle Books 1-3

The Recruit Series Bundle Books 4-6

The Shifters Series

Willow and the Wolf (Book One)

Ava and the Bear (Book Two)

Katarina and the Bird (Book Three)

Porter's Mate (Book Four)

Bria and the Tiger (Book Five)

Rosalie Undone (Book Six)

The Dragon's Mate (Book Seven)

Rise of the Jaguar (Book Eight)

The Draax Series

Reign (Book One)

Rule (Book Two)

Rebel (Book Three)

Harmony Falls Series

Sweet Harmony (Book One)

Perfect Harmony (Book Two)

Forbidden Harmony (Book Three)

Redeeming Harmony (Book Four)

Individual Books

The Necessary Engagement

Amelia's Touch

The Rancher's Daughter

Healing Gabriel

The Contract

A Home for Lily

Saving Charlotte

Shameless

The Fairy Tales Collection

Broken

An Unlikely Seduction

Holiday Romance

The Christmas Wife

The Christmas Rescue

The Christmas Nanny

Sordid Games

www.ingramcontent.com/pod-product-compliance
Lightning Source LLC
Chambersburg PA
CBHW071202250626
47159CB00001B/167